Copyright ©
All righ

For the people like Kelsey.

For the people like me.

You are not alone.

Prologue

I always imagined that when the world began, that the sky was red. Redder than a baby's face the day they were born, red as the dawn.

It feels almost poetic that the sky would be red, the day the world ends. The sky wasn't an orange-red colour. It was a dark red like the blood of the dead. Fitting, considering the world was dying.

Ash fell like rain and sparks rose upwards in an incredible vivid orange.

Thick, ink-black smoke cascaded across the ground like an avalanche across the Earth. I don't know where it was coming from. I can't see past it. It was raising up and it felt like I was drowning.

The world was silent. It wasn't quiet. There should have been screaming or people calling for their loved ones but there wasn't.

Blood.

It stained the shards of glass, scattered across the road, thick and gloopy. I blinked until my vision cleared to see the mangled carcass of my car ablaze. Smoke choked me as I tried to crawl away, wincing at the sharp pain in my leg.

We've lost.

Laying there alone in the road, all I could think about was her. I'm sorry. I fucked up. I thought they were after *me*. I should have never pushed you away.

Attempting to get to my feet, glass sliced my already bloody hands and the world span. Ice clawed at my flesh, reminding me that if I passed out, hypothermia would claim me. I laughed a hollow laugh that quickly laced with hysteria. Right, like hypothermia was going to claim me. The world's ending anyway.

He had been right. He was always right.

Phone… Call for help… Give them a chance to stop it… Arching my arm to check my pocket; I hissed in pain. It wasn't there. Panic and frustration slammed against my already aching skull. I twisted, shredding my skin against the shards to find my phone. It had snapped like a lollipop stick.

What do I do now?

I have to tell her.

I rolled, groaning in pain to peer into the tree line.

How long had those pale, yellow eyes been staring at me from the trees?

That malevolent apple-red smile shone in the darkness.

My heart rate sped up and I tried to stay still. Why hadn't I listened to him? He had warned me and now I would never see him again. I'm going to die here.

I'm never going to see Kelsey again.

One

Damn it, I'm starving and it's PE next. I ate my breakfast bar miserably, knowing full well that I should have saved more of my lunch earlier, but I was hungry, and we had very little food at home. I looked over to the raffle. I felt guilty that I hadn't bought a ticket yet because it was to help fund our year's prom but I didn't have any money today. The bell rang for next period, so I made my way over. Unfortunately, to get to the changing rooms, you had to go past the raffle.

"Kelsey!" Delilah called as I walked through. Her eyes were pale blue with long lashes framing them. Her face was oval shaped, and her lips were thin and smothered in nude lipstick. Her nose was a button and her hair; perfectly styled pale blonde waves that reached her shoulders. She was 5'6 and slender with slight curves. She ran the school and she was the one at the raffle. Delilah had hated me for years and she had waited for everyone else in our year to walk past before she called to me. I stopped and turned to her. "Have you bought a ticket?"

"No, I haven't got any money." I kept my tone even and polite, trying to ignore how my stomach growled.

She shook her head, tutting, and I already knew that she was about to guilt trip me. She sighed. Her friends were gathered around her and they were grinning, knowing what was to come. "Kelsey, are you going to prom?" She asked; her tone the epitome of condescending while leaning over the table.

"Yeah," I replied quickly. "My brother`s making me."

Delilah`s eyes bulged, and she lost the ability to speak. Her friends were in surprised silence for the moment and then laughed. "Yeah, Kelsey!" Phillip cheered, clapping. I left to avoid all other interactions. I was no longer sure whether I wanted to go back to the raffle store if Delilah was there. Delilah could be there and if I bought a ticket, I didn`t want her to think that she had any power over me.

"Is Freya sick today?" I asked my friend, Adria.

She shook her head. "No, she was caught by Mrs Veneman wearing more than one set of earrings, hoops, rings and a necklace. If she was wearing that hoodie she usually does, then she would probably be in inclusion for a month."

"And yet when Delilah sent photos of Miranda, passed-out drunk and naked around the school, she got off scot-free." I pointed out, pulling my PE shirt over my head.

"Mrs Veneman loves Delilah." Adria pointed out. "And she hates us. Especially Freya. I mean, you`re a nerd who has never rebelled in her life and she still hates you."

"I was sarcastic that one time in her office when she was supposed to be giving us information on a mental health organisation but gave every excuse not to."

"Oh yeah,"

We scurried to the sports hall and we picked up the badminton equipment. There was never really enough equipment so you`d have to be quick. Apparently, it was due to budget cuts, but they decided to give the humanities corridor a paint job. I say 'paint job' but it genuinely looked like they had coloured the walls in with a green highlighter.

I noticed Mason already playing with his friends: Mikey, Grant, and Brett. I had harboured a crush on Mason for ages.

Unfortunately, he was going out with Delilah. I knew she was different around other people, but it was so clear to everyone else around that she was stringing him along. His friends knew but they never said anything and even though Mason and I spoke every day; we weren't quite friends. If I said anything, it wouldn't make a difference. He was smitten by her. I wasn't really his type.

Even Adria had no idea about my feelings for him.

The entire school thought I had a crush on Grant anyway, because I tended to stare over at Mason. Grant was always next to Mason, so people seemed to think that I liked Grant.

In contrast to Delilah, I was pale, short, and curvaceous. I had boringly brown, unruly thick hair that tumbled to mid-back and brown eyes to match. I had more freckles than Delilah had brain cells and plump dark pink lips to match. Though I wasn't ugly, I wasn't exactly eye-candy. 'Boring', 'plain' or 'fugly' are words that people frequently use. By 'people', I mean Delilah.

It was strange to think that in my final year of school, as a major nerd, that PE was now my most enjoyable subject. Mostly because there were no teachers nagging me about homework or revision... Ok, completely because there were no teachers nagging me. I hated PE for everything else. It was boring and embarrassing between the insulting teachers, the revealing uniform, and the backhanded comments from other students. You know the ones; the students who your parents just said were 'jealous' of you. Like anyone ever believed that.

"Well, you have thoroughly kicked my ass." I told Adria after she had beaten me twelve times in a row.

"Yeah,"

"You two aren't slacking, are you?" Mr McGoo demanded accusingly. "You haven't even been on the court once, have you?"

"Yes," I snarled. He walked off. "What a dick!"

The people in the court next to us turned to me in shock. "Kelsey swears?" I noticed that Delilah was watching us closely. She grabbed Mason`s friend Grant and flounced out of the sport`s hall with him. She gave me a malicious smile. Of course, Delilah had no interest in Grant, just like she had no interest in Mason. She knew that she could get any guy she wanted because she was beautiful and manipulative. She was only friends with specific people because of what she could gain from them. I was yet to find someone she had gone out with just because she genuinely liked them.

Mason stared after her like a love-sick puppy. "Hey Mikey, I need to go and get the maths homework from Grant."

"You don`t do homework." Mikey pointed out; his eyebrows furrowed.

"Yeah, yeah," He waved his hand and followed the pair out.

Adria wheezed. "Kicking your ass is exhausting." I rolled my eyes. "Can you go get our water bottles?"

"We really need to remember to pick those up before class." I pointed out.

"But then we have no excuse to *leave*."

Rolling my eyes, I left the sports hall and made my way towards the girls changing room. I noticed Mason walking past the changing room doors and towards the old dance studio. Recalling Delilah and Grant`s swift departure, I decided that I was *not* going to get involved with that.

"What the fuck?!" Came Mason`s voice from right outside the old dance studio.

Despite my earlier claim, I found myself scurrying towards him. Was I a masochist, or something? "Is everything ok?" I looked into the dance studio, gasped and Mason covered my eyes. Something I was thankful for. Delilah`s pale blonde hair was a mess and her clothes were dishevelled. Grant was in the same state except he was shirtless.

"Mason?" Delilah breathed, covering her unbuttoned shirt just as Mason dropped his hand. "I..."

"How could you?" He stared in horror at the girl he thought was 'perfect' with his best friend. She tried to say something, but he interrupted. "No... I hope you're happy." He stormed off.

Delilah gave me a smug look while Grant just looked like he was going to throw up. "Sorry Kelsey, I know you like Grant..."

"No, I don't. I never did." I told her, pushing my thick brown hair out of my eyes. "You can have him. I don't want him. I have no interest in people who betray their friends." Grant flinched as if I had slapped him. I turned and scampered after Mason. We were just out of earshot and moving away from PE when I asked. "Are you ok?"

"Yes," He said automatically. That was always his response when I asked that question. Then shook his head. "No, I... I don't know what to feel." He sat down at a picnic table. "I thought she was..."

"I'm sorry,"

He frowned. "Why are you sorry?"

I laughed, a hollow laugh. "I don't know. I mean... I was never a fan of Delilah and I never trusted her. I feel like I should have warned you but..."

"You thought that I wouldn't believe you." He finished and I nodded. "I should have known that she didn't really want me. She never went out with guys like me before. Why would she now?"

"She is the one in the wrong here, not you." I assured him. He shouldn't be the one feeling guilty. "She manipulated you, not the other way around."

"And Grant..." Mason's hands rolled into fists and his jaw clenched. "That slimy little bastard. He was going to fuck *my* girlfriend. What the fuck is wrong with him?" I didn't know how to respond. "I trusted him, and he was going to fuck my girlfriend. I met her father! I bought her all that shit she wanted." I had seen the fancy Pandora jewellery. That stuff cost a lot. "I'm such a moron."

Mason was the smartest guy in our year, a sports prodigy and he had never once admitted to getting *anything* wrong. "She does this. You aren't a moron for trusting someone, you are brave for trusting someone. That takes guts." I continued. "So yeah, you trusted the wrong person. Next time, choose the right person."

He smiled at me. "Why are you being so nice to me?"

"Because you're good." I told him. "And you don't deserve what you're going through." I shrugged my shoulders. This wasn't the first time I had comforted one of Delilah's *playthings*. I had comforted two of her exes. I had comforted other people Delilah had tormented (girls like me). I had even comforted Precious Silverton (Delilah's supposed best friend) before she had realised that if she got a new boyfriend every week, she'd have her own status and power that would mean that Delilah couldn't abuse her to the same extent as the other 'giggle girls'. I pitied Precious the most. "And, I hate your girlfriend enough to see what she is truly like so I can understand what she is and how you must feel."

"I didn't know you didn't like Delilah."

"Trust me; the feeling is mutual." I ran my fingers through my hair, something I often did when I was nervous. "And, I feel guilty because the reason she was with Grant is that she thought I liked him."

"How is that your fault?"

"It isn't," I agreed. "Doesn't mean that I don't feel guilty."

"Don't feel guilty, Kelsey."

We sat there and chatted together for the rest of that lesson until the bell rang for tutor. We were completely oblivious to the pale blue eyes, glaring at us. "We better... Go get changed and get to tutor." I suggested, suddenly recalling that I was still in my revealing PE uniform, standing up too quickly and stumbling. He took my arm to steady me. "Thank you. Um... I'll see you in tutor?"

He dropped my arm and rubbed the back of his neck, not meeting my eyes. "Yeah. See you in tutor."

I got to the changing room where Adria was waiting for me with a smug look on her face. "So... You and Mason?"

My face glowed red and I ran my fingers through my hair roughly. "It... It's not like that!" I wish it was.

"Too right, it's not." I turned around and looked up into a pair of angry pale blue eyes. "He will never be yours."

"Back off," I growled. She was standing too close. It was a warning and it made Adria tense from behind me.

"Mason will never be yours. He only wants me!" Delilah continued, close enough to bite my nose.

"Back off," I warned. I wasn't backing away. That would be seen as a weakness and I would not let her think me weak.

"Why would a hot guy like him want the fat, nerd, plain Jane like you when he can have his future prom queen?" She laughed, her posse standing behind her.

"*I said back off!*" I shouted, stepping forward just as Adria moved between us.

"Kelsey, calm..." She turned to Delilah. "Delilah, go away."

Delilah glared at us and stormed off. "Take this as a warning, Alexander."

Her friend, Jennifer muttered. "That Kelsey is totally psycho."

Adria grabbed my forearm, to stop me from charging forwards. "Calm down, Kelsey. She`s just a brat. She probably has crabs or something. And not small ones; mutant crabs… the ones the size of small dogs…"

I snorted; my anger forgotten and rolled my eyes. "Let`s go to tutor."

The walk to tutor should have been a short one but with all the pushing and shoving made it a lot longer than it should have been. The fact that I was five-foot-one-and-a-half-inches tall made it harder. Taller guys like Mason or Rupert (an extremely tall asshole with a tendency to harass female students or encourage his friends to do it) didn`t have this problem. They just barged through or smaller people scurried out of their way. Unfortunately, my brother taught me manners and I didn`t have the heart to just barge through… Unless I was pissed in which case I didn`t care if the person in front of me was my height or six-foot-two. It wasn`t that Mason would push people out of the way; people tend to move out the way of a nearly-six-foot-tall, muscle-bound Year Eleven when they stomp forward. Unfortunately, the only time someone of my height had the same effect is when they have a 'scary' boyfriend. Neither Adria nor I had either the height or the man.

Not that I cared whether I had a boyfriend or not. I did fine without one.

We were knocked into walls and smacked around by students of all years.

The penalty of stopping growing in Year Eight…

"Hey Kelsey!" Mason shouted as the crowd parted for him to get to me. He looked next to me. "Oh, hey Adria."

She looked him up and down. "Hey, tall dark and gorgeous." She licked her lips. I laughed at the uncomfortable look on Mason`s face. Adria was a lesbian… but Mason didn`t know that. "Well… 'Dark' may not be the word for it with all that light brown hair of yours."

"Ok..." He smiled awkwardly: his eyes wide. He turned back to me. "Can I walk you..." He looked back over at Adria. "Wonderful ladies to tutor?"

I simpered, biting my lip for a second. "You may." I made my voice sound very posh. My nose crinkled with amusement. He held out his arm and I linked mine with it. He led us through the crowd and to tutor. I let go of his arm when we got to tutor. Delilah was watching us as we walked through the door.

She was sitting in my spot.

There wasn`t an official seating plan anymore but that was where I had sat exclusively for the last three years.

Mason took my hand and led me over to our table. He sat down in his usual spot and sat me down next to him. "So, Kelsey, are you still planning on skipping prom?"

"If I can get away with it, why?"

Mason shook his head. "It is a shame. I would have loved to have danced with you."

I snorted a laugh. "I don`t dance and you don`t either. I`d either crush your toes or we`d just embarrass ourselves."

He smirked. "That is true but we`d both have fun. Besides, I`ve never seen you in a dress."

I laughed. "And you never will." He laughed at that.

I was conscious of the piercing glare on the back of my head. "I doubt you could afford a dress anyway, Alexander." She hissed.

Mason and I turned to look at her.

Most of the people who lived in our area were very well off. I knew girls who had spent over £700 on a prom dress and I was yet to find someone who`d spent less than £200. I would never have even considered to get a dress over £50. Never. Admittedly, I had spent more on clothing before... On a pair of combat boots but they were from Camden Street Market and I had saved up for months.

"There are dresses that don't cost hundreds of pounds, Delilah." I told her.

"Yeah, but they are tacky and ugly." Delilah droned. Did she have a vocal range? She was completely monotone.

"There are dresses that cost £890 that look tackier." I pointed out. "How much did you spend on yours, again?"

Her eye twitched. "That`s none of your business."

She had been boasting about the price for weeks and I knew full well that it was exactly £890.

Our tutor called out the register, not that it stopped Mason from talking to me. I was silent throughout. My tutor was a good man. His name was Mr Clarke. He was kind and he had helped me out more times than I cared to admit. I had nothing but respect for the man so I wouldn`t speak while he was taking the register. "Mason," Mr Clarke asked when he had finished taking the register. "Your maths teacher wants to talk to you."

He nodded and stood up. "Ok," He turned to me. "Talk to you later, Kelsey."

I smiled awkwardly. "Yeah, see you,"

Just as he left, Delilah turned to me. "You may have won this war, *Alexander*." She spat out my surname with disgust. "But I will win the battle."

"Yeah, Alexander!" Her friend squeaked while the boys at the nearby table snickered.

Deciding not to correct her, I smiled. "Ok, Delilah. You will win the battle." The bell rang for us to go home and I was all too ready to leave. I said goodbye to Adria and turned to leave.

"What about English revision?" Adria inquired.

"It`s not compulsory. I`m not doing it." I answered. "Have fun in Hell." I waved and began my trek home.

"Later Kelsey."

The walk home was a lonely one. Nobody I got on with walked the same way I did, and it was a long path through trees and bushes. I spent my time daydreaming mostly. Thankfully, I had passed the large group of boys that used to follow me, shouting obscenities, long ago and the familiar sensation of anger and defensiveness had faded away.

Mason... Why was he acting like this with me? I wasn't that pretty or interesting. Was he just talking to me to make Delilah jealous? Did he...?

There was a growl next to me. I jumped and span to peer into the leafless bush next to me where the noise had come from. There was nothing there. I looked behind the bush and around it. There was nothing there.

Putting it down to my stress-fuelled imagination, I continued to walk home. My entire body was on edge. I was conscious of every sound around me. There were no birds singing. I was walking on a rural path, bushes, and trees on all sides. There were a*lways* birds chirping. Nothing. I felt eyes on the back of my neck and footsteps. "Kelsey!"

My eyes widened and I let out a sigh of relief. "Mason," I turned around. Nobody was there. Ice danced down my spine, goose bumps protruding from my flesh. I was certain that I had heard that. It had been right by my ear. I had felt the breath on my skin.

I sped up, quietly singing Back in Black to try and calm myself. It wasn't working. I looked behind me every few seconds. Nothing there. The voice was fresh in my mind and fear gripped my heart like an icy hand.

There's nobody there. There's nobody there. There's nobody...

"Kelsey!" I span around again. Nothing. I listened. I heard a baby screaming from the bushes. As I approached, the cries turned into a crow cawing. I breathed out a short-lasting sigh of relief. Then I heard a man screaming about a hundred yards away from me. My eyes darted there. Nothing. Just empty air.

"It is a great nothingness we fear." I laughed a shallow, emotionless laugh. "Oh, my English teacher would be proud." I scurried home, ignoring the footsteps behind me. I shivered. Once the familiar caravan park was in sight, I breathed a sigh of relief. Home was in sight. Almost as if the thing that had been taunting me knew that I was protected here, it stopped its games. I ambled through the park, waving at Mrs Harris and her pet ferret Tibbles. My caravan wasn`t particularly impressive and my room was barely big enough for my bed but that's ok. It was better than living at my old house. I quietly opened the door to be greeted by a monstrous furry mass, charging at me. "Hello Sergeant," I smiled, and she darted around, waking up my elder brother, who was dozing on the window seat by licking him across the face, resulting in David jumping and falling off. He groaned. "Are you ok, David?" I snickered.

He groaned again. "Morning Kelsey."

"Good afternoon, David." I meandered past and grabbed an apple off the side. "Has Sergeant been out this afternoon?"

He wiped drool from his chin. "Huh… No,"

"What time do you go to work?"

"I… Um… Nine. I`ll put dinner on."

"Yes please," I agreed. "I`ll take Sergeant out." I didn`t want to go back outside but Sergeant was waiting for me. There was a park with a field nearby. It wasn`t a big park and very few people went there. I could probably count on my hands how many times I had seen people there. Usually I was thankful for it but today I would have been comforted to see anyone. I threw a ball for Sergeant as she darted around, her massive ears bouncing. Her tongue spilled drool all over the place. She dropped the dripping ball at my feet. Grimacing, I picked it up and lobbed it away. I bent down to wipe my hand on the grass.

"Kelsey," Came my brother's voice. I looked around for him but he wasn't there. Was it that thing from earlier? I threw the ball for Sergeant for a little bit longer (because I didn't hear anything after that) and headed home.

I didn't want to be outside after dark.

My brother worked nights as a bartender at a night club, so I was usually alone in the evenings... Well, Sergeant was always there but she wasn't much of a conversationalist. Thankfully, we had a tv and Russell Howard wasn't leaving the screen any time soon. He never failed to make me laugh.

"Kelsey, dinner's ready." My brother told me when I returned.

"Oh, pizza," Again. "Pepperoni?"

"And barbeque," He smiled, throwing away the frozen box it came in.

I liked pizza, but we did have it quite a lot. It had gotten pretty boring. It was cheap; especially if it was frozen. But I did love barbeque, so that was a bonus. "Thanks, David." Dinner passed without conversation and David had to head off for work. "Seems it's just us, Sergeant." I smiled sadly. "Let's watch re-runs of Good News, shall we?"

Sergeant wagged her tail and I turned the tv on.

Two

When I entered school the next day, I noticed that everyone had their eyes on me. There was a lot of whispering all around me. I tensed. By no means did I *ever* want this much attention. Or any attention at all for that matter. I was more comfortable being ignored by everyone around me (walking around like I was the invisible man) than having any kind of attention.

"Did you hear?" One girl hissed.

"I know!" Another replied. "Kelsey Alexander... Who would have thought?"

Instead of heading to tutor, like I usually do, I turned towards them and strode over there. "What`s the rumour? I`m curious as to what people are saying about me."

They were shocked frozen for a second, their eyes widened, startled at my sudden boldness and then, they burst into a fit of giggles. "Delilah has been saying about your activities with the STEM Boys' Team, last night." They giggled again.

"Yeah, Alexander," The other one spat. "*Even* you could do better."

I felt sick. Were they...? "I`m sorry, what?"

"Sleeping with the entire STEM Team." The first girl accused. "Delilah told us about the whole thing. She saw it. All the boys are talking about it. I would never have expected it from you."

Overnight, the girl who had never been kissed was now the school slut. This was the first time I'd ever dealt with slut-shaming. I wanted to scream that I didn't do any of it but I knew it would just be a waste of air. I scampered off to tutor, my fists clenched and face red.

Delilah.

What the fuck is wrong with her?

Surely, she, a girl who'd been slut-shamed several times before, knew how much it hurt.

And the STEM Team?! I had never been anything but nice to them! How could they do this to me? I would get it if it were *just* Seth (another creep in my year-group), but all of them?! Don't get me wrong, if it was *just* Seth, I'd still be pissed but it would have been expected behaviour from him.

I turned away from Tutor and stormed off to the place where the STEM Team usually hung out to see one of the boys (Seamus) telling Mason what I had let them do to me, going into *explicit* detail, showing how much time they spent on Pornhub. Mason had a face like thunder. Seamus didn't seem to read the expression on his face. I stormed up to Seamus and socked him in the face. He fell onto his friends. "Which one of you started that rumour about me?" They all gave each other panicked looks. "WHO WAS IT?!" They jumped. Mason stood behind me, supporting me. I knew who had started it, but I wanted to see what they were doing.

"D-Delilah... She..." Seamus began.

"Why?" I demanded. "Why would you do that to me?"

"D-Delilah said that she would sleep with us if we spread those rumours." Billy told me. "Don't tell her!"

"D-Delilah said that she would sleep with us if we spread those rumours. Don`t tell her!" Repeated and I turned to Mason. He was holding up his phone with the recording app on it.

Mason turned to me. "I think we`re done here, don`t you? I think we need to have a conversation with Delilah."

I nodded and we walked away from the boys. "Thank you,"

He smiled at me but there was no joy behind it. "I knew when I heard the rumour that something was wrong. Your face was red, and you were looking away when another *girl* was half-naked yesterday. There was no way you were going to sleep with them. I went there to try and find out what was happening. If you hadn`t hit him, I would have."

Delilah was standing with her minions, laughing. She flipped her pale blonde hair as her minions vied for her attention. Delilah froze when she saw us approach and then smiled smugly. "Hello, Mason... Whore. Tell me, what does nerd cock taste like?"

"She wouldn`t know." Mason told her before I could say anything. "How about you tell us?"

"D-Delilah...She... Why? Why would you do that to me? D-Delilah said that she would sleep with us if we spread those rumours. Don`t tell her!"

The giggle girls stopped their giggling and Delilah`s smug look was wiped from her face. She turned to me. "You bitch!" She moved to slap me in the face. Bad move. I ducked and responded with a punch to hers. Her nose crunched under impact and she shrieked. "You ruined my face! You ruined my face!" She was holding her nose, blood dripping through her fingers. "You will pay for this!"

"*Kelsey*! *Delilah*!" Mrs Wilson shrieked.

That was where the problems began. Fifteen minutes later and we were sitting in the headmaster`s office with two governors. They were talking to each other as if we couldn't hear what they were saying. They kept the hushed tone but it could all be easily heard. "We should expel her, but she would give us much higher grades. We can't afford to get rid of her." The headmaster: Mr Small told them.

"We can't afford to do nothing." The male governor hissed back. "Delilah Delaney's father donated large amounts of money to the school. We can't be seen to do nothing."

"I have an idea." The female governor suggested. She was in her mid-forties with bottle-blonde hair and hooker red lipstick. "There is this behavioural camp that helps get teammates back to working together. I think that it will make them fast friends."

No. No. No. No. No. No. "How are we supposed to pay for that?" Mr Small pointed out. I had never been so glad to hear him say *anything*.

"I'll pay for it, myself." She smiled sickeningly. "I would be delighted."

They turned to us, like we couldn't hear the entirety of their conversation. "Miss Delaney, Miss Alexander, you both know why you're here. Would you like to explain what happened?"

We started to speak at the same time, but Delilah was significantly louder than me. "You ask Mrs Wilson; she punched me in the face! I was just chatting with my friends and she picked on me so I'd slap her and she punched me!"

"Why would you do that, Miss Alexander?" Mr Small asked. Seriously, he believed that?

"She told the whole year that I slept with the entire STEM team, so I gave proof that I didn't." I replied coldly. "She didn't take too kindly to that and I was always taught to defend myself."

"Why did you start that rumour about Miss Alexander?"
"She took my boyfriend."

"I did not! I comforted him after you broke his heart."

"I only cheated on him with Grant to hurt you!"

"Why did you do that?" Mr Small asked, baffled.

"Because she made me look stupid!"

"I`m sorry! I know you take pride in looking stupid all by yourself!"

"Enough!" The headmaster stopped us, like he didn`t expect something like this to happen. Moron. "You two will both spend the rest of your day in detention, your parents or guardian," He looked at me judgementally for the last part. "Will be contacted and you will be recommended to go to a behaviour reform resort. Mrs Wilson will escort you both over there."

The walk over was a long one. Less due to distance as Hornby Secondary was the smallest secondary school in the area but more due to the *people*. Everyone stared from their classrooms and both Mrs Wilson and Delilah were glaring at me. Mrs Wilson hated me. She hated me because she was an asshole that treated her students awfully. She was an art teacher and had before told me that my artwork looked like I had just learned how to hold a paintbrush and had repeatedly torn pages out of my sketchbook. I wasn`t the only person this had happened to and I was far from being the person who was worst treated. One girl that Adria hung out with wasn`t very good at art and all her pieces were ripped out. I was the only person willing to say anything. My displeasure resulted in my brother writing a formal complaint as my legal guardian (I didn`t know he was going to because he knew I would protest him getting involved), getting her in lots of trouble with other members of the art department. She spent a lot of time sucking up to me when I was around but the second my back was turned, she was glaring at me and causing problems (like not ordering my canvas for my mock exam). Honestly, the only reason I knew about the glaring is because she didn`t seem to notice the mirror in her own classroom and the only reason I found out about the canvas was because a friend of Adria's (different to the other one) had let me know that it hadn't been ordered while I was sick.

She escorted us to inclusion, which was not nearly as bad as staff made it sound. I wasn't particularly surprised. The room was messy, with a thick layer of dust on every surface and piles of folders and books that had never been put away. One thing I had noticed was a door in the back right-hand corner of the room. It was scrubbed clean to the point that it was shiny but the window on it was blocked by some kind of corkboard. It was blinding white, expensive-looking and had a large lock on it. I didn't know what that door could lead to. There was a tech classroom on the other side of the wall but, there were no doors there in that room and it was not far enough to be to another classroom. It seemed like a ridiculously expensive door in a school with huge budget cuts (most departments didn't have enough money for glue sticks) especially for something that could only be a large store cupboard. My stomach twisted just looking at the door.

I was placed in a cubicle with a desk and a small, blue chair. "You're classwork will be brought to you later." Mrs Wilson stated and marched out. On the other side of the barrier sat the guidance managers.

The guidance managers were far from being my favourite people. There was only one of them I liked (Mrs Marley), and it was clear that the others were trying so hard to fit in with my guidance manager as she was very close friends with the headmaster, and everyone else who has power in the school. They all wore silk blouses in horrifically bright colours (usually *florescent* pink) and ankle-breaker high-heels. Many of them bleached their hair blonde like hers too. I couldn't help but wonder how long it would take before they just looked like the same person at different stages. It was a clique of its own.

I think that my guidance manager (Mrs Veneman) never got past being the most popular girl in school. She was just like all the other giggle girls and cake faces... Just about 60 years of age. She acted like a teenage girl and often giggled creepily over things she had no business in.

Mrs Veneman handed us our classwork and her nagging seemed to go on for hours. She was nagging at *me.* She ignored Delilah`s flaws, just handing her the work and pretending that she didn`t see Delilah`s phone. There is a phone-ban on the school. Her voice was like nails on a chalkboard. I blocked out everything that she said.

One reason I also couldn`t focus on was my work was because I kept on staring at that door, wondering what the Hell was behind it. It was probably a giant filing cabinet and I knew that, but something about it that felt off. I slipped my phone out of my pocket and turned on the audio record, hoping that it may get something that would sate my curiosity.

Delilah hadn`t stopped glaring at me. "You won`t be with Mason for long." She hissed. "He doesn`t like fat chicks. You know your stomach is huge, right?"

I shook my head. "No, I can`t see my stomach over my boobs. I`m sure you don`t have the same problem." Her face was slowly turning from red to purple. If looks could kill, I would be ash on the ground. Instead of glaring back at her, I smiled pleasantly and got back to my work. I hadn`t bothered mentioning the fact that Mason and I weren`t together. The sadistic part of me liked that she felt threatened by me; how angry she was at something as simple as me comforting Mason. I didn`t think he liked me that way and a few days ago, I would have said that it was impossible for him to ever like me that way but after I talked to him about Delilah, he had looked at me differently.

He had looked at me like I was a woman and not some geek he talks to for fifteen minutes in the morning.

"She is in my year group!" Came a shrill voice from right behind me. "You had no right to help her! That's my job! Are you trying to take my job?"

I knew I wasn't supposed to, but I turned around to see Mrs Veneman shrieking at Mrs Marley. The other guidance managers just watched with venomous smiles on their faces. They surrounded Mrs Marley like hyenas, circling with their insidious eyes fixed on her short hair, her trainers and her hoodie. Mrs Marley stood her ground, her arms crossed tightly. "You weren't helping her. She had come to you, begging for help. It takes a lot for a girl like that do that and you just…"

"And you thought that meant you could steal my job?" Mrs Veneman continued. "Because a girl cried a little and told a dramatic story?"

Oh, bitch, you could write a dramatic story.

"That girl had scars all up her arms! Fresh cuts too." Mrs Marley argued. "And you sent her away! She needed a therapist and you gave her a cold shoulder!"

Mrs Veneman bristled. The other guidance managers' eyes widened. They were circling like sharks. "Do you think I'm incapable then, Mrs Marley?" She asked, cooler than a mirror left outside on a January evening.

Mrs Marley visibly paled at the blonde woman's tone. "No, Mrs Veneman."

"If you have a problem, maybe you should take it up with the headmaster." She continued. Mrs Marley was not stupid enough to do such a thing. It would be her word against Mrs Veneman's and everyone knew that Mrs Veneman was very close to everyone with power in this school: especially the headmaster. They had been friends for years (honestly, the way they behaved with each other was like they were having an affair; it was creepy), and there was no way that he would trust Mrs Marley over Mrs Veneman. It just wouldn't happen. *I knew that* and I was just a student. Mrs Marley would know far more about staff social exchanges than I would. She knew exactly what Mrs Veneman was suggesting and there was no way Mrs Marley would win. There was a good chance she would end up reported for something or other or she could lose her job.

And that was exactly why Mrs Veneman had suggested it. "No, Mrs Veneman. That will not be necessary."

"Glad to hear it. Get back to work and leave my students alone." Mrs Veneman hissed. The words '*snake in human skin*' came to mind.

You`re in trouble anyway; go for it. "Hey, Mrs Veneman," I called out before I had properly thought it through.

"Inclusion is a silent activity, Miss Alexander." She was now sat at her desk and she didn`t look up from her plastic, gemstone-incrusted phone.

"You should treat your colleagues with more respect. Someone could get hold of these conversations and record it on their phone despite the phone ban that you blatantly ignore, and they could post it on every social media they have. They could also perhaps, send it to the headmaster or the board of governors or the local newspaper..." I smiled politely with a sing-song voice. I tried to ignore everyone`s eyes on me.

"The phone ban is for students, Miss Alexander." She glared. "So, if you have your phone out then that is immediate confiscation." It wasn`t. The rule was that it was three phone warnings and a call to your parents before confiscation. I hadn`t ever been caught with my phone so I knew that I had never gotten a phone warning. By the school rules, she wasn`t supposed to take it but I knew that they didn`t *really* apply to her. Stopping the recording, I stood up. "Sit down, Miss Alexander, unless you want to be in more trouble." I subtly passed my phone with the recording on it to Mrs Marley. She saw it and slipped it into her desk drawer, saying nothing.

"I'm already being sent away. My guardian is already being called. I am already in here. Search me for a phone. I have already sent the video to the cloud. You won't be able to access it." I was lying (I honestly have no idea how to send that to the cloud) but she didn't know that.

Her blue eyes narrowed to slits. "What do you want, Alexander?"

"For you to be nicer." I told her. "For you to do your job."

She glared and she left.

Later, I requested to go to the toilet. Mrs Marley followed me out and stopped me just out of sight. She handed me back my phone. "Thank you, Kelsey." She told me. "But be careful. You're playing a very dangerous game."

I went to the loo and then returned to my cubicle.

The day was a long one… and a very boring one.

I did do all the work that was assigned but as I usually do in lessons, I finished it all early and sat there, contemplating the contents of the door. Nobody opened it. Just because Mrs Veneman refused to do her job, didn't mean that the rest of them were the same. They got on and took care of their assigned students.

I just wanted to leave.

But I wasn't looking forward to going home and telling David about what had happened today or the consequences. Though I didn't think he would be particularly angry with me, David had mastered the 'I'm not angry, just disappointed' speech. It took *a lot* for David to lose his temper. The first and last time I'd ever seen him lose his temper was when I was ten and even though it wasn't directed at me, it was scary.

It always is the quiet ones, was something I remember our father saying at the time.

I left school late. That seemed to be protocol for those in inclusion to leave later than the rest of the students. There were other students that left later than me. I was thankful to not be one of the students that were kept behind. I didn't want to hear Mrs Veneman's high-pitched shrieking any more than I had to.

It was the same walk home every day except there wasn't a single living thing in sight.

Nothing.

There were no birds, no obnoxious teenage boys, no dogs... Nothing. I couldn't even see the swarms of flies that always seemed to be at head height so they'd infest my eyes.

"Kelsey," My brother. I turned to look. Nothing.

It had started again.

Don't run. If you act like prey, it will act like a predator. *You don't even know what it is!* I didn't have to. Whatever it was, it was trying to frighten me (and was succeeding) and anything that wanted to frighten me couldn't be good. I started humming Back in Black again, but I stopped soon after. The idea of not being able to hear something behind me scared me even more.

Making sure that I didn't run, I sped up my step, looking to see if anyone was behind me every few seconds. There was no one there. That didn't stop the noise of footsteps tap-tap-tapping directly behind me.

"Kelsey!"
I turned. Nothing.
"Kelsey!"
Nothing.
"Kelsey!"
Nothing.
"Kelsey!"
Yellow eyes.

Before I could even think, I was running. Though my brain was screaming *you're acting like prey! You're putting yourself in more danger!* I couldn't stop. It was like my body wasn't my own anymore. It was probably too late to stop. My legs ached and my lungs burned. Those yellow eyes were all I could see; all I could think. What was happening? What was happening? What was happening? I couldn't think of what that could be. I had *never* seen eyes like that, and I couldn't bring myself to look behind me. I was too afraid of slowing down. I was too afraid of what I might see.

The caravan park was in the distance.

It was too far.

I felt the yellow-eyed creature's breath on the back of my throat. Tears streamed down my face. Was I going to die here?

My brother... I can't leave my brother. I can't die here. My brother was all I had left and, I was all he had too. I couldn't do that to him.

Not after everything...

I swung my elbow back and hit something solid. The pain throbbed down my arm but I couldn't feel the breath on the back of my neck anymore. I stopped just as I got past the gate to check behind me. Nothing. Empty air. I didn't know what else I expected.

Suddenly cold hand gripped my shoulder. I shrieked like a banshee and flailed about.

"Jesus Kelsey, it's just me." My brother groaned, rubbing the side of his head that I had thwacked. "What's the matter? You look like you've seen a ghost."

I had no idea what had been chasing me, but it was definitely corporeal... uh solid. How did I know that? Well, the blood dripping from my elbow, and rolling down my forearm was a hint. "I don't know. Some... *thing* was chasing me." I knew that I should have said 'someone' because there was no way that it could have been... and there was no way that he would believe that it was a *thing* but I couldn't bring myself to lie to David.

He frowned, concerned. "Did you see who it was?"

"No. It disappeared as fast as it appeared." I told him. I was shaking but I wasn't sure if it was down to fear or leftover adrenaline. My eyes darted everywhere but I couldn't see anything. "Let's go inside." We hurried inside our caravan to be greeted by Sergeant. She was ecstatic to see me... as per usual. I scratched her head, watching as her ears flopped around from the motion before sitting down in front of my brother. "David, I have something to tell you..."

"I know. School called. Do you want a chance to explain?"

I'd rather do *anything* else. Well, maybe not anything else. I had no urge to run into that yellow-eyed thing again. My brother's tone had been completely even and I couldn't gage his reaction. "Umm... Well... Delilah spread rumours about me. I proved that they were false in front of her friends and she tried to hit me, so I punched her in the face. Mrs Wilson saw me."

He nodded. "Are you ok? Did she hit you?"

I shook my head. "I ducked. That boxing club I used to go to really paid off." I ran my fingers through my hair and fidgeted with the fur underneath Sergeant's collar. "Are you angry with me?"

He laughed. "I know I probably should be but I'm honestly proud that you could defend yourself more than anything else." I was expecting him to react differently. "It's comforting to know that you can throw good enough a punch to break a bully's nose. Especially if I'm not around to protect you."

"I don't need your protection, David." I folded my hands across my chest. "I..."

"I know. I know. You are an independent woman. You don't need a man to protect you. Yah dah yah dah yah dah. I'm your older brother and it's my job to worry about you. It's my job to protect you."

"Yeah. Yeah. Yeah. Love you too." I rolled my eyes melodramatically.

"By the way. I told them that you can`t go without your dog."

I blinked. "You did? What did they say?"

"They agreed." I was surprised. "But I get the feeling that they severely underestimated the size of Sergeant."

I smirked. I could already see the expression on Delilah`s face. "Thank you,"

He smiled calmly. "I`ll take Sergeant out." Oh, thank God. "You can sort out dinner." I wandered into the kitchen and my phone rang, making me jump. It was Adria. "Hello?"

"Are you ok? I heard what happened! This is all bullshit! Veneman is such a prick!" She blurted down the phone.

"I`m fine." I assured her, covering up a laugh.

"This is all bullshit! It is Year Eleven for God`s sake! You shouldn`t be taking time out now! I will make sure that nothing like this will ever happen here again! They would never have pulled this with anyone else! Just because it is an honour student and Delilah Delaney. I will stage an uprising! A rebellion!"

I laughed. "It won`t make a difference, Adria. They`re adults. They only see us as children. Nobody will listen."

"I`m going to make them listen!" She assured me. "I`m going to go and work on my campaign speech. Talk to you later." She hung up.

I had never known Adria to ever be fired up enough to do something about anything before. It was kind of cool. I loved that she could be fired up enough to try and change something. She was usually the type to sit in the corner and deal with things. She may cry about it later and rant about it to me. She wasn`t timid but quiet. I felt proud of her.

I pulled out some of the old pizza from the fridge and grabbed two plates when my phone buzzed. I had never had so much noise coming from my phone.

I checked. The text read: *'Hi, Adria gave me ur number.'*

I wrote back, frowning. *'Who is this?'*

'Mason. R u ok? This is Kelsey, rite?'

'Yes, this is Kelsey. I`m fine. Thanks for asking.' God damn it, Adria! *'How are you?'*

'Good. Wanted to c if u r ok. TTYL.'

I finished serving up our dinner and looked out the kitchen window to see Mrs Harris and Tibbles. I waved with a smile. Strange, I thought as I walked away from the window. I was always sure that Mrs Harris had blue eyes.

Three

"You aren't bringing that fucking *thing* on here!" The bus driver snorted, glaring down at Sergeant.

"I am not going into the middle of nowhere without my dog!" I retorted.

"I don't care! That dog will take up half the bus!" He snarled, his fat face growing increasingly red.

I crossed my arms tightly across my chest and arched an eyebrow. Sergeant sat next to me, wagging her tail so fast that dust and stones were spraying everywhere. "I'm not going anywhere without Sergeant."

Mrs Veneman glared at me. "If you don't go on this trip then you're expelled."

I gave her a pleasant smile. "Great. I'll be heading home then." I span around just as Mrs Veneman stormed past me to talk to the driver. She whispered something in his ear.

He looked at her and then at me. "Get the both of you on the bus."

We made our way onto the bus. What did she say to him? I sat at the back with Sergeant so she could lay across the three seats as I attached her to her seat belt and harness.

There were only six of us on the bus (not including the dogs, Mrs Veneman, or the driver); Delilah, one of her giggle girls called Precious Silverton, a really creepy perv called Seth Hoyt and two girls I didn't recognise.

Precious Silverton had her bleach blonde hair cut into a bob with a fringe to match. She had a spray tan that made Donald Trump's look tame. Her face was circular with her hooker-red lips in a near permanent frown. Her eyebrows were significantly darker than her hair (though still blonde). Her eyes were surrounded by heavy eyeshadow and mascara. Her eyes were dark pink in colour (we were all certain that they were contacts) and they were covered by hot pink heart-shaped glasses that nobody was entirely sure that she really needed. She was tall; at 5'6 with extremely long legs but you couldn't always tell because she was always slumped. When asked it was because she couldn't be bothered to stand up straight. Her nose was wide, and her lips were narrow. She always walked around in short shorts, a grungy hoodie (the same one; it was never washed) and a unicorn top from a tv show for children. In her hand was her phone that would have costed as much as an average person's rent. She was sat on Seth's lap with Delilah next to her.

Precious was one of Delilah's favourite lackies, happy to do *whatever* Delilah says, and she made sure to fit in. There was just as many rumours about Precious as Delilah at any given time as both of them wanted to always be the centre of attention. Precious could have been Delilah in any other school. She had enough of the boys flocking to her (although I could not begin to understand why). Especially with that hoodie that must have been mouldy at this point. She never used to be like this, but she discovered the power that came with acting like Delilah, with being cruel. When Game of Thrones came out, she started calling herself the 'Breaker of Chains' because of how many relationships she'd destroyed.

She acted like she was proud but there was a reason why she never smiled.

Seth Hoyt was a sick pervert that got away with everything. Seth was shorter than Precious at 4'11. He was even shorter than I was, with a doughy, circular face and more spots than skin. His eyes were black, and he had long lashes framing them. He had a curly dark purple pixie cut and a straightened fringe to hide the fact that he was balding already. This hairstyle, especially the colour wasn't allowed but he got away with it. His body was slumped and covered with an orange hoodie. He was covered with piercings, concealer, and snot. In one hand he held his phone and in the other he had Precious's flat chest.

Seth Hoyt was the kind of guy that 'accidentally' walked into the girl's changing room the same day every week, halfway through the changing time. He was the guy that called every girl 'hey sexy' and offered to do her. He breathed down your neck in the lunch queue only for you to find out that he had a pre-packed lunch. There were few people who disgusted me more in this world.

I couldn't see much of the other two girls besides that one was blonde and the other had snow-white hair.

The conversation between Precious, Delilah and Seth wasn't one that I wished to overhear but snippets seemed to always float in my direction.

Sergeant was not happy about being on the bus. She wanted to walk around but for obvious reasons, I wouldn't let her. Her monstrous head rested on my lap. Though cute, it was slightly uncomfortable. Not moving my aching legs, I turned to look out the window. We had been driving through the woods for at least forty-five minutes now and I saw no sign for whatever camp we were going to. We were driving along a winding dirt road that the bus barely fitted on. Trees loomed over us ominously, branches grabbing at the roof like hands. Outside of the bus, I hadn't seen any sign of any other people. All there was to look at was the trees, mud, and bushes. I hadn`t even seen the wild horses. It was so dark that you wouldn`t believe it was still daytime. It was another hour before we saw the sign reading 'Joe`s Camp for Troubled Teens'. The post was rotten and covered with moss and dirt while the sign itself was still shiny. It made it impossible to tell how old the camp was.

Sergeant`s ears fell back, and her eyes shot around.

"You ok, girl?" I stroked her head gently and that seemed to be enough to snap her out of it.

Despite the sign, we drove for another hour before we actually arrived at the camp. There was a dirt road and a dirt path to match and due to typical English weather, it was so muddy that I wished that I had worn welly boots instead of the holey third-or-forth-hand walking boots. The cabins were only a little bit larger than the average garden shed. There would only be enough space for two sets of bunkbeds. Many of the wooden panels on the cabins were new and they stood out like a pink top at a gothic night club. Everything around was faded and green except the occasional replaced plank. There was an eating area with a barbeque and a small sheltered outdoor kitchen area. The kind of benches and wooden tables that you would find in parks were littered around. An assault course peaked out from behind one of the cabins and it looked so dilapidated and rotten that I was concerned that if I stepped on it, my foot would go straight through.

Certainly, would add more stakes to completing the assault course.

Other students were waiting for us there (though only a few), just enough to balance out the numbers between boys and girls.

"Hello campers!" Smiled an excitable man, jumping on one of the tables. The table groaned underneath him. "Welcome to Joe`s Camp for Troubled Teens! I`m Joe and I am the camp director here." He was a short man; five foot six at most. The puff of brown hair on his head was balding along with sprinkles of grey. He couldn't have been past his early thirties but he was skinnier than the average teenage boy. Harry-Potter-glasses rested on his nose, that one of the boys had made sure to point out seconds after our arrival with a snicker. He was slouched uncomfortably forward. "You all know why you're here and I want to tell you that your past mistakes don't matter here. You are here to learn, make friends and grow as people. You will take your usual classes with the work sent here by your usual teachers. You have all been assigned cabins so please go place all your things in your cabin and make your way to the eating area in fifteen minutes." There were three other camp leaders but they didn't really speak. Honestly, that was fair considering how much Joe did.

I hauled my things along the cabins. After scanning them, I found mine at the very end; Cabin 13. That bodes well. There was a sign out front that read: *Cabin Thirteen: Rin Anderson, Kelsey Alexander + Therapy Animal, Bianca French, and Precious Silverton. Please keep the cabin clean and do not invite members of the opposite sex into your cabin. You may not exchange cabins and you may not leave this cabin after curfew. Enjoy your stay.*

Opening the door, I discovered that everyone else had made it there before me. The other girls were the ones on the bus.

The one closest to me, sitting on the bottom bunk had short white hair in a similar style to that of Precious. She had Harry Potter glasses that hid amethyst coloured eyes and long lashes. She probably had the most beautiful eyes I had ever seen. She wore a hand-knitted jumper that was far too big for her. She chewed on her lower pink lip and fidgeted with the sleeve of her jumper. She was slim with average curves and slight features.

The other girl was sitting cross-legged on the other bed. She could have been Delilah's twin. I never thought I could find a girl that was prettier than Delilah but there she sat. She hadn't bothered with the make-up or the designer clothes. She wore a black off-shoulder top and flaring jeans. She was curvier than Delilah but still quite slender. Her hair was long and a natural blonde with a fringe similar to that of Precious' but it suited this girl perfectly. She had a petite nose and full lips with a smidge of lip gloss. Her eyes were hazel, and she had perfect cheekbones. She looked like she had fallen out an article on Britain's prettiest models. She looked up, revealing small hoop earrings, and smiled. She jumped down and strode over to me, hand outstretched for me to shake. "Hi, I'm Bianca French. You must be Kelsey, it's a pleasure to meet you." I was surprised at how tall she was; five foot, nine or ten.

"Nice to meet you too." I shook her hand.

"Wow, you have tiny hands." She seemed to be in awe despite the fact that her hands were perfect; small, slender with perfect nails.

"Yeah, I get that a lot." I pointed to Sergeant. "This is Sergeant, my dog."

She stroked Sergeant's head. "Hi. Is he the therapy animal?"

"She isn't a therapy animal. She's a pet. I don't know why they put that there." I answered honestly, but I was certain that nobody present believed that.

"Ok, well this is Rin and that's Precious." Bianca introduced us. I waved at Rin but Precious didn't acknowledge my presence and I didn't bother to greet her either. "The only bed left is top bunk. I hope you don't mind."

Good thing I remembered to bring Sergeant's bed. "Sounds good. It's nice to meet you, Rin."

Rin blushed at the attention on her. "Y-you too."

We unloaded our stuff and headed over to the eating area where Joe was waiting for us. He hadn`t moved from the table and I couldn`t help but wonder if it was because he was nervous to get off. I would be.

"Thank you for all coming back here so quickly." He told us with a smile. The man seemingly never stopped smiling. "We have a few rules to go over but first you need to turn over all cellular devices, apple watches and the like." There were groans of protest but after a few minutes everyone had given them up.

"It`s ok, Rin." Bianca reassured her.

Rin shook her head. "No, it`s not. Ricky is going to be so worried when I can`t contact him."

"Your boyfriend can go without you while we`re here."

"He`s going to be so worried."

Delilah strutted over to me. "I`m in this dump and I can`t even Instagram about it." She pointed a perfectly painted nail between my eyes. "This is your fault, you stupid tart, if you hadn`t…" As she stepped forward, Sergeant growled, stopping the girl dead in her tracks. Even under all the make-up she had on her face, you could see her face pale.

Shocked, I started down at my dog. I had never heard her make that sound before. It echoed through my chest like thunder. Don`t get me wrong. I could never be afraid of Sergeant, but I could understand why Delilah would be.

"Hey, hey, hey," Joe started, Sergeant still growling. "What`s all this fuss?" He turned to me. "Young miss, it`s lovely that you have your dog here but during activities he has to be in your cabin. Ok?" I nodded solemnly. I didn`t want to be parted from Sergeant but equally, the more Sergeant was around Delilah, the more likely she was to get in trouble. I couldn`t let Sergeant get hurt because of Delilah. I quickly took her back to the cabin, my stomach twisting with nerves at the thought of her being separated from me. Maybe she was a therapy animal.

Joe leapt back onto the table, making everyone around wince. He waited for me to come back before he started talking again. "Ok campers; rules! Rule number One: no wandering off. You could get lost and we don`t want that. Rule number Two: stay in your designated cabins. No mix-matching and no boys in girl cabins. No girls in boy cabins. Rule number Three: Complete all tasks to the best of your ability. You have to get involved otherwise you can end up staying here longer than the week." I honestly hadn`t thought to ask how long we were staying here for between the grumpy bus driver and the… Delilah. It was a relief to hear that it was only a week. "Rule number Four: remember to enjoy yourselves!" He jumped forward and off the table. The table made a loud cracking sound after he got off, making everyone but Joe flinch. This place had to be a giant safety hazard. "Ok, off to lessons. Let me show you the education cabin."

Classwork was as boring as it always has been. There was no real difference besides the fact that we were navigating the tasks alone instead of with a teacher telling us how. I think I preferred it that way. Not everyone felt the same, but I liked just being able to get on with it without the freeze moment of when a teacher looked over your shoulder. You`d think after four years of me being in that school, at least one of the teachers would have learned that I stop writing when they start staring. Once we had finished the tasks to the best of our ability, we posted them into a box where they would be sent off to our teachers at the end of the week.

Lunch was a little bit more eventful. I ended up sat with my roommates (minus Precious who was sat with Delilah, another girl and Seth). Joe came and sat with us, chatting happily. He seemed nice; harmless. "You can walk your dog around the camp but don`t go off into the woods and remember to clean up the dog's mess. There are bins all over the site. Use any one of them." I nodded my thanks and finished my cheese and ham sandwich. I didn't like cheese sandwiches and I didn't like ham sandwiches, but when put together, they were delicious. One of life's strange mysteries. They gave us all a cornetto. I was surprised that they gave us that but didn't question it. Joe sat there for nearly a minute staring at my ice-cream. He jumped to his feet abruptly. "I need me one of those cornettoes before I run off with yours." He told me.

What an odd man was all I could think as he tripped over a bin on his way.

"He's a little odd, isn't he?" Bianca voiced my thoughts after he left. Rin and I nodded in agreement. "He seems nice, though." I was glad that somebody else agreed with me on that. Rin excused herself to go to the bathroom, leaving just Bianca with me.

"Hey baby," Seth grinned, looking Bianca up and down hungrily. I winced, unsure what to say. "A beauty like you deserves the best seat in the house." He gestured to his lap, rubbing his legs.

"And a mutt like you deserves a shock collar." I interrupted the exchange. Bianca gave me a thankful look.

He smirked, moving between us, his hand too close to my shoulder for me to be comfortable. "Don't worry, gorgeous. There is plenty enough of Seth Hoyt to go around."

"We're not interested." Bianca insisted. He moved to touch her thigh, but she slapped his hand away.

"Feisty," He wiggled his eyebrows and licked his lips. "I like that in a woman." He moved to touch her again just as Precious Silverton skipped up.

"Come on Diddums. Come sit with me." They simpered off, his hands slowly going lower down her back.

"What a creep." Bianca glared at him.

"Yeah,"

We did some team-building exercises and I was partnered with Delilah *every single* time. It started with 'I feel that…' tasks.

"I feel that your hair looks like a rat's nest." She told me, smiling pleasantly.

"I feel that your nose is too big for your face." I replied, unfazed by her comment. My hair was always a mess.

Covering her nose for a few seconds, she glared. "I feel that you're a goblin."

"I feel that you're a troll." I countered, whip quick.

"I feel like those shoes are so outdated!" She screeched and I laughed.

"I feel that you can't walk properly in those heels."

"That's enough ladies," Joe was sweating nervously but he still had a smile. "How about we mix up the pairs now?" He paired me with Rin who had been with Precious.

We sat down opposite each other, awkwardly. "Umm… Do you want to go first?" I asked shyly.

She shook her head and pulled down her sleeves so that you couldn't see her hands. "N-no, y-you go."

I breathed out. "Umm… I feel that your glasses are seriously cool."

She blinked in surprise and stopped fidgeting. "Thank you. I f-feel that your top is really cool." I looked down to see my AC DC top.

"Thank you," I replied. "I feel that I'm jealous of your eyes."

She smiled, showing off her braces. "I feel that you have awesome hair."

"I feel that we are going to get on."

"I feel that we should be friends."

"I feel that I agree with that statement."

Eventually Rin and I dropped the 'I feel that...' and just had a regular conversation. She and I had a lot in common;

both liking Russell Howard, shounen anime and Team Four Star's Hellsing Ultimate Abridged. She and I sat there fangirling over the Morganville Vampires book series, until she told me about her boyfriend Ricky. Ricky was a rugby player and the tallest guy in her school.

She seemed smitten which was so sweet.

Afterwards there were trust falls and I was back with Delilah again. She didn't trust me enough to fall (not that I blame her as I was resisting the urge to move every time she started) and there was no way I was falling into her arms in this lifetime. Even if I trusted her to catch me (which I didn't), I did not want her to touch me. Next was a puzzle that we had to complete before all the other pairs. I ended up doing it on my own. I did still come second place, but Delilah still shouted at me over it. "Why are you so fucking slow?!" She screamed. "Are you retarded or something?!"

Joe gasped. "Delilah, we don't ever use the r-word here. Apologise to your friend."

"She's not my friend!"

"She's your neighbour on this Earth, making her your friend. Apologise."

"Forgiven," I told her. I had no urge to pro-long this experience.

"Very mature of you, Kelsey." Joe told me. "You're all dismissed for dinner."

Delilah glared at me murderously and I replied with a polite smile, pissing her off even more. You could almost see the vein throbbing in her forehead. Her eyes were on me all the way through dinner and afterwards when we were given free time to do with as we pleased. We were given a red ice lolly for pudding. Joe must really like his frozen treats.

I spent my free time walking Sergeant around the campsite. The forest, though dark, was beautiful and Sergeant enjoyed darting in and out of the trees.

"Abomination." Growled a low voice from nowhere. I froze. My eyes darted around but all I could see was Sergeant, ears back growling at everything and nothing. If it wasn't for Sergeant's behaviour, I would have thought I had imagined it. "Abomination." The voice repeated, closer now. "Seek. Destroy. Devour. Seek. Destroy. Devour. Seek. Destroy. Devour." The log next to me (that must have weighed at least three times my weight) flew from the ground and smashed against a neighbouring tree. Splinters sprayed through the air but somehow, none touched me. I fell back in shock, looking around. I hadn't seen anything touch it. I hadn't seen anything at all. I wasn't sure when I started to shake but I felt sick with nerves. Whatever it was… it was strong, and I had no urge to stay around and find out what it wanted to devour. I scampered off towards my cabin, hearing its voice still. It always seemed to be at the same distance away from me. "Seek. Destroy. Devour. She looks like her daughter. She looks like her daughter. Abomination. Seek. Destroy. Devour."

It was starting to get dark and everyone seemed to be already back in the cabins. The voice had gone silent and somehow that frightened me more. I felt eyes on me but I couldn't tell where from. As I opened the cabin door, I looked out into the trees.

Glowing, pale, blue eyes stared back.

I flinched and scrambled into the cabin, filled Sergeant's bowls and turned to the others. They were staring at me, startled. "Where's Precious?"

"She is in another cabin." Bianca replied, her eyes filled with concern at my behaviour. "She said she was bunking with 'Sethy'. Do you have any idea who that is?"

"Yeah. Creepy guy from lunch,"

"Oh, ew…" Bianca grimaced with a shiver. "Did you know that at lunch he offered us a seat with him?" She directed this at Rin and gestured between us. "And by with him, he meant on his lap."

Rin looked up in horror, putting down her book. "What a creep."

I nodded. "Seth has walked into the girl's changing room by 'accident' at least eight times this term. He sends pictures to every girl he knows. It's why all my social media doesn't have my name."

"Well at least Rin is in the clear." Bianca grinned. "Her boyfriend, Ricky made a big deal about kissing her in front of everyone when we arrived. He had a chat with Seth too. I reckon he was marking his territory." Bianca looked to Rin who was redder than Mrs's Veneman's lipstick this morning.

"Let's hope it's enough, huh?" I looked down at my muddy trousers. "I should probably get changed and ready for bed." I pulled my pyjamas out of my suitcase and walked over to the girl's toilets/ showers, keeping an eye out for everything around. I knew that it was risky leaving the cabin but with whatever it was being capable of tossing the tree like that, would have no problem getting into a dilapidated cabin. Besides, I wasn't comfortable getting dressed in front of my new cabin-mates.

The first thing I noticed when I walked in was a chair in the corner. Odd. I stepped inside and they sprang out. Delilah, Precious and the other girl they had been with at lunch. They shoved me into the shower stall harshly. I wrapped my arms around my head to shield myself from impact. This was going to hurt. I landed on my hip, the pain rippling through my body like a wave, and I cried out. They cackled and I heard them slam the door shut as they left the building. I crawled to my feet and hobbled to the door. They had blocked it with the chair. Who the Hell thought that outward-opening doors was a good idea? Especially at a camp for teenagers? Delilah and her cronies were gone, and I was left slamming my fists against the door. With slippery floors, I had to be careful how I moved otherwise a bruised hip would be the last of my worries.

Every second that past made the cubicle feel smaller and smaller and my breathing increased. Tears tickled the corners of my eyes. I could be in here all night, and it was December, it was cold. In a December night in the UK, this little building wouldn't keep me warm.

What if I froze to death in the night?

There was only so long that the shower's hot water would stay that way and I couldn't rely on that to keep me warm throughout the night. The adrenaline pumping through my body would keep me warm for now, but it would exhaust me.

My mind went back to when I was little, and I wanted to go camping in the snow. David had said that if you feel warm enough to fall asleep in this weather, you won't wake up.

A long creak told me that the door to the building opened. "Excuse me?" I called out still trying to be polite even in my desperation. Hope warmed my body. "Hello? Can you help me? I can't get out." I felt whoever it was yank out the chair and toss it away. I could hear the chair slam against the wall. My rescuer opened the door. "Thank y_"

Blue eyes.

I was greeted by the same glowing, pale, blue eyes as before. The chair was splinters on the floor and this huge man stood in front of me with those completely unnatural eyes. He was around 6' tall with broad shoulders. His hair was jet black and stuck out at every angle imaginable. He had plump lips and a strong jaw with a scattering of stubble. He was the only person I had ever seen that was paler than myself but he didn't look bad for it. He was like a marble statue from Roman times. He didn't move... at all. He wasn't even breathing. "Thank you," I corrected, trying not to show how afraid I was.

When he did move, it was predatory and far quieter than a man of his size should be capable of. "You're welcome,

Little One." It was the voice from before. I knew it would be. He reached for my face. I froze. He moved my face by my chin. My heart twisted with anticipation. I could feel his strength with every movement, and I was sure that he could rip my head from my neck if he wanted to. I trembled slightly but he didn't seem to care. "Just like her. Just like me." He dropped his hand faster than anyone I'd ever seen before, making me flinch. "Fear the dark, Little One and know that I am there defending you from it." I blinked and he was gone like he had never been there in the first place. Relief coursed through me but I couldn't bring myself to sigh. It was a strange feeling to fear something like him. It was strange that I wanted him to stay, to talk to me and at the same time, I wanted him as far from me as possible.

I got changed quickly and scurried back to the cabin, my eyes darting everywhere before I got inside. Logically, I should know that being inside the cabin didn't mean that I was safe, but I felt safer inside. Bianca was already asleep. Rin was caught up in her book and Precious wasn't there at all.

Sergeant wagged her tail at my entrance, and I sat there with her for a while, stroking her fur reassuringly.

Looking out the window, I watched as those blue eyes dissolved into darkness of the trees.

Four

"What the fuck?!" Blurted one of the boys from outside of the cabin. The sound jolted us out of sleep with a start. It was still dark outside. I could just see the outline of Bianca in the bed opposite me. We looked at each other and made our way down the ladder.

"What`s going on?" Rin whimpered, looking to Bianca.

"I don`t know." She replied, her tone calm and serious.

I rubbed sleep out of my eyes, and I looked to Sergeant. She was awake and staring out the window. I decided to keep her here, where it felt safer. We stepped sockless into our shoes and made our way outside, with the others behind me. We halted on the step on the step of the cabin. We stared in horror at the vehicles in a mangled heap in the centre of the camp.

How had we not heard it? How could this have not woken us all up?

The metal was torn and contorted at unnatural angles. It was in a heap. Cars twisted into each other. We should have heard it. We should have heard the vehicles being bent into each other.

"What could have done this?" The girl who was with Delilah before blurted.

Joe ran out in a purple dressing gown. "Good Heavens! Everybody remain calm. Let me make a phone call." He ran off back to his cabin.

"You have something to do with this, don't you, Alexander?" Delilah hissed. She was barely recognisable without her make-up on.

"How the Hell could I possibly be capable of that?" I pointed at the mangled metal. "You're so bitter, it's making you delusional!"

Joe returned. "I need to check something. Follow me." We were led to the outskirts of the camp where there were some telephone wires that were so well disguised by the trees that I hadn't even noticed that they were even there until now. 'Were', was the key word in that sentence as the telephone wires had been ripped to strands and there were bodies of other camp leaders littering the surrounding areas. "Oh crumbs! Children, look away!" I couldn't. Those people were bent into completely unnatural poses with their chests wide open and empty. Their lips had seemingly been ripped off.

My stomach twisted with nausea and for a second, I thought I was going to throw up. Someone nearby did but I couldn't see who.

"Everybody rem_" Whatever Joe meant to say was cut off with a roar and the lights all slamming off with a groaning sound. He screamed and we scattered. I made a beeline back to my cabin. Though it was the furthest away, there was no way in Hell that I was abandoning my dog.

Pitch black, and everyone was bouncing into each other. I could hear the screams as people were yanked off by whatever it was. Nobody ran as far as I did. Soon I was the only one left outside, besides something scuttling behind me. I flung the door open, threw myself inside. I slammed the door shut and shoved everything in the way of the door as fast as I could until I heard whatever it was fling itself at the door with a BANG!

Sergeant growled lowly and barked at the door. I wrapped my arms around her neck and shushed her, remaining quiet afterwards.

My heart was beating so loudly, I was sure that it could hear. I hoped that if I remained quiet then it would grow bored. Everything was so quiet. I was trembling, clinging to my dog like she was my lifeline.

It crawled across the roof, every step making a smacking noise. It was the only sound I could hear. I buried my face into Sergeant's fur. It was going to be ok, I assured myself but I didn't believe it. The nausea in my stomach was only getting worse and I felt like I was either going to throw up or burst into tears. It was going to get me. I was going to die here. There was nowhere to run, and it knew where I was hidden.

Then, there was silence. It unnerved me more than any sound I could have heard.

Its hand smashed through the wall next to me, reaching for me blindly. I shrieked as Sergeant latched herself onto it. It howled, knocking Sergeant away. She was back on her feet in an instance, a black liquid dripping from her jaws. I snatched up the bedroom lamp and slammed the lamp stand down onto it. It made a sound unlike anything I'd ever heard before. It pulled bloody limb back out through the hole.

Silence resumed. What was I going to do? I couldn't stay here. It smashed through that wall like it was tissue paper. There was nowhere to go. We were surrounded by miles of woodland in all directions. I'd never make it.

What the fuck was it anyway? The only thing that I could think of was the man with the blue eyes but he wouldn't hurt me, would he? No, he saved me. Although…

He didn't seem quite right and he was the only thing I knew of with the kind of strength to be capable of something like this.

What makes you think that he is the only dangerous creature among these trees?

Screams ripped through the silence, each stopped after a few seconds, ending abruptly as if some*thing* had torn the sound from their mouths. Had it killed them? Where was it? Where_? "Kelsey," Called an inhuman voice from outside the cabin. "Kelsey?" It sounded like a bad recording from fifty years ago; crackly and unnatural. "Kelsey... Come out, come out, Kelsey!" The voice sent chills down my spine and my eyes prickled with tears. How the fuck did it know my name? "Kelsey... I don`t want this one, Kelsey. His lips aren`t big enough for my tastes but yours..." I reached to my mouth, unsure if I did it to muffle a sob or to feel my lips. I did have plump lips; they were possibly my best feature but, in that moment, they were the last thing on Earth I wanted. "Your lips will be delectable..." It made a noise like grinding glass. It rattled through my bones. It took me a moment to realise that it was laughter. "Make this easy for me Kelsey and I might just let this one go..."

"Help! Please!" The boy begged, sobbing. I couldn`t even see his face but his voice was enough to tell me he was terrified. I was terrified. "I don`t want to die! I don`t want to die!"

In that moment, my mind was made. I crawled across the floor to find Precious` suitcase. Unzipping it, I rummaged through until I found what I was looking for: a lighter. I picked up the lamp again and began pushing all of the things in front of the door, out of the way. I crawled through the gap, leaving Sergeant in the cabin. She whimpered as I left.

I`m sorry, baby girl. Hopefully, this thing had no interest in dogs.

I made my way towards its voice. "Yes, yes, come here, Kelsey Alexander, come here..." I lit the lighter so I could see my way.

It stood there. It was tall, thin, gangly with every bone seeming dangerously close to sticking out of its skin. It had hard, sharp claws.

And it was alone...

It laughed again. "*Help! Please! I don`t want to die! I don`t want to die!*" I hadn`t spared the life of another person. I had fallen into the trap of whatever this *thing* was. It charged for me, moving too fast for me to outrun. I prepared for impact and to defend myself the best I could, the lamp shielding my face, before something dark slammed into the creature, sending it metres away. Sergeant burst out of the cabin behind me, and ran forward, barking and snarling. I looked up to my saviour. Glowing blue eyes looked back.

"Run," He growled.

He didn`t need to tell me twice.

I sprinted for the nearest cabin to me. In reality I was there in seconds, but the moment passed like hours. I couldn`t see what was behind me (not that I`d dare look back) and identify what was winning the battle taking place loudly behind me. I heard smashing, hissing and inhuman noises that I couldn`t possibly describe. I booted the door open. Sergeant and I dived through and whoever was in there with me slammed it shut behind us. I lit the lighter to see Rin and Bianca. They were alive. They gestured for me to be quiet and pointed to the window. I could vaguely make out the shape of that thing, but Blue Eyes was nowhere to be seen. It was several yards away and then outside the window in a flash. I fell back in surprise, yelping. "Three big-lipped girls... What a treat." It licked around its lipless mouth. Sergeant snarled at it, jumping at the window. It backed off, glaring at my dog. "Vile creature! Bah!" It slammed its fist through the window and slithered through. Sergeant attacked it but the creature just batted her away. She yelped.

"Sergeant!" I cried. "You son of a bitch!"

It had a grip on Rin's shoulder, yanking her towards its body where its sharp-clawed hand waited by her belly. She struggled, screaming but the grip was too strong. "That sanguisuge won't save you now. Too busy conversing with the voices in its head."

Was it talking about Blue Eyes?

I didn't care. It had hurt Sergeant and now it was hurting my friend. I picked up one of the shards of glass and shoved it as hard as I could into its eyeball. It screeched, dropping Rin onto the floor. "You little whore!" It batted blindly, knocking me to the ground next to Rin. Bianca scrambled forward and yanked Rin and I away by our shoulders. We made a beeline for the door, Sergeant slamming it open with her body as we opened it.

I clicked the lighter on the way, lighting the curtains on the way out. The cabin was ablaze in seconds. We ran to the cabin opposite to find Precious and Seth huddled in a corner with Delilah under her bed. I slammed the door shut and stared out the window. I watched in horror as it stepped out of the flames and pulled the shard of glass out of its eye, with the same manner I would pull a small splinter out of my thumb.

"You can't be in here!" Delilah hissed. "It's after you. It will know where we are now because of you. Stupid bitch!" She crawled out from under the bed and shoved me out the door. Before she could shut the door, Sergeant went for the arm that had pushed me. Delilah moved out of the way just in time and slammed the door shut behind me. I fell straight into the mud on the ground outside. It was coming towards me, grinning with twisted delight. I tried to get up but couldn't. The mud was cold, deep, and sticky, keeping me in place.

No. No. No. No. No. No.

I struggled, desperately to get out but I just kept slipping. I struggled and then I was on my back, as helpless as a new-born. My chest felt like my heart was slamming against it. I was so fucked.

I`m going to die. I`m going to die. I`m going to die.

If it didn`t kill me, I thought that fear might.

"Helpless little creature..." Came a melodic voice from behind the cabin. Blue Eyes. "Why do you fight death so hard, Little One?"

"Help... Please!" I could barely recognise my voice as my own with the level of fear and shakiness in it.

He cocked his head, looking more creature than man. "Are you stuck, Little One?" I don`t know if it was his company that brought me out of the blind panic, but tears stopped rolling down my face and I stopped struggling.

I breathed, trying to calm myself. "Yes. You said you would defend me from the darkness. Did you mean that?"

His brows furrowed. "Did I say that? I don`t recall. Have we met before, Little One?" I nodded, trying to ignore the sensation of my hair trapped in the mud. "Interesting. Perhaps they are keeping things from me... So, confused!" He sounded frustrated, desperate. "You do look so familiar, Little One." It... He looked up from me and at the creature skipping towards me. "Abomination." He growled. "Is this what hunts you, Little One?" I squeaked and nodded. I don`t know how he knew that I answered because he hadn`t taken his eyes off the creature. He stepped forward, pulling me from the mud with ease on his way. I fell forwards at his movement, my hip giving way on the way down and I landed clumsily on the steps of the cabin.

"Thank you,"

I struggled up, my pyjamas wet and heavy. He didn`t answer, instead he stalked towards the creature coming towards us. He moved so silently that his feet didn`t even squelch in the mud. Everything about the way he moved was predatory. He was hunting the thing that was hunting me. He slammed into the creature, sending it back several feet before they charged into each other again. They moved too fast for me to see properly as I stared in a mixture of terror and awe of what was in front of me.

It took me a few minutes to snap out of the trance and run to the cabin door. I hammered my fists against the door. Bianca opened it and yanked me inside. She turned to Delilah. "You will not push her out again. You hear me?" Delilah glared at the taller girl but said nothing.

I peered out the window, running my muddy hands through my muddy hair. The area illuminated by the burning cabin. The blue-eyed man had the upper hand, pinning the creature into the dirt. Then he grabbed the sides of his head and cried out. "No. It wasn't me! No! No! The earth and the sky will merge in the nether realms. One two…" He was rambling and rocking back and forth. "No! He took the only thing worth taking. He took the only thing worth taking. He took the only thing worth taking…"

I couldn't see anybody around him but the creature but he seemed to be speaking to empty air.

The creature danced towards the burning cabin and picked up a burning piece of timber. It danced a long, lighting the cabins, singing 'London Bridge is Burning down'. I watched in horror as one of the students ran out to escape the fire. It grabbed her and I watched helpless as it fed on her.

She screamed while it ate her insides.

It stared at me while it devoured her.

"It can't be hungry after that." Delilah reasoned, seemingly unfazed by what we just witnessed. "It ate the camp guy and her and all those people. It can't still be hungry."

"That thing isn't human." Bianca replied, unable to tear her hazel eyes away from the scene in front of us. "It shouldn't have been hungry after the first person but there's no telling of how much it eats."

Rin rubbed the scratches on her arm. "It's fast too. It will need a lot of food to keep up with its metabolism."

I shivered. "Please can you all stop talking like that." I looked at the limp body of the girl, lying there alone on the ground outside the burning cabin. "They aren't food. They're *people*."

"They're dead now." Delilah told us bluntly, rolling her eyes. "And we need to get out of here unless we want to join them." Though I hated to admit it, she was right. The creature was creeping around the campsite, setting the cabins on fire, and eating whoever ran outside to escape the flames. We had to get away while we still could.

"We need our phones." Precious insisted. We all turned to her. "We can't call for help without them and there is no way we're getting through those woods without a car."

She wasn't wrong. "Someone needs to get the phones." Seth pointed out. "Where would they even be?"

"The camp director's cabin." Rin stated. She pointed at the cabin two doors down from where the creature stood. "We're going to need a distraction."

Everyone turned to stare at me. "What? Why?"

"You have survived an attack from it at least three times now." Seth said. "It wants you. It has to be you."

Turning to my dog, I rubbed her head. Her ears flopped around, and she grinned, oblivious to the plans happening around her. "Ok, I'll do it. Rin, can you please take care of Sergeant for me?" She nodded solemnly, her eyes tearing up slightly.

I dropped my hand from Sergeant's head, turned and opened the door.

One step outside and it stopped its dance. Frozen, facing away from me. "I wondered how long it would take for you to come out, Kelsey Alexander." It was in front of me in a flash, blood still oozing from its eye as it looked down at me.

"Run. You all taste better when you're scared." I kneed it in the stomach and sprinted off... into the woods. It laughed. "Run little lamb... Run..."

Why did I think running through the woods at night was a good idea?

It wasn't running after me with any kind of speed. It strolled a long, singing. "*Ring o ring of roses.*" The creature wanted me to be afraid. I knew that was why it was behaving the way it was. It's trying to frighten me.

Well it's doing a damn good job, isn't it? Came an irritated voice from my head. *Use your head!*

It was hard to think of anything when I was screaming on the inside and my heart was beating so loudly that I couldn't hear my thoughts over the thumping.

I just want to go home. I want to be at home with David and Sergeant, watching Russell Howard on the tv with the crappy pizza we have all the time.

"*She smells just like roses.*" It sang. I can't see where it's coming from.

It was faster than me. That was never in doubt. I couldn't outrun it and fighting it only slowed it down. My best shot was to hide. My eyes scanned the area, hoping to see if there was anything around to hide in. Think! Think! Think! My best shot was to climb the large pine tree in front of me. It had a lot of branches so it would keep me concealed but the only problem with that is that it wouldn't be challenging to climb. If I could climb it, so could that thing.

Scrambling to the top, I was both thankful and nervous over the fact that I couldn't see the creature.

"*Ah-tissue, ah-tissue!*"

In theory if I can't see it, it can't see me. In reality, I was human, and it was anything but. There was no telling the limitations of its senses. I couldn't see in the dark but maybe it could. I tried to slow my breathing, to stop the trembling that was slightly shaking the tree I was clinging onto. I was hoping that it couldn't hear me. I was praying that it would think that the rustling sound my trembling was producing would be mistaken for wind. I was hoping that there was enough mud stained into my blue pyjamas that I would blend into the tree.

Part of me wished for Blue Eyes to run out of those trees and rip the creature into pieces but I knew that was unlikely. Blue Eyes was fighting his own demons, ones that I couldn't see.

The idea of something being able to make something as powerful as Blue Eyes like that; so afraid and trembling on the ground, was a very disturbing thought.

"*We all fall...*" It stopped. It was close. My eyes darted all around the forest floor to no avail. Where was it? "Down!" It yanked down hard on my leg. I screamed, dangling from the branch above me, clutching it as tightly as I could with both hands. I kicked at the creature with my other leg.

"When lions devour lions, the lamb is obsolete." Came a low voice from below. Blue Eyes... His gaze was fixed on the creature. It was as if he had heard my thoughts.

"Little puppy is sick in the head." The creature pointed out, letting go of me and smoothly dropping down to the forest floor. "I think it's time to say goodbye to the puppy. It needs to be put down."

"Run to the flock, little lamb." Blue Eyes ordered. It was directed at me but once again, he didn't take his eyes from the creature. "The realms of men are no longer your sanctuary. The brutality of nature is your only hope." They slammed into each other once more, a blur of claws and teeth. I scrambled down the tree and back the way I'd come.

The others were standing at the edge of camp, shouting at each other. Every cabin was on fire. "*We are not leaving without Kelsey!*" Bianca snarled, with Rin nodding in agreement. "She's the reason we got out of the cabin before it caught fire, you mythic asshole!"

"If we stay here, we all die!" Delilah snapped. "You aren't in charge here!"

"Neither are you." Bianca thundered. Her arms were crossed firmly across her chest.

I stumbled out of the trees, my knees knocking together. "We need to go." I pointed. "It's that way! Hurry. He can only buy us so much time."

"Who?" Bianca frowned, rubbing her arms.

"The blue-eyed man." I replied.

"What blue-eyed man?" Rin continued; her tone concerned.

"The one from earlier... You know... Didn't you see him out the window while I was outside?" I asked, confused. They had to have seen him, right? Didn't they look out the window to see them fight before?

"The only *thing* other than you outside was that creature." Delilah pointed out. "So, you're crazy... Whatever... Let's just get the fuck out of here." We ran down the small road we were driven down. "Precious, call the police."

She dialled the number. "There's no signal."

"Use a hotspot."

"It isn't working!"

"Well keep trying!" Delilah hissed. Our path was lit purely by phone light. It only lit the muddy path and the trees felt darker and taller around us. Though I knew that it could probably see us because of that it was our only...

"I have an idea!" Rin interrupted my train of thought. "We're all tired. It moves faster than us, it can clearly see in the dark and we are all running low on energy."

Seth scoffed. "What's your point?"

Rin flinched. "Well... Umm... I..." I gave her a reassuring look, a nod, and she stood up straight. She stared into his eyes. "We build a boma."

"Rin, that`s brilliant." I agreed. She gave me a thankful smile.

"What the fuck is a boma?" Precious sassed, rubbing her arms.

"A boma is a thorny wall Africans use to keep out lions." I explained. "We make it as high as we can, and we light a fire inside its walls." Honestly, the idea of fire was a welcoming one because all of us were purely in our pyjamas. Though nobody was in underwear, it was thin fabric and not enough to keep us warm through a December night. "Two of us stay awake on look out while the others sleep. We take shifts. It should keep that creature out and if it doesn`t, we set the son of a bitch on fire."

"There are brambles everywhere through these woods." Bianca nodded, clenching the sleeves of her pink pyjama top tighter. "If we survive until daylight, we can make our way through these woods far quicker and much more safely. It would give us much more of an advantage." Everyone nodded. "But we will have to do this quickly. God only knows how long we have before the creature comes back."

Funnily enough, it *only* took the threat of a violent death for Delilah to learn how to work. And despite everything, that was actually kind of funny.

With six of us all working as fast as we could, it took is just over half an hour to build the boma (we were very motivated). It was five feet tall and not as thick as I would have liked but it was too cold, and we were too tired to do much more. Delilah had a lighter, so she set a fire in the centre of the boma circle and she curled up to go to sleep. I decided to take first watch with Seth. It didn`t feel safe enough to fall asleep with him there. His eyes were hungry, and they shamelessly looked me up and down. Just his eyes on me made me feel like I needed a long shower (though that could have also been the mud). Sergeant glared at the boy, daring him to come closer. He didn't. He didn't make any lecherous comments or gestures. He just sat there staring.

I had never found him creepier.

For several hours, I sat closely to the fire and let the mud dry so I could dust off the mud. It took forever to get it dried and scraped off. It still felt horrible and my shirt was stuck crinkled at an angle. It felt sharp but it was better than the sloppy, wet mud, squelching against my back.

"Little One," I flinched at the voice by my neck and span around. Sergeant growled at Blue Eyes and my heartbeat calmed when I realised that it was him. Yes, he was frightening and there was no doubt that he was dangerous, but I felt safer with him here. How stupid is that? It was comforted by the presence of something that could rip me to pieces because I didn't want to be alone with the school perv. What could Seth really do? "How clever to build yourself a cage. The birdy cannot get out if the cat cannot get in."

"How did you get in here?" I demanded, sounding more confrontational than I intended. The sound of my voice woke everyone else up. They stared at Blue Eyes but said nothing.

He didn't seem to mind. "Pain is an old friend." He held up his bloody hands and I watched in twisted fascination as the cuts closed up, leaving scarless, blood-stained skin. "Be careful not to let a fox into the hen house." He eyed Seth, who trembled under his gaze. "The lion devours the fox faster than the fox devours the hens." It was a threat. Seth knew it was a threat and his black eyes widened in fear, and his lip wobbled. Blue Eyes turned back to me. "Remember; when lambs devour lions, the balance changes." Most of what he said was cryptic or nonsensical but there was a lot of intelligence behind what he was saying. It felt like he was talking in code that he knew I could understand without the others cluing in. Or that felt like the intention because much of what he said left me confused and nervous. "Happiness defends the island."

He got up to leave. "He comes for you all. Which will arrive first, I wonder?"

"Wait!" I protested, scrambling to my feet. He froze, inhumanly still, reminding me of a praying mantis. "What's your name?"

Confusion twisted his face as if I had asked him if he believed in aliens. "My name?" He seemed to think for a moment. "I have been called many over the years. I do not recall the first." Blue Eyes turned away from us and walked to the edge of the boma. "She used to call me 'Ben'."

"Goodbye, Ben." I smiled sadly at his tone. "Thank you for your help."

He grabbed the side of the boma and jumped over it.

"So, he was the blue-eyed man you were referring to earlier." Bianca stated once he was gone. "I get the feeling that he wasn't wearing contacts."

"That man was insane." Delilah blurted, her eyes still as wide as a deer in headlights. "Nothing he said made any sense!"

"Yes, it did." I protested, feeling rather defensive. Everyone turned to look at me like I was the one that was crazy. "Not all of what he said made sense but most of it did."

"Then explain 'when lambs devour lions…'." Precious snorted.

"He was suggesting that the longer we live, the more damage we do to that monster, the less power it has over us." I explained. Delilah didn't look very convinced. "He was telling us that the longer we live, the less confidence the creature has that it can beat us. It starts to doubt itself and vice-versa."

Bianca rubbed her head. "How did you get that from *that*?" I shrugged. "I guess it doesn't matter. What about the fox thing?"

"It was a threat."

"Huh. To who?"

'*Whom*' Rin mouthed, with an irritated look but, she said nothing.

"Seth,"

Precious looked like she had been slapped. She held his head to her chest. "Why would he threaten my Sethy-poo?"

The rest of the girls (including Delilah) all looked at each other. We all knew why.

"Well, at least we know that if he comes back," Bianca began, making herself comfortable on the damp ground. "We can use Kelsey as a human translator."

"Good night, Seth. I love you." Precious cooed.

"Night. Love you, too." He replied.

We swapped shifts around an hour later but I couldn`t sleep. Even after Seth was snoring, I couldn`t sleep. BI-Ben was right. There was danger inside the boma too. Sergeant`s nose nudged my hand. I knew what she was telling me. 'Go to sleep. I`ll watch over you.'

I think that her beautiful brown eyes were what comforted me enough to close my eyes.

Crack!

My eyes opened at the sudden noise to see cold eyes looking down at me from the tree above us. "Wake up. Wake up!" I scrambled to my feet as the creature leapt down into the boma with us, bringing the branch it was on crashing down with it. We scattered, rushing to the edges of the boma and tugging at the tangled brambles. At least it had protected us until daybreak. It charged for Seth and Precious first. She screamed. "Seth! What do we do?!"

He pulled the boma apart... And shoved Precious at the creature. "Bye," The creature gutted her in an instant.

We sprinted through the trees, running as fast as we could until we just couldn't anymore.

We all looked at each other, eyes wide; frightened and angry. Standing up straight, I strode over to Seth and punched him as hard in the face as I could. He fell to the ground with a cry. "What the fuck?!"

"You killed Precious!" I snarled, my body shaking. I wanted to hit him again. I may not have liked the girl but I didn't want to see her dead. "You son of a bitch!"

"You all should be thanking me!" He hissed, clutching the side of his face. He stumbled to his feet, manoeuvring further away from me (and closer to Bianca). "I'm the reason we got out of there. It was distracted enough to let us go! Besides... What was she to any of us? You three hated her! Delilah used her and to me she was just a good fuck_"

Bianca knocked him back down, her hazel eyes blazing with anger. "You're a fucking murderer and you sicken me." He didn't dare meet her eyes.

We started trekking through the woods again, listening for any sound. Whenever I had walked through the woods before, I heard birds rustling through the leaves and singing in the trees. There was none of that. It was just silent.

How hadn't I noticed before?

Delilah said nothing. She was abnormally silent. She just stared blankly at the floor. It didn't take us long to realise that Precious was the one with the bag full of phones. They must have been back in the boma. There was no way we could call back.

There was no way we could call for help.

We're *thoroughly* fucked.

Though we had been walking for at least two hours, we had yet to see the creature or Ben. Nothing. It should have found us by now.

"Where do you think it is?" Rin whispered to me.

I hated to say it. I hated even thinking it, but I thought that perhaps the creature was taking all the bodies back to its lair. I was reminded of 'Rogue': a horror movie about a large crocodile that only stopped attacking one point during the day when it was in its lair *eating*. In this scenario, the creature was the crocodile, and we are the stranded people, swimming across a river with no real idea where it was. It could be waiting for night so it could use the cover of dark to hunt us more effectively. It was only down to Ben and dumb luck that we had lasted this long. We all knew that, but it was something that none of us would say out loud.

It hadn't given up. I have no doubt about that. It had hunted us so relentlessly so far to have given up. It seemed to be dead set on me. There was no way it was giving up just yet. Especially considering it would be hours before we find help.

Perhaps Ben had bought us more time? "I think_" The ground left from under us before I could finish my sentence. We landed awkwardly in a pile of dust and broken wood. "Ow."

Bianca, Sergeant and Rin were down here with me. We looked at each other and somehow, none of us were any more injured than we were before. We looked up to see Seth and Delilah staring down at us, their eyes wide. "Let's go, Delilah." Seth insisted, tugging the sleeve of her pyjama shirt. "It will have heard that and the more time it spends eating them, the less time it has to hunt us."

"Agreed," She nodded. A malevolent grin crossed her face and she shoved *hard* him into the pit with us. He landed far roughly than we did, face-first and onto the ground. He shrieked, his nose dripping nastily with blood and the dirt was smothered across his face. He was sobbing uncontrollably and clutching his nose. It must have been broken because the blood was oozing out between his fingers and dripping onto the ground. "You killed my *friend*." A single tear rolled down her cheek and dripped down. "*I hope it takes its time with you.*" She hissed and stepped away.

"Delilah!" Bianca protested, calling after her. "Delilah! Don`t leave us here! *Delilah*!" She was already gone. "That *bitch*!"

"Where are we?" Rin questioned, rubbing her head. Dust fell off her hair and to the ground. "What is this place?"

I looked around us. It was shockingly dry and warm down here for December. Wooden beams held up the sides and it was definitely man-made. I saw shimmers of glass on the floor. To the left there were dilapidated steps going down into darkness. "It`s an abandoned copper mine."

Rin shook her head. "No, there aren`t any in the New Forest." She looked around again. "Perhaps you`re right. I can`t think of another explanation."

"Maybe it`s an illegal copper mine?" Bianca reasoned. "That could be why no one knows about it."

I stepped towards her and jumped at the crack beneath my foot. I peered down at what was underneath my feet and nearly gagged. "It isn`t abandoned anymore." I told them.

"What do you mean, Kelsey?" Bianca`s brows furrowed. I raised my foot. Bianca`s hand covered her moth, eyes wide. "Is that_?"

I nodded. "Human bones," I kicked at the dirt around us, revealing more. "I think we know what happened to the miners. Do you know what this means?"

"We have found the creatures lair?" Seth gulped, shaking blood off his hands and onto the floor.

"Well… Yes, but the bones… Do you know what they mean?" Bianca and Seth looked at me like I had just suggested that licking a porcupine's butt would give them magic powers. Rin, however, knew *exactly* what I was talking about.

"We're by the entrance!" She reasoned excitedly, jumping up with a clap. Everyone turned to her and her face turned bright red. I nodded.

"How did you get *that* from that?" Seth spat irritably, spraying blood onto Rin's pyjamas. Bianca glared at him in response.

"Predators often put the bones of their victims near the entrance of their lairs to make them obvious to other predators. It is territorial marking." Rin explained, looking to me nervously. I nodded reassuringly. "This also suggests that there isn't likely to be others out there."

"God, I hope so."

"Which direction do we go?" Bianca asked me, gesturing to both directions.

I grinned humourlessly. "We follow the bones."

Seth was right and we all knew it. The creature would have heard the fall with all the cracking wood and the large 'bang' of us falling in. It was like a beacon telling it exactly where we were. My only hope was that we made it out before it got to us.

To think that only a week ago, my biggest worry was staying out of Mrs Veneman's way (and possibly finding a way to talk to Mason without putting a foot in my mouth).

It felt like a lifetime had passed since then.

The mine was almost pitch-black. We had to feel our way along the walls. Though the fact that it was gradually getting lighter was *very* comforting. "Kelsey…" Called a voice from the dark. "Is that you?" I couldn't see where it was and the mine echoed so much I couldn't distinguish which way it was coming from. "Ah… Fear… Such a delicious smell…"

Great, it's close enough to smell us. That is just *wonderful*.

We started to sprint towards the exit. "Yes, yes, run Kelsey run!" It sang with sadistic delight. Is it right behind us or a hundred yards away? I can`t tell. We sprint around the corner to see the bright light of the entrance.

And the creature standing in it.

"Oh Kelsey, did you miss me that much that you had to run into my embrace?" He asks with the same voice a boy may use greet to his girlfriend when he comes back from a long trip. I felt sick. Before I could move to run away, it had me. It gripped my throat like a vice. My legs dangled and I kicked anywhere I could reach but it didn`t seem to notice.

Sergeant lunged but it just moved out the way. "How about we have a chat, my dear?" It moved so fast that I couldn`t see anything we passed and seconds later, we were in another part of the mine with just a little sunlight cracking through the wooden boards making up the ceiling; just enough to reflect off of its fangs.

No light reflected from its eyes.

"I`m going to take my time with you." It grinned, licking around its mouth, where its lips should have been. "Nowhere to run. No one to save you. No hope left for you. There is only me!" It yanked me close and inhaled. "Oh, you do smell like roses. I wonder if you taste like…"

Ducking to the floor, I snatched up a plank of wood. I hit it over the head with the wood as *hard* as I could but the wood just crumbles. "Fuck!"

It laughs, a cool eerie laugh. "Did you really think that would work? Metal lamp stand? Sure. Rotten bit of wood?" It laughs again. I snatch up the next hard thing my hand finds: a bone. I smack the creature with it and it actually flinched. It felt like poetic justice; a victim helping another one fight back. "Wow. That actually hurt." It smacked the bone out of my hand and grabbing my hair, it slammed my head against the wall.

Black.

I can't open my eyes.

Those were the first words that came to mind when I woke up. My face *hurt* and all I could think was 'am I still with it?'. Where I was laying was hard and uncomfortable and there was something damp and cold over my eyes.

Why hadn't it killed me?

"You're awake." Came a familiar voice.

"A-A..." I couldn't say anything. My throat hurt.

"It's ok. You don't need to speak. Your throat is really bruised." I lifted my arm to take the cloth off my face. I stopped immediately. *That hurt.* "It's ok. It's gone."

I pulled the cloth off from my eyes and sat up, wincing. I rubbed my eyes and blinked them open. The world was bright and blurry for a few moments, making me dizzy. "W-what h-happened?" My voice sounded as if I smoked six packs a day at some points and others it sounded almost whistle-like.

"See for yourself." She pointed to the body of the creature with a monstrous hole in its chest. It was dead. "They say it will turn back soon." As if the creature heard her, it spasmed. We jumped and scrambled back as its body contorted and twisted... Until it was back to Camp Director Joe with a big hole in his chest.

"Holy shit."

"Yeah... They said it would do that." Rin told me, breathing a sigh of relief as the body stilled. "After it took you, two men arrived. One of them killed that *thing* and the other pulled you out. I'm pretty sure one of them was..."

"Schitzo." Delilah finished. "The other was *gorgeous*."

Rin cringed at Delilah's description. "They saved us, called the police and said that they shouldn't be here for when the police arrive so they left."

"What did that guy do to it?" I inquired, curious to find out what could have stopped that thing... And made that massive hole.

Delilah snorted. "Bitch please. Enough with your *whoring*. That hottie didn't even see your face with that cloth over it the entire time. He has no interest in you, *skank*."

Seriously? That was where her mind went? "I don't care about that. I want to know how he killed it."

The group shrugged and turned back to me. "They just went into the mine and when the first one came out, it was with you with a cloth around your face and when the second came out, it was with its corpse."

"Why didn't it kill me while I was unconscious?" I asked.

Bianca shivered and grimaced. "They said that the reason it didn't kill you was..." She watched as Sergeant curled up into me. I cuddled into her fur and scratched behind her ears "They said the reason why it didn't eat you while you were unconscious is because it wanted you to be awake while it ate you."

I shivered. Then I laughed. It was the kind of laugh that breathed madness. It bubbled up at the back of my throat and exploded out. They turned to me with concerned looks. I knew that I sounded insane. I just didn't care. Despite the odds, despite everything; I was alive.

The police found us there an hour later, shivering in muddy and torn pyjamas. They asked us a myriad of questions. We all told them the story we'd all agreed on earlier. That the camp director went mad and decided that he wanted to eat us, and some men we didn't know tried to stop him, and they accidentally killed him, running away before the police arrived.

We were all very vague as to which direction. I had a genuine excuse as I was unconscious. I had a concussion, my head and face were bleeding heavily, so I was told to wait at the hospital until David arrived.

When he did, his eyes were wide and full of panic. He sprinted towards me and wrapped me up in a hug and spun me around like he used to when I was little. "I`m so glad you`re ok, Kels." He put me down and looked me up and down, checking for injuries. He sighed in relief but not all of his tenseness disappeared.

"What is it, David?" I inquired as he wrapped me up in the coat, he`d brought for me.

"I`m really sorry."

"Why are you sorry?" I laughed humourlessly. He didn`t know that Joe was going to do that. Why would he be sorry?

"Kelsey, it`s about your friend Adria..." My heart stopped. "I`m sorry but she took her own life when you left. I`m really sorry..."

Five

I don't remember anything after that.

There are two months in my life that I remember next to nothing about. David says I spoke to the police a few times after I got back. David told me about Mason coming to visit me every day after school. He told me that I clung to the cloth from the *incident* like a lifeline.

The only thing I remember is the note.

It sat on top of the chest of drawers in my room. I couldn't bear to look at it. I remembered reading it, I remember the anguish but I couldn't remember the words.

I think it was the news of a girl called Nina Bowers going missing that snapped me out of it. She wasn't the first person to go missing since my return (in fact she was the sixth) bit she was the first child. "I want to go looking for her."

Mason blinked in surprise. Then he smiled. "It's nice to hear you talking again." I blushed and ran my fingers through my messy hair. "Are you going to join the search party?"

I shook my head. "No... I..." I breathed out. "Adria's dad will be there... I..." I scratched my arm nervously. "Adria's dad will..."

Mason nodded. "I get it. So, we go alone, then?"

"You're coming with me?"

He smiled kindly. "Yeah. Is that ok?" I nodded. "Should we take your dog?" We turned to look at Sergeant, who was on her back and snoring in the corner. "Or not..."

I snorted. "Trust me just say 'walk'," The dog's ears perked up, and she rolled to face us. "And she'll be awake." Sergeant trotted over and put her face in my lap. "Do you want to find Nina, girl?" Sergeant wagged her tail and tried to lick my face. "I'll take that as a 'yes'." We decided that it was best to put Sergeant on the lead (I didn't usually bother because she was so well behaved) so we could focus on looking around for Nina instead of keeping an eye on Sergeant.

We decided to walk through the woods (somewhere I hadn't been since the camp) because it was right by the play park where she'd gone missing. If she had wandered off, then that would be the place where she'd have most likely have gotten lost. "We shouldn't split up." Mason suggested as we got there. I arched an eyebrow at him. Splitting up wasn't on my agenda. "If there really is someone out there who takes kids then it is best that we're together when we come across him."

Yes, *someone*. It's a person. It has to be a person.

I agreed.

"Hello, Little One." I flinched at the familiar voice as Mason shoved me behind him, shielding me with his tall frame.

"Who are you?" Mason demanded, staring down the taller man. Ben wasn't intimidated by Mason in the slightest. In fact, he seemed irritated in a similar way to how a German Shepherd appears when a Jack Russell barks at it; annoyed without the slightest fear. Not wanting to see how an angry Ben reacts to Mason, I stepped out from behind him to greet Ben.

"Hi, Ben, how are you?" I smiled gently. His gaze softened on me.

"'Ben' that's what she used to call me." I felt Mason tense behind me. "Is that what I asked you to call me?" I nodded. "Your scars don't show from then." I nodded again. He was right; my face hadn't scarred up but it was still a little tender. "Those who sell their souls for power are an abomination, no better than a monster. Monsters that prey on children are the worst of all. Once you fight the darkness, you can never truly escape it." He told me. "Put your dog on a lead. Not all is as it seems." He stepped forward and kissed the top of my head gently. "I'm glad to see that he got there in time." As quickly as he had arrived, Ben disappeared.

"Who was that?" Mason questioned, clearly unsettled by the exchange.

"Ben. He saved my life at the camp." I explained.

Mason looked at me. "Was he the one who killed that man?" I shook my head. "Then who was he? He's far too old to be one of the students... He can't have been a member of staff. There is no way they'd let someone that mentally unstable..." He then recalled the reason we'd given to the police that the camp director acted in a certain way. "Oh."

"He wasn't a member of staff." Mason seemed very relieved by my statement. "He just seemed to be around. He helped me out a few times and a few of those times involved him fighting off the camp director." I told him. "I think he has more of an idea of what is going on than anyone else. He is clearly super intelligent..." Mason arched an eyebrow. "None of his advice has ever led me wrong."

"He just told you to put your dog on a lead." He gestured to Sergeant. "She's already on a lead."

"He wasn't talking about Sergeant." I stifled a laugh, my nose crinkling. "He was talking about you. Ben was telling me to keep you close because there is something dangerous about."

Obviously offended by the 'dog' comment, Mason bristled. "Why couldn't he just say that?"

I shrugged. "I guess he speaks in a certain way. He knows I understand. He only really seems to talk to me."

"Thinking about it, Delilah did talk about a crazy guy. I just assumed she was talking about the cannibal." He reasoned. "Are you two related?" I shook my head, confused. "It's just that you look sort of alike." Turning back to the trees, he scratched the back of his head. "So, he says that we're in danger in these woods, then do you want to go back?"

"You can." I told him. "But I want to stay and look for Nina. If there is something dangerous out here, then it's better that we find her before it does." He nodded in agreement and then laughed. "What?"

He rubbed the back of his neck. "Everyone thinks you're just this quiet little nerd but the more I get to know you the more I realise; you are seriously brave." I blushed. "You are probably the bravest person I've ever met." He took my hand in his, catching me completely off guard. "Let's go find Nina."

I found it ridiculously hard to concentrate on looking for Nina when Mason was holding my hand. Part of me was panicking; what if my hands were too sweaty or too cold? His felt nice. They were so much larger than my own and they were soft and strong.

Sergeant abruptly started to bark, shocking me out of my head. I followed the direction she was barking at until I saw a little blonde head. She was so still and so pale that I at first thought she was dead. It was when she blinked that I realised that she was still alive. "Nina? Are you ok?" I asked delicately, sighing with relief that she was still alive.

"Ok…" She repeated. She stood up awkwardly like her limbs weren't the right size. How long had she been out here? How long had she been sitting there? She must have been freezing. I shrugged off my hoodie and pulled it over her head. Mason was shouting, hoping to grab the attention of the official search party. They shouldn't be too far from here. They found us quickly as the majority of the people looking were in these woods or by the park. Nina's father sprinted forward and wrapped his little daughter up in his arms, sobbing. "Thank you... Thank you,"

They took Nina away and we smiled.

"I guess Ben was wrong," Mason continued. "She must have just been lost."

My brows furrowed and I thought back to what Ben had said. He'd never been wrong before. "No. She was left there for us to find. We had been walking in here for fifteen minutes. She could have found her way out. There is a reason why she didn't."

"Yeah," Mason nodded with a short laugh. "*She's six* and she's alone. That fifteen-minute walk to us is more like a forty-five minute one to her. She got lost and was too afraid to move. Case closed."

"I guess you're right." I didn't think that at all. My gut told me to trust Ben. Besides, why had we found her when the search party is so much larger and was looking around here? That bright pink top stood out like a beacon. It just didn't make sense.

"Come on, Sherlock," Mason grinned jokingly, wrapping his arm around me. I swallowed a squeak. "Let's go back."

My eyes were everywhere on the way back. Why was she out there? Mason had been right about one thing; it was a long walk for someone with such little legs. So, if that was the case, then how did she get so far into the woods in the first place? What six-year-old wandered off into the woods alone? I couldn't think of a viable reason as to why she would have wandered so far into the woods without insidious assistance.

Perhaps Mason was right. She was young. She could have just been chasing a butterfly. Except that it was February. There were no butterflies for her to chase.

After what happened at camp, I could have just as easily be seeing monsters everywhere. And Ben wasn't exactly the most stable source... and yet when had he been wrong?

No matter how I looked at it, there was no way I could fathom how this couldn't have some kind of malicious intent.

Mason dropped me off at my caravan and headed home. I could still feel the warmth of my hand from his.

I was thankful he left, however, because I was determined to do some research. I had to know more. I had to know *what* that creature was. I couldn't just move on.

"Hey Kelsey, I'm going to go off to work." David called.

"Ok, see you later." I replied with a smile.

He blinked. "You're talking again?" He beamed and wrapped me up in a hug. "I love you so much. Be safe."

"I will." He released me and left. I went on my brother's laptop. He never complained when I used it, as long as he could use it when it was needed. As I scoured the internet for any information, I found myself surprised at how much there was about things that people didn't believe existed. Titles such as *Ghost Chases Family out of Home, Woman is Determined that Her Son is A Changeling* and *Ghost Hunters Find Body Buried Under House* were disturbingly common. Though I had found many articles, there weren't any on what I had experienced at the camp. None with *real* information.

In fact, there was nothing on the camp from before we went there.

"I have the answers you seek, Little One." Came a low voice from my window. I jumped, tripping over the sofa in my panic. When I looked up, a pair of pale blue eyes was peering through my window.

"Ben," I breathed a sigh of relief and picked myself up from the ground.

"You found it, didn't you?" He continued. "I smell *rot* on you." The woods were a place where lots of things rotted but I wasn't a fan of smelling of rot. And 'it'? Was he referring to Nina? I guess he really wasn't human? "I have a gift for you." He carelessly dropped a massive, old, leather-bound book through the window. "This should contain the answers that you seek. Do not let *anyone* find it. The dark does not wish for you to know its secrets and the light will see only madness."

"Thank you," I told him, looking up from the book to see that he was gone.

That seems about right.

The book had no title and seemingly no author. It had a large lock bolting it shut… and no key. Damn it. The book wasn't much use if I couldn't open it.

I was no locksmith but even I could appreciate the artist's work in crafting that. It was bulky but it had intricate patterns in a Celtic-like style. I ran my fingers over the patterns. The lock clicked and the book flung itself open.

The first page was revealed. It was blank for a second, but ink soon seeped into the page reading: *The Personal Grimoire of the White Witch Amyelia Locks. Beware; magic takes a toll on body, mind, and soul. Human bodies are not built for magic. Proceed with caution.* The writing was beautiful but old. It was smudged in places and there were places where the ink had run. Had this been written with an actual ink pot? And how did it appear like that?

The book started to flip through itself and it stopped almost half-way through. The page once again started off blank but soon ink flooded in.

The Soulless

These beings were of human origin but sold their souls to a dark power such as a demon or a higher-up in the unseelie court, usually for power. Though they can take the form of their old selves, their second form shows the rot inside with the capacity to do whatever they sold their soul to.

The book showed a drawing in a similar style to what you'd find in a Grimm's fairy tale book with a small note underneath it. *One example of what a soulless could look like. This is Joseph Norris, possibly one of the eldest soulless I've ever encountered. He sold his soul for the ability to overpower humans so that he could carry out his cannibalistic fantasies.*

My eyes ran over the creature in the picture. It was Joe. I knew it. Despite how dark it had been when I had seen the creature, it was a face I could never forget.

The soulless are often far stronger than the average human and they can appear completely normal to unsuspecting people. Most supernaturals (especially those with heightened senses) can tell what they are. The majority of supernaturals will not allow the soulless in their territories. Despite their strength and stamina, the soulless can be killed the same way humans can be. Though the most effective methods would be the removal of the head or the heart. So that was how those men had killed the creature. They removed the heart.

How did those men know to do that anyway?

Who were they?

I looked over to my drawer. That was where the cloth sat. I couldn't bring myself to get rid of it. I knew it was silly but I was determined to find those men so I could thank them. I knew I'd see them again and until then, it was a reminder that good people were out there, vanquishing creatures like Joe.

The book moved again, flipping through its pages, closer to the front. Ink seeped into the page, revealing a word in bold '*Vampires*'. It flipped through again though not too far. *Vampires are creatures that have been on this Earth for thousands of years, but some bloodsuckers are older than others. Unfortunately, part of this is down to me. I created a new species of vampire from possibly the worst of them all; the Frozen. I returned one of the Frozen's soul. Though not dissimilar to the Frozen, these vampires that people have taken to calling 'the Returned' have the ability to not only turn humans into ones like them but also make more Frozen too. Their souls can be both a benefit and a curse. Some things that they can do, that they do despite their souls are despicable and they no longer have the excuse of no soul. What I have done? I have yet to decide whether it was right or wrong to return the soul of a vampire to its body.*

As I read through certain things stood out to me such as *'unnaturally pale eyes', 'high intelligence', 'strength'* and *'speed'.* All of which applied to Ben. It also taught me about some of their other abilities such as the ability to bend others to their will, hyper senses and depending on their bloodline, they can fly, move things with their mind, transform into animals or even read minds. The limit on their abilities were small and it all seemed to revolve around which bloodline they came from. Apparently, the bloodline showed through eye colour but it didn't say much more on the topic. What was Ben capable of?

I hid my book under my mattress (original; I know but there isn't anywhere else to hide anything in my room) and tried to get some sleep.

School the next day, was flooded with whispers all on the same subject: Nina Bowers. I couldn't hear much but the looks on people's faces was enough to tell me that it couldn't be good.

Mason strolled over to me, his face gloomy and brows furrowed. "Hey Kelsey,"

"Hey Mason, what's the matter?" I asked, concerned.

He blinked in surprise. "You haven't heard?" I shook my head. "Kelsey, the Bowers were murdered last night, and the killer ran off with Nina."

"Shit," I blurted. "Do the police have any idea who did it?"

Mason shook his head. "No, but reports say that the bodies were partly eaten."

A chill ran down my spine. Was it... could it be...? Was Joe back? There was no way... those men killed it. The police confirmed that it was dead but... This thing was supernatural, and it had made a deal with a demon. There was no telling the limit of its abilities. My fists were clenched so tight that I could feel my nails in my skin. "Did they say anything about the lips?" I demanded.

He frowned. "No... why?"

I grimaced. "That was the part that Joe liked best."

He visibly shivered. "That's fucked up." I nodded. "How did you_?"

"Know that was the part Joe liked best?" I finished. "Because i-he told me. He wanted me for my lips. It... He was obsessed with me. He was determined that he would eat my lips. Though it hunted the others, he wanted me. I was what i-he really wanted. He wanted me to suffer."

"That's fucked up." Mason told me. I wondered then how he would react if I told him the really fucked up part of the story; how he would react to me telling him what happened in the mine and the only reason why I was still alive was because the creature was extremely sadistic. I decided that I wouldn't tell him that part; he didn't need to know and there was enough horror today.

"Yeah." I agreed. I need to see those bodies. I had to know if Joe was back or not. If its back than what could I do?

How would I find someone to stop it if those men who knew how to kill it, couldn't?

"Have you noticed that whenever you get involved in anything, Alexander, someone gets eaten?" Delilah asked, skipping over. "First you go to a camp and the camp director decides that he has a serious case of the munchies and now you find a girl in the woods and her family become some psycho's midnight snack." She bats her eyelashes at Mason. "Hey Mason," She kissed him on his cheek. He froze. He looked like he was torn between excitement and throwing up. The malicious skank he was still in love with had just kissed him on the cheek in front of the girl said skank had been tormenting for the last thirteen years. He was torn between enjoying her attention and being disgusted by how her.

"Delilah..." He managed; his voice strained. He sounded like he was being strangled and his face was turning red. My heart twisted in my chest. Would he ever get over her?

"Delilah," I smiled pleasantly. "It's nice to see that you don't change; even after we survived a near-death experience together."

"An experience that I wouldn't have had to be a part of if it wasn't for you." She snapped, her blue eyes flashing with rage. "It was your fault that I was sent there, and it wanted you. Precious's death is on you."

I glared at her. "Precious's death is on Seth. I never touched her." I crossed my arms over my chest. "Joe had a vendetta against me, but he would have tried to eat you regardless of my presence."

"*Don't say that name!*" Delilah hissed. So that was how you can make "You spiteful cow! It's no wonder that he wanted to wait until you were awake to eat you alive!" She stormed off.

Mason was pale. I wasn't sure whether or not it was over the fact that Delilah had kissed him or what she had said. "He wanted to..."

I guess I had my answer. I nodded. "Yeah. He wanted to eat me while I was awake to watch."

"Fuck."

"Yeah." I rubbed his arm reassuringly. "Everything`s fine, Mason. He`s dead and I`m alive."

He shook his head. "Aren`t I supposed to be the one comforting you right now? It was you who went through that." He asked incredulously.

"I have had plenty of time to process."

"What did Delilah mean about Precious?" Censoring the parts about the supernatural creature, I explained what had happened. "That slimy little bastard. Why the fuck is he still at school with us? He should be in fucking jail!"

I nodded in agreement. "Yeah, but apparently our statements weren`t enough because I was completely out of it, Delilah was in shock and they put the statements down to that; shock."

"I thought there were two other girls there."

"There was but it was all put down to shock." I told him. "Innocent until proven guilty and there wasn`t enough evidence. Eyewitness testimonies aren`t enough evidence. They aren`t reliable, especially when people have had time to talk about it."

"That and the Hoyt family has money coming out of their ears." Mason continued. "They get away with everything and there are some seriously nasty rumours about things that the Hoyt`s have done." Thinking about Seth Hoyt, I wasn`t surprised. He clearly wasn`t accustomed to the word 'no'.

Thankfully, I had learned that it was easy to keep out of his way. The only class he was in with me was P.E and he was easy enough to avoid.

The bell rang for tutor and on went our usual routine. Mason and I still sat together for tutor and for the most part, Delilah left us alone (small blessings). We chatted animatedly and I wondered if this made us friends. Besides Adria, I didn't really have any friends. Adria had plenty of friends, but they were her friends; not mine. They had tolerated my presence purely for her benefit. After Adria's death, I had sat alone in the library with only Mason visiting me. I think he just thought that was what I would be doing while I was so out of it. It was a routine that I would probably continue. The library used to be a near-silent place when the old librarian was there. She was a harsh woman with a sharp nose. I was her favourite and she *still* wasn't nice to me. As a result of budget cuts, she was one of the people they let go and the library now was busy and *loud*. The library had used to be a safe-haven for us freaks 'n geeks, a refuge from the brainless bullies but now it was as bad as everywhere else.

Part of me still clinged to what the library used to be. I still went and sat in my usual spot and pretended that there weren't screaming children all around me. During my first two years of secondary school (when I had no friends at all); I spent every spare moment reading in the library. I knew that it was no longer a comfortable environment, but I wasn't sure where else I could go.

Mr Clarke (my tutor) had let people like us stay in his tutor room during break and lunch (despite the fact that the rules clearly said that we weren't allowed in there) because he knew how uncomfortable it was for all of us outside of there (he had seen enough of the bruises and heard enough of the stories about what other students were like). He had been defending us from other teachers, saying that we weren't supposed to be in there for years and until a few months ago, I hadn't had any idea. The school board had created a 'safe space' for us to go at breaks and lunch but I had been in that room many times and it was a very uncomfortable environment with judging looks, tense voices and possibly the most disturbing: Seth Hoyt. All of us avoided the room like the plague. We no longer had an excuse to stay in my tutor room and that those of us who used to stay in there with few options. And I wasn't sure where else I could go.

Mason, though very nice, had his own friends to hang out with and they weren't the kind of people that were picked on or felt uncomfortable with the other students. The idea of approaching that table felt like tying a lump of meat around my throat and leaping into the lion exhibit at the zoo.

School continued as usual.

Textiles: a blend of confusion and Rupert making comments as he came through the textiles room to get the same equipment every single lesson. Honestly, he was just a better-looking version of Seth. The teacher in charge of the technology (Mrs Wilks) was a judgemental and hypocritical bitch making comments such as "they are all so lazy! They come in for extra time for their art subjects but it's like they don't even try with this subject. Those girls will be lucky to get a pass!" It was a mass of frustration as I had taken to coming in for at least four hours every Saturday and often two after school on Monday so that I could get a *passing* grade. My textiles teacher was a lovely lady, but she seemed to be under the impression that we had been taught more than we actually had (the last three textiles teachers had been useless in one way or the other) and only I seemed to be the one to explain anything. My textiles teacher was kind, but her subject was so *frustrating*, she never seemed to see me as in any other mood than anger.

Art: the empty seat next to me felt like a hole in my chest. Mrs Wilson's comments about my work were cruel as she brought out examples of grades from other years. "Kelsey, sit over with the grade fours. I really want to see you push for that grade four!" I had been predicted a grade six by the previous art teacher. The urge to draw a stickman and turn it in with a smile was overwhelming. I painted a thunderstorm instead and ignored whatever feedback I was given. I just didn`t care anymore.

Maths: my least favourite subject (excluding textiles)... but with one of my favourite teachers. She had a real passion for her subject, made jokes and worked really hard to make sure we were ready for exams. Yes, she used a lot of exam questions and submitted a lot of practise papers, but she didn`t do it to torment us. She did it because she wanted us to pass. Mrs Kent made sure that she didn`t pick on me for answers too often because she knew that I was uncomfortable talking too much in class and if I knew the answer; I would write it down. She knew how to treat each student to make us work at our best. She was a fantastic teacher and I was beyond lucky to have her. No more yelling for an hour.

Biology; a wonderful subject with a wonderful teacher. She was funny and kind.

English: probably my favourite subject and the one that I was best at, but the strict teacher did know how to make it high stress for her students. I don`t think she meant to.

That was my day. It was the same every Wednesday and very few other days were any better. Thursday was the worst with a double of Textiles, then a double of Geography (which was horrible and there were at least two students asleep at any given time) with a final lesson of art.

Any day was better than Thursday.

"Would you like me to walk you home?" Mason offered.

I blinked. "You live in the opposite direction to me."

"Yeah, but we both know that I`ll be visiting you in an hour anyway." He insisted, with big grin. "Besides, I thought that maybe, I could take you to the park we went to yesterday and buy you ice-cream... If you want?"

"Are you...?"

"Asking you out? Yes."

My brows furrowed. "I thought you were still..."

"Enamoured by Delilah." He finished. "I am. But I really like you and I don't want to miss out on you because of her."

"O-ok." This seemed really risky and, though I really wanted to go out with Mason, I had a feeling that this was going to end in pain. "One date… We will have to see where it goes from there."

He grinned. "Awesome." We started walking home. "Did you like my use of the word 'enamoured'? I learned it when I was at a book shop."

"You were at a book shop?" I asked teasingly. "Who are you and what have you done with Mason?"

He shook his head. "I went to the book shop looking for that 'Infinity' book you recommended me."

"Y-you remember that?" I had talked about Infinity about last year… probably over six months ago.

He smiled. "Of course,"

"Kelsey," I jumped and looked around.

"Did you hear that?" My eyes were darting everywhere. That voice… it was Adria's and that was impossible.

He frowned. "No… What?"

I shook my head. "It's probably just my imagination." The yellow eyes in the trees told me otherwise. The yellow eyes followed me but didn't get any closer. It stayed at least six feet away at any given time. Close enough to be threatening but not close enough to do me any harm. What the fuck was *that* thing? I hadn't seen it since I had returned from the trip, although thinking about it, I was so out of it, I probably wouldn't have remembered if I did.

Once we had gotten back to the campsite, I got changed into something more comfortable, told David where we were going and then we left for the park with Sergeant. It was a pretty warm day for February so ice cream wasn't that bad an idea.

"Hey Kelsey," The owner of the ice-cream shop smiled. "Your usual?"

"Yeah, thanks, Giuseppe." I replied. He took Mason's order and Mason looked over at me, arching his eyebrow. I rolled my eyes. "So, how is my favourite cousin?" I asked Giuseppe. Mason's mouth turned into an 'oh'.

"I'm good," Giuseppe handed me my ice cream. I pulled out my wallet to pay him. "Kelsey, don't be ridiculous. You don't pay to eat here." Mason pulled out his wallet. "And you, as long as you are with her, you don't pay either. Kelsey doesn't have many friends. It's nice to see her with people her own age." Please stop.

"See you later, cousin." I grinned, with my best John Wayne voice. It was terrible.

"You too, cousin." He replied with a laugh and a much better John Wayne voice.

Mason and I sat together on a bench on a little hill outside the park with a view of the entire park. We weren't talking for long before I saw Liz Spencer, a little girl I used to babysit, walking towards the woods. I looked to try and see her parents but I couldn't see them. Concerned, I stood up and marched over to her, Mason right behind me. "Hey Liz," I waved. "What 'cha doing?"

Liz smiled at me and pointed at the woods. "I was going to play with Nina." A shiver running down my spine, I span to look into the trees. There was nobody there. "Oh, she's gone."

I looked to Mason; whose face was as white as a sheet. "Should we call someone?"

"I don't think they'll believe it... Not without proof." He shook his head. "Why don't we go and take a look? For Liz's sake." I nodded and sent Liz back over to her parents, who'd miraculously appeared after the crisis was over. We ventured into the trees for the second time. "Look." He pointed down.

Footprints... They were the right size but the way they were ridiculously far apart... I couldn't stretch *my* legs that far. Mason could barely. I don't think a girl that small could jump that far. "I think that's enough evidence."

We called the police and they made their way down to where we found the footprints. The officer told us to wait there and when he came back, he told us that he followed the footprints, but they were a dead end. He thanked us and he left.

"Sorry our date kind of became more like an episode of Sherlock." Mason rubbed the back of his neck.

"I like Sherlock." I smiled and he replicated it.

"Maybe next time we should try a restaurant?"

I smirked. "Next time?"

"Well yeah... if you'd like."

"I'd love to."

"Great, I'll walk you home." He did just that. He kissed my cheek once we got there and began his walk home.

It took me a moment to return to this reality, my hand on my cheek but I scurried inside to find the book. It flung open at my touch. I needed to find a way to break into the morgue to find the bodies.

I had to know if they still had their lips.

The book span open to a page that read: *astral projection. Astral projection isn't difficult for those with witch blood (those without may find it more challenging), but it does have its risks (especially for witches). You have to make sure that you're grounded and you have protection. Demons may try to take your body and it is likely that one may latch onto you. You cannot get lost. It is impossible. What you may see is never guaranteed. Do not have sex with a demon. It is a transfer of energy that is never good. You are likely to be very tired during astral projection and afterwards.*

I read through the rest of the information and laid back on my bed. Was it really a good idea to do this? Demons...

There was nothing that could sound scarier. I didn't have anything to ground myself. The book said witch blood made all the difference but I didn't have witch blood (although my Aunt Jenna could make me question that). I lay back and closed my eyes. I focused and nothing for a few minutes... I opened my eyes and stood up. Maybe I missed something? Deciding to look through the grimoire, I turned back my bed to pick it up. My body laid there.

"Holy Hell," I blurted, stumbling back from my body. Not knowing how much time I had, I made my way towards the morgue. It was a mile-long walk which didn't seem very far usually but today that felt like a big deal. Once I left my caravan, I could see things; pitch-black shapes like very tall men (varying from 6' to 7'), just staring at me. It was like walking through a field of statues. I felt an overwhelming sense of dread and I wanted to run, but it's too late to turn back now.

Why were there so many?

I turned to look behind me. The ones behind me had moved to stare at me. At least, I think it was staring. It had no eyes, but I could feel it peering at me. I was so tense; every breath was sharp and short. I felt so cold, seeing my breath in front of me. "*Witch blood,*" Came a very deep voice from everywhere and nowhere all at once. I looked around and it took me a minute to realise that it wasn't one voice but all of these shadows talking at once. "*Witch blood. Yours can give us life and let us leave.*" They didn't have features so I couldn't see lips moving. I couldn't see anything moving.

"I'm not a witch." I insisted, doubt niggling its way into the back of my skull. How else could I have gotten here so easily?

"*Your soul glows bright with the colours of your magic, witch.*" I felt so cold. Why was it so cold?

Staying here felt like a bad idea. I started to sprint towards the morgue. It wasn't a long run but I felt myself getting increasingly tired. There were shadows everywhere, all staring at me and chanting "*Witch blood*".

The morgue had more of these shadows than anywhere else. It was a tight fit to get through them without touching them. I didn`t want to think about what would happen if I touched them. I made my way to the file room and dug my way through. I pulled out the folder on Mary Bowers (Nina`s mother) and opened it. The first page had a photo of Mary`s corpse.

The lips were still there.

I checked through the rest of the Bowers` folders. They all had their lips. I breathed out a sigh of relief, returned the folders and turned to leave.

The shadows were blocking my exit. "*Witch blood,*" I backed up, expecting to hit my back against a wall. When it didn`t, I looked behind me. I was half-way through the wall and outside. I scampered the rest of the way through the wall. On the other side waiting for me was *something* else. It was a creature with long claws, made of thick black smoke with malevolent yellow eyes. It charged for me, letting out an inhuman, ear-splitting roar. I sprinted towards my home, it hot on my heels. I could feel it right behind me. I zig-zagged through the shadows. They retreated at the sight of it, no longer interested in me. Its claws ripped into my shoulder. I screamed. It *burned*. There was a berry tree in front of me. I made a beeline for it. I needed something in between me and that thing. Even if it was a spindly little tree. I snatched a stick from the ground below the tree and smacked the creature around the face with it as hard as I could. My shoulder protested. The smoke dispersed. Relief coursed through me, but it was short-lived. It was gathering back together rapidly. In an instant I was running again, clutching the stick like a lifeline.

Suddenly, a wave of exhaustion washed over me. I nearly fell over. I was so *tired.* I blinked and slapped myself in the face, sprinting harder.

I don't know if I have the energy to make it.

The caravan park was in the distance, but the thing was right behind me again. I blindly flailed the stick behind me, hoping that I would hit it and slow it down just for a *second*. It occurred to me then that not only could it get *into* my caravan, but my helpless body was just *lying* there.

It could hurt me.

It could kill me.

The first thing that came to mind was salt. I remember reading somewhere that evil couldn't cross salt. We should still have some on the side in the kitchen. I ran as fast as I could towards the caravan, swing harder at the creature to slow it down.

Every second counted.

I charged through the caravan door and snatched up the salt, surprised that I could touch it. I rushed to my room and poured the salt around my bed.

It was in there in seconds. I wished I'd had the time to make the line of salt thicker but it was too fast. It charged forwards, bouncing off an invisible force-field. In that moment I was far too aware of my own size. The creature loomed over me like a giant and I felt so small, like it could crush me. Had it always been so big?

I poured down more salt, thickening the line. It kept on slamming against the barrier, the force of it shaking the caravan. I couldn't help but flinch every time. I had emptied the rest of the salt. It didn't feel like enough. I stumbled over to my body. I wanted to return to my body. I laid down over the top of myself and focused on returning. The next time I opened my eyes, there were no shadows outside my window and the creature was gone.

Another wave of exhaustion hit me, and I fell back onto my bed. I was asleep before my head hit the pillow.

The next morning, I woke up to immense pain in my shoulder. There were large scratch marks where the creature had got me. I made sure to sweep up all the salt before David saw it. By the time David gets back from work, he is so tired that as long as he sees that I`m in bed, he didn`t care about anything else. Usually when I woke up, David was still asleep. This morning, he was awake and sat on the sofa.

"David, are you alright?" I inquired.

He shook his head. "Hey Kels, another kid has gone missing."

"Who?" I breathed out.

"I`m really sorry, Kelsey."

"Who is it, David?" I demanded.

"Liz Spencer."

Liz Spencer. I had babysat her since I was fourteen and I had known her family for years prior to that. "Do the police think it`s the same person as before?" My brother nodded. "Then she`s still alive."

"What makes you so sure?" My brother frowned.

"Whoever it is, they want the family too."

I ate my breakfast in my bedroom (something I don`t usually do) so I could read the book. It flung open to a page about a tree *Rowan wood is sacred and wards off evil. It will burn witches.*

That was as far as I got before it flung to another page; a poem called *Six Months*.

There are many mistruths about the old gods,
Lies they told about each other,
But in a way, Persephone beat the odds,
And Hades was once again betrayed by his brother,
The biggest lie was of Hades and Persephone.

Zeus and Poseidon feared their brother`s power,
So, they banished him to a prison of his own making,
In the Underworld, most others would cower,
But Hades became king,
Hades never wanted to hurt his brothers.

Kore as she used to be known faced her own kind of prison,
For Demeter had seen how the world treated little girls,
So, she kept her from everyone,
Kore obeyed every command her mother hurls,
But Demeter forgot Kore was a goddess too.

Her power didn`t die out, it imploded,
Kore`s soul split in two,
She was like a gun fully loaded,
Though she tried to be gentle, she knew,
If she stayed, she`d hurt her mother.

Fearing the monster inside, Kore ran straight to Hell,
She could not kill what was already dead,
To Hades her heart fell,
He told her she could stay but said,
Never eat the fruit that grows here, or you can never leave.

He let her do as she pleased,
Her chaotic spells seemed to stop,
When he walked by, her heart squeezed,
And she almost fell over the top.

Before long staying there forever didn`t seem so bad.

Hades loved her like no other,
And was shocked to find she loved him too,
But he soon heard word of her mother,
What would you do if they would take your love from you?
Demeter went to Zeus and Kore begged to stay.

Hades issued a plan,
Kore ate the pomegranates,
They have to do all they can,
Because the power of Zeus can explode planets,
But Hera would protect marriage.

They were married when they came,
Zeus demanded that Kore was returned to her mother,
Kore hid behind Hades large frame,
While Hades said, "No brother,"
"She is an adult. She can make her own choices."

Demeter shouted; "You kidnapped her!"
He did no such thing,
The argument continued from there,
Kore stepped out in front of the kings,
And from her rose Persephone.

The gods tried to subdue the destructive force,
She was lightning in a woman`s form,
They screamed until their voices were hoarse,
It was Hades who calmed the storm,
For his love did not waver for a second.

To avoid this happening again,
Zeus divided the chaos in two,
Half the year she was with Demeter as she was more tame,
Demeter could accept what her daughter had turned into,

So, Persephone stayed with Hades.

Demeter would never look on Persephone,
Hades kept the destruction where she couldn`t hurt anyone,
He loved her whole-heartedly,
Though what happened could not be undone,
For six months she`s free to love, to choose, to exist.

-Persephone`s Book.

Next to it was an illustration of a book. What did that have to do with anything?

It flipped around again to another page; *Skinwalkers. Skinwalkers are man-eating creatures with the ability to mimic voices and changed their form to any of their choosing. They use this ability to isolate and devour their victims. They are highly intelligent, and hard to kill. Taking its heart is always a good bet and burning it is a good way too but saying its name (as with all things) gives you complete control of it. Do not let this thing know your name. Thankfully, they are located over in the United States so...*

I breathed out a sigh of relief, staring at the picture in the book. "So, it`s not a skinwalker."

Why did the book show me all that? The rowan made sense. It was the same tree from the night before but I couldn`t understand why it showed me the rest. Perhaps it was trying to explain what happened while I was astral projecting (something that I didn`t want to experience ever again).

School was, once again, full of whispers. This time it was about Liz. All I could think about was the fact that she would never grow up. Those big brown eyes of hers...

Her eyes!

She saw Nina yesterday. It was so obvious now. Liz was about to follow Nina into the woods when I stopped her. That was how whoever or whatever it was, was taking the children. It used another child or... The word 'skinwalker' was burning into my mind.

That grimoire was written centuries ago. Now we had planes and we had reliable boats. The skinwalker could have easily travelled to the UK where people would have no idea what it was and children wouldn't have heard stories about them.

If it was a skinwalker then...

Shit.

If it was a skinwalker then I hadn't rescued Nina Bowers and taken her home.

I had put a man-eating creature in the Bowers home.

My stomach twisted, and nausea spread through my body in a wave. I scrambled for the girl's toilets. I got there just in time to throw up into the toilet.

I flushed the toilet and washed my hands and face. This was the perfect excuse. I could leave school for being sick and I could research that skinwalker. Find out if it actually was a skinwalker and how I could find out its name. There was no way in Hell that I was going to get close enough to a skinwalker to cut out its heart.

Matron was a cold woman; rude and cruel. The majority of students wouldn't go to matron at all because she was so awful. I had experienced many unpleasant encounters with her, but I never backed down. She had learned that I was a very honest person so even though she gave me a hard time, she didn't give me nearly as hard a time as she did everyone else. She called up my brother and I curled up on the sofa in reception.

David was there in a matter of minutes. Being a very empathetic person, my brother would probably coddle me for the rest of the day. I explained to him that I'd been sick and school rules had made it so I couldn't be at school for the rest of the day. I told him that I felt a lot better.

He didn`t buy it.

He tucked me into bed, placed a bucket next to me and a glass of water on the drawer. He told me that he was going out to buy some Lucozade to get my energy back (being sick was physically draining so he always bought Lucozade to give energy back). "I`m taking Sergeant. I`ll see you in half an hour, ok?" Once he left, I leaped out of bed and grabbed the grimoire. It flipped to the page on skinwalkers again. *Skinwalkers can often be found in graveyards. They dig up graves. Do not look into their eyes because it is rumoured that they can possess you. They walk on all fours more often than not. They were once human, but they committed a horrible deed to become a skinwalker (such as killing a close family member) and the appropriate rituals. The name you must repeat is the one they had when they were human.*

She didn`t have anything else on the matter. I guess that made sense considering the witch who wrote this was probably British and it wasn`t a short journey to America back then.

How do I find out its name?

The book flipped through once again. *Invading someone`s mind through telepathy is a dangerous thing. Especially if the one you seek to read is a supernatural creature. They can dig into your mind instead and it can even result in possession. Humans are easy enough. The basic spell is…* I stopped reading. There was no way I was risking being possessed by something that ate human flesh.

I needed to know if there was a skinwalker around. The book flipped again to a location spell. *Fill a goblet ¾ with water. Place four blue candles in around you in directions North, South, East and West. Use jasmine too and chant 'Hermes help me find what is lost', holding what you need to find in your mind and look into the water. Chant as long as you have to. Witch bloods will see it in the water. Non-witch bloods will see it in their mind.*

I didn't have any blue candles, jasmine, or a goblet. What I did have was a blue wind-up torch, a blue night-light from when I was four, and we had two blue lamps. I set them up as instructed and poured water into a mug until it was ¾ full.

"Hermes help me find what is lost." I whispered and looked into the mug. Nothing. "Hermes help me find what is lost. Hermes help me find what is lost. *Hermes help me find what is lost.*" The water glowed red and rippled into an image.

It was the graveyard by the primary school. I could see someone walking strangely... Not someone... Liz. It was the skinwalker in the form of Liz. It stopped abruptly and turned.

It was looking right at me.

It's hand shot forward, no longer resembling anything human and shot out the mug, grabbing at me.

I shrieked and scrambled back. Slowly it seemed to be pulling itself through the mug. What the fuck do I do? I snatched the blue wind-up torch and turned it off. The hand froze and fell out onto the floor.

Just the hand.

I kicked it. It just rolled.

Black blood stained the carpet.

Looking into the mug, I waited to see its face again. Nothing. I breathed a sigh of relief. What the Hell I was going to do with a hand? I moved all the blue things to their original places and emptied the water into the sink. When I returned to my room, the hand was still *there*.

"I haven't seen a skinwalker in a long time." I jumped and span.

"Jesus, Ben, you frightened me!"

His nostrils flared. "But I don't scare you. I'd smell your fear if that was true." He was in my room in a flash. "You really should ward this place against vampires. Anyone could get in."

"What about you?" I asked.

"You should ward against me, Little One. Not every day I will see you as friend, some days I will see you as a delectable little morsel." I shivered. "Don`t show me weakness, Little One. Predators devour the weak." He picked up the hand. "I will dispose of this. It knows where you are, Little One. Don`t let it inside. The butterfly and the moth may appear the same but only one will fly away with your soul."

He disappeared again.

Looking at the big black stain on the carpet, I decided to get out my pencil case.

David had bought me a quill and a pot of ink for my birthday one year. If I spilled that over the blood, he`d smell the ink instead of the blood. I didn`t want to ruin it but how else was I going to explain this? I poured a little over it and grabbed a bucket, sponge and filled the bucket with soapy water. I scrubbed it hard, knowing that neither substance was going to come out of the carpet.

There was a knock at the door. I made my way to it to see Mason standing there. "Mason, what are you doing here?"

"Why don`t we go and take a look? For Liz`s sake." He replied, monotone.

I backed up. "You`re not Mason."

The skinwalker smiled, impossibly wide. "You`re not Mason." It mimicked my voice.

I slammed the door shut and backed away. As if this was a horror movie, I watched as its flesh squeezed through the gap in the door frame like a liquid. I scrambled to the kitchen, making a beeline for the lighter. With any luck, a lighter would be enough to make it back off.

It wasn`t.

The creature melted and formed a face I hadn`t seen in six years. His eyes were identical to my own, taller than me by nearly a foot. "Peter?"

How did it know what he looked like? Even I hadn't seen him for years. "It's been a long time, Little sister." It was just like his voice. How did it have his voice? How did it know Peter?

I kicked it in the stomach and tried to get away. It grabbed my leg and flung me across the caravan. I hit my head against the thin wall and crawled to my feet. The room was spinning. Did I have a concussion? It was in front of me in seconds. It snatched my hair and lifted me up by it. I screamed and struggled. It was no use. It was stronger than me.

I should've grabbed the knife.

It just laughed at my struggling. Its mouth twisted, revealing rows of needle-like teeth.

It was going to eat me.

Before I knew it, there was six other people in the caravan, all shouting. These big burly men were my neighbours and they were determined to save me. "Put her down!" Karl Timbers shouted, waving around a massive pizza knife. The creature dropped me and backed off. It charged through the side of the caravan, leaving a large hole it is way.

"Th-thank you," I told them.

The men (who I'd known for years nodded). Karl looked to a man called John Phipps and said "You call the police. I'll call her brother."

The police were there in minutes. They started asking me a lot of questions when my brother arrived. "Kelsey!" He charged past the police officers and wrapped me in a hug.

I burst into tears.

They found Liz later that day and by the morning, her family was dead, and she was missing. The police couldn't understand it. How had someone managed to get past all the officers surrounding the house?

Because we were renting, the landlord just moved us into a different caravan. Considering our old one was scrap metal now. We just moved our stuff (which wasn't very much) into the new caravan. It was identical to the old one.

I had looked up wards against evil in the grimoire and had carved them around the caravan (out of sight). The men who'd saved me had made sure to keep an eye on me. I was so lucky to have such brave and kind neighbours otherwise I'd be dead.

The skinwalker scared me more than ever. I was going to hunt it down.

With an axe.

It was the morning when news of the Spencer's had reached me and I was determined that I was going to kill the skinwalker. It would pay for killing the Spencer's. It would pay for destroying my home. It would pay for showing me Peter's face again.

My only thoughts were how did it know about Peter? The only place you could even find a photograph of him was at my parent's house or the police station near my parent's house and both of which were over an hour's drive away. Well, there would be photos of him in the police databases but how could a skinwalker get a hold of that?

The police knew it couldn't be Peter because he had a rock-solid alibi.

I had told them that I didn't believe it was Peter but someone who just looked eerily like him.

I stared into the mirror. Brown eyes stared back. I was so short and plain.

Nobody would ever guess me to be a monster hunter. No monster would ever find me even remotely threatening. I wasn't even sure if I could reach the right angle to cut the thing's head off. And if I did, what then? If I got caught, I would go to jail… for life.

But it would be worth it, wouldn't it?

If I didn't kill this thing then it would keep taking children. It would keep killing families. It was my life for possibly hundreds.

Was this what those men were thinking when they saved us from Joe?

My brother and I didn't own an axe but there was a B&Q nearby. The only problem I could see with this was that I was sixteen and there was a good chance that they wouldn't sell an axe to a teenager. My thoughts went to Ben.

If I took him with me and kept him from talking perhaps, he would be able to buy the axe.

With my money, of course.

It was just a matter of finding him.

Six

Turns out, finding Ben was the easy part. He had just been outside the caravan when I was leaving. I tried to ignore how excited he was by the prospect of me buying an axe. The vampire followed me around B&Q, eyes on everyone who walked past. "Once again, you bring the wolf into the hen house." He muttered.

"Thank you for doing this." I told him. "I need to stop the skinwalker."

"Clever, clever girl." He grinned. "Lambs devouring lions... The lion came for you last night." It wasn`t a question but a statement.

"How did you_?"

"I can smell it on you."

I shivered. The idea of it being on me made me feel sick. Peter`s face flashed through my mind. It had barely left my mind since last night. Why had it taken that form? "Why do you help me, Ben?"

"Ben..." He mumbled. "That`s what she used to call me." Ice ran down my spine. "You... I... I don`t..." He rubbed his head hard.

"Hey, hey, hey..." I tried to soothe him. "It`s ok."

Ben looked back up at me. Those eyes of his were soft for a second but in an instant, they were cold, hard, and predatory. It was like he was a different person. He licked his lips. "What are you doing so close, Little lamb?"

"Ben… Are you ok?" I asked, concerned. He had never directed *that* look at *me* before.

He flinched. "You know me?"

I nodded. "Yes, we`re friends."

"I don`t have friends."

"You have me." I assured him. "At the moment, we`re out shopping for an axe to kill a skinwalker with. Don`t you remember?"

"Oh, a skinwalker…" He licked his lips. "A dangerous thing for a little human to hunt. Why would something so delicate fight something like that?"

"It`s killing people in my town." I told him gently. "And it came for me."

He growled. "And I let that happen?" His hands moved oddly, looking sharp and grabby: not like that hands of a man but more like talons. "Why would I do that to my friend?"

"You tried to warn me." I thought back to our conversation. "You hid it`s hand."

He laughed a dangerous laugh that dripped madness. "You removed its hand? Was it with a spell, *witch blood*? Yes, yes, a spell. Magic is a dying art… Who taught you?"

"You gave me a grimoire."

"Me? Spreading witchcraft?" He seemed shocked by the idea. "Interesting… Kelsey… You… Little One."

He seemed to be returning to himself. "Ben?"

"Ben? That`s what she used to call me." Ben`s eyes were back to normal. I breathed out a sigh of relief and wrapped him in a hug. It was like hugging concrete. "You`re hugging me? What did I do?"

"You weren`t yourself."

"Or maybe I was more myself than you`ve ever seen."

I shook my head. "I don`t believe that. You`re my friend…"

"Friend? Is that what I am, Little One? I thought I was your protector." He bent down to my height. "'Friends' mean trust, but you can *never* trust me. Next time I don`t know your face, you may not be able to talk your way out of it."

I shook my head as he returned to his full height. "Regardless of trust; you`re my friend. You are a good man."

"I am neither good nor a man, Little One." He insisted. "Now, let`s go find your axe. Death is near and you won`t outrun him for long. The child does not learn if the father does it all." We found an axe that was big enough to do damage, small enough that I could easily carry it and cheap enough that I could afford it.

We made our way to the check out. The look in Ben`s eyes made the worker hesitate. He held his hand over the axe but didn`t scan it, just stared at Ben like he was frightened of what would happen if he let Ben touch it. Ben shifted in front of me, like a glitch on a screen. It made me flinch and I found myself looking around to make sure nobody else had noticed him move like that. They hadn`t. Ben leant forward over the till and looked into the worker`s eyes. *"You`re going to give the girl the axe for free because you are an incompetent prick."*

The man looked dazed, swaying slightly. *"I`m going to give the girl the axe for free because I`m an incompetent prick."*

He handed me the axe and we left. On the way out I heard the worker talking to another. "Why did you give her the axe for free?"

"Because I`m an incompetent prick."

"What does incompetent even mean?"

"I don`t know."

I snorted and stuffed the axe into my bag. It was a tight squeeze, but I managed it. "Thank you, Ben."

"You're welcome... my friend." He stumbled over the words like they were a foreign concept. Who knows? It could have been. He disappeared again and I began my walk home.

It occurred to me once I saw the primary school that the graveyard wasn't far away. Even if the skinwalker wasn't there, I could at least visit Adria.

I hadn't been to her grave since the funeral and I couldn't even remember the funeral. It was almost like I would be seeing her grave for the first time. I decided to stop by into the local corner shop to buy her some flowers. I picked up a bunch of carnations in a variety of colours. I thought she'd like the myriad of colours. I twisted through the graveyard to Adria. I wasn't sure how I knew that was where she was. It was like my body was on autopilot. Her gravestone read '*Adria Kelley. Loving daughter. Kind friend. We hope you find more happiness in the next life.*' A tear ran down my cheek as I lay down the carnations.

"Why didn't you do anything?" Snarled a voice from behind me. I flinched and turned. Adria's father. He strode quickly at me, fists clenched. I stumbled back, grabbing the strap of my rucksack. I stumbled to avoid stepping on Adria's grave. "You were with her all the time!" He grabbed my shoulders and shook me a little. "Why..." He sobbed. "Why didn't you do anything?"

My lower lip trembled. "I- I didn't know..."

"Bullshit!" He howled, shaking me harshly. "Were you too lazy?! Did you not think it mattered?! That it was all a joke?! My baby killed herself! Why didn't you do anything?!"

"Why didn't you?" I demanded, smacking his hands away from me. "I didn't know! You were with her just as often as I was! Why didn't you do anything?"

That was the first time I'd seen a grown man cry. At least... it was the first time I could remember seeing a grown man cry. He looked so much smaller now as he hugged his stomach and bawled. Guilt twisted my stomach.

I didn`t know what to do.

How do you react when you make the man who was shouting at you seconds ago, cries?

Unsure of how safe he was, I manoeuvred my body behind the gravestone, and I crossed my arms across my chest to grab both of my biceps. Doing so didn`t really make me feel better but I didn`t trust him not to do something. "She wouldn`t want you to be upset. She was never like that. We will never really know what drove her to do it, but we can live *for* her."

"I wish it was me instead." He choked.

"She wouldn`t want that." I insisted shakily. It was really hard to sound confident in front of a man who had been shouting at me seconds before hand. Usually when someone had shouted at me, I didn`t try to comfort them; I tried to defend myself. But this man was the father of my late best friend and he was in a lot of pain. "She would want you to *live.* She would want you to live your life to the fullest and try to be happy."

"How can I be happy when she`s gone?"

What the Hell was I doing? "I`m not saying it will be easy and I can`t even begin to imagine what it is you`re going through. I know the pain will never fully go away but… you have to try."

He wiped his eyes and sat up. "I`m sorry for shouting at you. You didn`t deserve that. My daughter was lucky to have a friend like you."

My eyes fell from his to look at the gravestone. "I was lucky to have her."

The conversation (if that was what you could even call that interaction), stopped there and we stood in front of her grave for a while. I knew I had to find the skinwalker but, I didn`t want to leave Adria just yet.

A scream ripped through the melancholy silence.

"She's gone! She's gone!" Came the hysterical voice of a young woman.

"Who's gone?" I asked calmly, rushing over to her.

"My mother! She's gone!" She pointed at an open grave. It had been dug up, the coffin smashed open, and the body had been removed. Splinters littered the ground like snow, a muddy trail where something had been dragged started at the hole and ended in the beginning of the woods. As I looked around the area, I noticed several other identical graves.

How would I have reacted if it had been Adria?

So, the skinwalker had been here. Had it gone far? Was it still here? I looked around and the only person I could see was the woman. I observed the way she was moving; thought back to the way she spoke.

I think… she's human.

At least I wasn't chancing lobbing her head off.

It must have left into the woods. Do I follow it? I looked to the others… No. I can't leave them here. And if I did, it would look too suspicious.

The police were called… again. I could tell from the way they were looking at me that they were thinking 'it's her again'. I knew that it was only a matter of time before they started asking me questions.

Questions that I didn't have answers to.

It wasn't a long walk home but I still had lots of time to think. What were the chances of me running into all these weird things in the last few months when I hadn't seen anything for the sixteen years prior? It was like I'd been marked.

I decided to return home, to look at the grimoire. Every sound around me snatched my attention but it was never the skinwalker or the yellow eyed thing. I needed to deal with the skinwalker before I looked into the yellow eyed thing. Hopefully, the grimoire will have something more than just the poem.

I couldn't let another child go missing. If another child went missing, I felt like that was on me.

Who else could do anything? At the camp there were a dozen kids who had no idea how to fight that thing. Those were kids from a dozen different families and none of us knew *anything*. We were all from the same area. That didn't exactly bode well for the rest of the community knowing anything about any of this either. I couldn't rely on anyone else... and Ben was a vampire. Yes, he seemed to care for me, but he looked at everyone else like they were food. He wouldn't care to fight a skinwalker. *A child will never learn if the father does all the work.* Came to mind.

So that's what he meant.

I had to learn to fight for myself.

Re-evaluating my strategy, I considered the woods. That was where I had seen it both times. Not only that but the woods seemed to be where it had gone after destroying the graveyard... Although the idea of being alone amongst a maze trees wasn't exactly a comforting thought. While walking, I did consider bringing Sergeant with me but if she died then I'd never forgive myself. There was no way in Hell I could chance that. There was that blue wind-up torch somewhere in the caravan. It would be dark soon.

Because hunting a skinwalker when it's dark in the woods is *such* a good idea.

I'm *so* going to die.

I opened the door to our new caravan to see David sitting in front of the TV. "Another kid went missing."

"Who?"

"Jake Phipps." That was the name of the son of one of the men who'd saved me from the skinwalker the night before. One of my neighbours. "He left a note this time."

"What did it say?"

"Don't know. The police took it and won't tell anyone." I had to know what was on that note. "But they did say to keep an eye on you."

So, it was about me. I wasn't as surprised as I probably should have been. "I... I think I'm just going to go to my room."

"Are you ok?" I heard it in David's voice; he was guilty. He must have felt like he shouldn't have told me any of that.

I nodded as I walked through. "Yeah... I just hope that they find Jake. This has to end soon. It just has to." Who would have thought that the drama club thing I used to go to would actually come in handy? Convinced, he went back to the tv, allowing me to continue to my room. Sergeant followed me there and gave me a disappointed book when I shut the door behind us. "Sorry girl," I whispered. "I need to find out what that note says without anyone else knowing."

Pulling out the book, it reacted to me instantly. The book flipped open to an all too familiar page: astral projection.

Fuck that. There had to be *anything else*.

The book flipped through until it reached another page: *familiars.*

Having a familiar is a big step into witchcraft. It is a step in which there is no coming back from. There is no limit to how many familiars you may have. Though you can make non-supernatural animals your familiars; the fey are far more helpful for more witch-related tasks. Other spirits can be used but the fey would be my recommendation. Summoning a familiar is an incredibly challenging spell and potentially an extremely dangerous one. I would not recommend it to be attempted by humans at all.

I looked to Sergeant. She wasn't really suited to this task and I wasn't sure if I wanted to permanently involve myself in witchcraft.

My mind wandered to little Jake Phipps and his family. I couldn't let them die.

I looked to the spell. It involved no ingredients; just me. Deciding that it was best for Sergeant to not be in the room, I opened my bedroom door. David was just leaving. As the front door shut, I shooed Sergeant out of my room and shut the door behind her. Guilt gnawed my stomach at her sad eyes but if I summoned something dangerous then I didn't want her anywhere near me.

I began chanting, feeling the tingle of energy in my fingertips and the fatigue in the rest of my body.

Magic takes a toll on body, mind, and soul.

I could feel my lungs and how they ached. It was almost as if someone had reached into my chest and grabbed a hold of them so I couldn't breathe properly. Sweat dripped from my forehead, to my nose and to the floor. I didn't remember it *hurting* so much before.

I opened my eyes to see a small creature on the floor. The book flipped through to a page that read: *Fairies; puca.* I had never heard of such a thing. *They are shapeshifters and although they can be helpful, they can also be very dangerous.*

It opened it little mouth to speak. "*Speak my name and to my beak, to my tail to my claws, I am yours. Speak your name and mine you shall be. Bound to me for all eternity.*"

How do you find out a fairy's name?

His name is Sage. Call out for Sage. Stated a voice in my head.

"Sage. I name thee Sage."

"*Then I am your eternal servant, little witch. Your wish is my command.*" Sage's voice was very deep and gravelly for something that was six inches high.

"I need the letter the skinwalker wanted me to find."

"Done." It transformed into a raven and flew out of the window.

I opened the door, collapsed onto my bed, and decided to rest my eyes until Sage returned.

When I woke up, it was pitch black outside. How long had I been asleep? I was still tired. That amount of magic I had used, had taken all the energy out of me. Sage had just flown back through the window, landing on the drawer next to me. I sat up in my bed. Sergeant was laying at the end of my bed, crushing my legs, and though she stared at Sage, she didn't bark or growl.

"Here's your letter." Sage, who was still in the form of the raven, handed me the letter.

Kelsey,

I know your name. I know your name. I know your name. I know your name. I know your name. I know your name. I know your name.

You're mine. You're mine. You're mine.
Did you find my little treat in the graveyard?
Will you find my latest toy?
Perhaps you should look where it all began? You know where.

XXX

My first thought was to go back to the woods where I found the skinwalker when it looked like Nina, but it occurred to me that the police knew where that was. *They use this ability to isolate and devour their victims.* It didn't mean there. The police would think that too and it didn't want the police. It wanted me.

"Does it mean Joe's camp?" I turned to Sage, who was watching me with beady little eyes.

Sage transformed back. "The skinwalker is no longer in these trees." He gestured in the direction of the woods. "It wants you back *there*."

I was unsure of how Sage knew about that but I didn't question it.

How do I get back there?

It was a long drive and I couldn't drive. My brother was working and there was no way he would take me back there even if I asked. Even if he would take me there then there is no way he'd be back in time. I had no way of contacting Ben and even if I did, who knows if he could drive? I did consider calling the police, but they didn't know what a skinwalker was and there was no way that they'd believe me if they did. Furthermore, there was no chance in Hell that they'd take me with them.

That left one person.

But if he drove me it would be highly illegal. I wasn't sure if he'd even do it.

I pulled out my phone and he picked up on the third ring. "Hi, sorry to call you so late but, I need a favour. Do you think you can drive me somewhere? I... I need to go back to the camp, and it can't wait."

I left a note (written by me, not the skinwalker) on the kitchen side. I kept the note in my pocket. I left the caravan just as the Toyota land cruiser pulled up.

"You ok?" Mason asked as he leaned over to open the door. I slung off my bag and dumped it on the floor of the car. I sat next to him.

"Not really," He started driving. "Sorry for doing this."

"I know you have your reasons." Mason told me. "Even if you can't tell me them."

"Sorry about that... But there is *no way* you'd believe me." I insisted, feeling guilty that I couldn't tell him. It wasn't like he believed me. I wouldn't have. Mason didn't ask me any more questions on the matter and for that, I was thankful.

It was so dark now and the lights on the back of other cars hurt my eyes. I wasn't really sure how Mason could see to drive but I didn't really have any experience with driving so what did I know? I had remembered to bring the axe and two torches (it was always good to have a spare). There were matches and a flask with a bottle of oil (screwed up as tightly as possible). Sage had crawled in too, quietly curled up in an old knitted hat in the form of a grey mouse.

It was a strange feeling on that drive. There was a good chance I would fail (especially considering what happened last time I ran into the skinwalker). I knew I was putting Mason at risk and I felt horrible about that. But what else could I do? I would ask him to turn around once I get there. I could call him once it was done.

It was a good thing that I had a password or the skinwalker could call Mason using my voice.

"I can`t thank you enough." I told him, running my fingers through my hair.

"Anytime." He smiled.

"When we get there, you should turn around and drive away. Maybe wait in the nearby town for an hour or two?"

"You`re about to do something dangerous, aren`t you?"

"Yeah,"

Mason gave me a look that made me think for a moment that he was going to protest. "Ok, then. You want back-up?"

Yes. "No,"

I knew that he knew I was lying. Mason was far from stupid and he knew that I knew that he knew I was lying... Thankfully, he didn`t point it out. "Ok,"

I breathed a sigh of relief. "Also… If I call you up… We need a codeword."

"Why do we need a codeword?" He asked, arching an eyebrow.

"Um…" I had no answer for that. "Because I`m a James Bond wannabee?"

He snorted a laugh. "*Right*," He dragged out the 'I'. "Because I`m sure that you told me that you`d *never* seen James Bond."

"Damn you and your eidetic memory."

"I get that a lot." He didn`t really have an eidetic memory but it was a rumour that went around that he did. He never confirmed or denied it so I honestly wasn`t so sure. "How about 'eidetic'?"

Perfect. "'Eidetic' it is." I agreed. "Just make sure I say it. It doesn`t matter whether or not it`s my voice. Only pick me up if I can say the word."

Mason was clearly unsettled by this conversation, but he promised that he wouldn`t come for me unless I said the word. My stomach twisted more and more, the further we got into the trees. By the time we had reached the camp, I felt like I might throw up over Mason`s car. Mason stopped and I thanked him as I got out (making sure that I had picked up all my stuff). Mason drove off and it was quiet and dark again. Sage crawled out of my bag while I pulled out the torch. It only illuminating a small circle in a monstrous forest, not nearly enough. The light scanned the trees, revealing nothing.

If I survived this, I was never coming back here *ever* again.

I creeped towards the camp. The place was still covered in ash and fenced off with police tape. There were red-brown stains against stone pathways and half-scorched wood. Was that blood? My stomach twisted again.

Those poor people.

Those people were bent into completely unnatural poses with their chests wide open and empty.

My chest tightened and my eyes couldn`t move from the stain.

It`s over. It`s over. It`s over.
It crawled across the roof…

My vision blurred and I started to shake uncontrollably.

"Kelsey..."

I grabbed at my sides, trying to stop the shaking.

How the fuck did it know my name?

Was it always this cold out here?

"Kelsey... I don't want this one, Kelsey. His lips aren't big enough for my tastes but yours..."

I couldn't see anymore... It was all blurry.

"Your lips will be delectable..."

I can't breathe.

She screamed while it ate her insides.

My fingers gripped my throat. I can't breathe.

It yanked down hard on my leg.

I'm going to be sick.

The creature gutted Precious in an instant.

Can someone please stop the ringing?

"Yes, yes, run Kelsey run!"

My fingers tingled and I grabbed my stomach.

"They said the reason why it didn't eat you while you were unconscious is because it wanted you to be awake while it ate you."

The world was spinning so much, I had to sit down.

"They said the reason why it didn't eat you while you were unconscious is because it wanted you to be awake while it ate you."

Was I dying?

"They said the reason why it didn't eat you while you were unconscious is because it wanted you to be awake while it ate you."

I tried to slow my breathing. What was happening to me?

"They said the reason why it didn't eat you while you were unconscious is because it wanted you to be awake while it ate you."

"Hello, Little One,"

I flinched but the voice seemed to snap me out of whatever was happening. "B-Ben,"

He stepped out of the trees. What was he doing here? Did he follow me? "Ben. That's what she used to call me." He said. "What are you doing so close, Little Lamb?"

I got to my feet, rubbing my bicep. "I'm looking for the skinwalker."

"A dangerous thing for a human to go up against." He said.

"I know." I assured him. "You…" Realisation flashed through me. "You told me."

Ben's face twisted unnaturally, his smile literally reaching from ear-to-ear, like it had been cut into its face, thin and malevolent.

I stumbled to my feet, regaining my composure seconds later. "Where's the boy?"

"Here… There… Everywhere…" This voice wasn't one I'd heard before. It was low, hollow, and *wrong*. Was that its real voice? "Let's play a game."

"Let's not."

It smiled again, making me wish that I'd stayed silent. What am I doing? I'm not a monster hunter. I'm a bookworm. "Who will find who first? Will you find the boy before I find you? I will give you a ten-minute head start and this clue. Then I will come and find you." It gave me a look that said, 'understand the rules?'. I would be insulted if I cared what this creature thought of me. "*Follow the bones.*" Oh God. It's in the tunnels. "Go."

I scrambled through the trees, remembering exactly where to go like I'd never left.

Then I stopped to climb the tree with the best view.

You didn't really think that I was going to do this by this creature's rules, did you? If I played by its rules, then it had the advantage. No… I was going to play this game by my rules. I pulled the axe out of my bag, realising then, that Sage was still with me. He had been sitting on top of my bag. "Sage…" I whispered. "Do you think you could give me a location on the skinwalker?"

Sage crawled from my bag to my shoulder before shifting into the raven and flying off.

Leaving me completely alone.

You really didn`t think that through, did you, Kels?

I can`t see anything in the trees and I the only thing I can hear is my own breath. It was like even the wind was stopping to listen.

Sage was back two minutes later but it was the longest two minutes of my life. He landed on my shoulder and shifted back. "It is following its rules, but I suspect that it will have your location in a few minutes. Quite a predicament for you this puts."

"I`m going to kill it."

"The upper ground you have but the advantage you don`t. If you stumble, kill it you won`t." Sage assured me.

"Thanks for the vote of confidence, my friend."

"Though your familiar I shall be, so these rules do not apply to me; never thank or apologise to the fey for that is a debt in their say. The things that they will ask of you, you will have no choice but to do and even I cannot protect you."

That is definitely good to know.

"Why is it that sometimes you speak in rhyme and others you don`t?" I inquired. It had been something that had been slightly bothering me since he appeared.

"Mind your fucking business." Sage snapped, crossing his arms across his tiny chest. I wasn`t sure whether or not he was joking so I said nothing. We sat there in silence, scanning the trees for the skinwalker. I kept looking down, fully expecting it to be there, grabbing my ankle like Joe had. Before long, I saw it, wandering through the trees. I held my breath, determined to keep silent. My heart was thundering so quickly, I was sure that it would hear, and my cover would be blown. I waited for it to walk by the tree…. Closer…. Closer… I leapt onto it, swinging the axe down at it as hard as I could.

"*Kelsey,*" My muscles tensed, and I fell, missing the creature entirely. I landed on my back with a loud thud. That hurt. "*Kelsey,*" I tried to get up, to attack it again, but my body wouldn`t obey. I couldn`t even wiggle my fingers.

What was happening?

I wanted to jump up and hit it with the axe but I couldn`t move.

"*I told you…*"

Saying its name (as with all things) gives you complete control of it. Do not let this thing know your name.

"Stand up."

I stood up, leaving my axe there on the ground. No. No. No. No. No. No! My mind screamed for my body to move, to free myself, to take up the axe and smash the creature`s skull with it… But I couldn`t. My body was no longer my own, the only thing I had left was my mind.

"*Come to me.*" No! My left foot took a shaky step forward. I fought as hard as I could, but I was slowly walking towards it. "*You`re fighting me. That`s good. But you don`t know the secret… So, you`re mine.*"

As a feminist, I resent that statement. I would have said that if I could move my mouth.

I took another step forward.

I wanted my big brother… Or Ben. I was so scared. I was walking towards a cannibalistic monster that had control of my mind. I`m going to die here.

It stroked my cheek… It wasn`t gentle and it`s hand felt like sandpaper grating against my face. Its claw glided down my cheek, slicing into my flesh. It hurt so much but I couldn`t flinch or pull away. I felt my eyes water and I felt so cold. I can't believe I'm going to die like this. "How can something so small cause so much trouble? Will they miss you when you're gone? I don't think so... There's that brother of yours; but he's ashamed of you. You haven't seen the rest of your family for over six years. That vampire probably won't even remember your name after a month... He may even convince himself that you were just another hallucination. And that boy of yours... He never really got over the other girl, did he? You hope that he will, but you really know that he hasn't. That he never will. Perhaps I should put you out of your misery. After all, ... Your negligible existence will be soon forgotten." Its claw moved up and down my throat, each stroke getting harder and harder.

I'm going to die. I'm going to die here... alone is these *fucking* woods. They won't find the body and I'll be here forever in these fucking *woods.*

I felt it's claw dig into my flesh, just enough to draw blood when something knocked the skinwalker off of me, sending it flying into a nearby tree.

The creature was that had knocked it off was huge. As big as a horse with teeth like a saber-tooth tiger. Its body reminded me of a bull mastiff, but its muscles were huge, and its ears were more like that of a beagle. It stood between me and the skinwalker, its tail wagging like a fan. "Take the name." What? That was Sage's voice. Really not the sound I was expecting from such a large body. What name? "Take a name. You'll move once you take a name." Did he mean like a nickname? I was so confused. "Pick your witch name."

What name...? I... Only one name seemed to fit.

Adria.

My muscles relaxed and I stumbled forward, free at last. I scrambled for the axe and turned back to the skinwalker and Sage.

"I can't hold a skinwalker for long." Sage warned me. "And I'll turn back soon. You have to take it from here."

There is a time-limit on Sage's transformations? Oh, come on! Give me a break!

Sage slammed into the skinwalker again and again. The skinwalker was covered in thick black blood. It grabbed Sage by the throat, and I watched in horror as he shrank back into his bruised fairy form. It violently tossed Sage to the side and turned back to me, revealing large shark-like black eyes on me with a malevolent grin. "*Kelsey,*" That voice was back again; it sounded so inhuman. I didn't look human anymore. All the tears in its skin revealed pale grey, veiny flesh. Its limbs were bent at the wrong angles; inverted knees and forearms that are far too long.

I raised my axe.

It smiled, and stepped back into the trees, dissolving into the darkness. *"Where's the boy?"* It said that in my voice, and I charged forward in the direction where it had been, and it was gone.

Plan B: I needed to get to Jake before the skinwalker did.

I scurried to Sage. "Sage, are you alright?" He was at the base of a tree, bruised and bloody. Are those bitemarks?

"I'll be fine, Adria. Find the child."

I scooped up his tiny body and delicately placed him back in my bag. At least he would be safe there. Wait. Had Sage called me 'Adria'? I had never said the name out loud.

Walking to the entrance of the mine would take over an hour, so I charged through the trees, axe gripped tightly in my hands. The mine was huge. There *had* to be another way in. I remembered these woods enough to remember the look of the inner parts of the mine. I could never forget. I recalled which direction the mine was going; I just hoped that I could find another way in. I hoped I could get their faster.

It doesn't want the boy; it wants you. Don't forget that.
But why does it want me? I'm nobody.
Witch blood.
I can't hear anything.
No birds.
No crickets.
Not even the crunch of any footstep but my own.
I'm not alone.

Frozen in place, my eyes dart around the trees, my torch light flickering everywhere. There was nothing. But there's something here. I can feel it. I clenched my hands tighter around the handle of my axe to stop them from shaking. My stomach twisted and ice was shooting through my veins. Every hair on my body was standing on end (I must have looked like an electrocuted monkey). A shock went down my spine and I span around; there he stood.

Two identical boys stood in front of me. Grey eyes stared at me, blonde hair rustled in the wind and their tiny bodies shook in the cold night air.

Which one's real?

"Kelsey, please help me. I don't understand." Came the voice first.

"Don't listen... It's me. Please... I'm scared."

Shit. What do I do? They're identical but I barely knew Jake. I couldn't tell the difference.

If Sergeant was here, she could tell me which one's which, but I could never put her in harm's way... So, there I stood... In the woods in front of a young boy and a cannibalistic monster. The pair completely identical. I was being deceived by a fucking mimic...

That was when it came to me.

"Jake... Copy everything I say."

"Ok..." There was uncertainty in the voice.

What words do children rarely say? Um... "Picture." I took one step forward.

"Picture." They replied.

"Halloween." I took another step forward.

"Halloween."

"Obnoxious." Another step.

"Obnoxious." Said one, retaining the child`s voice. The other one followed a mere second later. You wouldn`t have noticed unless you were listening for it.

I span quickly and swung my axe at it. It dodged, shedding its appearance for a far more menacing one: Rupert. His grey eyes glinted. "Oh, the things I would do to you, Kelsey Alexander." His voice. It`s Rupert`s voice.

It stepped forward and I swung the axe. It grabbed my forearm. It squeezed tight, forcing me to drop the axe. It twisted my arm.

I screamed.

That *hurt*.

It eyes glinted grey with excitement. If I didn`t know better, I would have thought it was Rupert. "Oh, the things I`m gonna do to you." It was still Rupert`s voice.

Kicking out, I hit it straight in the crotch as hard as I could. Its face turned pale purple, releasing my arm. I snatched the axe with my left hand and scrambled away from it. How was I going to fight this thing with one arm?

Jake was crouched behind a tree, staring with wide frightened eyes at the scene in front of him.

The skinwalker grinned malevolently at me, matching Rupert`s smile so perfectly. Was Rupert the skinwalker? It marched forward, faster than I could manage when I ran. I swung the axe down, moving in between its arms so it wouldn`t grab me again, and get close enough to hit it. I lodged my axe in its shoulder.

It stumbled.

It looked up at me with those shocked pale grey eyes. I think it knew then that it was going to die; that I had won, that I was going to kill it. Those pale grey eyes returned to a watery black. I swung the axe again, as it fell onto its inverted knees. I hacked into its neck and swung again and again and again until its head came clean off and its body flopped onto the ground. After a few seconds it shifted...

Back into the bus driver from the trip.

I looked it up and down, waiting for it to get back up but it didn`t. As I looked it up and down. It`s shirt had edged up and I noticed something on its stomach.

Hesitant to get closer, I stepped forward and raised its shirt with the edge of my axe. There was a symbol carved into its stomach. Was that a spider? I pulled out my phone and took a photo of the symbol.

Maybe it meant something.

When did the bus driver become a skinwalker?

Was it before we went to the camp or afterwards? I shivered. Was it there when we were being hunted down by Joe?

I eyed the scar again and pulled out the matches and the bottle of oil. I poured the oil all over the body and set it on fire. I moved over to Jake. "Are you ok?" He nodded and we watched the skinwalker burn. I waited for it to burn up more and then I dialled Mason`s number. "Eidetic."

David told me that I would be grounded for the rest of my life but somehow, he seemed to have forgotten that I was grounded after a week and a half. He never could stay angry with me for any period of time; especially after I saved the life of a little boy.

The Phipps family treated me like a hero but from what I heard, they'd gone to stay with a family member until they could move somewhere else. I think David was thinking about it but we couldn't afford to move. He needed his job and I was in my final year of secondary school. It was only a few months before my GCSEs started anyway.

My arm was dislocated at the elbow. It hurt and it was bandaged up, but it would be fine.

The oddest thing though, was that when I searched for that symbol in the book, but there were no spider symbols to be found. I couldn't understand why that skinwalker had that symbol on its stomach.

Why a spider?

As far as I know, skinwalkers have nothing to do with spiders so why was it there? Besides, who carved that symbol onto its chest? Surely, it wouldn't have done that to itself because it looked extremely painful. Though perhaps something that painful to me wouldn't be that painful for something like that? I don't know.

"Kelsey! There's someone at the door for you!" David shouted, startling me out of my thoughts.

"Coming!" I scurried from my room to find David staring out our front door with a smug look. At the front door stood Mason with a stunning bouquet of sunshine-yellow daffodils. "Mason,"

"Hey Kelsey," He waved, eyeing my brother warily for a second before thrusting the flowers towards me. "These are for you."

"Thank you," I smiled awkwardly. I looked to David who was shaking with silent laughter at our awkward encounter.

Mason had met David before, when he was visiting me after Adria died.

"We never finished our date." Mason stated. "I was wondering…" He looked to David and back at me. David was grinning, clearly enjoying how uncomfortable his presence was making us. "I was wondering if you would go out with me this evening to a restaurant with me?"

I turned to David to ask his permission. He shrugged as if to say, 'go ahead'. "Sure,"

"I`ll pick you up tonight at six?" He asked, looking between me and my brother.

I looked to David who shrugged again. "Ok,"

He smiled brightly. "Ok; I`ll see you later."

"Bye," As the door shut, my stomach flipped. What do you wear to go out to a restaurant? The closest thing to a restaurant I had ever been to was eating out at the local pub or McDonalds. Do I wear make-up? Do I wear heels? I`m not even sure if I know how to wear heels!

Noticing the panic on my face, David laughed. "Maybe I should call up Kyle. He and I haven`t been out in ages."

"I haven`t seen Kyle in forever." I told him, smiling. I liked Kyle. He was funny.

David shrugged. "I thought that snogging my boyfriend in front of my little sister would be kind of weird."

"Thank you for that." I sighed. "What do I wear to a restaurant?"

"A dress?"

I wasn`t even sure I *owned* a dress. Admittedly, outside of my school uniform I only really wore three different band t-shirts that were all too big for me and I got from the charity shop, two different pairs of jeans and occasionally a pair of joggy-bottoms that were too short for me and looked awful. I did *own* other shirts but few that I liked, and I did own other trousers but most of them I had owned since I was ten and most didn`t fit comfortably or weren`t suitable for English weather most of the year, let alone in February.

Deciding that I should dig through my chest of drawers, I left for my room and started digging through. Eventually, I discovered a flowy purple summer dress. I think I remembered being given that by my late grandmother back when I was twelve. Though I had owned it for four years, I don`t remember ever wearing it but I was pretty sure it would still fit because I`d stopped growing around that time anyway.

I tried it on. The dress was beautiful: long and flowy and suited my shape. The purple colour made my boring brown hair look more like a dark auburn. The dress was beautiful and made me look beautiful. I looked beautiful but I didn`t look like *me*. I looked like a completely different person.

Just as I was about to take it off, I hesitated.

I wanted to look pretty for my date tonight and this was the best way to do it. What else could I wear? I could hardly show up in jeans.

Deciding that this was the best option, I kept it on. People wear make-up for dates to restaurants, right? Unsure of what make-up I actually owned, I dug through my drawers until I found the small bag full of the make-up that I had been bought by family members when I was younger (most of which didn`t know me very well). There was one lipstick in there that I liked; a dark wine red but that wouldn`t go with the pale purple dress I had on. I rummaged through it to find a pale pink lip gloss, some mascara, and a tube of something the same colour as my skin. I applied it all as best I could (none of which was particularly good, so I had to try it again several times). I looked in the mirror again. I looked pretty but it was like I was looking at another girl. Was I ok with that? I decided that I was, and I sat down on my bed.

I hadn`t seen anything even remotely supernatural (besides my fairy familiar) since the thing with the skinwalker.

People were still going missing but there were no bodies or anything, so the police had nothing to go on. I don't know where these people were going and with there being no bodies, I had turned to the grimoire, but it flipped to so many pages that it left me very confused.

Sage had taken to taking the form of an adorable grey mouse and riding Sergeant around. If Sergeant knew that Sage was a dangerous supernatural being, she didn't show it. She loved her little fairy buddy and though Sage would huff and puff about 'stupid mutt', I was certain he loved his furry buddy.

David still didn't know about Sage, who was more than capable of hiding in Sergeant's long fur.

I had taken to reading a little bit in the grimoire each night. Sage had tried to open it before for me while I grabbed a drink, but it seemed that I was the only one who could open it. I had learned a few more spells (my favourite being the one that allowed me to throw my voice to anywhere I wanted... the amount of times I had tricked Delilah into thinking I was following her in the vents was admittedly shameful) and I had taken to collecting different plants for different spells.

I guess I was a full-fledged witch now.

Despite the fact that I could find witches online (and I had scoured the internet for people like me), the kind of witchcraft they used was completely different. I had looked through the grimoire for information on this and the grimoire suggested that it was humans practising witchcraft and that what I was and what I was doing was something else entirely.

Though my witchcraft would have to remain a secret, it felt like since the skinwalker was gone, my life was getting better and better.

"You look really pretty tonight." Mason told me at our dinner.

I smiled nervously and sipped at my water. "Thank you. Y-you too." I mentally slapped myself. *You too?* "I-I mean! I mean you don't look pretty! Not that you look ugly! I mean you look handsome." I stumbled, feeling my face burn red. Crap, had talking to Mason always been this hard? Hell, had speaking English ever been this hard?

He laughed. "Thanks," I breathed out a sigh of relief. "How's your meal?"

Boring. "It's good. How's yours?" He had taken me to a restaurant, and it was *ridiculously expensive*. I had bought a salad because it was the cheapest thing on the menu (still over seven pounds) and they didn't have a burger and chips like they did at the pub that David usually and I went to.

"Good,"

Our conversation was far more awkward than it usually was, but I learned a lot about him. I learned that his birthday was exactly a week before mine (mine was October thirty-first and his was on the twenty-fourth). His favourite colour was green, he loved ribs and his favourite videogame was Red Dead Redemption. I learned a lot about him.

As the date went on, my mind began to panic. What if he wanted to kiss me? I wasn't sure I was ready for that level of intimacy. I was uncomfortable to have the majority of people hug me. Though with Mason, I thought I'd be comfortable with a hug. What if he wanted to go further than a kiss? I *definitely* wasn't ready for that.

He walked me home. I wasn't sure how happy I was when it came to the fact that he would be walking home alone in the dark; especially after everything that had happened with the skinwalker.

I was no longer ignorant lurked in the dark.

But he was.

Mason insisted that he was fine. I looked up at the caravan. David wasn't home yet. I turned back to him. He leaned forward.

My stomach twisted. Was he going to…?

He kissed my cheek and I couldn't help the sigh of relief. "I know you're not ready for more. Your eyes say it all. We can go at the speed you're comfortable with." I smiled shyly.

"Thank you," I gave him a quick hug. It was nice. "Have a nice evening."

"You too," He grinned and walked away. I closed the door behind me.

What was wrong with me?

I liked Mason. I liked Mason, *a lot*. I wanted to be in a relationship with him and I wanted to kiss him, but I was so awkward. How long would he wait? I knew that he had been in a sexual relationship with Delilah so how long would he be comfortable to have less than that with me? I didn't have a problem with that kind of relationship but I just wasn't ready yet.

I wasn't sure when I would be.

Making sure to text my brother that I was home before I went into my room and tore off that stupid dress and wiped off that make-up. I put on my Star Wars pyjamas and lied down on my bed. Suddenly, the room got really cold. I sat up so I could shuffle under the covers and opened my eyes.

Floating in front of me was the spectral form of Adria. "Adria?"

"*Kelsey! Kelsey!*" She was looking straight through me like she couldn't see me but knew that I was there. *"Kelsey! You have to stop them! You have to stop them, Kelsey!"*

"Who, Adria? Who must I stop?"

"*Kelsey, you have to stop them before they kill someone else! Kelsey! Kelsey! Stop them!*" Didn't she hear me?

"Stop who?"

She disappeared as fast as she had appeared.

What the fuck was I going to do?

Seven

It had been a week since Adria's ghost had appeared to me. I hadn't seen her since and I had found nothing. Honestly, I wasn't sure what I was looking for. Originally, I had planned to use a Ouija board (the grimoire showed me how) but I watched the Conjuring 2 with Mason on our most recent date at his house so I had decided that I would *never do that*. I read more about it in the grimoire later and it was seven shades of disturbing stuff. The grimoire had suggested astral projection but that would be my last resort. Not after last time. Sage had stolen Adria's file from the police station and it had told me that she had died of blood loss. However, I had seen the picture, something that left me sobbing all over again, and there had been barely any blood in the water.

She hadn't died there.

How had the police not seen any of this?

The suicide note…

It occurred to me that I hadn't read it recently. I hadn't read her note since I had that black-out period. Guilt twisted my stomach at the thought of how little I remembered since then.

Maybe if I re-read it, I could find something else.

The world felt more sinister than it ever had. More and more people were going missing. There were too many people for me to keep up with. Everyday there seemed to be a new poster or report about somebody who'd missing. Six people had gone missing in the last week. There was no way I could keep up. I didn't even know who or what was taking them.

All I could be was thankful that none of them were children.

"Hey, Kelsey, over here!" Mason waved from his usual lunch table. His friends looked over at me in surprise. Nobody was more surprised that Mason was calling me over at lunch in front of his friends than me. I wandered over shyly. He stood up and rested his arm over my shoulder. "Guys, this is my girlfriend, Kelsey." *Girlfriend?!* I was girlfriend-ly?! We hadn't had this conversation. I covered up a blushing smile. "Kelsey, these are my friends. I'm pretty sure you know all their names." I nodded shyly and gave an awkward little wave. "Do you want to sit with us?" Not at all but I didn't have anyone else to sit with and Mason knew it. I had no excuse to get away and it would be rude for me to refuse.

"O-ok," I sat down with the (on the end and next to Mason). We were sat with Mikey and Brett from before but Grant wasn't there. That was the first thing I noticed. There were a few other guys there too, but they rarely spoke; just laughed at something that Mason, Mikey or Brett said. It was clear who was in charge in the group.

I sat there staring at a stain on the floor, nibbling nervously on my stick of celery.

"What do you think, Kels?" Mason asked.

"I'm sorry, I spaced. What was the question?" I replied, somehow managing to keep my tone even.

"Which 'It' movie is better?" Brett repeated. The condescending look on his face and his tone clearly said that he didn't think I would be able to answer the question.

"The new one, in my opinion. Bill Skarsgard is super talented, and his ability to look at the audience and the other characters simultaneously is pretty awesome. It's much freakier than the old movie." I took a swig of my water.

The look on Brett's face told me that he was one of surprise. The look on Mikey's face told me that I had earned his respect. Mason just looked smug like he had proven some past point or wanted to show 'look, my girlfriend likes horror movies'. Thankfully, the bell rung for PE before anything could continue.

I'd never been more thankful for a twenty-minute lunch break.

PE sucks without Adria.

My arm was mostly back to normal so there was no way I could get out of it.

I got changed and as per usual I decided that I would go to badminton (the other two options were football outside and dance). It was February so I wasn't going outside willingly and dance... I wasn't good at that and it was full of assholes; usually Delilah and her cronies; although she occasionally joined badminton to play with the boys. And by play, I don't mean that she actually plays badminton; she doesn't. She plays with the people.

"She's really your girlfriend?" Mikey asked Mason. I stopped in my tracks, staying out of sight.

"Yeah, she is." Mason replied, his tone defensive. "Why?"

"Because you were so obsessed with Delilah and Kelsey's..." Mikey hesitated. "Nothing like her."

"Yeah," His friends agreed, nodding.

"It's not that we don't like Kelsey..." Mikey continued. "I actually really like her but are you sure that this isn't you trying to get over Delilah by dating her opposite? Like an overcorrection."

"How is Kelsey Delilah's opposite?" Mason demanded, crossing his arms tightly over his chest.

"Delilah's blonde. Kelsey is a brunette." Mikey started.

"Delilah's tall. Kelsey's short." Brett continued; his tone not nearly as gentle as Mikey's.

"Delilah's a bitch. Kelsey's real nice." Mikey resumed.

"Delilah's skinny." Brett finished. "And Kelsey is kind of fat."

I flinched. I don't want to hear the rest of this conversation. Making sure that I wasn't seen by Mason or his friends, I turned and scurried to the dance studio. Tripping over my own feet was better than having to hear the rest of that conversation. I wasn't *fat*. I was chubby... curvy... I wasn't... I'm not...

In that moment I wished that I wasn't wearing that stupidly tight P.E kit and I felt sick with the emotions bubbling back. Perhaps when you're insecure about your weight going into a room full of skinny dancers and mirrors isn't the best course of action.

The dance teacher always really liked me. Mrs Terry knew me well after year nine when I was in her dance class. None of my friends (or even Adria's friends) had been in that class with me and because it was all group work, Mrs Terry had to insert me into specific groups. Nobody was happy about this because I had never been an even moderately talented dancer; continuously falling flat on my face and failing to accomplish even the most basic of dance moves. Despite all this, I think the reason why Mrs Terry had grown to respect me was because I always tried, I always got back up and I always offered to help her tidy up (or whatever else she may need help with) at the end of class.

Being back in dance class was not something that I ever thought I'd choose to do. But there I stood. In the middle of the new dance studio, appearing like a chubby ghost among the slim, tanned girls. In a room full of chatting people, I stood completely alone.

God, school sucks.

Long story short, I left that class with many bruises and my self-esteem in tatters on the ground. "How are you, Miss?" I asked after my classmates had left. It had been a while since I`d spoken to her. Barely seen her since year nine.

"I`m fine Kelsey." She smiled kindly. "How are you?"

"I`m ok," I`m not. My self-esteem is fucked and I`m on my own again. "Do you need help with anything?"

She looked around the dance studio. "No, I think I`m o-actually, would you mind taking those hangers to the PE office?" She pointed across the room to a pile of colourful hangers with some netball bibs hung haphazardly on them.

I nodded, scurrying across the room to pick them up. "Have a nice day, Miss."

"You too, Kelsey and thank you."

There weren`t too many hangers and the PE office was just outside the girl`s changing rooms. The door had a huge padlock on the front of it but because Mr McGoo was an idiot (trust me, I`m being nice by *only* calling him that), it was always unlocked. The PE office always smelled of gone-off milk (something that I had been told was also Mr McGoo`s fault) and it was cluttered full of netball bib piles, rugby jumpers and old hockey sticks scattered around haphazardly across the floor and underneath the volumes of unfiled paperwork you`d find the occasional tennis ball; perfectly placed for you to trip over.

Just as I`d dodged the first avalanche of rugby jumpers, a scream rang out from the girl`s changing room. It was the for-show scream that girls made when someone turned off the lights. I couldn't help but roll my eyes.

I`d just had enough.

I reached across the mountain of jumpers, stretching to try, and put the hangers in the right place but I just couldn`t help. There was no way in Hell that I would put my bare leg in that pile to get a better reach. I was frightened as to what my bare foot would touch.

Suddenly a second scream ripped through the air like an alarm. I dropped the hangers and sprinted towards the girl`s changing room, leaping over piles of junk like an Olympics athlete. I flung the doors open to find the lights flickering, girls huddled in the corners, shaking and eyes as wide as saucers. In the centre of the room, a girl I didn`t recognize just lying there.

Hesitantly, I stepped forward, staring at her. I don`t know what I`m looking at. Once I got close enough, I realised who she was. It was Katherine Holt, but she looked... Deflated.

Katherine Holt had been severely overweight and now her skin lay on her like a pancake resting over a wooden spoon. Where had her fat gone? It was literally just skin and bone.

"Someone call the police." I ordered. The girls just looked at me blankly, confused. "*Now!*" They jumped into action, scrambling for their bags, and yanking out their phones.

What could have possibly done this to her?

Ice ran down my spine... What if it`s still in here with us?

My eyes darted around the room; what was different? Jennifer, and four others were calling the police while the others had returned to the corners. There was still chewing gum everywhere and bags scattered across the ground. The only thing out of place seemed to be Katherine and blood... Dripping from the ceiling. I looked up and... were those bloody handprints. They were large and animal-like. They reminded me of velociraptor footprints from Jurassic Park mixed with something ape-like.

"What`s going on in_ *Oh my God!*" Mrs Terry jumped. "Girls get out of here! Call the police!" She pulled her phone out of her pocket.

It was a stampede of teenage girls charging out of the room. As Delilah and her cronies passed, I felt my head smack against the wall. I bounced off it and fell onto the ground into something sticky and clear. What was that? I smelled my hand... was that *fat*?

I made my way out of the room and washed my hands in the PE toilets. In there, the heckles along my spine stood up. I wasn`t alone.

I made my way along the cubicles (most of which were hanging off the hinges).There was a scraping sound and I looked up. Four of the ceiling panels had been taken down. They were in a crumbled pile over and in a toilet. I could hear something moving above my head.

What do I do?

I`m unarmed and I can`t reach up there.

Climbing up there would be reckless and stupid.

Deciding that it was better for me to learn what I was up against and return prepared, I left the girls toilets and stood out in the PE corridor with the other girls.

The police arrived twenty minutes later. They eyed me as they arrived but didn`t say anything. None of us were sure what to do. How are you supposed to feel after seeing your classmate dead on the floor?

"Kelsey!" Mason called, jogging over as the boys were released from their own changing room. "Are you ok?"

I flinched at the sound of his voice and turned to him. "I`m fine."

He reached me and scratched the back of his neck while resting his other hand against my bicep in a reassuring motion. "I heard about Katherine. You were there?"

I shook my head. "No, I heard the screaming and got there afterwards. I saw the body, though." I grimaced at my own words. 'The body' sounded as if I had reduced her to an object.

She was a person, a human being. She was a shitty human being, but she was a human being. She didn't deserve that.

He gave me a hug. I couldn't help but tense. "I'm sorry, Kels." People were staring and the attention made me more uncomfortable than I could begin to describe. What were they thinking? Were they thinking what Mikey and Brett said? That I wasn't like the other girls he had dated… That I was fat… That I was… "What happened to Brett's face?"

I had seen it over Mason's shoulder; a bruised and bloody nosed Brett. Was his nose broken? Mason pulled away from me and scratched the back of his neck, not meeting my eyes. "Well… um… Brett and I had a little bit of a disagreement… We're good now and he realised that he was being an ass." A smile flickered over my face. I tried to cover it up, but he caught it and his eyes widened. "You heard the conversation, didn't you? That's why you weren't in badminton like you usually are."

Looking to the ground, I ran my fingers awkwardly through my hair. I nodded. "I didn't mean to eavesdrop but your friends are *very* loud."

"They didn't mean badly by it…" Mason insisted. I raised my gaze back up to him and arched an eyebrow. "Look; they're just worried that I was rushing into a relationship after Delilah."

"Are you?" I blurted before I could stop myself. Fuck. I covered my mouth with my hand. Mason looked like I'd slapped him. "Sorry, I shouldn't have said that. I didn't…"

"No." Mason stopped me; his face was tense, and his brows were furrowed. He was angry. "I get it. I would probably be pissed if I overheard that conversation between you and your friends about me. Look: I like you. I really like you. Can you just trust me?" He was talking so loudly, and people were staring. I was frozen. I didn't *want* people staring at me. Noticing my discomfort, his voice softened. "Maybe I am rushing this, but I am not going to miss out on trying this..." He gestured between himself and me. "Trying us; I think I'd regret it for the rest of my life. Please *trust* me."

"Oh please!" Delilah interrupted. "Everyone knows that you're only dating that freak to get back at me! You've had the prom queen... Nobody believes you're interested in Plain Jane."

Mason turned away from me and to Delilah, the anger returning to his voice. "Delilah, I know this may come as a shock but not everything in this world is about you."

Delilah flinched like he had just slapped her. Everyone was staring and some giggled. Was this really the right time? A girl just died, and everyone is focusing on... *whatever this is*.

My mind wandered to how Katherine could have died. My grimoire was my best hope to find out what was going on. "Kelsey Alexander," A police officer began. "Were you here when that girl was killed?"

"I..." Mason squeezed my hand reassuringly. "I was in the PE office when I heard screaming. I wasn't in the room at the time."

The police officer nodded. "What happened then?"

"I um... The first scream was a jokey scream... The kind of one that you get when someone turns the lights off, so I ignored it..." Can someone please stop the staring? Since when are interviews conducted in front of other witnesses? It causes problems with reliability of eyewitness testimonies. I don't like all this attention I was getting from him and *everyone else*. "I was trying to get to the other side of the PE office so I could put the hangers down in the right place. Then I heard the second scream and I knew that it was real."

The police officer arched his eyebrow. "You can tell the difference between the meaning of screams?"

I couldn't meet his eyes. "I... I was in a... um... a... I was at the camp... with the... um... cannibal camp director."

The police officer nodded. "I know. Are you going to answer my question?"

Mason squeezed my hand. "Didn't she just?"

The police officer. "I don't like your tone, young man. A girl is dead. I ask the questions and unless you want me to take her down to the station, I suggest you keep quiet." Mason glared but kept quiet. "Continue." He instructed me.

"I still have nightmares about the screaming." I told him. "I can tell the difference because I hear those screams every night."

The police officer's eyes flashed with guilt for a second as if its remembered why he had chosen to interrogate me in the first place. He wasn't looking at me like I was a suspect anymore. He swallowed. "What happened next?"

"Um... I ran into the changing room. The girls were huddled in the corners and Katherine was just lying there. I told them to call the police and then Mrs Terry came in."

"Why did you run in?" The policeman enquired.

Frowning, I answered. "People were screaming. Someone had to be hurt. If there was a chance that I could help them, I had to get there."

"Despite the fact it could be dangerous?"

"That hadn't occurred to me. I just wanted to help." I rubbed my bicep and looked at my feet. "Is whoever killed Katherine still here?"

The police officer looked uncomfortable. "I can't tell you that." So, yes. Whoever killed Katherine was still here. "Um... That's all for now. You should head home. We will contact you if we need further information."

Mason, still holding my hand, pulled me away from the group and towards the exit, his jaw clenched, and eyes focused on getting out of there. I almost had to jog to keep up with his pace. He only slowed down once we were outside of the gates and heading in the direction of my home. "Are you ok, Mason?"

He let out along sigh. "He shouldn't have spoken to you like that."

"I've had worse." Like from your friends or your ex. "Besides, he was only doing his job. He's stressed. A girl is dead and all he knows is that I seem to be everywhere a body is found. It's reasonable for him to be sceptical of me."

His hand was tense but he wasn't hurting me. Had we ever held hands for this long? "That's not your fault. You don't deserve to be spoken to like that."

"I'm ok," I promised, squeezing his hand reassuringly. "If you want, we can go by my place, drop our stuff off and get ice cream?" I suggested. His eyebrows raised: eyes slightly wider than usual. "What?"

"It's always been me to ask you out. You've just…" His lazy smile returned. "I just… Never mind. Let's go." We ambled down the road like it was a beautiful day in the summer holidays when there was no worries or school.

But it wasn't. It was February, my best friend was dead, and her ghost wanted me to do something and I had no idea what. Something had killed one of the schools most notorious bullies and had sucked *everything* out of her and I hadn't the first clue what. And what's more, I still all the witch stuff going on and you just know that Sage has something smart to say about it when I ask him about it later.

Also, the coat I was wearing was third or fourth hand, thinning and it was completely freezing.

"Crap," Mason stopped so suddenly that I nearly tripped. There were roadworks taking up the pathway I usually went down to go home. He turned to me. "Is there another way?"

My stomach twisted. "The only other way that doesn't take over an hour is through Maddison Gardens."

"Oh," Was all he said and her turned back to the pathway, his eyes scanning for a way through that didn't involve us falling into the hole, the stinging nettles on either side of the pathway or the stream. There wasn't one. "Um... Will we have to go by the um...?"

"Yeah,"

I could see the gears turning in his head. "I'll call my brother to give me a lift home afterwards." There was no way in Hell that *anybody* would walk by that place on their own.

"That's probably a good idea."

Ok, some context; at 43 Maddison Gardens, there's a house. There's nothing particularly unusual looking about the house but the *feeling* you get when you walk by that place was enough to make up for it. Something happened in that house. Nobody could really tell you what happened, but the Jackson Family used to live there. As I said, nobody is really sure what happened, but it resulted in the children and the husband found dead and the wife being taken to a mental institution. Every time a new family moved in, they either moved out again within the month or you'd hear horrible stories of how those people died.

Long story short; nobody goes near that house. The people who used to live on either side of that house had put them up for sale and moved. Eventually, the houses close by were torn down, leaving the Jackson's House lonely in the middle.

I don't know why it was never torn down like the others, but I suspect it was because builders were too frightened to do so.

Mason and I walked along the opposite side of the road to the Jackson's House. We tried to ignore it but both of us couldn't help our eyes making our way over to the empty window.

I felt sick with the 'butterflies' in my stomach feeling more like bats. I'm sure Mason felt the same. The house always did have that affect.

Though it felt like an eternity, we eventually got out of Maddison Gardens. With any luck, the roadworks would be done by the end of the day and I would never have to pass this place ever again.

With my luck there was more chance of lava rain.

It wasn`t such a long walk home after that. Actually, it was quicker than the way I normally went. That did not mean that I would take this route after the path was fixed. No way. I would not pass Maddison Gardens if I had a choice.

Mason and I eventually reached my home and we dropped off our bags. There was a quick word to my very smug looking older brother before we made our way to the park, and the ice-cream place. "Your tastes in ice-cream are weird," Mason stated as I ordered my usual of rum and raisin.

"Rum and raisin is my favourite." I told him, licking my ice-cream. I accidentally got some on my nose, the cold shocking me. He laughed at whatever look I had on my face as I wiped it off. "But you go to an ice-cream parlour with twenty different flavours and you pick strawberry. The most boring and artificial flavour there is. No account for taste, my friend." We were joking and he wasn`t taking it offensively. But I just want to point out that strawberry ice-cream doesn`t even taste like strawberries! It tastes fake and covered in plastic.

"I chose you, didn`t I?" He replied.

"As I said: no account for taste." He rolled his eyes and we made our way to our booth. "Although I am thankful for your decision and I *do not* mean the strawberry ice-cream."

He smirks. "I guess it is good that everyone has different tastes." He took a bite of his ice-cream. "That can be a good thing. If we both liked the same thing then we wouldn`t be together."

"Agreed."

"So, what do you think killed her?" Mason asked, suddenly changing the subject. He took a bite from his ice-cream.

"I don't know." I stated. "What do you think happened?"

He shrugged. "No idea. I'm surprised you don't have some kind of theory. You usually seem to have more of an idea of what's going on than the police or anybody else."

Yeah. That's because I'm a witch who has been seeing all kinds of creatures and monsters since a cannibalistic camp director tried to eat me alive in a mine shaft. Because he'd believe that. "Maybe I am the reincarnation of Sherlock Holmes?" I suggested, taking a lick of my ice-cream. Seriously, who could ever say that rum and raisin was bad? "After all, it's elementary, Watson, elementary!"

He snorted and rolled his eyes. "Well it seems the game is afoot, Holmes."

We enjoyed our ice-creams and Mason walked me home. He kissed my cheek at the door. My eyes widened in surprise and my stomach did a back flip. He looked at me with a smug smile and left in silence. Wasn't he going to call his brother?

Refocusing on what's important, I scampered inside and darted for the grimoire. It span open before I'd even got there, and to a page that said. *If in doubt; decapitate, use silver, or set it on fire. If none of these options work; just run.* "Sage, what does this mean?" Sage made his way over to me in his usual form.

"The book doesn't recognise the creature you are hunting, Adria." I shivered. Sage glared at the pages. "You'll have to write it in when you figure out what it is."

Me? Write in the book?

David had left for work before I'd gotten back and had made sure to write a note telling me that Sergeant had been walked so I texted him to tell him I was home.

The question was, did I make that walk in the dark past Maddison Gardens to get to the school and try to hunt down what killed Katherine, or did I not risk it and wait until school tomorrow? "Sage, could you find out if the pathway to my school is walk-able or will I have to go by Maddison Gardens?" He transformed into the sparrow (though I had expected him to turn back into a crow) and he disappeared through the window.

I flopped down on my bed and flipped through the grimoire; hoping to find something that could explain what had killed Katherine. As if the grimoire was sulking that I didn`t trust it, it didn`t reveal the contents of its pages and a handwritten word appeared in the centre of the page.

'*Rude.*'

If I wasn`t so concerned about what killed Katherine, I would have thought it was funny. Sage was taking a long time, so I decided to lay down for a bit… Just rest my eyes…

I blinked awake. It was morning. Guilt twisted my stomach, making me feel nauseous.

"You were so tired," Sage told me. "I didn`t want to wake you to see you go past *that place* in the dark." I was touched (and surprised) that Sage actually cared.

David wasn`t home yet, so I googled to see if I was going into school today. Surprise, surprise; I was. Even when someone is murdered in the school grounds, Hornby secondary doesn`t shut down.

There was no way that I would be able to hide my axe during a day at school… it was too big to fit comfortably enough in my bag without people asking questions. Besides, you just know that if I brought that in, Delilah would find out about it and I'd have to deal with Mrs Veneman. At the same time: how can I go into school where a girl was killed without a weapon? After I got changed, I put my deodorant in my bag (another thing that was banned) and grabbed a lighter out of the drawer (also banned). I made sure to put the lighter in my blazer pocket and not in my bag. No need to risk any freak accidents. Hopefully if this works, I'll have a DIY flame thrower. I was just about to leave when I turned and snatched a knife from the knife block and shoved it into my lunch box.

You can never be too careful.

Hornby secondary school may be the smallest in the area, but it really did seem to have more problems than the rest of them combined... actually, at least Hornby doesn't have a drug problem like St Paul's (I know; ironic).

Sage transformed into a woodlouse and crawled into my pocket as I left the caravan. According to Sage, I would have to walk via Maddison Gardens again. I found myself thankful that Sage was with me. If I had to go past that place, at least I wouldn't be alone.

Making sure to walk on the other side of the road from the house, my hand was in the pocket with Sage. "*Adria,*" called a voice... no, not a voice: *her voice*. Adria. I turned... it was coming from that house. "*Adria,*" I sped up. Was it that yellow-eyed thing from before? Or was it something from the house? Was it both?

"What is that?" I hissed to Sage.

"You know what it is." He replied. "You've seen it before. It is the latest infection in *that house*. Never go past that house alone."

He won't need to tell me twice. I tried to ignore the voice calling my witch name. How is it that it knows that name? It was as if it was written in neon above my head.

It wasn't a long walk to school from there and the first two lessons went as usual. Art was miserable and maths was monotonous.

"Kelsey, can I have a word?" Mrs Kent enquired just as everyone else was leaving. Tensely I nodded and she sat down on the table in front of me. "Is everything ok? You seem to be struggling. I know it's been a hard year for you but it is your GCSE year. If you need extra help, you can come here after school on a Friday. Maybe you can get Mason to come a long and do his homework while you're at it." She laughed gently.

I smiled back. "Thank you, Mrs Kent."

"You're welcome, Kelsey."

Part of me wished I could take her up on her offer but there was no way I'd have time. GCSEs didn't feel so important anymore. Not since Adria died. And after the skinwalker, GCSEs seemed completely irrelevant. Before all of this, I'd feel extremely stressed if I felt even fractionally behind but now... it just didn't seem to matter.

Before I went to have my break, I decided to see if I could get into the PE block. It had been fenced off at the beginning of the day with at least three teachers on guard at all times. It was easier to sneak past Mrs Wilks (the head of technology) than it should have been. She had to have seen me. I'm not exactly stealthy. She must have hated me more than I realised.

The hallway to the changing room was completely empty. There were no teachers or police officers in this corridor. There was police tape blocking the door like a fence but there were only four lines of it, so it was easy to get past. I barely had to duck to get under it. I opened the door, making sure to cover my hand with my too-long sleeve (although I wasn't really sure what difference it would make). The room showed no sign of anything out of the ordinary, except that just walking across the floor made my shoes stick to it. Every step I made sounded like ripping from whatever substance was on the ground.

I pulled out my phone and took several photos of the room, hoping that I would find something I had missed before. I tried to take photos of the sticky substance, but it was clear and didn't show up on camera. Sage crawled out of my pocket, onto the ground and turned back into his normal form. He sniffed the ground. "I don't know what that is. I've never smelled anything like it."

"What should we do?"

Sage jumped up onto my shoulder. "Don't touch it."

He didn't have to tell me twice. "How can we find out what it is?"

"There's probably no point." Sage told me. "There's nothing to compare it with in the grimoire even if you could." He turned into a woodlouse and crawled back into my pocket.

I had to be getting back before someone noticed I was gone. There was no way I'd be able to subtly kill any monster.

Honestly, subtly never was my forte.

I snuck out the way I came (thankfully without nothing chasing me) and I met Mason with his friends just as the bell went for the next class (typical). They were nice and chatted about something I wasn't paying attention to. We walked together, hand in hand, until a little boy (couldn't be more than twelve) grabbed my elbow and looked up at me. I let go of Mason's hand and turned to look at him.

I had never seen such intense black eyes in such a young child. "Be careful."

My eyebrows furrowing in surprise and the intensity of his words. Was he talking about the monster? Did he know something? "Of course. You too…"

He let go and made his way back to his friends, disappearing into the maze of people.

What a weird encounter.

"What was that about?" Mason laughed once I caught back up to him.

"Not a damn clue."

There were another two classes before lunch time because having lunch time at twelve was too sensible a decision for the senior leadership team. As a result, lunch took place at 1:30. Seriously, if both primary schools and colleges can succeed in having lunch at a reasonable time, why couldn't Hornby Secondary manage it?

Class three of the day was English (one of my favourites) and we had the supply teacher. That was good as it meant that the class wouldn't be as intense and the teacher would be so busy trying to manage the class that those of us who wanted to do the work, could do so independently. Does anyone else have that pet peeve of when someone is looking over your shoulder to see what you're doing? I've always hated it. When I was younger, it used to make me so nervous that I would freeze up so when I got older, I realised if you just crossed your arms and waited for them to leave, they would soon get the memo.

It wasn't often that I was rebellious at school, but somethings were harder for me to put up with.

Class four of the day was geography, where the teacher was an asshole and I was sat on a table of four with Delilah, her minion Jennifer and Rupert. Oh Joy.

Mrs Wesley was... ugh. Whenever she spoke there were at least three people in the class asleep. No joke: she had to move one boy to the front of the class to wake him up every time he fell to sleep (which was every five minutes). Though this was something that originally frustrated me, after Rupert was moved to sit next to me, I was thankful for how monotonous the class was because he would fall asleep. She also has a weird hero-worship thing going on for a few politicians and she would go on about politics for at least half an hour... all of which was completely biased and came from a place of financial privilege, and she guilted people who didn't feel the same way she did.

Another thing about that class; Rupert was someone who genuinely frightened me. He was known for harassing female students and as someone who had never had to deal with that (thank God for being Plain Jane), it came as a shock when he started making comments. I was never sure how to deal with it. He would whisper things in my ear about how I looked and what he wanted to do to me. If he was threatening violence, I could say something back but the shock of these kind of comments had me frozen in place like a statue. Out of all the shit I've been through, you wouldn't think that it would be a sixteen-year-old boy that frightened me the most. When he spoke to me it was as if I was chained to my spot. I'm frightened every time that I'll start crying or I'll throw up.

I've yet to do either, focusing my mind on being like the stone Mrs Wesley harped on about at the front of the classroom.

"Hey sweetheart," Rupert whispered, far too close for me to be comfortable. He always sat too close.

I shuffled my chair as far away from him as I possibly could, until the chair leg hit the side of the table. Oh Gods, I don't like this. I don't like this. I don't like this. Why did she have to sit me next to him? "Good morning, Rupert." I said stiffly. I tried so hard to see emotionless and I wished that I didn't sound as terrified as I was but I couldn't seem to help it.

"So formal," He laughed, sliding closer. If he got any closer then, he'd be on top of me. "Am I making you nervous, *Sweetheart*?"

You could just leave. The more rebellious voice in my head said. *Leave and don't come back.*

"No," I growled, sounding more like a feral dog than a teenage girl.

"Is that so?" He smiled malevolently, his hand landing on my thigh.

I stood up with jolt. "*Don`t touch me*!" I shrieked.

"Kelsey!" Mrs Wesley was startled. I wasn`t sure she`d even realised what I said: just heard the noise. Her hands were on her tiny hips. "You interrupted *my* class! Stand outside, now!"

I picked up my bag, on overwhelming sense of relief at getting away from him. "Gladly," I stormed out, making sure to slam the door behind me. The sound echoed through the corridor and moments later, the surprised faces of several teachers looked out. Miss Steward tried to stop me. "Kelsey, where are you going?" I dodged her hands, shrugging her off and kept walking.

Why did I bother with this bullshit? There were serious things going on in the world around me! Why was I dealing with school shit, classes, and grades when I should be finding out what happened to Adria and Katherine? Why should I care about this shit?!

Then it hit me. Mr Clarke would have to deal with phone calls from Mrs Veneman because of my behaviour. Guilt twisted my stomach like nausea, but it was too late now. He`d still get the phone call, even if I did go back.

I won`t go back.

Katherine`s killer was still out there, and I was no closer to finding out what happened to Adria. This was my chance to do some digging.

I am going back to the changing room. I`m going to find the monster that killed Katherine.

And then I`m going to kill it.

Eight

Mrs Veneman was looking for me.

I could hear the clip-clop of those horrific high heels stalking around the school like a glittered gremlin. She shrieked my name every now and then (like a banshee) but there was no way I'd answer he. She'd ruin my mission. She'd take me back. I couldn't allow that.

I was in the changing room and I knew that she wasn't allowed in here. Despite that, I knew if she decided that she wanted to come in here, that wouldn't stop her. I tried my best not to move when she got close for the fear of the sticky substance on the ground making that sticking sound.

"Hi, I have an 888 crisis." Mrs Veneman screeched down the phone. "Kelsey Alexander has run off. I want all exits shut and I want all guidance managers out looking for her."

I should go to inclusion. They won't be in there and I can find out what is behind that door.

Part of me realised that my door-obsession was ridiculous, but it was unlikely I'd ever get another chance. I may be able to find some files on Adria and Katherine. Though I have no idea what I could find, any information could be helpful. I waited for Mrs Veneman to reach the sports hall side of the PE corridor before I darted to the other side and out into the open. Every teacher would have been informed about me. I couldn't afford to be seen. I crawled by the drama classroom CA1, on the other side of the astro turf. Resisting the urge to peek in through the windows, I kept just underneath them, out of sight but high up enough to move quickly. Just as I got to the other side of CA1, I heard one of the guidance managers clip-clop past. I pressed myself against the wall and held my breath.

She didn't notice me.

Once she was far enough away, I breathed out a sigh of relief and darted towards the next building. The problem with the next building is there was not so much space to hide. It was longer too so I'd have to be faster. I crouched and rushed down the side of the building. My eyes darted all around.

Shit! Mrs Wilks was coming around the corner. I squeezed through a gap between two bushes, turned and pushed myself into the gap between the bush and the brick wall. She walked by and entered the building behind me. I sighed in relief. Thankfully, it seemed that she wasn't looking for me.

I scurried out of the bushes, scampered down the side of the building and slipped around the corner. If the window blinds are covered, I could sprint to the end and get straight into inclusion. I crouched below the first window, looked up; the blinds on the first window were down. Standing up as quickly as I could, I sprinted to the next window. Yes! The blinds are down so sprinted to the next window. The blinds were also down. The third window's blinds were up and there was a set of double glass doors. I waited for the teacher (Mrs Green) to move to the back of the class, out of sight before crawling past the door. The rest of the windows in the row were covered so I sprinted to the end. Nobody was around the corner, so I crept up to the door of inclusion and peaked in. It was completely empty.

Stepping inside, I checked for students in the rest of the room; nobody. That was strange seeing that Mrs Veneman liked to punish as many students as possible. It was usually overflowing with students being punished. So, why was there nobody in here?

I rushed to the other side of the room, towards that door. I snatched the handle and twisted. It was locked. Where would they keep the key?

I eyed the door. It looked fancy; important. I scurried to Mrs Veneman's desk. One by one, I made my way through the drawers. They were full of half-done paperwork. I flipped through the first draw but no key. The second drawer was full confiscated objects such as phones and dangly earrings. There were keys in there. Who takes keys from students? None of them would fit in the door so I discarded them. Some of them were student locker keys but some of them have to be front door keys. Why would she have those? It was in the third drawer that I found a box. It was covered in dark pink velvet and plastic gems with gold latches. I opened the box. Inside was a gold key. I quickly pulled it out, rushed to the door and unlocked it. It was a tiny room. Maybe two foot by two foot but there was a chair in the middle and dark red-brown stains on the carpet.

What the actual fuck?

I pulled out my phone and took a dozen photos.

What was this place? It looked like some sort of torture chamber.

"She should be in here." Stated a voice from outside. "That's what showed on the CCTV." Someone is murdered and CCTV does fuck all, but I goes on a wander, CCTV leads them right to me.

I darted to the desk and dropped the key into the box, shut the drawer and scampered behind the door. I swung it nearly shut behind me and for the last inch I slowly closed it.

Just as they entered the room, the door was finally shut. Thank God they went the long way around. If they went the other way I wouldn`t have heard them until it was too late.

I couldn`t hear *anything* from inside the room. It must be soundproof, because with Mrs Vallance`s shrieky voice I should have been able to hear her at this range. The floor was sticky, and the liquid gelled itself to my hands. I sniffed it. The metallic twang rang up my nose like a church bell shakes the eerie silence of a funeral. It was blood. It had to be blood.

I turned from the floor to the door. There was no handle on this side of the door. It was smooth.

This can`t be happening.

The first day I break the rules of school and I think I`m going to die here. I think I`m going to die here in this fucking torture room at my fucking school! If they don`t open this door then I`m going to starve to death. If they don`t open this door then whatever happened to whoever was in here before me could be what happens to me.

I have to call Mason or David. There is no signal in here; none. Internet was down and for some strange reason my mobile data wasn`t working. What had they done to this room?

David, I`m sorry but I think I`m may be leaving you.

Time has run away from me. It`s four o' clock.

What had they done in this room?

I can`t stay in here. It will be safer to get caught and make a break for it than staying in here. I pushed the chair into the corner, pressed my back against the wall and tried to push the door with my legs but my legs weren't long enough to get a proper push. The floor shifted. What's happening?

Shit!

The floor gave way and I fell down a winding staircase. My hands snatched at the stairs but I couldn't get a grip. There was no bannister to catch me as I tumbled off the side. I grabbed at the steps. It was like time froze for a second.

Then my fingers slipped.

I was falling again. I didn't grasp at the air; I curled up and tried to cover my head with my arms. I landed with a thump, pain shooting up my side as I landed on my hip. "Ah!" I yelped. Thankfully, my arms shielded my head.

Where… I was in a dark room with that spider symbol carved into the wall. Candles were littered around the room but they weren't lit. The only thing lighting up the room was my phone that somehow hadn't broken after the fall. There was a table (more like an altar) in the middle with a dark purple blanket over the it. There was massive leather-bound book open in the centre.

My God… What have I found?

Pain shot up my leg when I tried to stand. I whimpered and stumbled. Pulling myself up, using the corner of the table, I grimaced but managed to get to my feet. I had to find a way out and I intended to take as many photographs as possible. I looked at the book. It read; *how to make a monster that can crawl across walls.* I flipped through the pages: *how to create a creature with all the capabilities of a skinwalker.*

Someone made these monsters?

Was the page that was open what they made?

I scanned it. There was no indication of how to kill it and flipping through each page showed me more and more horrors; *how to become super strong by using the blood of men, how to make humans succumb to your will* and *how to make yourself look younger.*

This place... what was this doing under the school? And with that spider symbol that was on the skinwalker painted and carved everywhere: every inch of every wall and along every surface. There was no way this could be a coincidence.

I had only taken three or four photos before someone opened the door above. I scampered behind the staircase and huddled at the bottom. Hopefully, nobody looked this way because I was not as well-hidden as I'd like to be. I couldn't see much from where I was crouching. People trailed into the room, gathering around the table in front of me. I couldn't see all their faces from underneath their black robes but I recognised several (some from a sliver of their face and others from voices); Mr Small, Mrs Little (a guidance manager), Mrs Wesley, Rupert, Delilah and Mrs Veneman. "You failed, Rupert and now she's missing."

"She freaked!" He protested. "What was I supposed to do? Chase her?"

"I gave you every opportunity to get the job done," Mrs Wesley snarled. Jesus! I knew she hated me, but they *wanted* him to harass me. She moved me to be near him. What is it that they really wanted from me? "You fucked it up and she's clearly terrified of you. There's no way that she is going to go anywhere willingly with you now!"

"Who says she has to go anywhere willingly?" Chill shocked down my spine. What did they want with me? "What is it that is so special about this girl, anyway?" Rupert continued. "Nobody knew her name until she started dating Mason."

"We think that she was the one that killed our skinwalker. We think she's *Adria*." Mrs Veneman stated. "And she is getting too close. She is stronger than we could have imagined, and she will only get stronger. We are too close for her to get in our way now."

"If she's as powerful as you say then she'd make the *perfect* sacrifice." Delilah smirked, malevolence shining in those blue eyes of hers.

"Exactly," Mrs Veneman agreed. "So, Rupert, get her here by any means necessary. Her file is on my desk. Take it."

He stepped away from the others and headed upstairs.

"Do you really think it's wise to leave something like this to *that* boy?" Mr Small asked.

Mrs Veneman shook her head. "Of course not. That is why we summoned the creature. If Rupert fails; it will not." They spoke a little longer, but I struggled to focus. What did they want with me? I'm not anybody special! I'm just a teenage girl with a grimoire. And how did she know so much unless…

The symbols around the room, the creature that they summoned, and they want me… Why would they do all this? Why would they summon monsters to kill people? What's the purpose behind all this death? I don't understand how a group of people could be so hateful.

What were they going to sacrifice me to?

I was so caught up in my thoughts that it took me a whole to realise everything had gone silent.

I looked up. It roared in my face. Jumping back, I scrambled out from under the stairs as it grabbed for me, scraping its claws down my calves. I had to use the stairs to pull myself to my feet. "Get her!" Mrs Veneman ordered as the creature scuttled after me. I ducked arms and dodged fists and started sprinting up the stairs, my hip screaming at me as I did so. I have to get out of here! They're right behind me and more importantly the creature is too. The door's left open, and I slammed it shut behind me.

Rupert is at Mrs Veneman's desk.

He looks up, a malevolent grin twisting his features before charging forward. I sprint for the exit. He's right behind me. It's dark outside already. My fingers had just gotten hold of the handle when I heard that fancy door clatter to the ground. Both Rupert and I halt to turn. The creature had ripped the door off. It made some weird clicking sounds and scuttles forward like a giant spider. I slam the door shut behind me again but that didn't slow it down this time. I yank my bag off my shoulders and tried not to slow down as I rummaged through it for the can. The second my fingers grasp the cold aluminium, I dropped the bag, pulled the lighter out of my pocket. I span around and blasted the creature's face full of fire. It shrieks like a banshee, making everyone chasing me stop to stare. I picked up my bag and pulled out the knife as it crawled out from the flames.

Fuck.

Fire doesn't work.

I slashed at it and duck behind the side of the building to crouch behind the closest bush. It scuttled past, sniffing around. Hearing a yawn from my pocket, I was reminded that Sage's still with me. He crawled out of my pocket, still in the form of a woodlouse.

"What did I miss?" He shifted back to his original form.

"There are teachers in a cult controlling the creature that killed Katherine and they are trying to kill me!" I blurted, slightly louder than intended.

"Lovely," He stretched lazily. "Get the fire out."

"The fire isn't working!"

"Oh shit," He got off my lap and his body started to morph, contort, and stretch into that thing he used to fight the skinwalker. "Run, Adria." He didn't need to tell me twice. Sage towered over the bushes and slammed into the creature just as it found us.

I dove from out of the bush and sprint through the school. With the screeching of the creature and Sage in the background, I almost forgot that there were *people* chasing me too. I could hear their steps behind me.

David! I need to call David! I can't outrun them forever. I pulled my phone out of my pocket and tapped in the password mid-run. Thank Hades I changed it to a short one. I didn't slow down so it took longer than it normally would. His phone number was the first one to appear on the screen. I pressed the button, hoping that Sage would get to me soon because it's only a matter of time before he'll turn back. "Where the Hell are you?" My brother demanded.

"Help, David; they're after me!" I pleaded.

"Where are you, Kelsey?" His voice was panicked.

"The school. I'm running out towards home!"

"I'm on my way." I could hear him running. "Don't hang up."

Sage flew over and landed on me. "It's still coming."

I slam against the gate and yank it a few times. It's locked. There's no way I can climb that! There's a car next to it. I ran around the side, leapt onto the car, and tried to use the roof of the car to get over. I'm not tall enough. Just then I was yanked backwards. Rupert was gripping my ankle. "Did you really think you were going to get away from me, fat ass?"

No. I slammed my foot into his face as hard as I could. He fell backwards and I jolted up, jumping to the next, taller car, and climbing onto the fence, launching myself to the other side. I landed on my knees with a yelp. I turned to look back. They'd all stopped.

Still as statues, they stared at me, the creature disappearing behind those brick walls. It was like I had pressed pause. Why had they stopped?

There's no way I'm staying to ask! I sprint down the road, only stopping once David pulled up. "Kelsey, what's going on?" He rushed, getting out of the car.

I launched myself into his arms like I did when I was little, crying with relief. "Let's just go." I pleaded. "Let's go. Let's leave this town. We can go anywhere you want. *Please*. Let's just go." I didn't want this anymore. Why did I have to deal with this? Why was I the one that had to save everyone? I didn't want this. I just wanted to go home.

"What are you talking about, Kelsey?" My brother stroked the back of my head gently. "What happened?"

What could I say? That the school covered a... *cult*? That Mrs Veneman wanted to sacrifice me? That they had summoned a creature that I was pretty sure killed Katherine Holt and that they were going to use it to come after me? Not to mention that they knew where I lived and there was no way that David and I could fight of a group of people that large... especially when that creature was on their side. I was fucked.

So instead of saying anything, I just cried.

I sobbed like a child with a scraped knee.

He took me home.

Though David was concerned, still trying to comfort me, once we got home, I got directly into the shower. I couldn't wash the feeling of his hands off me. It was like he was still there with his hands on my ankle.

Why can't I stop crying?

I went to bed early. Collapsing face-first. Gods, what a day.

"Adria," Came …. Voice.

"Who are you?" I demanded, sitting up from my bed. He had the most beautiful face.

"I am your soulmate." He replied. "You are in great distress so as a witch, you can summon the soul of the one who can give you the most comfort. Someone you can be completely honest with."

"I would have thought that would have been David or Ben."

"You can't tell your brother anything about the supernatural world." The man replied. "And a vampire has no

soul. Ben may have had his returned, but it cannot withhold that level of strain."

"When will I know you?" I inquired. His voice was entirely comforting. Clearly my subconscious knew exactly what I needed.

"I don`t know." He told me. "If I didn`t contain my memories from my past lives then I`d be trying to kill you so."

"Why?" I asked.

"I hunt witches. I`ve only known evil witches in this life. I don`t know that good witches can exist." He told me. "After you wake up, you will not remember my face or my voice. You will remember my words. But natural reincarnation won`t have you recall your previous life."

"Is this the face that I`ll know?"

"It`s the face you`ve known a thousand lives before and I hope you`ll know my face again in this life." He told me. "I just hope you`ll be happy."

"I don`t know if I can be happy," I admitted. "People keep on dying and I don`t know what I`m doing. I`m a nerd. I`m not a hero."

"Those things aren`t opposites." He said. "You`ve saved people. You`ve stopped monsters. You`re a hero. What you choose to do is up to you."

"I have to go back, don`t I?" I sighed. "I have to stop it."

"You`ve done enough, Kels." He insisted. "You can run, or you can fight. It`s up to you."

I stand up. "I`m going to fight. No matter what it takes. I`m going to stop them."

He grinned. "That`s my girl." I turned but he caught my wrist. "Before you go, I know that vampire`s your friend but you cannot trust him."

I shook my head. "I won`t abandon him."

"I know," he stroked my cheek. "But just be safe. He is a vampire at the end of the day."

163

My eyes fluttered open and the world was oddly tranquil. My pillow was still wet from last night.

I cannot tell you how he looked or how his voice sounded. However, I could remember the emotions that came along with it and I could remember the words. I hope I can see him again.

I guess it's time for round two.

"How are you doing?" My brother asked, concerned, as I entered the living area.

"I'm ok," I told him. "I'm going to school."

"It's an inset day," He argued.

Was it? It doesn't matter. I have no intention on staying there for long. I was going to kill that creature and I was going to bring down Mrs Veneman and her cult with it. "That doesn't matter. I'm still going." He gave me a strange look but said nothing. I scurried to my room, got dressed, plaited my hair, and pulled out the Grimoire.

The pages span and it opened to summoning. *There a multitude of dimensions and creatures can be summoned to do your will from any one of them. There is no telling what can stop them if they are not of this world. Try beheading, fire, or silver.*

It was basically nothing that I didn't already know.

Despite what the man in my dreams said, I wanted Ben with me. He was the only person I could call for back-up and he was strong.

I shoved my axe into my spare bag. I don't own any silver so I can't take any. With any luck, that would kill it. I don't know what else I can do.

Sage was sat on top of Sergeant, watching as I moved around my room. "Can you get Ben to come with me to meet me at the school?" I asked. He transformed and disappeared, saying nothing. I made my way outside.

"What are you wearing?" My brother cocked his head. "You look like Lara Croft."

"Thanks," I grinned. Is there a higher compliment?

"Your welcome." He paused. "Are you sure you`re ok?" I nodded. "Ok. Be safe."

I wish I could promise you that.

I hurried towards the school. Thankfully, I didn`t have to go via Maddison Gardens and it wasn`t long before I found myself in front of the school gates. I started to tremble. What if they were in there waiting for me? What if this doesn`t work?

Snap out of it! You have a monster to kill and people to save.

"Little One," I flinched. Ben stood behind me, under the shade of a tree despite it being an overcast day. "You asked for me."

"I am about to go fight a creature I do not know how to kill." I told him bluntly. "It was summoned by my guidance manager who wants to sacrifice me."

"You took the name." He stated: his voice completely even, ignoring what I`d just said. "It shines from you like moonbeams."

"What do you mean?"

"Your body screams it out; *Adria*." He flashed forwards and held onto my shoulders. "Your name defines your fate."

What does that mean? "I... uh... Do you have my back?"

Instead of answering, he flashed over to the gates ripped off the chains that held it shut.

Wow, that`s handy. We entered the ground and that wave of melancholy I always felt when I entered this Hell hole seemed stronger now. "The smell of oppression," He sighed. "This place should have been bathed in fire the day the rot set in."

Easy for you to say.

We wandered through the school (with Ben keeping to the shadows), waiting for that creature to ping out and attack me. It didn't. "A threat to it, Ben shall be," Sage materialised by my shoulder. "It shall not appear if him, it can see,"

Why is he rhyming again?

So, I had to separate myself from Ben. Nothing could terrify me more. False. If I saw Rupert skulking around, then I wasn't sure if I could... "Ben, can you stay in the canteen? I want to see if it will come after me if you are not there."

He nodded and blurred into the canteen. The creature did not materialise. I marched towards the changing room. This was the first place it appeared. Perhaps it would appear here again. I pulled the axe out of my bag (knowing full well that I really should have done that earlier) and approached the changing room door. It was locked. The key would be in the PE office. The PE office was around the back. I scampered around the back and up to the door. There was a padlock on it. I twisted the numbers, my ear pressed against the metal block. Click. The first number was three. I twisted again. Click. The second number was nine. Click. Click. The numbers were three-nine-four-six. I yanked it off and shoved into the room. Now, where would a conceited asshole such as Mr McGoo keep the key to the girls changing room? Come to think of it; why wasn't it locked yesterday?

Then it hit me. They kept it unlocked because they knew I'd hide there. They thought that I would have stayed hidden in there so they could catch me. They didn't expect me to follow the screams.

So why was it locked now?

I span around, ducking the creature's claws. "BEN!" I shrieked, swinging the axe at the creature as hard as I could. It landed in its ribcage but it didn't even flinch. I yanked it out and I rolled out underneath it. I swung the axe at its head. It dodged with ease. I had to get to the shadows, where Ben could reach me. I swung it at its neck, slicing its head clean off. The creature's head bounced and then rolled across the ground. I breathed a sigh of relief... and then it blinked. "Fuck!" I yelped, falling back as its head melted and reformed with its body.

Fuck that.

I sprinted away as fast as I could and just as I got to the shadows, Ben materialised. "Ben, run! Beheading doesn't work!" He scooped me up like I was a baby and moved through the school faster than I could see. One second, we were in the school and the next we were in front of the gates. He dropped me roughly and I landed on my backside, my head spinning. "Thanks," I grunted, getting back up to my feet.

"The silver solution would come next." Ben suggested.

"I don't have any silver."

Just then, a couple walked by. Ben flashed towards them, making us all jump. He looked at her chest. "You smell of silver." He snapped her neck in an instant. The man screamed.

"Oh, my gods!" I shrieked, rushing across the road to Ben. "What have you done?"

He ripped the silver necklace off her corpse. His hand bubbled, fizzed and smoked before he dropped the necklace into my hand. "You have silver now."

"You didn't have to kill her!" I exclaimed, my entire body shaking. Her blank eyes were looking up at me.

"I'm a vampire, Little One." He pointed out. "Don't mistake my fondness for you as humanity." The man, that was still frozen in place, was snatched up by Ben and before I could do anything, he was gone in a flash.

I stared down at the silver necklace in my hand, a shining symbol of the crime I allowed to take place. It felt that my soul was tearing itself in two. On the one hand, Ben killed someone for it but on the other, this may be my only chance to get silver and kill that creature before it killed anyone else. I pocketed the necklace, feeling sick with shame and made my way home. Hopefully, there would be something in the grimoire that could tell me how to weaponize silver.

Sage and I made our way back. I could see yellow eyes watching us from the treeline but once again it didn't get any closer. It only seemed to come out when I was completely alone. Why?

Perhaps this thing lived for my fear. It knew that I would be more frightened if I was alone.

Sergeant greeted me ecstatically when I got home. David was snoring on the couch. I tip-toed past my brother, motioned for Sergeant to follow me and crawled into my room. I pulled out the grimoire and it flipped open instantly. I looked down at the metal in my hand, my stomach twisting with guilt. The page flipped to one titled *Silver Essence*. It melted the silver down to the essence of it that was toxic to those creatures.

To weaponize silver; all I needed was a wooden bowl, salt, water, three black candles and a container for it afterwards. Black candles was something I actually had. Adria had bought a set for Halloween as decorations for her house last year. Because it was my birthday, she'd let me keep three.

We didn't have a wooden bowl, but I could use one of my drawers. I pulled one out and emptied the contents on my bed. I poured a salt ring around the drawer and put three black candles equidistant apart. Placing the necklace in the middle of the drawer, I poured water over it and placed an empty jam jar next to it. I turned for the matches only to find the candles lit.

Freaky.

Suddenly my skin felt like it was covered in ice and I began to chant. This magic, it was stronger than anything I'd tried before. It felt like I was being pulled into the drawer with the stronger I pulled back, the more it yanked me forwards. I wanted to move but my body demanded that I did not. I couldn't stop chanting, no matter how much I wanted to stop. Blood started to drip down from my nose, past my mouth and dripped from my chin. Then, everything froze like the ice had won. I fell onto my side like all the energy I had was sucked from my body. I pushed myself up on shaking limbs. It worked. The necklace was liquid in the drawer. It looked like silver paint, but it had a strong metallic smell. I raised my hand and the liquid followed, moving with my fingers, and fell it poured itself into the jar, the lid twisting by itself. I pushed it under my bed, along with the grimoire before the cold and the spinning became too much and I passed out on the floor.

"Kelsey!" I woke up to my brother`s concerned voice. "Kelsey, what happened?"

I blinked awake. "Sorry, I tripped. I think I hit my head." I rubbed it.

"You`re bleeding." He told me and rushed to grab some tissues. "You must have hit your nose. It`s bleeding like crazy." He looked at the floor. "What were you doing in here?"

"I read about these DIY candles. You burn the wax and cover it is salt. As it burns, it is supposed to smell of the ocean." I have no idea whether or not that`s true or not but it was the only explanation I could come up with. "When I tripped, I made a mess."

He sighed and passed me the tissue. "Try to get some sleep, Kels, I think you need it. If this happens again, I will take you to the hospital." He pulled me to my feet and helped me into bed.

I nodded. "Thanks, David. I`m sorry I frightened you." My head hit the mattress before I could hear his response.

The next time I blinked awake, it was morning. I rolled out of bed and cleaned up the mess. I walked past the mirror and froze.

I looked different. My acne had completely cleared up, no spots marring my face and I was certain that my hair was at least a shade darker.

Was I imagining it?

I pulled out the grimoire, nearly knocking the jar over in the process, and it flipped open. *Once you have taken your witch name, your body will go through changes to match your soul and your name. It`s like a second puberty.* Seriously? Not this shit again. *The more magic you use, the quicker the changes will happen. It can be as subtle as the change of hair colour, eye colour or as drastic as changes in bone structure, height, or build.*

On the bright side; at least my acne had finally cleared up.

I pulled out the jar and the pages flipped to the second part of the silver essence. Bonding the silver essence to a weapon was an easier spell. You just poured the silver essence onto the blade and named the weapon aloud.

I unscrewed the lid and poured just enough silver essence on the blade for it to cover most of it but not to spill onto the floor. Now, for the name... What do you call an axe? "*Fluffy,*". The liquid sank into the axe like it was a sponge instead of metal, the colour changing to almost white. There was still plenty of silver essence in the jar, so I tucked it back under my bed. "Well Fluffy," I looked down at it. "It seems that we`re going to school." I squeezed it into my bag.

"Where have you been?" Mason demanded the second I got there. "I called you and called you. Why didn`t you answer?"

I hadn't realised. "I'm sorry. I must have missed them." I pulled out my phone and showed him my empty caller history. "There must be something wrong with it."

The tension left his body and he sighed. He pulled me to his chest in a tight hug. "I was worried."

"I'm sorry," I told him. "I didn't mean to frighten you," He released me and nodded. We walked to tutor together.

"What's that in your bag?" He asked.

Damn. Covering up the axe clearly hadn't worked well. I wish there was a spell that allowed me to change the size of the axe at will. There probably was a spell and I should probably look for it when I get home, but I was still a bit wobbly from all the magic I used yesterday. I could quite easily go back to bed right now and fall asleep instantly. There was still a creature out there and Mrs Veneman and her cult had to be stopped.

Just as we reached our tutor room door, a scream ripped through the peace.

I darted in the direction of the scream. Please don't let it be too late. People were huddled around in a large crowd. I barged through to find another body outside my old maths classroom. I hadn't known this little girl but her body was in the same state as Katherine's had been.

I didn't know what I had been expecting.

A naïve part of me believed that the creature would leave other people alone while it was fixed on me. It clearly hadn't.

Idiot.

The maths teacher hurried us all into the library and the police arrived quickly afterwards. Even after a traumatic event, the librarian held no sympathy for any of us. Her glares were more than distracting and if anyone got too loud (such as a young girl in year eight who kept on saying "how could this happen?"), she'd shh our group loudly (hypocritical if you ask me). She didn't, however, dare to behave this way with the police officers. She'd glare but she'd say nothing about the noise of their interviews.

"Kelsey Alexander," Came a familiar voice. It was the police officer who'd spoken to me when Katherine had been killed.

And I have an axe in my bag.

I just can't catch a break.

"Hello again, Officer," I smiled politely. "I'm sorry to see you again under these circumstances."

He nodded, as if pleased by my greeting. He motioned for me to follow. Mason squeezed my hand in goodbye (I hadn't even realised he'd been holding my hand) and I waved my hand behind me. The officer and I made our way to the table in the corner of the library. It used to be my favourite spot but with the talking and the sobbing, it felt like a different room. "Can you tell me what happened?"

I shook my head. "I just heard a scream and we ran over and saw the body."

"Who were you with?"

"Mason," I replied. I wasn't nervous like I had been the first time. This police officer wasn't eyeing me like I was a suspect, but his co-workers definitely were.

"Your boyfriend? The kid from last time?" I nodded in response. The police officer nodded back. "Where were you?"

"We had just walked up to my tutor. We were outside the door… It was the outside door. The room is labelled S2. We heard the scream, so we turned and ran to the…" I thought about it. I was never good with my left and rights. "Left and round the bushes, through the patio and to the crowd. I pushed through because I knew someone was hurt and nobody seemed to be doing anything. That's when I saw the body."

"What did you do then?" The police officer continued.

"Nothing. The police had already been called and it was only a few minutes before the teachers sent us all here. There was no time for anything else. I`m not sure what I`d do if I`d been there longer."

The look he gave me said 'fair enough'. "Did you know the victim?"

I shook my head. "No. I`m not sure if I`ve even seen her. Obviously, she goes here but I don`t recognise her. Is it the same person who killed Katherine?"

"I can`t divulge that information."

"Sorry,"

"Why is it that you`ve been at all these crime scenes?" His voice was a mixture of half curiosity and half pitying. He was clearly trying to maintain a tone of authority, but his curiosity was getting the better of him.

"I don`t know,"

"It`s probably best you don`t." He sighed. "Be careful,"

I nodded, knowing full well that it was a promise that I couldn`t keep. Just like with David, I couldn`t say the words. He let me go and once again, the school had been shut down. Mason`s interview had finished before mine. I guess they had less questions for him than they did for me. He was waiting for me.

"Are you ok?" Mason asked.

I nodded. "Are you?"

"Yeah," He replied. "Want some ice cream?"

I laughed. "Yes. At this point, it has almost become our ritual after a murder." It wasn`t funny but he laughed back.

"You may have a point." He agreed. "Homicide cream,"

"That sounds like something you`d get from the chemist." We were walking back towards my home to drop our stuff off before heading to my cousin`s ice-cream shop.

It seems that after hours is when my hunt begins.

Nine

After the events of earlier today, I didn`t want to bring Ben with me.

Was it reckless? *Yes.* Would I regret it later? *Probably.* But it was too late to turn back now. I was alone as I had asked Sage to follow David. Just in case the cult members decided to come to my home looking for me. I couldn`t take the risk of David being undefended.

I had spent an hour making some simple defensive charms after I got back home. I had learned that sugar was good to keep energy up while doing spells. Thankfully, simple enchantments like the ones I`d chosen didn`t take as much energy as making silver essence. Or seemingly any at all. After I`d had a coffee I was good as new.

Thank the gods.

It was freezing outside, and the darkness was thick. I didn`t dare to turn on my torch. Nobody needed to know I was here.

I held up my first enchanted item: a key. If it works, then it should unlock any door. Please work.

I pushed the key into the lock and twisted. It clicked and opened. Breathing a sigh of relief, I opened the gates and entered silently. I had barely made it through reception before

I tripped over something. My hands landed in more of that sticky goo and I pushed up to see what I'd landed on. I yelped and scrambled away. "Mrs Wiley?" She was just the same as how Katherine and the other girl had been. "Shit," I hissed. Getting back to my feet, I looked around. The only thing around was the windows to Mr Small's office.

Mr Small's office... he's a part of the cult, this was too good an opportunity to pass up. I stuck my key in the door (not really sure how long the enchantment would hold up) and it clicked open. Sighing in relief, I entered the room. Just as I stepped in, I heard the door slam. I jumped and looked behind me.

Rupert had been waiting for me. "We knew you'd be coming."

I scrambled backwards, angling the desk so that it was between him and me. My legs were shaking. What was it about this fucker that frightened me so much?

"What is it about you that bothers them so much?" He's stalking around me like a predator. "First they thought it was that Adria girl that would bring us down but now... they say that Adria is you... Why don't you explain that to me?" He lunges forward, reaching for me. I bounce back, shoving Mr Small's computer at him. It smacked him square in the chest, knocking him back. Taking this opportunity, I yank out the axe (that I really need to start taking out immediately) and rush towards the door. He snatches my ankle as I pass and pulled me to the ground, crawling towards me. I kick out blindly until he let go, scrambling back to my feet. As he stood up, he laughed. "You aren't going to swing that at me. You don't have the stomach to kill a human being."

"You say that like it's a bad thing." I lower my axe and he charges for me.

Just as I planned.

I pulled back my sleeve, revealing a blue beaded bracelet and I shoved my hand at his face. Electricity shocked through him, launching him backwards and into the desk. A burned smell filled the air. I smirked. Rupert was down for the count.

That charm worked far better than I ever could have imagined.

I opened the door and left Mr Small's office. I don't want to chance staying around Rupert for anything. I didn't bother locking it behind me. You could unlock it without a key from the inside.

Time to find the creature.

I pulled out my torch and shone the light around.

Nothing jumped out at me. The part of me that was focused purely on self-preservation wanted me to stay silent, to back away and leave. I'd be lying if I said that I actually wanted to find this creature, that I wanted to fight this creature. I wasn't shaking anymore. My body was too tense to shake. This was the third time that I would be coming up against this thing. An irrational part of me believed that it couldn't be killed; that I should just run.

The other, more logical part of me knew that any living thing could die and if I didn't stop this thing, it would just kill another person. If silver didn't stop it then I would just have to find something else that would.

I have to stop it, whatever it takes.

The hair on the back of my neck suddenly stood on end and I span around. "*Shit!*" I yelped, falling backwards as the creature scuttling across the ceiling dropped down at me. I raise my axe, but it knocks it from my hands. Just as I made a grab for my axe, it lodged its teeth into my forearm. A scream tears from my throat like an alarm. I tug but it won't let go. I feel it sucking. Oh gods... It's going to... I shove the hand with the bracelet at its head and the electricity launches it off. My right arm was now useless. I think the bone's broken.

I'm right-handed.

I snatched up my axe with my left hand and jump to my feet. It's back in front of me in an instant and I swung the axe as hard as I could at the creature's head. Furious, it swipes at my stomach, batting me through the hall. I land not too far from Rupert's feet. He made a groaning sound. He's waking up. I scramble to my feet, wincing and wobbling at the pain in my side and my arm.

Do I run straight for the monster or do I knock Rupert out again?

The creature took that decision from me as it charges through the hole in the wall. I electrocute Rupert on my way past, using the desk as a shield. It doesn't work. The creature leaps over the desk just as I swing the axe at its head. It lodged straight into its skull, stopping the creature in its tracks. Is it dead? I stood there, frozen. It moved, and I flinched just as the body dissolves into a pile of grey sand. "Self-cleaning. Nice."

Rupert groaned, rolling. I pushed around the table and hurried out of there. Nobody ever needed to know that I was here. The CCTV camera was linked to Mr Small's computer that was smashed on the floor. There was no evidence.

I rushed down the road and away from the school, only slowing when I was far enough away not to worry about Rupert chasing me. Thankfully, David was still at work so I knew that there would be no awkward explanations as to where I'd been. The walk home was as lonely as ever and I couldn't help but think what every snap, crack or rustle could be.

Walking anywhere alone now was terrifying.

Just as I had reached halfway, I heard it. "Kelsey!" It was Rupert's voice. No! I spun around; axe raised.

Empty air.

The yellow-eyed creature had found me again. I sped up. There's a rowan tree not far from here. A stick from that tree should ward it off... I think.

"Kelsey!"

I clutched the handle of the axe in my bag. Just in case.

"Kelsey!"

It was closer so I span around. Yellow eyes and black smoke reached for me. I yanked out my axe and swung it across the smoke. The smoke dissipated.

"Holy shit," I breathed. I didn't expect it to disappear like that. Was it a trick? Had I killed it? I wasn't taking any chances. That had been too easy.

I hurried back home, feeling eyes on the back of my neck but whatever it was didn't get any closer. I kept looking back but I saw nothing.

Sergeant was ecstatic to see me, her tail wagging so hard that her body was wiggling too. I ruffled her fur and entered my home. Sage was still out with David, so it was just us. I pulled out my grimoire and it flipped to the page about healing. It seemed to be a relatively simple spell to make sure there was no infections and that the wound healed; and it was but it still hurt when I touched my arm. I held my arms out to see that my right forearm was bent at a weird angle.

It must have broken when the creature bit me.

The grimoire's pages flipped again to healing broken bones. The spell was more complicated and required a bowl of water. I went to the bathroom (that didn't have a bath) and filled the sink with cold water. Laying my forearm in the water, I began to chant. Once I opened my eyes... nothing had happened. My forearm looked and felt exactly the same. I tried it again... also nothing. My head span and I landed on the toilet seat. Damn. I must have used too much magic.

Stumbling back to my room, I kicked the grimoire under my bed and collapsed on top of my mattress, falling asleep instantly.

The next morning, I made a point to fall out of bed with a loud thump and told my brother that I'd landed on my arm. He took me to the hospital, and we found that my forearm had been broken in two places. They straightened it; something that hurt more than the time I'd actually gotten the injury. We got home at four 'o clock and my brother immediately passed out on the sofa.

Sorry, David.

When I looked into the mirror, I found that my hair had grown darker again.

I had to wonder; what would I look like when the magic had finished changing my appearance? Would I still look like me or would I not recognise myself anymore?

When school started again (a week after the death of Mrs Wiley), it was hard to believe all of what happened. Rupert was back in school. Though I wasn't there to find out what really happened. Apparently, he was found in Mr Small's office and the police arrested him. The police had suspected him to have been the person responsible for the murder of Mrs Wiley because he was the only one there at the time and he had enough marks to show that someone had fought back.

They couldn't keep him, however, because they didn't have a murder weapon or a motive. Innocent until proven guilty.

"I have an announcement," Mr Clarke told us in tutor that morning, cutting through the chatter and leaving silence. "Due to the amount of days that we've had off due to the murders, the Senior Leadership Team," They were the members of staff that ran the school: the headmaster, the deputy, the assistant headmaster and unofficially; Mrs Veneman. "Have decided that you will be coming into school over half-term for normal classes."

Groans of protest echoed through the school like the world's most miserable choir. While the other students were furious that we lost our break, I was busy wondering what Mrs Veneman was planning. Surely if she has that chamber under the school, wouldn't she want us out of the way so she could spend more time doing whatever they do down there undisturbed. This couldn't have been by accident; not now. What did she want?

I could feel eyes on me every second of the day like needles dancing on my skin. The people watching me were Veneman's cronies. I recognised some of them from the last time and most of them were not very skilled in the art of subtlety. With my arm broken, I couldn't help but feel vulnerable.

Though jewellery wasn't allowed (beside single stud earrings; a rule that Delilah got away with ignoring every single day), I made sure to keep the taser bracelet, tucked under my sleeve. I had updated it with a permanency charm so it would always have the tasing ability. After I had tased the creature while it was biting me, I had wondered why I hadn't been electrocuted. Turns out, because my charm was a defensive charm, it meant that the wielder can't be electrocuted by it. Neat.

Some days I wondered why I should go back to school. I wondered if going back would get me killed but I knew I had to pass my GCSEs. It wasn't like I could transfer to another school in Year Eleven. If I didn't pass my GCSEs then I couldn't go to... yes, I could. I could go to college. I only had to be able to pass maths and English. It would make my life significantly harder, yes but at least I had a back-up plan.

I asked Mrs Kent for me to move to the back of my maths classroom. It was an odd request (most seating requests were to be near another student instead of away from other students), but I found that if I rubbed my broken arm slightly and nibbled the corner of my lip, I looked nervous enough that she complied. I hated to manipulate such a kind woman but friends of Delilah and Rupert were in this class and I didn't like the idea of them sitting behind me where I couldn't see what they were doing; especially while my arm was broken. Not when I knew that the cult wanted to sacrifice me.

Unfortunately, I knew that this wouldn't work with all my classes. I knew for certain that Mrs Wesley was part of the cult and she had me sat right next to Rupert. There were several other people in that cult whose identity was unknown to me. They could be teachers. They could be students. They could be strangers. Either way, they wouldn't be behind me in maths.

Thank the gods for Mrs Kent.

"Is everything alright, Kelsey?" Mrs Kent asked me once the others had left. "You seem... distant." Her concern probably hadn't been helped by my strange request.

I nodded. "I'll be ok,"

She looked at me sceptically but allowed me to leave.

I walked to my usual seats with Mason and the others at lunch. We chatted every day now. It was almost as if they never made comments about my weight. It was almost as if we were friends. "I have to go." Mason said, suddenly standing up. "I'll be back later." He abruptly left through the side door of the canteen and headed towards the PE building.

I frowned. "That was weird." I stated. "That *was* weird, right?"

The boys nodded. "Yeah," Mikey agreed. Their eyes followed Mason as he moved across the school and entered the PE building. "That was weird. What`s with him?"

Unable to think of a reason why he would be going into PE right now, I just frowned. He had to have a reason.

The bell rang for the next class and I moved on. The day was calm. No monsters, no nothing. Glares from some students and teachers but that was no new thing. It felt easy. Too easy.

On the way home, I found myself walking past Maddison Gardens. It was as if something was pulling me there, feeling dazed. *You`re a masochist.* One part of my mind hissed. *You miss the pain. You miss the action. You miss feeling like a hero.* Did I? I wasn`t sure anymore.

It felt like something was pulling me that way. Like there was a lasso around my middle and someone was pulling me from the other end.

Maddison Gardens was as ominous as ever. It was still abandoned. One thing was different, though. One light was on in the downstairs window. It was one of those yellow-orange lights like a fire. I peered through the window, but the room seemed to be empty. Did an estate agent leave the lights on? Suddenly someone was up against the window, making me stumble back. It was a woman, slamming her fists against the window, her face grey with terror. Her mouth was wide, screaming but I couldn`t hear anything. 43 Maddison Gardens was the last house that should have had sound-proof windows. She was abruptly yanked away from the window by an unseen force and the light was extinguished.

I darted for the door, running purely on autopilot. I didn`t speak. I didn`t think. I just reacted. The door was open, so I scrambled through. Not stopping to question why the door was open now, I charged for the door of the room the woman was in. Just as I got it open, the front door slammed shut.

"Fuck!"

You idiot.

The yellow floral wallpaper next to me ripped and red writing began to appear underneath.

Got you.
Got you.
Got you.
Got you.

Was the woman even real or had this always been a trap? I rushed to the front door and yanked on the handle. It was locked and it wasn't giving anything. "Fuck!" I snarled again. "Fuck! Fuck! Fuck!"

"You couldn't resist the siren's song!" Came a voice from behind me. I flinched and span around, but nothing was there. Was this the yellow-eyed creature?

I abandoned the door and hurried over to the other door again. It was unlocked this time.

Maybe the woman had been real. Maybe she wasn't. Nobody was in the room. There was no sign that anybody had been there for a long time.

"Why did you let it kill me?" Came a soft voice. I span around and there the woman stood.

She was so pale that she looked almost see-through. Who was she? *What* was she?

"Who are you?" I asked gently.

"You let me move in here! You *knew* it would get me!" She shouted. Then she stopped. She was almost static. "It is coming for you now. Try to get out if you can. The living cross over frequently here."

She flickered and disappeared.

"Well that wasn't at all cryptic."

What was *it*? Besides an awesome movie with Bill Skarsgard in it? I tensed. Now *really* wasn't the time to be thinking about *anything* to do with Stephen King. My reality was freaky enough. I rushed to the other side of the room. It must have once been someone's office so I snatched the computer monitor and slammed it into the window. Again, and again and again.

"That's not very nice." Came a deeper voice. Startled, I dropped the monitor and turned to face where the voice was coming from. The man in the doorway was pale. "You're breaking my house."

I knew who this man was.

Mr Jackson.

The man who died here twenty years ago.

And the axe in his hand looked *very* real.

Ten

He slammed the axe down at me and I stumbled back, falling onto the desk. I tried to get off and I ended up falling off the desk and crashing down onto the floor behind it.

"You. Are. In. My. House!" He shrieked, walking through the table to swing the axe at me on the floor. It chopped through the floor between my legs. There was no space for me to move so I pushed the chair at Mr Jackson and shuffled out from behind the desk. I jumped to my feet.

I have to get to the door so I snatch the monitor and threw it as hard as I could at him. It went straight through him.

I don`t know what else I was expecting.

I scramble for the door but found myself launching across the room, slamming into the wall behind me and smacking my head *hard*. He didn`t even touched me and I`ve been flung across the room. "You can`t go until I say you can go!"

"Bossy, aren`t we?" I smile, my mouth tasting coppery. *Yes, Kelsey, sass the homicidal ghost. That seems clever.*

His face twists in rage and his axe shot at me. I duck but it still clips my ear.

The man may not be corporeal, but that axe certainly is. I leap to my feet and with my working arm, I start yanking at the axe in the wall. I pull on the axe, again and again, and again. He's glitching closer. I eventually get the axe free and sprint for the window. I swing the axe and the glass shatters.

Not skipping a beat, I dove out the window. Dropping the axe immediately, I fled down the road. People stared but said nothing.

They didn't have to.

We all knew that I was running from 43 Maddison Gardens.

Why did the axe work when the monitor didn't? I guess it doesn't really matter.

What possessed me to go anywhere near that Hell hole? Maybe I was really going insane. Hell, I'd fought monsters... perhaps I'd gone insane a long time ago. I scurried home and nothing calls for me. Thank God.

David opened the door for me before I'd even reached for my key. I walked Sergeant, made dinner (pizza) and David left for work. Once again, I sat on the sofa for a re-run of Good News. It felt unnervingly normal until I saw something out the corner of my eye.

Abruptly, I stood up, crept up to the window and peered out. Grey eyes stared back at me. I flinched back, horror twisting my heart.

Rupert was outside my home, and I was alone.

That malevolent grin twisted his handsome features, and he waved jovially. In his hand was my pale blue bracelet.

Shit. I grabbed my wrist as if to check that my eyes weren't betraying me. How did he...? He must have done it in the science corridor. So many people bump into me through there that I wouldn't have noticed him take it.

He slowly made his way around the caravan, towards the front door. That ominous grin never faded from his face. The door was locked. He cannot get in. "Don't think that a locked door can keep you from me, Sweetheart." He laughed the second he saw the relieved look on my face. "You didn't think that your taser was the only thing I took, was it?" He held up my key.

Fuck.

I rush to the kitchen and snatch up a knife just as I hear the click of the door unlocking. I turned just in time to see the door open and Sergeant launch herself through it. I rushed over to find her pinning Rupert to the ground, snarling at him.

"A fox shouldn't attack a wolf cub." Ben materialised behind me, his voice making both Rupert and I look at him.

"You must be Kelsey's older brother." Rupert groaned, still as cocky as ever. "I can see the resemblance."

Ben grinned, his fangs showing. "Not quite."

About an hour later, I was in a cabin (that I didn't know existed) in the middle of the woods with Rupert chained to a chair and a vampire hungrily grinning down at him. I had my things back, my arms folded across my chest, displaying the pale blue bracelet proudly. "What did you expect when you knock on the door of a witch? When you knock at the witch's door, did you not expect chaos to answer?" Ben was enjoying this. I could tell from his voice. "Do you taste as disgusting as the contents of your soul?"

Rupert's cocky demeanour had evaporated long ago (just after he discovered that Ben was a vampire) and his face was getting paler by the second. "You're insane."

"Oh yes," Ben's voice dripped madness. "And you are a predator who's just met a deadlier animal. Do I frighten you, you little piece of shit?"

The look on Rupert's face was a good enough answer. A sadistic part of me was enjoying watching someone who enjoyed terrifying me so much be frightened of Ben. A part of me liked that Ben could install so much fear in Rupert. It was almost like revenge, like karma. I looked to Ben, noticing how those pale blue eyes were ablaze with anger.

My stomach twisted.

Was Ben going to kill Rupert?

Did I even care? It wasn't like I could stop Ben if he chose that he was going to have a Rupert kebab.

"What was your intention when you came to her home?" Ben displayed his fangs. It almost looked like a smile but with the rage in those blue eyes of his, there was no way it could be mistaken for happiness. Rupert didn't answer, he just whimpered and shook like a leaf in the breeze. *Not so fun when someone bigger than you decides you're their plaything, is it?* "Are you going to make me repeat myself?" Ben's tone was slowly changing from madness to that sinister voice I heard in B&Q.

Rupert was trembling. "Mrs Veneman wants her dead. She said that I could do whatever I wanted as long as she ended up dead."

I shivered. *Whatever he wanted.* "Why?" I demanded.

"Mrs Veneman said that Adria was the only one who could stop us," Rupert couldn't take his eyes off Ben. "Then she said that it was you after you took the name." How did he know? "She said we have to kill you too before it's over."

I tensed. "*You killed Adria?*"

His eyes went back to me. "Y-your hair..." Strands were moving through the air like snakes. "You... Mrs Veneman..."

The cult had killed Adria.

My body trembled with rage unlike any I'd ever known, my vision stained red and my fists clenched. "*You're the reason Adria's dead!*" I roared.

Ben made a strange noise and I turned. He had a disturbingly proud look on his face.

The rage in my body was making me dizzy. I wanted to *rip* Rupert apart. I wanted to scream. I wanted to run. I wanted to cry. I wanted this all to be over.

Before I could decide what action, I would take, Ben flashed forward and Rupert's neck was in his jaws. He was held up from his neck... not by Ben's hands but only by Ben's powerful jaws. Rupert looked like a large doll, no longer human. He was dead within seconds; his eyes hollo grey orbs and his skin fading to grey. I can't move. I can't breathe.

I should have felt frightened.

I should have felt angry.

I should have felt disgusted.

I should have felt guilt or relief.

I felt *nothing*.

Ben's face was dripping with blood. He'd never appeared less human. He unlatched his jaws from Rupert's neck, dropping the body, roughly onto the ground. His neck was bent at an unnatural angle and I could see bone.

Ben turned to face me. His eyes weren't blue anymore. It was like a thousand blood-red veins had stretched across the white to reach his pupils. As he looked at me, the veins retreated slowly. His eyes may have gone back to normal, but his face was smothered with a thick layer of blood, it was covering half his face and rolling down his neck. "The rot in his soul had seeped into his blood."

I threw up into a plant pot.

Ben didn't blink. He didn't wipe his face. He kicked the body out of the way as he made his way towards me. "Let's get you home, Little One."

He escorted me calmly through the woods, leaving the mangled body there in the middle of the cabin floor.

Days like these I wonder if I left my humanity in the woods when I killed Veneman's artificial skinwalker. I knew I should feel *something*. Rupert had tormented me and he wasn't going to stop. Rupert killed Adria. Rupert had been someone who'd frightened me like no other. I should have been relieved that he was gone or sad for the loss of a human life.

I was neither of those things.

Just before we left the edge of the woods, I fell out of my trance and stopped Ben from stepping out of the trees. "Ben, you need to wipe your mouth." He looked at me, confused, cocking his head like Sergeant did when I spoke to her. "You have blood all over your face and it will draw attention to *anyone* who sees us. There's a stream over there. Let's wash your face." I took his hand and guided him over to the stream, like a parent dragging their child over to the bath. I pulled out a scrunchie from my pocket and dipped it into the stream. Using it like a cloth, I started wiping Rupert's blood off his face. When the blood is wiped off his skin, the shocking white of his skin more striking next to the red blood. It was the first time that I'd ever felt older than Ben. Those blue eyes of his were wide and innocent, like that of a child. It was easy to forget that he had just killed Rupert moments ago and could easily rip me in two.

After I had finished wiping the blood off his face, we finished our trek to my home in silence. He left me at the door and dissolved into the darkness.

For the next hour, I laid in my bed, cuddling with Sergeant. Soon, I was asleep.

"Kelsey, wake up!" David shouted, rushing into my bedroom. "Kelsey! Kelsey!"

"What's the matter?" I jolted upwards, wiping the sleep from my eyes. "What's happening?"

"A child's been taken, Kelsey." David told me. "Kyle's little sister," He was trembling. "I know that you can do things... Things that you haven't been able to tell me... I won't ask... But please... Can you save her?"

He knew? Since when?

"I can try," I promised, rolling out of bed. "Um..."

"Right." He stood up. "I'm going to join the search party and you... do your thing." He quickly left the room, closing the door behind him.

I pulled the grimoire out from under the bed and it opened instantly.

Dark Witches.

There were dark witches and light witches? Turns out, a dark witch is a witch that uses dark magic. *They are often more powerful than witches that use 'good magic' because their power builds up much more quickly but unless they have a lot of natural magic power (well above average), they will start to rot while they are still alive.* Oh, gross. *They'll die younger than the average witch and they'll be easy to spot as they cannot hide the rot unless they are extremely powerful. They may be able to hold up a glamour but it's easy enough to look past.*

A newbie witch vs a dark witch. What could possibly go wrong?

I needed to find some spells that could protect me against another witch. If they could use magic, then an axe clearly wouldn't work. I looked to Fluffy... yeah, I'm going to bring the axe anyway. Just in case. But I'd never killed a human being before. That's what witches are, right? Just humans with the ability to use magic. Perhaps this was one for the police?

But then again... she could use magic and she was a child snatcher... what did she intend to do with Kyle's little sister? The police can't stop a witch. Did someone like that really deserve to live anyway?

I don't want to kill anybody but I'm not going to allow another person to die either.

I needed to find her; to do a tracking spell. Though I was far from thrilled to try that again after last time, I didn't seem to have much of a choice. What else could do? I set up the spell and sat there. *"Hermes help me find what's lost."* The spell's results this time were instantaneous. I could see her. I knew that room. I knew *that house*.

She was in the office in 43 Maddison Gardens.

Seriously? Couldn't she be *anywhere* else.

I read through three defensive spells but none of them were appropriate to practise in my home (not that I really had time to practise anyway). I just have to hope that I can replicate them when the time came for it. The spells involved a lot of hand movements that I had briefly practised in my room.

Why was it always children that were taken?

Sage stood up, blocking the doorway with his tiny frame. "Don't go, Adria. You can't fight another witch. You aren't strong enough."

His concern surprised me. "The witch has taken a child." I reminded him. "I can't sit around and wait for the body to show up. I can't do nothing and I won't."

"This is a trap." Sage cautioned, his voice pleading. "She knows that you are here. She knew what would bring you out. She didn't take the child for the sake of a child, she took it to get *you*. A witch can absorb another witch's power through their death. You have a lot of power with little experience. You are the *perfect* target, Adria. Don't go."

"I'm sorry, Sage."

"I knew you'd say that." He replied solemnly. "If you are to die, the one by your side will be I."

"Thank you," What else was I supposed to say in response to that? "We have to hurry." We marched from the house and out of the caravan park in the direction of Maddison Gardens. "*Adria,*" I turned. It was already there. I swung the axe through the smoke. It dissipated and reappeared almost instantly.

Run.

It seems like the silver-tipped axe isn't working anymore. I thought it was gone. How naïve could I be?

We sprint as fast as we can, not really paying attention to which way we're going. It arrogantly ambles after us, in no rush. I can still feel where its hand had scorched my skin before. The scar had never faded; still as red and raw as the day it had branded my skin. It was the only thing that still marred my skin now (unless you included the broken arm).

Rowan.

There was a rowan tree not a hundred yards in front of us. We just have to make it to the tree. *The axe doesn't work anymore. What makes you think the tree will?*

It has to.

As if it noticed that I'd seen the tree, it flashes forward, moving shockingly faster. I swing the axe blindly behind me but it's not slowing down. The second my hand reached the tree, I gripped it like a vice and yanked myself forward, shielding myself with the tree. I snatched a stick from off the ground and swung it at the creature. It halted. I held up the axe and the stick in front of me in a cross as I moved in the direction of 43 Maddison Gardens. Though the creature was smoke, it seemed to grin before it disappeared.

I kept a hold of the stick.

The streets around me were vacant. It was like a ghost town or something out of a zombie film. I didn't see another living soul the entire way to 43 Maddison Gardens. Perhaps they were all looking for Kyle's little sister. I wonder what her name is.

Green seemed too gentle a colour for the front door of 43 Maddison Gardens. But then again, what colour could really represent what hid behind it?

Once again, the door was unlocked.

Oh, that bodes well.

I stepped inside, my entire body tense. The door slammed shut behind me, hitting my back as it did so. I had expected that. I didn't jump... much. I opened the door of the office. It was empty. The girl wasn't there. The wallpaper had been peeled back and writing was on the wall but it wasn't the same handwriting as last time. *If you want the girl, come to the forest at midnight. Where you found the skinwalker. Come alone or she dies.*

The witch must have written it.

"You came back," Echoed a familiar voice. It came from everywhere and nowhere all at once. *Why can't I ever catch a break?* "Nobody ever comes back."

"I get the feeling that few people ever had the privilege of leaving." I said to no one in particular. He launched the axe through the air by my head. I ducked and spun. When did he get that axe back? Mr Jackson was waiting for me by the door I'd just entered. I knew he would be. "Hello again, Mr Jackson."

"You're in my house!" He roared. He held up his hand and the axe soared through the air again. I ducked.

"And I'm sorry about that, Sir." I smiled politely, though it didn't hide the sarcasm in my voice. "I'll let myself out."

I move towards the door but he glitches in front of me again, blocking my path. "You can't go until I say you can go."

"I heard you the first time." I tensed, resisting the urge to back off. Backing off is a sign of weakness. Gods this is frustrating. "Why don't you let me leave if you don't want me here?"

"You can't go until I say you can go!" He shouted.

"Yes, I know. You've said that already." Gods, this guy makes Ben look positively sane.

"Adria," Sage began. "The window," I looked to my left and found that it was still shattered so I darted for it, Mr Jackson howling like a banshee from behind us. We dived out the window again.

This is starting to become a habit.

Once again, I was running down the road away from 43 Maddison Gardens. This time there was nobody there to watch. There was nobody there to see me. Why do I keep having to go back to that fucking house?

The second I got back to the caravan I started the tracking spell again. I had to find out where Kyle's sister was. I couldn't afford to wait. *"Hermes help me find what's lost."* It felt like I'd been hit by a truck. I was launched across the room and I slammed my head against the wall. What just happened?

The grimoire slid out from under my bed and it flipped open. *Anti-tracking spell.*

"No. No. No. No. No." If I couldn't track Kyle's sister, then I'd have to wait for midnight to come around. God only knows what could happen to her before then.

Maybe I should go to sleep. If I was going to fight the witch, then I should have the energy to fight at midnight. I knew that Kyle's sister couldn't hear me but I couldn't help but repeat the words 'I'm sorry' over and over in my head. I laid down just as David opened my door. "Did you find her?"

"No," I told him, sitting up. "I am meeting up with the one who took her tonight."

"I'll come with you."

"No, you won't," I protested. "They told me to come alone. I can't risk it."

"Kelsey," I did not like the tone of his voice. "I know you do this kind of thing a lot and I know there are things going on that I don`t know about... that you think I can`t understand what`s going on but trust me... I can take it."

I held up my hand, recalling the words from one of the spells. Sparks danced from my fingertips and gold smoke twisted from my hands. "You were saying?"

"Um... How? What? I..."

"Witchcraft." I told him. "And the person who took Kyle`s sister was a witch too. If you go with me, I fend off another witch and protect both you and Kyle`s sister. I will be more at risk." He hadn`t moved. He was frozen, staring at my hand. "Please stay here. Trust me."

"I..."

"You don't have to say anything," I interrupted. "You can forget I ever said anything. You can forget we ever had this conversation."

"I don`t think I can, Little sister." He smiled awkwardly. "I won`t go tonight." Liar. "But promise me you`ll be careful."

"I will." Liar.

Just then, there was a knock at the door. Both of us tense but we made our way over. I opened it. "Mason, hi!" He was standing there with a bouquet of tiger lilies.

"I got you these." He grinned.

I took them and pretended to smell them. "Thank you, they`re beautiful. What`s the occasion?"

"I want to take you out this evening." He looked between me at David. "To see a movie?"

"Sounds good," I breathed. "But it can`t be too late. I have a family thing tomorrow and I will need *all* my energy to survive that."

He laughed. "Ok, I will make sure to have you back before ten."

I turned to David. He shrugged. "Go ahead."

"I`ll be here to pick you up at seven." Mason told me and I nodded before he left.

"You hate lilies." My brother pointed at the bouquet. "And you`re allergic."

"He doesn`t know that." I pointed out and then sneezed. "Geez, these things work fast... What do I do with them?"

"Isn`t there a spell you could use to make the pollen die?" My brother suggested.

"Not that I know of," There probably was an anti-allergy spell. "And I need all my magic for tonight."

"I`ll put the snot flowers in a..." We didn`t own a vase. "A jug and put them outside."

"Thank you," I sniffled. Gods, out of all the flowers the Earth has to offer, Mason had to pick lilies. I decided to get some sleep before the before the big night. I needed to be on my A-game.

Eleven

"That movie was awesome!" I grinned, bouncing with excitement, as we stepped out of the cinema. "Good choice, Mason."

"I swear, Kelsey," He smirked back, pulling popcorn out of my hair. I hadn`t even eaten any popcorn but there it was. "You are the only girl I know who goes on a date and wants to watch a zombie movie."

"Those girls are sorely missing out."

"Can`t argue with that,"

Just then, David pulled up. "Thought I`d give you two a lift."

"Thanks," Mason smiled.

"Thanks, David." The drive to Mason`s home was a short one from here. He really had been going out of his way to walk me home. His home was a good-sized house. I wasn`t really sure what I`d been expecting. Most of the people in our area were very well-off so it shouldn`t have been a surprise that Mason was no different.

"I`ll see you tomorrow, Kelsey." I hope so. Mason then leaned forward and gave me a quick peck on the lips before getting out and striding inside his home.

I made some kind of squealing noise that I didn't know I was capable of, and David snorted. "I take it you two have not done that before?" I slowly shook my head and he laughed. "You two are adorable."

David drove us home and something quickly occurred to me. "Hey, David?"

"Yeah?"

"Whose car is this?"

"It's Kyle's. He heard that you were going out tonight and he didn't want you to go missing too."

"That was nice of him."

"Yeah, it was."

Once David pulled up, I darted inside. I shed my date night clothes and pulled on my 'Lara Croft look' as David had dubbed it. I practised the hand movements for the spells until the clock turned 11:30. "You ready to go?" My brother called from the doorway.

"Yeah," I held my hands up. "*Sleep,*" David fell back, and I caught him as best as I could. *Damn, for a slim guy, he's heavy.* I dragged him over to my bed.

I couldn't risk David coming after me and there was no doubt in my mind that he would have followed me the second my back was turned. Guilt gnawed at my stomach, but I ignored it and slipped out the front door. Sergeant whined. I flinched at the sound and Sage jumped onto my shoulder. "I can't talk you out of this?"

"No,"

"I thought not."

"The full moon is beautiful tonight." It illuminated my path, making it appear like a silver ribbon. I wondered if the moon could affect my magical ability or maybe hers.

I heard a noise from behind me. I spun. "*Adria.*" The yellow-eyed creature was back. And it was far bigger than last time. I reached my hand out towards the rowan tree and a stick flew through the air and slammed into my hand. I swung it at the smoke, and it evaporated again.

"Is this what is going to happen every time I leave my home?"

"Until you trap or kill it; yes." Sage told me, as per usual he didn't bother with sugar-coating anything. "You should probably ward your home so it doesn't get in while you sleep."

"And on that terrifying note; let's go." As we entered the tree line, my blood turned to ice. I hadn't been back into these woods since everything with the skinwalker. Why did I have to go back here? I guess it could have been worse. The witch could have set us to meet in the forest where I killed the skinwalker and the whole thing with Joe went down.

The first thing I noticed when I reached the spot where we found fake-Nina was that the log nearby was gone. The witch was nowhere in sight and there was no sign of anybody else. I stood there frustrated, looking around for a few minutes when a white light appeared to my left, beckoning me further into the woods. *Don't look into the light.* I quietly crept in the direction of the light to find a clearing with that log in the middle, sticking out of the ground like the tree it once was and tied to it was a young girl. It must be Kyle's sister. She looked up at me. Her eyes widened and she hissed. "We have to get out of here. The lady's crazy and there's *something* in the trees! Please help me!"

I scanned the trees to make sure I wasn't going to be ambushed, before scurrying over to the girl. "What's your name?" I began, trying to keep her calm with calm conversation.

"Sarah. Please hurry!" I started to try and untie the chains. Damn, these knots held tight. "What are you_ *Ah!*" She let out a blood-curdling scream, making me duck just as something large swiped the air where my head would have been. I span around and raise my axe.

"Holy fuck! Werewolf!" I shrieked, rolling out from under the things arms and swinging the axe at its side. It dodged with ease. "Fucking full moon!" It should've been a warning. The creature's blue eyes were fixed on me and its grey fur shone in the moonlight. It was seven feet high, towering over me and its canines were the length of my thumbs. It snarled and charges at me like a bull. The thing moved just as quickly as Ben does.

I swing the axe at it, but it seemed to blur away. How does something so large move that quickly? I swing the axe blindly, hearing it on all sides of me all at once. How could I save Sarah?

The werewolf launched me forward and I landed flat on my face, smacking my nose against the damp earth. I rolled, shrieking at the pain in my arm as I hit it again. *Can't it just heal already?* I held up the axe as the werewolf dives down on top of me. The silver burns its skin with a loud fizz, and it bounced back with a yowl of pain. That hesitation lasted no more than a split second before the werewolf's on me again. Sarah's screaming and I'm waving an axe around like an idiot.

"Sage!" I shout. "Untie Sarah!"

"What about you?" Sage calls back, his skin rippling as he was part way through changing form.

I shove out my hand. Electricity zaps the werewolf's face, launching it back several feet. "I'm fine." Gods, that bracelet is fucking awesome. I leap up to my feet just as the werewolf charged forward again. *"Hephaestus' flame,"* Fire ignites like an orange storm from my hands, my body blocking Sage and Sarah from the werewolf and the flames. "Gods, fire in the woods is *such* a bad idea." The werewolf continued to catapult its body at me. The thing is on fire. It is burning alive and it doesn't seem to care. It's so obsessed with killing me that it shrugs off the pain of burning alive like I would a grazed knee.

How the Hell was I supposed to fight this thing?

It leapt at me again. Instinct took over and I flinch backwards, trying to get away but I slipped over the damp ground, landing painfully on my back. It bounced over me and landed just above my head. It span around. Its blue eyes glistened with insidious excitement. Its mouth widens open to take a bite, but I shock it one the nose, launching it back. "Did you forget the bracelet already?" I laughed humourlessly.

Its fall put out the fire and it`s scorched body`s healing supernaturally quickly. Roaring with frustration, it leapt at me again and I met it with a blast of flame.

No. No. No. No! My vision is starting to blur, and I was wrestling to find the energy to stand up. The cold of the mud felt less and less unpleasant as my energy faded. The price of using magic seemed unprepared to wait for the end of the fight. I haven`t even seen the fucking witch yet and I was just running on fumes. How much energy did that defensive spell take?

The creature isn`t slowing down. What if I passed out before this is over? "Sage!" I twisted and chucked the axe at the werewolf. It dodges the blade with ease. "How`s the rope coming?!"

"Just…a… Got it!" I heard Sarah fall down. She darts for the trees.

Noticing the easier prey, the werewolf gives chase.

I spring up too quickly and I nearly fall back over. My head spins, dizzy with exhaustion.

It`s faster than Sarah and it`s on her in seconds. I stumbled, using the trees around me for support. Don`t pass out. Don`t pass out. Don`t pass out. I reached the axe as and breathe a sigh of relief as I got to the werewolf, smacking it hard in the back with the axe. The fizz was as loud as the roar of agony it let out. It spins around to face me, my fingers slip on the axe, leaving it lodged in the werewolf`s skin. I cannot see Sarah`s tiny body from behind its hulking frame. It grinned as it shakes the axe out, landing with a squelch on the ground behind it.

Well fuck.

I jolt out my hand to electrocute it, but it snatched my wrist. I brought up the other arm "*Hephaestus` Flame.*" The force of the flames may not have been as strong as before, but it was enough to send it far enough away from me that I could snatch the axe.

I staggered back, black spots dancing across my vision. I blinked them away and swung at it with the axe again. It . It caught the handle of my axe with an arrogant smirk. "*Thorns!*" Cuts slash across the werewolf`s chest but they heal almost instantly. It grinned again. "I`m sorry?"

It swipes at my head. Its attacks seemed less animalistic now. It wasn`t leaping, it`s slashing. It slashed my shoulder and I shrieked. Fear gripped at my lungs making it hard to breathe and my energy had left me. I fell back and it`s on top of me. I shoved my hand in its face to electrocute it off of me, but it had sliced through the bracelet with its claw the second I moved my arm and knocked it away.

The werewolf is learning.

It pinned down my hands with its own, blocking me from sending magic anywhere. None of these spells had been strong enough anyway. "BEN!" I shrieked, tears streaming down my face. "BEN!"

He`s not coming. You`re alone.
You`re going to die.
David, I`m sorry.

Sage charges out of the trees, in the large form he used to battle the creature before, and knocked the werewolf flying. "Run, Adria!" He roared and springs into battle. I scramble to my feet. Guilt twists my stomach, but I run. I dragged Sarah up and pulled her onto my back, twisting to keep her on. Thankfully, she`s small enough to carry. I just have to get to someone who can help her. I fall into trees, using them to keep me up. Keep going! It's just a little further. I collapsed into the mud.

"Can't run forever." I felt Sarah stand up and step away from me.

"You're not Sarah." I groaned.

"Ding. Ding. Ding." She smiled. The air shimmered and Sarah was replaced by a young woman in her late twenties. "Any witch worth anything should see through a glamour."

"Then perhaps you should remove your next layer." I coughed. I can't move my body. "You're not fooling anybody."

"I fooled you." She dropped the second glamour and I wished I hadn't said anything. Her body was gaunt and *rotting*. Her eye sockets were empty, and her hair was thin and white.

"Geez, I'm sorry!" I laughed, trying to cover my fear with humour but I couldn't cover the tremble in my voice. "Put the glamour back up. I didn't realise you're a walking corpse."

The witch kicked the side of my head, sending my limp body rolling across the ground. "Adria, it was so easy to plant the idea in that Kyle's head and your idiot brother just ate it up."

"*Thorns!*" I raised my hand limply at her. Nothing. My arm drops. She laughs.

"Oh, Sweetie," Her fingers rest on the collar that was gripping her neck. "You ran out of magic energy fighting the dog. Look around, sweetie. He's gone. He's only there when I want him." What do I do now? Sage cannot help me. If he wasn't injured, he would have used all his magic up fighting the werewolf by now. I'm alone.

"Why are you doing this?" I demanded. "What do you want?"

"It's not about what I want." She adjusted her collar.

"Veneman…" I grunted, trying to get up again but my limbs just wouldn't obey. It's taking every ounce of willpower I have just to stay awake. "You're working for Veneman."

"Yes again!" She smiled, clapping her hands. "What a clever Little One you are!"

"Could you be more condescending?" I groaned. Get up. Get up. Get up. "Why are you working with Veneman? What has she got on you?" She adjusted her collar again and the bell goes off in my mind. "Is that your collar? Has she chained you up like a dog? It must be so frustrating for a powerful witch like you to be under the control of a mere human."

The witch shrieks like a banshee with a flick of her wrist, she launched me into another tree. I yelped. My back *hurt*. "You little shit."

"Killing me won`t relinquish her control over you!" I choke. "She`s not going to stop! Why would she give up the power of a witch?" I manage to shuffle myself up into a sitting position against the tree. "Let me help you. We can stop her."

The witch cackles and shakes her head. "You? You can do *nothing*. You`re barely a witch! Do you really expect *me* to think *you* can help? You`re going to die, you pitiful excuse for a witch." She held out her hand. "*Mortis*," I started to choke, and my vision blurs. The pain was indescribable. I couldn`t cry out or scream. It hurts far too much to scream. I coughed. Is that blood? I`m coughing up blood.

I`m dying.

I`m dying.

Something knocked her away and suddenly I could breathe again. My clothes are drenched in my own blood. Where`s the witch? What took her? Was it the werewolf? I couldn`t move to look. There`s no strength left in my body. Who saved me and what was that spell she used? Had I been saved just for something else to kill me?

Out of the corner of my eye, I could see something large approaching and then black.

I blinked my eyes open to see a pair of cold, dead, grey ones. I yelped and scrambled back. Seems that my energy has returned. "Little One,"

"Ben?"

"Ben; that`s what she used to call me." He replied and sat down in front of me, blocking the mangled body from my vision. "You howled and howled so I came. Someone`s spent too much time playing with a dog that you didn`t see past the mask."

"That about sums it up." I agreed, shuffling to a more comfortable sitting position. "Thank you. What happened to the witch?"

"Little birdie flew away... But like a pigeon, she`ll return once again." Ben rambled, his eyes moving across the ceiling as if they were following an invisible bird. "Perhaps it`s time for you to flee the nest too... Just fly far away... Why return to Hell?"

"People are dying, Ben."

"Ben; that`s what she used to call me."

"I can`t walk away." I continued, wiping the mud and blood off my clothes (or at least trying to). "Veneman isn`t going to stop and nobody else is going to stop her."

"They don`t deserve you." He stated, his voice more stable than I`d ever heard it. "Why oh, why oh, why does the little bird serve the cats that would break her wings for the joy of seeing her flap around helplessly?"

"Not everyone`s like that." I crossed my legs. "Some people don`t want to hurt anybody and yeah, there are a few assholes out there but you shouldn`t let a few rotten apples ruin the whole batch." I was being a little bit hypocritical here. I once bit into an apple that was rotten on the inside and I was terrified to go near the fruit bowl for nearly a year afterwards. "I can`t abandon all the innocent people because a few of them are assholes. They can`t defend themselves against the supernatural." Ben rolled his eyes and I giggled. "What can you tell me about how to defeat a werewolf?" I inquired. "Because I was throwing everything I had at that thing and it didn't even slow down."

"The cerulean" Doesn't that mean blue? I'm sure it meant blue. Well, the werewolf does have blue eyes, I guess. "Will be here for two nights more." His accent had changed. I think it was Irish but I wasn't entirely sure. I was never good with accents. "Silver will burn the witch's spell. Aconitum is the bane of the wolf." Aconitum... I knew that word. Where did I know that word from? "You played the game in their territory. The next game, you should play in ground you know best. Beat the wolf; weaken the witch."

As far as Ben goes, that wasn't hugely cryptic. "Thank you."

"I will escort you home." I looked down at Rupert's body and couldn't help but want to ask what was going to happen to it. It was far more mangled than I remembered. Something told me that I didn't really want the answer to that question.

Ben was quiet but I was thankful that he was there. Something felt wrong. He stopped suddenly and I stumbled, almost falling into his back. "Ben, are you ok?"

"I'm *hungry*," He turned to look at me in a flash, his eyes turning red from those veins. "And you smell delicious."

"Thank you," I replied. You have to stay *calm*. Panic will make him attack. "Ben, shouldn't we be going? That werewolf is out there and we're out in the open. You were escorting me home to make sure I wasn't attacked, remember?"

"Ah... My *friend*." The way he said 'friend' sent chills down my spine. He recognised me but felt seemingly nothing. "I am *protecting* my *friend*."

"Yes," I agreed with a gentle smile, trying to ignore the twist of anxiety in my stomach. "You are. Did you keep Rupert because you were hungry?"

"Rupert… Rupert… The grey-eyed little morsel who thought that he was the predator but became prey?" He laughed, hollow and ominous and licked his lips.

"Yes," I nodded. "Is that why you kept him?"

"No, no," His voice was so different. "I drained his tainted blood the second I found him. I have plans for him… yes, yes. Let`s get you home, *Adria*." I was tense. I was covered in blood, I was battered, Ben wasn`t feeling like himself and had already told me that he had the munchies. That didn`t exactly bode well.

He halted again. "Ben, are you ok?"

He blinked. "Ben; that`s what she used to call me."

"Oh, thank God!" I launched myself at him, wrapping my arms around his chest. He was so tense; it was like hugging a marble statue. I released him and we made our way back towards my home. Once again, he had disappeared before I could turn to say goodbye. The sun was coming up and there was no point in going back to bed. I`d have to be at school in two hours.

"You knocked me out." David accused when I opened the door. "You look awful. What happened?"

"Kyle`s sister doesn`t exist." I sighed, slouching against the kitchen side. I was too dirty to lie on the sofa. "She planted the idea in Kyle`s head. It was a trap."

"For you?"

"For me," I confirmed.

"Shit," He ran hands through his hair nervously. "What do we do?"

"I stop her," Sergeant tried to put her massive head in my lap (despite the fact I was still standing) and the weight made me stumble. "Free the werewolf and stop Veneman."

"Wait... Werewolf? Did you say werewolf?"

"Yep," I told him. "I need breakfast and a shower... Food first." I sat up and made my way to the kitchen.

"But *werewolf*?"

"I fancy bacon." I told him, opening the fridge to find it waiting for me. "Do you want some bacon?"

"Are we not gonna talk about the werewolf?" He blurted.

"Your sister is a witch and all you can think about is a *werewolf*?" I snorted, pulling the bacon out of the fridge. I picked up a frying pan and got on with cooking the bacon while my brother continuously muttered 'werewolf; there are werewolves' in the background. I made us each a bacon sandwich, had a burning hot shower and he drove me to school early.

There was a crowd around the gates.

I barged through and stopped when I could see it.

Rupert's body was hanging from the gates.

Twelve

My day was consumed with sleeping, plotting and summoning aconitum (which turned out to be wolfsbane... figures), I was sitting in my bedroom with my grimoire in front of me.

It was time to banish the yellow-eyed creature. The grimoire flipped open to a page titled 'banishing'. There was a list of ingredients: fire, salt, and iron. I hurried to the kitchen and took a spoon from the drawer. I poured salt all over it and pulled out a lighter. *"I banish the one who follows me."* I held the creature in my mind as I repeated it a few more times and lit the spoon. I was shocked that the spoon actually caught fire. It must have been because of the magic. Once I opened my eyes, the spoon had disappeared. Had it worked? There was no way to tell... except maybe when I left my home.

The time was six 'o clock and we'd had our dinner (pizza again). David left for work and Sage and took Sergeant for a walk. It felt incredibly normal.

Unfortunately, I hadn't seen Fluffy since our first encounter with the werewolf. I must have left it in the woods. As a result, I came armed only with a freshly made taser bracelet, rope soaked in wolfsbane and a few more spells. After finished our walk, we dropped Sergeant off at home and we made our way in peace to set up the trap.

I guess the banishment spell must have worked.

I stood outside the gates of my school. It was just getting dark.

Ben had suggested that I fight in familiar territory. What was more familiar to me than the school where I`ve spent every day for four years? It should be empty now and I could lay a trap. With any luck, I could lure the werewolf into the cult`s lair. Two birds with one stone.

So that`s the plan.

Once again, I used the enchanted key. It opened up and we made our way inside the gates. "We need to make sure nobody`s here." I told Sage once I`d locked the gates and we`d gotten to the centre of the school. "You do the side with Inclusion. If the cult is there, then they are less likely to see you. I`ll do PE side." Sage shifted into a little robin and flew off in the direction of Inclusion without a word.

Now that Sage had left, I was hyperaware of how quiet my surroundings were. There didn`t even seem to be a single pigeon or seagull (birds that flocked to our school because of all the food dropped by students). Had they flown away because there had been no students today to steal chips from or had they disappeared because of all the monsters in recent years?

There was nobody in the canteen, canteen kitchen or English building. I made my way over to PE and towards the Sports Hall. It was the largest room in the school and there were lots of small rooms leading off from it. From the window on the door, I scanned the sports hall to make sure it was empty before entering. I made my way to the first room attached to the sports hall. It was just a storage room, but it was full of large mats and gymnastics equipment shoved haphazardly in there, resulting in a lot of places to hide that could even fit something as large as the werewolf. I wouldn't put it past the cult to have left a nasty surprise in here for me. With any luck, nobody would know that I was ever there and hopefully the cult didn't think I'd be here and wouldn't leave any nasty surprises.

I peeked my head around the corner. Nothing was there. Sighing with relief, I began my time slipping behind gymnastic equipment to make sure that there was nothing in there. Thankfully, I found nothing.

Leaving the first room, I scanned the sports hall again before moving towards the next room. It was full of metal beams to hold up badminton nets and there was a storeroom that led off from it. There was a loud slam from the storeroom and a groaning sound. Somebody was in there. Were they hurt or was it something more sinister? I adjusted my arm so the taser bracelet was at the ready. I resisted the urge to put my other arm down as I raised my broken arm to grab the doorknob. I gripped it tight, hesitated and then opened the door quickly. They screamed and scrambled back.

Delilah and Mason. Both shirtless.

"Kelsey!" Mason blurted, snatching up his shirt as if he could disguise what I'd already seen. Delilah didn't even have the decency to look ashamed. She looked proud, smiling at me smugly with a twinkle in her eyes that said; 'I warned you'. "I… I'm sorry."

"So am I," I snapped, spinning around. "Goodbye Mason," I was *not* going to cry in front of *them*. I fucking refuse. How could he do this to me? He knew how much this hurt him! I was the one who comforted him when Delilah did this to him! How fucking *dare,* he?

You should have known, my mind replied. *She'll always have her claws in him. She's not going to let him go. This will happen again and again and again. You're just the first in a long line of victims.*

As I exited the other room, I shrieked. The werewolf was in the sports hall and it was darting closer. "Kelsey I... What the fuck is that?!" Mason blurts as we all bundle back into their storeroom. I shove boxes of sporting equipment in against the door. The door is thick but I`m not sure how well it can hold against a werewolf.

It had to have followed me here. How long had it been watching? I had intended to lead it here *after* I had set up the traps, but none had been set and I`m stuck in *here* with only a wolfsbane rope and a taser bracelet. Inside a storeroom with my now ex-boyfriend and the girl who`d hated me since pre-school with a psycho werewolf outside was the last place in the world I want to be. Mason sat their frozen, staring at the door, shocked into silence; something I was glad for.

"We knew you`d be coming." Delilah cackled, pulling her top on lazily. Why couldn`t she have been shocked into silence too? "Did you really think that we wouldn`t have planned this? You`re going to be eaten *alive*."

"Delilah, you dumb bitch!" I snarled. "If that thing gets in here; it`s going to eat you too!"

"No, it won`t," She protested. "I`m one of the *chosen*. It won`t eat us. It serves us."

"It serves the witch." I replied with an angry laugh. "Who was enslaved by Veneman. Are you really *stupid* enough to believe that the witch would have enough control over the werewolf so that it would spare you? Do you really believe that the witch cares enough if you die if she could? It gets in here, you die too."

"But Mrs Veneman said…"

"Veneman is a psychotic troll." I interrupted tersely. "She wanted you here to make sure that I was distracted while the witch put the werewolf in here. How can you not see that?"

"Why do I always end up hunted by some psycho when you`re...?" The werewolf slams against the door, making us all jump.

"Shut up," I growled, low and quiet. The werewolf slams against the door again. "Keep fucking quiet and hopefully it will lose interest so we can get out of here."

We`re all far too close for my liking and after a few minutes listening to the werewolf slamming against the door and praying that it would hold, everything went quiet. Delilah jumps up. "Can we go? Is it gone?"

I shook my head. "It`s waiting. It hasn`t left."

"How can you possibly know that?" Mason snorts, trembling. It seemed that he was back in reality again. Perhaps in his shock, he hadn`t heard my conversation with Delilah. Or maybe he had heard and didn`t care. "How do we know that you aren`t lying to scare us and that isn`t David or Ben outside in a bear suit? If Mrs Veneman got Delilah here to make sure you don`t break in, then you must have pulled shit like this before."

I have never wanted to hit someone more in my life.

"Why don`t you explain, Delilah?" I smiled pleasantly. God, I just want to leave. Maybe I should just take my chances with the werewolf. "Why do we know that the werewolf isn`t just my brother in a bear suit? Go on; tell him."

"Because we brought it here." Delilah admitted. "Kelsey was here to kill it."

"To catch it," I corrected her. "It`s a human being underneath all that fur. I won`t kill it."

"Didn`t stop you from killing Rupert, though, did it?" She countered with a hiss.

"You killed Rupert?!" Mason blurted, eyes wide and more frightened than ever before. The werewolf slammed against the door, making our barricade shake.

"No," I glared daggers at Mason for being so loud. *Moron.* "A vampire killed Rupert. What was he expecting, coming out in the middle of the night, alone and unarmed?"

"It was that pet vampire of yours, though, wasn`t it?" She spits.

"Ben isn`t a pet. He`s my friend." I snarled. "But yes. He did. I can`t control what he does, and he protects me. Rupert may have been an asshole... Hell, I think he is just as much a monster as Seth or Joe!"

"Don`t say that name!" She shrieked. The werewolf slams on the door again.

"I *hated* him. I didn`t want him dead but I won`t mourn his loss." I finished.

"How do you make that vampire so loyal to you?" Delilah smirked haughtily. "Are you sure that Mason was the first one to cheat?"

I tried to ignore how hopeful Mason appeared when she said that. Gods, I want to hit him. "Funnily enough, not everyone gets people to do as they want them to with the promise of sex." I deadpanned. "Some people are loyal to you because they care and you`re kind to them. Ben is my friend, regardless of humanity, blood, or payment. Not everybody is like you." She jolted forward to slap me, and I block her... with the hand with the taser. She launches backwards, slamming into the barrier. "Shit!" It toppled down like an avalanche, covering Delilah. The door swung open lazily.

The werewolf grinned, its blue eyes glinting. There is nowhere to run.

Instinctively, I blocked Mason with my body, I held out my hand. "*Thorns.*" Cuts glide across its chest like invisible blades but the werewolf didn`t move an inch. It didn`t even flinch. Not missing a beat, I untwist the rope from around my waist. "*Thorns.*" I repeat and launched the rope at the werewolf, the rope landing along the cuts that hadn`t quite healed. It roars in agony, falling to the floor, pinned by the rope. "I can't believe that actually worked." I let out a short laugh of relief. It struggles and I know it cannot hold it for long. I turn to Mason, keeping my voice clipped. "Stay here with Delilah. Build the barrier back up and stay here until dawn."

"What about you?" He asked, eyes wide.

"I think you've already established that you don't give a shit about me." I can't control the anger seeping into my voice. I have to protect them even if they are scumbags. "Stay in there. If I trap it, I will come back to let you out. If not, it should turn back at dawn." I slammed the door shut before he can answer me and sprint towards the door of the sports hall. *You have limited magic left. Be clever.* I had gotten half-way across the sports hall when I hear the werewolf break free and start to charge after me. *"Hephaestus' Flame."* I swing my hand out behind me, hoping that the magic might slow it down enough for me to get on the other side of those doors. My legs burn and my lungs felt too tight. There is no way in *Hell* that I'm slowing down. I reached for the door and propel myself forward. I dived behind the door and slam it shut behind me. The werewolf stops to stare at me through the window.

Its hand smashes through the glass, reaching for me. I shriek and stumble back, nearly tripping over. *Run.* I hurry down the corridor towards the set of double doors at the end that will let me outside. "The werewolf's here! Sage! The werewolf's here!"

"We aren't ready." He complained, materialising out of nowhere. "Why did you bring it here so early?"

If I could give him an irritated look, I would have but I'm too busy running. "Veneman brought it here. Not me!"

I heard the doors crash to the ground behind me. Splinters of wood sent flying, some hitting my back. I won't look behind me. I can't risk slowing down.

It's faster than me and I could hear it catching up with me. I'm not going to make it to the end of the corridor. I needed to get to the old dance studio. It's closer but the doors wouldn't hold. There was a door into the theatre in there. I just have to get through the next doors and into the theatre. If I get through, I could into *another* drama room. That would be a shortcut to the tech building that contains inclusion... just on the other side. I just hoped I could get there before the werewolf ripped me in half.

Survive the maze, you may survive the night.

I yanked open the door but before I could shut it, the werewolf's claws were in my shoulder. I slam its arm in the door, releasing my own from its clutches. I needed something to put through the door handles... There was a weights bar (without the weights) lying on the floor. Quickly, I slammed my palm into its hand, knocking it back. I ducked, snatching it up and shoving it through the handles just as it slams against the door with a loud crunch. That doors going to last seconds. I scramble to the other side of the room.

To the untrained eye, you would just see a wall of black curtain but behind the curtain was a heavy metal door to the theatre, I yanked the surprisingly heavy curtain upwards and slide underneath it as the door shatters.

The werewolf is in the room with me.

Holding my breath, I slowly crept towards the door. It's sniffing the air and I'm sweating bullets. It roared. I tugged the door open as it slashed through the curtain next to me. With a shriek, I propelled myself through the metal door and slammed it shut behind me. I rushed up the stairs. The metal screeches as it contorts and bends from the strain the werewolf was putting on it. It's pitch black in the theatre and I'm not confident that I can navigate my way through here blind. However, I'm pretty confident that the werewolf doesn't need light to find me.

I scurried across the stage, pulling my phone out of my pocket to illuminate what was in front of me. Just in time, as I'm about to fall down the next set of stairs. I leap down and sprint into a storeroom.

Crap. I had forgotten about the storeroom and I'm not sure which door could get me out of there. I hear the slammed of the metal door crashing down. I tug open the first door: office. I scurried to the next door: office. It has to be the third! Office. I swing open the door of the fourth, relief filling me when it is the drama classroom.

I never thought I'd say that.

Once again, the door's at the end of the room, so I started sprinting for the door. Crap. The door is locked. I'm a dead woman.

I scanned the room. There is a chair in the corner. I snatch it up and rush to the window. I slam it against the window, sending a myriad of glass shards everywhere. I knock out the bottom shards before crawling through. The gap is too small for the werewolf to get through but considering a metal door didn't stop it, I'm certain that this wouldn't slow it down.

I tumbled down and my knees crunch into the glass. I yelp and turn to see the werewolf reaching for me.

Shrieking, I scrambled back, cutting my hands in the glass. It grins. Not missing a beat, I pushed to my feet and hurry towards the food tech room. How do I get in? "You, fucking idiot," I snarled, reaching into my pocket. I had the enchanted key. I unlocked the door and hurry through the kitchen. I pushed through the next set of doors and into my old English classroom.

My old English teacher used to insist that this room was haunted. With what Veneman had been up to, she may have been right. There's no telling how long she's been doing all this. I had just reached to the door when I heard glass shatter.

The werewolf is in the building.

I swung the door open and I'm in the hallway. Just two more rooms. The werewolf had gotten into the classroom in a matter of seconds and I'm running. The doors swing open behind me and it's on me before I could turn to look. It pinned me to the ground, growling by my ear. I could feel the glass in my legs pushing further in and I cannot help but whimper. I twisted my arm and the taser knocks the werewolf off. I pushed to my feet. *"Thorns!"* I held my arm up behind me as I rush towards the next set of doors. I flung them open and throw my hand behind me. *"Thorns!"* I launched through the next set of doors and twist into the next room.

The wood-shop was difficult to cross on an average day with all tables placed too close together and equipment was always scattered everywhere. Instead of trying to squeeze in between gaps, I leapt on top of the nearest table and bounced from one to another across the room. There was a door on the other side of the room next to Mrs Wilks' desk. Making sure to kick her computer off the desk as I jumped off, I opened the door to inclusion. The werewolf tossed tables out of its way as I slammed the door behind me. I twisted round the wall and through the rows of desks towards the door.

I reach the door and tried to pull it open.

It's locked.

The werewolf is in the room, so I sprinted towards Mrs Veneman's desk. The werewolf leaps onto it, knocking the table over, splinters scattering across the floor. W

I ducked under a desk, using it as a shield as the werewolf swiped under it at me. "Sage?!" I called. "Where are you?"

He materialises next to me, crawling through the gap. "Why didn't you use the enchanted key?"

I take it out of my pocket and hand it to Sage. "Wasn't going to get there in time. Can you unlock the door without the werewolf noticing?" I ask, clutching to the sides of the desk. I'm so glad that these desks have three sides and Inclusion is jam-packed otherwise I would have nowhere to go.

But a wooden desk wasn't going to last long. It will realise soon that it can't reach me like this and will just take to smashing the desk and I'll have nowhere to escape.

I don't have any time.

Sage nods and crawled out. I shocked the werewolf's hand with the bracelet and it jolted back but the shock knocks it into the cubicles and smashes the top of the desk as its legs thrash out. The wood smacked my head into the side and the world span for a second, but I blinked it away and scrambled out. "The door's unlocked!" Sage shouted and disappeared.

I leapt through the open door and slam my feet on the red-stained floor, and it gives. I tumbled down the stairs... again. The werewolf dived on me just as I land at the bottom of the stairs. Smacking my hand at the werewolf, the electricity launched it back again, its claws sinking into my cast, ripping it open as it was flung back. I choked down the sob of pain, crawled to my feet and rushed back up the stairs. I held my hand out behind me. *"Hephaestus` Flame!"* I held onto the magic instead of letting it go, so it projected as an extended barrier so I could get to the top of the stairs and escape. *I didn't know I could do that.* I pulled the floor back up and shut the door behind me.

Sage materialised out of nowhere, holding the rope. "Did you recall the spell?"

"Yes," I told him, taking the rope, and resting it down in front of the door. "We need to wait until he turns back to do the spell. I'm going to go and release Mason and Delilah while we wait. Could you stay here and make sure it stays put? Find me if something goes wrong." He nodded. I sat on another desk to pull out the glass from my body. Why should I rush? There are hours until dawn.

When had this become normal to me? When had the pain of pulling glass out of my knees and hands become less of a worry and more of just another job on the list?

I feel numb.

Was it because of Mason and Delilah or because of the werewolf? I don't know. I don't think I care right now.

I'm not tired either. Not to the extent I was last time or to the extent I should be. I'm tired but it was the kind of tired you feel when it's a bit past your usual bedtime instead of the 'I'm going to pass out where I stand' that came the last time I did battle with the werewolf.

After removing all the glass, I calmly strolled back to the sports hall. I was covered in sweat and blood drenched my torn clothes. My cast dangled from my arm, not supporting anything anymore. I must have looked like hammered shit.

Who cares? I haven't got any interest in impressing *anyone* here.

Fuck them both.

I'd be lying if I hadn't thought about leaving them in there until dawn. Who wouldn't consider about it in my position? But my mind was made up. I would be the bigger person here. Just because they were both assholes doesn't mean that I would be too. I calmly made my way across the sports hall and knocked on the door of the storeroom. "It's trapped. You can leave." I made my escape (making sure to walk away calmly so they didn't think they'd hurt me) as I heard them tearing down the barrier and flinging open the door.

"Kelsey!" Mason called after me, rushing to catch up with me. I clenched my fists. "Kelsey!" I didn't turn around or even slow down. I only stalled when I felt his hand grip my wrist. Turning to look at him, I kept my face blank; emotionless. Inside, I was screaming and resisting the urge to rip his hand from my wrist and return it with a fist to the nose. "I'm sorry. I know I fucked up... What hap-"

"Understatement of the century." I interrupted, removing his hand from my arm to cross my own. The anger was seeping into my voice like venom.

"I know why your pissed. I fucked up. I was hoping we could still be friends."

I laughed humourlessly. "If you had broken up with me and got with Delilah, *then* we could have been friends. You *cheated on me.* Did you stay friends with Grant?" I stopped bothering with trying to hide my anger. I couldn`t anymore. He tried to say something but I didn`t let him start. "I know you didn`t so don`t start with the 'well' or 'but'. Enjoy what time you have with Delilah, Mason, while it lasts." I turned to walk away.

"I`m sorry!" He repeated, not moving from that spot.

It took every ounce of my control not to punch him in the face then.

"No, you`re not."

Fuck you, Mason Baird.

"Veneman is going to be here soon." Delilah smiled maliciously, clearly enjoying the interaction. "That will teach you for tizing me!"

"Do you mean tasing?" Mason frowned.

"That`s what I said!" She shrieked, shoving past us and out of the sport`s hall.

I followed out behind her to head back to Inclusion.

"Kelsey_" Mason tried.

"Goodbye Mason." I finished. "Enjoy your walk home." I didn`t turn around. I didn`t stop walking. The walk to Inclusion was peaceful up until I re-entered the building. I could hear the werewolf slamming against the door before I was even in Inclusion. Sage was staring at the door. "Are you ok?"

"Your enemy draws nearer." Oh, come on! Seriously? "We cannot stay here."

"What do we do?" I inquired.

"We need to get out of here. Leave the wolfsbane and let them find the werewolf." Sage stated.

"Is that a good idea?"

"We could set fire to the school." He suggested.

I snorted a laugh. "If you said that when I was thirteen probably would have asked you for a lighter." Sage gave me a concerned look. I laughed. He didn't. "Yeah… let's go."

We turned to leave Inclusion. We had just gotten to the door of Mrs Wilks' wood shop when Sage pulled me back. I turned to ask why he'd pulled me back when he put his index finger to his lips. "Shh…" He pointed to the door and then to his ear.

I pressed my ear against the door. "Have you chained up all the exits?" Mrs Veneman sounded like she was partaking in an interrogation instead of just walking through the school.

"Of course," Mr Small squeaked. "I made sure to get those numbered padlocks so she can't use that enchanted key of hers." How do they know about the key? Wait… CCTV. Just because they cannot see my face, doesn't mean that they cannot see what I've been up to. I'd always been so concerned about concealing my identity to the police if necessary that I hadn't thought about what they'd see and learned about me. "She won't be going anywhere."

They're walking this way. Unsure where I could hide, I hurried back towards Mrs Wilks' desk. I ducked underneath it, stepping over the broken computer as I crouched underneath her desk. Thankfully, it was another three-sided desk, but I hoped that they wouldn't see the soles of my shoes under the wooden board at the bottom. I held my breath as they entered the room, her high heels clip-clopping as they got closer. I looked to Sage, but he was gone. Where is he?

"Adria," Mrs Veneman cackled. "Did you know that fairies are hugely weakened by the colour red? If it touches them for too long it can even kill them." I scrambled up from under the table to find Mrs Veneman holding up Sage with a red glove like a rag doll. "You don't want to cast a spell on me, girl or you'll kill your little friend."

"Let him go." I demanded, staring at his limp body in her hand, surrounded with a blood-red cloth.

"No," She smiled sickeningly sweetly. "Adria, did you forget to look for Mr Small?" I span around to find Mr Small behind me with a bottle of chloroform and a damp cloth. Without thinking, I blocked his approaching cloth with the taser hand, and knocked him back, smacking his head hard against the wall. The bottle tumbled with him but though I expected it to shatter, it bounced. *Everything* is made of plastic these days. I turned back to Mrs Veneman. "You shouldn't have done that."

"I apologise for knocking out your boss." I replied. I knew that he wasn't her boss; perhaps in regards to him being the headmaster while her only a guidance manager but in regards to the cult, it practically *reeks* of Veneman. "But you should really use glass. The plastic is likely to end up in the ocean."

"He's not my boss." She replies, ignoring my comment about plastic. Why am I not surprised that she doesn't care about recycling? "He's my lover."

That's all kinds of *ew*. "You're married!" I blurted. Then I point to Mr Small's unconscious body on the floor. "He's married! And not to you!"

Veneman stepped forward. Whatever anti-wrinkle cream she's been using, it seems to work supernaturally well. "My husband is *old*." The way she says 'old' is like she's disgusted by the very idea of aging. "And I'm going to live forever."

I laughed. She doesn't. "What? Did you find the fountain of youth?"

"In a way," She really did look different. The crows feet around her eyes were faded and her hair was thicker. "Others die so we may live. Enough souls and He will return, and She will grant us immortality as a reward for our service and loyalty." And I thought Ben was crazy. "Join us, Adria. You can live forever. Never grow old. Never die." She smiled, her eyes widening with madness or excitement. "Join us. End this senseless violence."

"Did you really think that your offer would tempt me?" I demand, anger and confusion bubbling up in my voice. "Do you really think I would *want* that? Why the fuck would I want to live forever if the people I love aren`t going to be there with me? You killed my best friend!" I snarled. "I will make sure that you *never* gain eternal youth. You will *fail*, Veneman. I promise you, I won`t let you get away with murder."

Her face twisted with disgust. "You`re a *fool*, girl."

"And you`re a spiteful troll." I growled; my fists clenched. "Release my familiar and I will leave your shithole now or you don`t release my familiar and I *burn* it to the ground. The choice is yours. Either way, I will have my familiar returned to me."

"Or" She steps forward. *Back off!* "You crawl down into our chamber with me and I don`t crush this little *imp*`s neck."

What do I do? I could... What if I concentrated hard on the spot on her wrists with the thorns spell? Maybe I could chop Sage away from her?

I glanced behind me to make sure Mr Small was still down. He is. I held up my hands as if I`m surrendering, ignoring the pain in my arm. I glare at her wrist. "*Thorns!*"

She shrieked, tossing Sage to the ground. His body`s limp. "You *bitch*!"

"Witch," I corrected. "*Hephaestus` Flame!*" I created a wall of fire and scrambled forward. *I warned you I`d burn this place to the ground.* I pulled Sage into my arms, cradling him like an infant. He wasn`t moving. I have to get home. I need to heal him. He`s still breathing but it`s so quiet. "*Hermes, grant* *me safe passage home.*" The words flowed from me as easily as breathing. I didn't have to think. I just knew the words. The flames split, blocking Veneman from me. She hurried over to the fire extinguisher. I rushed down the pathway that seems to be highlighted by a glowing gold line. It stopped at the locked gate. The lock glowed gold. "Shit." He's the God of thieves. There must be a spell to unlock it but it didn't come to me and I had no idea where to start. "Um…" I started to twist the numbers with my ear pressed against the lock. "I'm so sorry, Sage. We're getting out of here." Click. Twist, twist, twist. Click. It's taking more time than I wanted it to, and I don't know who is waiting in the shadows.

I didn't know how much time Sage has.

I had just gotten down to the last number when I heard "Hello, bitch!" I ducked as Delilah swings an axe at my head. It clanged against the bars. "You bitch, stand still!"

"Why?" I laughed, dancing away from her with Sage still motionless in my arms. "So, you can chop my head off? Not a chance! It's nice to know that even though I saved your life, despite the fact you slept with my boyfriend, that you still won't change your ways." I replied, dodging as she swung the axe at my stomach.

"You took him first!" She shrieked like a banshee. "He. Was. Mine!"

"You cheated on him!" I point out as she swings the axe at me again and again. "I never *took* him. You basically chased him off!"

She swings the axe at my head again. I ducked and rolled, shielding Sage with my body. I don't have time for this. I hate her but I didn't want to hurt her. I don't think I can use my magic without hurting her.

I'm starting to think I don't have a choice.

"And yet he came running back to me. Clearly you weren't good enough." She smirked, swinging the axe at me again.

I ducked and I electrocuted her in her chest. She dropped the axe as she's flung backwards. "Axes are my thing." I picked it up and swing it at the lock. The lock fell off. Yanking the gates open, the gold path reappeared. Veneman charges out of the tech block just as I start sprinting down the hill. "Sage, just hold on." I plead. He doesn't answer.

I am thankful they didn't chase after me. I'm thankful that the yellow-eyed creature doesn't appear.

No matter how fast I run, there seemed to be a man in a black hoodie a hundred yards away from me. On an average day I would have walked in a circle around a block to see if he's actually following me but with Sage limp in my arms, I cannot afford to take any detours.

The gold path followed my usual route and I was thankful to make it home in record-time.

David wasn't home so I rushed straight for the grimoire. It flip open directly to a healing spell. "Apollo, help me heal." I open my eyes. There was no change. "Apollo, help me heal." No change. "Apollo, help me heal." I sob. No matter how many times I repeated the spell, no matter how much *power* I put behind it, nothing was happening. Eventually my words just turned into sobs.

Help him, please. He's dying.

Sergeant was whining behind me. She knows.

I don't know what to do. I still have magic power so why can't I heal him?

"Little One," I spun around with Sage still cradled in my arms. Ben. "Why do you cry?"

"I-I c-can't h-h-heal h-him." I choke out.

Ben took him from me, and slices open his own thumb with one of his fangs. He shoved his thumb into Sage's mouth. "Vampire blood allows us to heal. It may heal your familiar."

"But it's red." I protested, frozen in place.

"Supernatural laws always have loopholes, Little One." He told me. "Especially with the fey." I stare down at Sage, praying that he's going to be ok. *Please* let him be ok.

His eyes blink open and I let out a sigh of relief. "Oh, thank the gods you're ok."

"He'll require rest." Ben insisted. "Let him sleep."

"Thank you," I hugged Ben and took Sage from his arms and to Sage's bed on my chest of drawers. Sage fell asleep in an instant. "Why couldn't I heal him?" I asked Ben once Sage was settled.

Ben takes my hands and holds them palm-up on top of his own. "These hands were not meant for healing."

Ice rolled down my spine. "What were they meant for?"

"Chaos."

Thirteen

Even after Ben had left, I couldn't stop staring at my hands. What did he mean by them being meant for chaos? Was it literal or metaphorical? I hope it's metaphorical. My hands were so *small* and pale, with lean fingers and chipped nails. They used to be my favourite thing about the way I looked but now, they felt like they didn't fit my body... Or maybe it was just that they didn't fit my mind. Regardless, they didn't look like they were capable of damaging *anything* let alone producing chaos. But then again, I don't look like I can produce fire from my hands either.

Last night I had used more magic than I ever had in my life but even today I was fine. Regardless, I had made sure to make myself a cup of coffee in the morning.

Sage used to be extremely independent but now I had to find food for him. Turns out that he liked grain and muesli which is surprisingly expensive but thankfully, he is tiny, so whatever I buy will last a while. We don't usually buy cereal but while walking Sergeant, I made sure to buy some. I'd set up his bed with more pillows, put books by his side and a bowl of muesli.

I pulled out the grimoire again and sat cross-legged on my bed. I needed to find a way to stop the witch. If I can't trap the werewolf anywhere long enough to use the counter-curse for the werewolf, then I'm certain I should take out the witch first. If I stop the witch, then perhaps I can save the werewolf (without it eating me). How could I be strong enough to fight her?

The grimoire flipped open to a new page: wands.

Wands do not enhance your power, but they will allow you to use more of it in one go without putting as much strain on your body. Ok, so I make a wand. The pages flipped to 'how'. *Find a tree. Ask the tree for some of its wood. You may do the incantation then or you can find some kind of stone to reinforce the power and do a second incantation.*

Making sure to take Sergeant with me, I left to look for a tree. What wood do I pick?

We went for a walk in the woods… Yeah, yeah; I know I said that I didn't want to go there ever again but what's the best place to look for a tree?

Then I realised: rowan. Why not rowan? Rowan was the tree that had saved my life several times. I cannot think of a better tree.

I meandered in that direction and over to the tree. It was beautiful. A myriad of luscious green leaves and bouquets of coral-coloured berries held up on the end of each branch. I reached out my hand to touch the trunk. I am supposed to ask, and it felt like I should rest my hand on it to ask. My hand touched the trunk and it *burned*. I shrieked and yanked my hand back. It felt like I had dunked my hand in boiling water. Why? I didn't try to take anything… I put my hand up against it and it burned… Just the way it had burned the yellow-eyed thing.

Wondering whether or not it was the same with all trees, I walked over to the closest tree (a birch). It didn't burn at all.

I looked down at my hands.
Chaos.

I should go and look at the grimoire. I turned to rush home, but I bumped into a man in a hoodie. "Sorry,"

"It's fine," The man replied blandly.

I started jogging again. I grabbed my key from my pocket and yelped. My hands were burned, and I had only noticed once I'd tried to pick up the key. Wincing, I used the tips of my fingers to take it out of my pocket because I couldn't move my broken arm to unlock the door. I managed to unlock the door with the tips of my fingers and open turn the door handle with my elbow. I knew I'd have to treat my hand but I wanted to look at the grimoire first. I stepped into my room and the grimoire slid out from under my bed, slipping open. I could read the words before I'd even entered the room; *rowan burns witches.*

I guess that means I'm not a witch blood anymore. I was just a witch now.

I looked at the burn on my hand. Don't get me wrong, the burning had *hurt* but the burns were far worse than I expected. I ran my hand under cold water which dulled the pain for a little while. I cleaned it with some antiseptic and wrapped it in bandages. What's the point in wasting magic on trying to heal myself when I knew it wouldn't work?

It was time to go back to the woods. I couldn't let this stop me from making my wand. How else could I stand a chance against the witch? There was no time to slow down. I wasn't sure how much time I had.

Sergeant and I returned to the woods. Making sure not to touch any rowan trees, I battered around. There was a black stone on the ground. It was smooth, flat, and oval shaped. I could see my face in it like a mirror.

I guess I found half.

Picking it up, I continued to look around. I saw a dark red flower. I made my way over to it: a wild rose. Not like a dog rose but a classic red rose growing in the wild. It felt right. It felt like *me*. It was pretty, the petals arranged delicately, but if you grabbed it too tight, it would cut your hand. I stared at the roots of the plant. It was surrounded with sticks from the plant. "Um… may I take a stick to graft into my wand… um, sir?" Gods, this is *awkward*. The rose swayed but there was no wind. Unsure if that was a 'yes' or a 'no, I hesitantly, I picked up one of the sticks off the ground. The tree didn't move again so I took that as confirmation that I could take it. "Thank you," The thorns, though sharp, didn't prick me and the wood was a beautiful dark colour. Sergeant looked at the stick in my hand and wagged her tail. "No," I warned. She tucked her ears back and turned so we could walk home. Part of me felt guilty but one; this was going to be my wand and disrespecting by letting my dog play with it, probably wasn't the best idea. Two; this stick had thorns on it, and she could hurt herself if she played with it.

On the walk home Mason returned to my mind like an echo of pain. Gods, Mason, *why* did you have to do it? You've left me all alone. A part of me had known that it would happen, that he would hurt me in the end. I *should* have known that he would choose her. I should have known that he wouldn't let me down easily.

He had texted me since then, a hundred messages of apology. I hadn't replied once and I wasn't going to reply. Why should I? I owe him *nothing*.

Besides, what did he want from me? He was dating Delilah for the time being as far as I knew. I say the time being because I knew it wouldn't last. This was another ploy for her to hurt me and once she was bored of him, she'd drop him. Maybe he knew that. Maybe he wanted me to stay close to him so that when Delilah dropped him, he would have me instead. Maybe he was genuinely sorry. Or maybe he was trying to get close to me so Delilah could hurt me again.

Would she be that petty? Yes. Could she manipulate him? Absolutely.

Perhaps she'd already left him now that the damage was done. Maybe that's why he was messaging me because he knew that he would be alone now. If he thinks that I can be strung along like a puppet then he never knew me at all.

I guess it doesn't really matter because *I don't care*. I'm annoyed that I ever went out with him in the first place. I'm annoyed that I ever gave a shit about him. And I'm annoyed that he got my first kiss. Stupid gentlemanly nice-guy charm got me once, it would not get me again.

Some people say it's good to forgive and forget. Some people act like when you don't forgive, you're as bad as those who have wronged you. All I could think was sometimes forgiving and forgetting was like handing the person who'd wronged you a loaded gun, saying 'please don't shoot me' while you're still bleeding out from the last time they got a little bit trigger-happy. Forgiveness is my choice. Maybe one day I'll forgive him but I won't be naïve enough to forget what he's done.

As if she could sense that I was upset, Sergeant nudged my hand with her nose. I smiled at her and ruffle the fur underneath her collar. "Good girl,"

I opened the door to the caravan to see a familiar hoodie standing there. I freeze like a deer in headlights. The figure turns to me. Its eyes are crystal blue.

I should have warded my caravan because in front of me stood a vampire. "BE…!"

The vampire yanked me inside, covering my mouth with its hand. Sergeant snarled, leaping for its arm. It shook her off as if she was no more than an insect. "Adria, I am here to talk… No more." I glared at it, making sure to avoid its eyes. The last thing I wanted was to be compelled into doing something horrible. What do I do? I can't fight it. Not without my magic and I needed to speak for that. Ben couldn`t hear me to help me. What else could stand a chance against a vampire except another vampire? "Let us sit down and perhaps your friend will come and join the conversation." It grabbed my chin and shoved my gaze up to meet its own. "*No magic. You will not speak unless I ask it of you.*" It released me and I moved to talk. I couldn`t. My voice wouldn`t obey. "Good girl,"

Fuck off, I replied… In my head.

"So, your friend… I wonder what he calls himself to you; is it…" The vampire stopped. "Your friend is my brother… at least, by *blood*." It showed off its fangs. I pointedly rolled my eyes. "So, tell me, where is he?"

"Who are you talking about?" I asked. Yay, I can talk again… Ben, he must be talking about Ben. I lowered my gaze.

"He`s had many names." It yanked my face up to look at it again. "I can see why he chose you. You look just like her… You know of whom I speak of. Where is he?"

"I don`t know," I answered. It is the truth. Who knows where Ben actually lives? Sure, he made a meal of Rupert in that shack, but I doubt that he actually lives there. Is 'lives' even the right word for it? 'Undeads?'… '*Resides*'?

"You know something." It insisted. "*Tell me. Where is he?*"

I glared up at him. "*Behind you.*" The vampire turned around and was greeted by a pair of bright blue eyes, identical to its own.

"How did you get in?" The vampire dropped me like a toddler does a doll, and Sergeant hurried back over to me.

"When you call and call… such a sweet song… You sing and sing but you don`t see the music." Ben smiled, his fangs showing. I still can`t move. I`m frozen in place.

The vampire laughed. "Dear brother… You still have a brain like a box of screws… All loose." Honestly, neither of you two sound remotely sane. Then again, they`re vampires. At this point I'm starting to wonder if insanity comes with the job description. "You have ignored you summons. Why?"

"Seraphine, the Vampire Queen of London... She wants me to fight the Beast." Ben laughed maniacally. "She's going to lose. The Beast could destroy half her army alone. With an army at his side? Her days are numbered."

"You are sworn to her." The vampire countered with a growl. "*You made an oath.*"

"She broke hers," Ben argued. Their interactions remind me of when I was younger, and I used to bicker with my siblings. This must be how my mum used to feel. "I'm under a new oath. It is not to her but *her*." His eyes met mine. "I protect her." His eyes returned to that of the vampire. "You hurt her."

"*N...*" Ben had his hand gripped around the vampire's throat before he could finish whatever he was going to say. Ben holds the vampire up for a few seconds before the vampire snatches Ben's wrist and rips it off.

Vampire blood sprayed everywhere but if the loss of a limb hurt Ben, he didn't show it. The vampire didn't fall over or gag despite the fact that its throat has been crushed. The neck made crunching noises and it twisted and contorted until its back to normal. I resisted the urge to throw up. It just handed Ben back his hand. Ben reattached his hand and it healed up instantly. "Thanks for the hand."

The vampire laughed with an amiable smile. "Anytime, brother." It laid back onto my sofa. I still couldn't move. Even the crushing of its vocal cords, didn't release me. "You aren't leaving here, are you?"

"No," Ben confirmed. "And release *her*."

The vampire stood in front of me before I could blink. "*You're free,*"

My body relaxed, able to move once again. I punched the vampire in the jaw. It didn't move and my hand *hurt.* "Jesus Christ!"

The vampire blinked at me incredulously. "If you weren`t under his protection, I`d eat you, witch."

"Noted," I snarled. "Get out of my house." I pointed towards the door.

"Hardly a house…" The vampire protested, his tone surprisingly offended. "You`d kick me out?"

"You compelled me to do whatever you said, broke into my home and you hurt my dog away!" Honestly, Sergeant seemed fine. She was still growling but she was calmer now that Ben was here and more so since the vampire was no longer touching me.

"He was biting me!"

"Sergeant is a girl!" I shouted.

"Oh," The vampire turned to the still-growling dog. "I`m sorry for misgendering you, Miss." I blinked in surprise. The vampire turned back to Ben. "We should go. We need to talk." Ben disappeared and the vampire turned back to me. I tensed. If it wants to hurt me, now would be the time. Why did I have to sass the vampire? "He`s going to kill you, Adria." I couldn`t help but shiver. "He`ll kill you by accident or when his mind slips. It will destroy him all over again before he inevitably forgets who you are… Just another ghost whispering madness in his ear." I hadn`t realised how much its words upset me before I felt tears dripping onto my chest. "Don`t ever turn your back on him." The vampire then disappeared out the door.

I let out a shaky sigh of relief, still feeling sick with the knowledge that a creature that could have killed me if Ben hadn`t got there in time could just enter my home. I locked every door and window in the caravan before I fell back onto the sofa, sobbing.

This is too much! This is all just too much! I`m sixteen years old. I should be grieving the relationship destroyed by my back-stabbing boyfriend, not fighting witches, and acting as witness in an argument between vampire siblings. Why do I have to be the one dealing with this shit? Why did it have to be me?

The words echoed in my mind like a chant. It felt like I was losing everything: Adria was gone, Mason betrayed me, Sage was so injured that I was frightened a strong wind could blow his life away, and I knew that I couldn't trust Ben no matter how much I wanted to.

Get up. My mind ordered with a snarl. *Get the fuck up. You aren't done yet. This isn't over yet.*

I wiped the tears away. Sergeant was resting her head on my lap. How long has she been there with me? "Good girl," I smile, ruffle her fur, and stand up to pick up the stone and the stick that rested on the floor where the vampire had first grabbed me. I hadn't even realised that I'd dropped them until that moment.

Hastily, I marched to my room and the grimoire flipped open. The spell was simple. Hold them together and just project your power onto it. I didn't even need words. Who knew there was magic like that? I sat there for seconds with my eyes closed before I felt the change: the surge of power like electricity coursing through my veins. The stick moulded in my hands, feeling like damp clay, no longer resembling wood at all. It shifted and contorted in my open hands. When I felt it dry, I opened my eyes to look at it.

It was beautiful. The wood was darker than when I picked it up; auburn and wrapped around itself and the stone as if they'd never been apart. It even had a handle that fit my small hand perfectly. In my hands, it felt right, like an extension of my very being. Even though it rested in my burnt palm, it didn't hurt at all.

The grimoire flipped to the page about creating wards. You draw the symbols with the tip of your wand, they should glow white and then disappear. I looked at my wand.

The first spell was going to use with my wand was to keep my best (only) friend from coming into my home.

Gods, I feel like a dick.

I wish it could be different.

I wish a lot of things could be different.

I made my way around my home, tracing the runes from the grimoire into the sides of the caravan. The grimoire said that no vampire could enter unless it was invited. I guess that must be where the myth comes from.

Sage was still fast asleep. Somehow, he had managed to sleep through the whole vampire situation. I have no idea how it was even possible to sleep through all that. He had woken up earlier (though I only knew that because of the empty bowl) so at least I know he isn`t in a coma or anything. I place the bowl in the sink in the kitchen to wash up later, before returning to my room.

Perhaps I should try and find some better defensive spells considering the first two don`t seem to be helping me at all. How else could I go up against the witch?

Take out the witch, save the werewolf, stop the cult. What could go wrong?

I flipped through the grimoire to try and find some more spells that could fight the witch. The ones I chose involved more enchanted objects. I did find a spell that would tattoo me, but David would freak if I tried that. If I was going into the woods again, I was not going to be unprepared this time.

The sun began to set, and the sky looked like it was made of fire. The witch was waiting for me in the tree line. She hadn't bothered with the glamour this time and her face was even more slashed up than from the last time I saw it. My first thought was that it was probably from Ben, but it could have been from the werewolf.

What if the werewolf had been let out?

She smiled, her teeth were brown and rotting. "So, the little witch got her first wand... Isn't that cute?" She holds up her hand. "*Mortis*," I smirked and reach into my collar and revealed a bumblebee necklace. "Oh, an anti-hex charm. Clever girl," She giggled but it didn't sound happy. It sounded irritable. "It won't last forever girl... Enough magic *presses* against it and it will shatter like glass."

I know. That's why I needed to finish this quickly. "*Thorns,*" The spell rushed through the wand and sliced into her gaunt flesh. It cut far deeper than any spell I'd done before. The wand is working. "*Hephaestus` Flame.*" The witch held up her hands, muttering something I couldn't hear. Our magics pressed against each other, pushing for dominance and it felt like fire on my skin. She's stronger than me and she pushed it back towards me. I am losing. I may be able to use more magic than before, but I was still no match for her. I had two choices; either drop the spell and moved or let her overpower me and get a face full of fire. I dropped the spell and dodged hers. "*Shatter,*" My aim was perfect, and I cast the spell before she had time to adjust her aim. It's a perfect hit.

The collar shattered into splinters, exploding outwards. I ducked, dodging the splinters as best I could but several lodge themselves into my flesh. She's free. The witch blinked in surprise. "You... You freed me."

"Yes," I told her. "You're free. You can leave this place."

She cackled a bone-chilling laugh. "Oh no, it`s not over yet." She turned and waved as she walked away. "Tell Veneman I will see her soon." She stopped and raised her hand. "Oh, and I suggest you keep an eye out for that vampire of yours. Not all the missing persons reports in this shitty little town are due to Veneman`s cult."

I followed her into the woods, but she dissolved into the darkness before I could catch up. Do I turn back, or do I keep going?

Deciding that I`d continue, I meandered through the trees until I reached Ben`s shack. Maybe he`s here. Maybe his vampire friend was. Deciding it was worth a look, I entered the shack. It was empty. There was a bloody trail where the body had been dragged out, but it split in two different directions. One headed towards the school and the other headed further into the woods.

You don`t want to follow it. You know you won`t like what you find. I followed the trail further into the woods. The world around me felt colder the longer I followed the trail. Was it just the world getting colder or was it the dread bubbling in my stomach? I was following the footprints and the bloody trail for what felt like an age. I had never been so deep into the woods. I didn`t even realise that they went this far.

Then a smell hit my nose and I nearly doubled over right there. *What on Gaia`s green Earth is that smell?* I ventured further, covering my mouth and nose with my sleeve, trying to block out the smell. *I wish I`d brought a scarf to cover my face with.*

I made it into a clearing. *I wish I hadn`t.* There was Ben. His vampiric friend was gone. So many of the people who`d been going missing… People I had thought the cult had killed… People that hadn`t been reported as missing… They were here. They were piled up, dead. Dead bodies lying there like a pile of dolls from child`s toy box. It was a mountain of death. As if the universe wanted to make sure that I knew it was Ben's doing, he was gulping blood from the neck of a familiar person: Mrs Wesley.

Horror shook my body and I threw up into the closest bush and my head spun. "Little One?" Ben looked up from the mangled corpse beneath him.

"What fuck have you done?" I blurted, clinging onto a tree trunk for support. My knees were shaking so much that I thought I might fall over.

Was this fear? No. My body was a cocktail of grief, anger, sadness, and horror. I knew that I should be afraid. I should be more than terrified but I couldn't. He was my friend and I couldn't be frightened of him. I couldn't decide what the grief and sadness was more directed at. Was it the grief of these people's death or was it the grief of the knowledge that Ben was the one to kill them? Was it the grief in knowing that my best friend…? He has killed people before. I knew that but the knowledge and the visual were two completely different things.

"I'm a vampire, Little One." He replied.

You hunt monsters. Are you going to kill your best friend? You know you should.

I know I should. It's not as if he's going to stop killing people unless someone stops him. But I can't. Saying nothing, I turned around to walk away. He's going to kill people, but I can't be the one to kill him. Somebody is going to have to stop him one day. It isn't going to me. I just can't.

Just when I thought that school couldn't get any worse, it did.

Once again, when I entered the building, people were staring and whispering. There's no point in delaying it. I strode over to the STEM team. They'd been terrified of me since the first incident, avoiding me in class with wide, frightened eyes. That felt like a lifetime ago and in a way it was. How much had changed since then? How many people had died since then? "So, what's the rumour?"

Seamus trembled and looking between each other. "Y-you ch-cheated on M-Mason w-w-with Rupert b-b-before h-he d-died." Of course, I did. "And…" And? There's an 'and'?! "Th-they say y-y-you ac-accepted m-money f-from him a-and others…"

"Others?" I demanded, my fists clenching.

"Grant," Of course. "R-Rupert's dad," *What?* "Mr Small…"

"*Ew!*" I blurted, unable to stop myself. "Are there more on that list?" The boys nodded. "I don't want to know. Let me guess, Delilah?" They confirmed it again. "Is Grant confirming this?" They nodded again. "Is," I hesitated. I didn't really want the answer to this question but I had to know. "Is Mason?"

"I'm sorry, Kelsey." Seamus told me. "He's with Delilah and they're discussing the *romantic tale* of how you cheated on him and *Delilah comforted him* afterwards."

I felt sick. I want to go and confront them. I want to scream at Mason, and I want to knock Delilah's teeth out but what would be the point in that? She'd won. She'd warned me. This time I had no proof of anything and honestly, I wasn't sure if I cared about the rumours. People could think what they wanted. What really hurt was that *Mason* helped spread them.

I saved his life. I'd expect this behaviour from Delilah but not Mason!

I headed to tutor and sat in my usual spot. *Just try and sit in your usual spot, Mason Baird*, I challenged in my head. Usually tutor is pretty full already but it wasn't today. *Probably because they're all in the canteen, listening to Delilah's stories.*

I pulled out a notebook from my bag and started mapping out plans.

"How are you, Kelsey?" Mr Clarke inquired once he entered the room.

Crappy, the rumour is that I'm exchanging sex for money and my cheating, scumbag of an ex-boyfriend is helping to spread it. "I'm ok," I replied with the most realistic smile I could manage, shutting the notebook. It was probably best that my classmates don't see that. "How are you?"

"I'm ok," The bell rang, and people trailed in. Mason eyed me the second he entered the room. I ignored him. He went and sat with Delilah, giving me the kicked puppy look from across the room. I resisted the urge to glare at him and the urge to shout at him. Then Mr Clarke spoke. "Kelsey, you need to head over to inclusion."

"Uh... Ok... Um, thanks." I frowned. *Fuck.* I picked up my bag and headed towards inclusion.

The fire had spread through much of the tech building so one side of it was fenced off but *somehow* inclusion was completely untouched, despite the fact it was directly next door to where I set the fire. That has to be more than shitty luck.

I hesitated outside and stepped into a corner, out of sight of passers-by. I pulled out my phone (that I should have turned off earlier) and turned on the video-camera. I side-stepped into the girls bathroom and pulled out toilet paper. I covered my phone, just leaving the camera partly visible. Hopefully, it will be enough to keep the phone hidden while recording everything. I don't know how much use recording everything will be, but it was nice to know I'd have some sort of alibi or back-up.

I opened the door to Inclusion, made my way inside and there sat Veneman. Inclusion was *empty*. It's never empty at this time of day. It's *always* full. Mrs Veneman always had people crammed into the cubicles like prisoners, scolding them over the half-wall in between them and her desk. Today, it was just Veneman's cronies and... Mrs Marley. She was wearing fluorescent pink high heels and a highlighter-yellow silk blouse... I guess she finally gave into peer pressure.

Everything had been fixed. There were no scratch marks or splinters. It looked completely normal besides how empty it was.

The second I stepped into that room, I wasn't a student, I was the enemy. They circled me like hyenas, their lipstick-smiles promising malevolence and spite. "You should have accepted my offer." Veneman cackled. I froze. Her goons are behind me now.

I hated to admit it but whatever she'd been doing, she looked like she was over a decade younger. The wrinkles on her skin were completely gone and her hair was far more luscious than last time I saw it.

"Why can't you be like every other mortality-obsessed person and go on a quest around England for the fountain of youth?" I crossed my arms lightly across my chest.

"Because killing people is so much fun." She replied, her eyes appearing almost reptilian. *Eyes are windows to the soul.* "Get her!"

They pounced like hyenas. I yanked my wand out of my pocket I held it out in front of me. "Don't think I won't use this!" I snap. They laughed maniacally and all held up their left arm. They each wore identical bracelets. Anti-hex charms. "Well, fuck," They continued their stampede and I aimed for one of the charms. It's worth a try. "*Shatter,*" It doesn't. The charm bounced off and smacks the wand out of my hand.

Veneman snatched it up and shoved it into her desk drawer, slamming it shut. "I'll save that for later." They grabbed my arms and opened the door, before flinging me down the stairs. I shrieked. It felt like I hit every bone in my body as I tumbled down. "It's time for phase two, Adria." Veneman smirked from the top of the stairs. "We don't *have* to kill everyone in this school... But we will... After all, why waste such *power* for the life of any of these brats? We'll save you until last and you can *watch* your classmates die and know that you failed to stop it."

"I'll stop you," I groaned, wincing as I picked myself up from the ground to glare up at her.

She cackled like a witch and held up my enchanted key (that one of her goons must have stolen in the struggle) like a trophy. "You need to get out first. Once I shut this door, the enchantment will keep it shut. You can watch the action from that mirror." She pointed a perfectly manicured finger and I turned. The mirror was seriously fancy-looking, and it shimmered to show a birds-eye view of the school. "And keep Fluffy company, won't you? He's been ever so lonely since you abandoned him here." I turned to see a dishevelled man, suspended from the wall with silver chains, hissing and burning his skin. The werewolf.

I moved to charge up the stairs but the second I put pressure on my ankle, I fell over. Veneman laughed and shut the door.

Fourteen

The man (werewolf) didn't have a mark on him (besides the areas under the chains). Though his flesh sizzled and smoked, but he didn't make a sound, not even a whimper. How long had they kept him here? Had they kept him here since I trapped him? He was a big man with blue eyes... not like Ben's. They were a smoky blue. Like a bright blue sky made pastel from a snowstorm. What little clothes he was wearing were ripped and burnt to tatters. "For the record, my name isn't 'Fluffy'."

"Oh, I uh... I didn't think it was." I shrugged off my blazer and hesitantly stepped forward. I wrapped it around his hips as best I could without touching him.

"Thank you," He nodded to the blazer. I smiled awkwardly and backed away. "You're Adria," I tensed. "You're the one who imprisoned me." He pushed against the chains and I took another step back. "Thank you,"

I blinked. "What for?"

"If it wasn't for you, I would have killed many people last night." He began, his voice sad and sincere. "That infernal *fucking* witch... I need to go home. If I'm not there, the tree is undefended... I need to get out of here."

"What tree?" I inquired.

"You're new at this, aren't you?" I nodded. "The tree is the Heartfelt Tree. There are a few scattered across the world. There is at least one in every universe, in every reality. They have incredible power, and if someone like Veneman got hold of it, there is no telling what kind of chaos she could unleash on the world. I am the guardian of one of the Heartfelt trees in this reality. In a place called Persephone's Garden."

"Like the goddess?" I blinked.

He grinned. "Hades built it for her, and she grew the place… So, the legend goes."

"Where is this place?" I continued.

"Scotland." I wasn't expecting that answer. I kind of expected him to say Greece. He wasn't Scottish. In fact, I was pretty sure he wasn't English either. I didn't recognise that accent. He was also very tanned for someone who lives in Scotland… Not that it really mattered. "I need to get back there. The only one there to defend it at the moment is my twelve-year-old son. He's a good boy but he's no warrior."

"I'd love to help," I told him. "But I don't even know how to get *myself* out of here. As you said, I'm new at this. I may be a witch but I'm a pretty shitty one."

He laughed. "Do you think that because you couldn't beat Daphne?" I frowned. Who? "The witch who imprisoned me. Because I should tell you… She's over four-hundred years old. Witches can live for hundreds of years if they're clever enough and power only grows with age in your kind. You're what, sixteen?" I nodded. "An average sixteen-year-old witch that would come up against a werewolf like me would have been ripped apart in seconds. An average hundred-year-old witch that fought against Daphne would have died. For a little witch your age, your abilities are impressive. If you were the same age as Daphne, she wouldn't have tried to fight you at all. You are far more powerful than you believe."

"Veneman took my wand." I protested.

"She's a sixty-something-year-old woman so afraid of a teenage girl that she had to imprison her in a dungeon below the school with a werewolf and she still felt like she needed to disarm you. What does that tell you?" The werewolf continued.

I hadn't thought about it that way. "I- I frighten her?" I couldn't help but be reminded of 'Interview with a Vampire', but this felt more like 'Therapy with a Werewolf'.

"That whole speech at the top of the stairs was a power-play. She's trying to look stronger than she actually is, make you think you have no chance." He insisted. "She still knows that you could win this and she's terrified about what will happen when you realise that too." He looked me dead in the eyes. "*Melt the chains.*"

"How?" If I used my fire spell, it would burn him.

"Use that fire spell of yours. If it hits me, I'll heal but these chains will melt away. You need to hurry. They're sealing the school." I turned to look at the mirror. The cult was in full robes, walking around and closing all the doors and gates with thick chains and dozens of padlocks. And there were more of them than I'd ever seen.

"She's locking everyone in." I blurted. Not missing a beat, I turned and focused everything on the chain. "*Hephaestus` Flame,*" He groaned but I didn't stop until the silver was dripping onto the floor, he ripped it away.

"Clever girl," He grinned, the burns healing up instantly. "Do a healing spell on that ankle of yours and we can get you out of here."

"I... I can't do healing spells." I told him.

"What?"

"I can't do healing spells." I repeated. "I've tried a dozen times... On myself, on my familiar... It never works."

"Your name... You can't..." Fear flickered in his eyes for a fraction of a second, but it evaporated so quickly that I almost thought it was my imagination. His fists balled and his

248

jaw clenched, and his eyes filled with grief. "You… You`re just a little girl…" He choked

"I`m sixteen." I snorted. "Hardly a little girl."

He looked as if he was in agony before he unclenched his fists. Why is he so upset? "You can do anything you want. You can *be* anyone you want to *be*. You *can* heal yourself. Try."

I frowned but rested my hands over my ankle. It would be easier if I had water but that wasn`t an option here. "Apollo, help me heal." My ankle did not change. I couldn`t help but be a little frustrated. "Apollo, help me heal."

"You`re getting frustrated." The werewolf cautioned. "Healing magic requires calm energy. Try to remain calm." I genuinely cannot recall the last time I was calm. Also, I am in an underground dungeon with a semi-naked werewolf while my teachers sealed off the school with the promise to sacrifice me. Probably best that I don`t look in the mirror right now. *Calm… Calm…* How do people do 'calm'? The werewolf laughed. "Right… Ok, how about we make a splint?" He ripped off the sleeve of my blazer, snatched a fancy-looking feathered pen off the table and strapped it to my ankle. I couldn`t help but think I looked like I was trying to cosplay as Percy Jackson and failing epically. "Perhaps it will work better when we get your wand back?"

I doubt that but I nodded anyway. I turned to head up the stairs when something in the mirror caught my eye. "Crap,"

"What is it?" The werewolf inquired, following my gaze to the mirror. "Oh, that`s not good."

The witch had entered the building. "If she finds you, she`ll have control over you again, won`t she?"

"Again?" The werewolf snorted. "If she flexes her magic enough at this distance, she`ll have me."

"I know a counter-curse."

"With a witch as powerful as Daphne, the counter-curse will only be helpful if I can get far away from her afterwards. It would only buy me time to leave."

"Ok," I thought for a moment. "I find my wand and I could try a teleportation spell to get you back home. Scotland's far enough away that she won't be able to control you, right?"

He nodded but furrowed his eyebrows. "But don't you need help here?"

"Yes, but if she controls you again, then I've already lost." I pointed out. "I can't beat you when you're all wolfed-out."

"Wolfed-out..." He chuckled. He gave me that amused look an adult gives a child when they say something adorable. "Right. Ok, I bust us out of here and I break the gates. You then try to teleport me out of here."

"That sounds risky."

"It is." He agreed. "You game?"

I grinned. "I'm game."

He helped me up the stairs and once we got to the top, he slammed against the hatch. It groaned and a pale blue forcefield appeared. "She wasn't lying about that enchantment but look there." He pointed. There were cracks in the shield. "She can't produce magic powerful enough for this to hold. I slam against it for a while and it will shatter."

"That seems to be the case for a lot of enchantments." I stated.

"Magic may not have limits but the amount a person's body can use does." He slammed against the forcefield again, making the whole chamber shake. The cracks spread. "Human bodies aren't built for this kind of magic. She can't use as much of it in one go as you can." He slammed against it again and the cracks got larger and deeper. I doubted it could hold against one more.

I was right. It shattered under the next one like glass. The shards fell like blossom and then melted away into a glitter-like substance, flying away into nothing. "I like that the majority of her magic is self-cleaning." He snorted at my comment again with an amused grin, before pushing the lid of the hatch up. He jumped through it and then pulled me up into the creepy little room, one-handed. Nobody could say that the werewolf wasn't strong in human-form. He turned to the door and kicked it. I expected it to fall down but the power of his kick, launched it across the room, toppling to the floor as it bounced of the entrance.

Inclusion was still empty. The ominous feeling twisted at my stomach. The werewolf scanned the room, still blocking my body with is, before we entered. He still stood next to me like a bodyguard as I limped over to Mrs Veneman's desk and I pulled open the drawer. My wand wasn't there. "Shit. Do you think she has my wand on her?"

"Probably," He nodded. "Don't worry about that."

"How can I not worry about that?" I blurted. "It gives her a power boost!"

"*Really,*" The werewolf continued, moving back over towards the creepy little room. "Don't worry about that." He jumped back down the hole. I limped over to see what he was doing just as he rematerialized in seconds with the mirror. "We can use this." He knocked everything off Veneman's desk. I'm not going to lie, hearing Veneman's computer smash on the floor made me grin. "Right... The cult is all around the perimeter of the school." He pointed. "Can you see?"

"Yes," I peered closer. "They're doing the barrier spell, aren't they?"

"Yes," He confirmed. He could see it better than I could. "With all of them together, I may not be able to break the barrier but that vampire friend of yours... It definitely could. It's old enough and strong enough to shatter it. Can you contact him?"

I shook my head. "I'm not sure. I can call my brother who can wake my familiar... But Sage is injured, and I don't know if he can do it."

"Call him."

I pulled out my phone and turned off the camera. I scrolled through to my brothers number. "There's no signal."

The werewolf took my phone and examined it. "Veneman is blocking the reception. You can't contact the outside world via phone."

"Might be for the best." I sighed. "Ben has killed a lot of people."

"He's a vampire." The werewolf reminded me. "They've *all* killed a lot of people. I'm not saying it's the good guy. I can promise you it's not. Vampires kill people and I doubt it even sees you as much more than a pet," I flinched at that. I couldn't help it. I hope that's not how Ben sees me. "But if you have its loyalty: keep it. Sometimes it's better to have something big, bad, and powerful on your side. There are few things more dangerous than an old vampire." He hesitated. "But whatever you do, *don't trust it*. It's a vampire at the end of the day."

How do I contact Ben? "I could use a tracking spell. Theoretically, he could see me, and we could speak through it." I turned back to the mirror. "Where's Daphne?"

He searched the mirror and pointed. "She's there."

I froze. "We need to go... I need to go. You stay here... I need to get there."

He frowned. "Why? What's there?"

"That is my tutor. There are twenty teenagers and a teacher in that room." I watched in horror as Daphne blasted fire at the wall. Bricks flew through the air, smashing nearby windows. "Shit! I need to stop her!"

I darted towards the door. "When it rains, it pours." The werewolf sighed. "I'll keep eyes from above."

"Thanks," I said at the door before walking outside. Immediately I could see the cult members around the fence and students sprinting around blindly. I don't blame them. They've heard a loud bang, seen a blast of fire tear through the building while the fire alarms scream like they're being tortured.

In every fire drill we were calm, but this was anarchy.

I weaved and pushed through the crowd, ignoring the pain from my ankle and the elbows slamming into my shoulders and sides. I stumbled but I didn't fall over. Students tried to get through the gates and away from the blaze, but they bounced off the forcefield like tennis balls against a wall.

The cult members then turned and pulled out scythes from under their cloaks. They each looked like the grim reaper as marched forward in unison. Students scrambled back, their expressions a cocktail of fear and shock. "Mr Small, why are you…?" They swung down the scythes. Blood sprayed through the air as students fall. The majority of the kids darted back away but others couldn't move fast enough and splashes of blood splattered up.

The world was shocked into silence.

What the fuck did I just see?

They just murdered students! "Run!" I shrieked as children scrambled in all directions, knocking people down.

The werewolf was outside and next to me before I could think what to do next. "They just started killing students. They're coming from all sides. Where's a big space with few doors?"

The sports hall was easily large enough, but it had far too many doors. The canteen had massive windows that could be easily smashed in. The next largest room had been the food tech room but that had burned down. Inclusion was out of the question… That left the new dance studio. There were two sets of double doors, but it's large, the windows were too high up for people to get through and there were mirrors a long one side. Maximum visibility. "The new dance studio. How can I get all these people there?"

He just nodded and advanced forward. The cults kept swinging and people couldn`t move out of the way to evade death. People crushed other people in their desperation to get away. What spell could I do to help? I couldn`t think of a spell that could take out the cult members without hitting a student?

The werewolf doesn`t have that problem. He leapt over the swarm of students in a single bound. The ground trembled when his monstrous form landed. His arms and hands thickened, claws sprouting from his fingers, thick dark hair sprouted along his arms. He ripped into a cult member, dropping their mangled corpse in front of the others. Mrs June? Mrs June had killed a student?

It was as if the world was frozen. Everyone stared as this non-human man stood in front of the wall of murderers, unsure whether he was their saviour or just another monster. "Get to the dance studio! Hurry!" Students surged forward like a wave of chaos. When the cult started to march forward, the werewolf took one step forwards too. The cult hesitated. He had just ripped Mrs June in half in a second. They no longer had control over him, and he`s stronger and faster than any of them. They looked to each other nervously and then began to march forward, swinging the scythes at the werewolf. He reached up and smashed the scythe closest to him with ease. "I`ve got this area. Go! Save those kids!"

"Thank you!" I called back.

Daphne or Veneman?

I turned towards the burning building. Daphne was burning down my tutor. I may not have ever gotten on well with the majority of people in my year but if there was one person trapped in that building then I`ve got to save them from a fiery death. If not, then perhaps I could get Daphne to leave or at least lead her away from the werewolf.

Yeah, I know. Fat chance.

With the forcefield up, if the werewolf turned under the control of the witch, nobody would make it out of here alive. It would be a massacre. Of that, I was certain.

I snatched up the nearest fire extinguisher and entered the building. If David found out that I'd willingly walked into a burning building, he'd crucify me. I fumbled with the extinguisher and I sprayed down as much fire as I could get to.

Daphne stood in the centre of the corridor as it burned around her. "Adria," She sang. "You took your time."

"Why are you here?" I demanded.

"I'm not here for you." Daphne frowned. "Not really... You see Veneman wants immortality. She wants to awaken *Him,* so I'll kill everyone first... She will not awaken Him, and she will not get her reward."

"Or you could just save every one?" I suggested.

She laughed. "This way she can't get her wish and I'll gain more power." She grinned. Geez, she needs to learn how to floss. "You're with me or you're against me, girl. Come on; you know these people don't deserve your protection. How many of them have hurt you in one way or another? How many of them ignored it when they saw that little shit lay his hands on you? How many of them spread those rumours about you? Think of that *boy* who betrayed your trust, the Delaney girl who'd do anything to spite you, all those people who abandoned you in your grief. Why protect them? *Kill them*, take their souls, grow in power."

"No,"

Daphne smirked. "You'll learn one day." She blasted flame at me, and I sprayed the fire extinguisher back at her.

It wasn't normal fire. It lit up the foam in seconds and I ducked. I had forgotten about the pain in my ankle until that point, making me yelp and stumble, falling onto my already bruised and cut knees. The splint held properly but it *hurt.*

Thankfully, I landed under the blast, fire spreading inches above my head. "*Artemis, protector of women,*" I whispered. "*I ask for your assistance.*" My eyesight seemed to sharpen and immediately my eyes were drawn towards every weak point on Daphne. My eyes flickered to anything that could work as a weapon. It was as if the fire extinguisher was glowing. I snatched up the extinguisher and tossed it through the air towards Daphne's neck. Shocked that I hadn't used magic, her eyes widened with shock. Panicked, she shot her magic at it; a thick, purple smoke to knock the fire extinguisher away but she wasn't fast enough and the extinguisher slammed into her jaw. She fell backwards, landing hard on her back. The shock on her face was quickly replaced with anger.

She floated upwards and landed on her feet. "*Mortis!*" She shrieked at me. The magic bounced off my necklace, but she kept pressing.

"*Thorns!*" I countered and she dropped her hex to block my spell.

"You like quaint spells, huh?" She revealed a venomous smile. "Here's a quaint spell. *Zeus' light!*" A bolt of lightning ripped through the air, launching me backwards. It felt like every cell in my body was on fire. The necklace shattered and I clash into the wall of lockers. I bounced, landing directly onto my face. The lockers crashed down on top of me. Fuck! That *hurt*. I pushed against the lockers, but I was pinned. Daphne laughed and strolled forward, knocking more lockers on top of me as she did so. "Now, I don't know what its like to be human." She began. "I never was one, but I wonder… Is your body witch enough to survive the smoke long enough for somebody to save you?" Who's going to save me? The werewolf cannot and will not come this way and there were more people in this school that hated me than those who even tolerated me. Nobody would walk through a burning building to save me. There's nobody coming. Daphne knew that. You could tell from the smug look on her face and her earlier words echoed in my mind like a curse. "Enjoy the barbeque." She laughed and disappeared into the smoke.

I pushed at the lockers, but I couldn't even see how many were piled on top of me. The fire was getting closer and closer. Every second, they grew faster and faster. If the smoke didn't kill me then the fire would burn me alive. I squirmed and the lockers slipped and landed on my ankle. I shrieked. That hurt like Hell. I struggled to get my foot loose but I couldn't dislodge it. I yanked at my shirt, shrugging it off to wrap it around my face.

I reached out and grabbed a hold of my magic and pushed. Dark red dust spilled out and pressed at the lockers. I couldn't move to look at where my magic is moving. It was surprisingly difficult to do magic if you can't see what you're doing. It made this far more challenging. Come on, come on… Then I heard someone rush in. "Is anyone left in here? Hello!"

"Help!" I coughed. Footsteps. Someone was running towards me. Who? By that point they were just a large grey silhouette in the smoke. With the assistance of my magic, they pushed the lockers up enough for me to slip out. They pulled me to my feet, and we rushed out of the burning building.

"Are you ok?" It's Mr Clarke. I nodded. "Let's get to the new dance studio."

My head hurt and it felt like I was walking through tar. I unwrapped my shirt from my face and pulled it back on.

"Adria!" Called a familiar voice.

"Adria?" Mr Clarke questioned as we turned to look at where the voice was coming from. His eyes widened to the size of saucers at the sight of a semi-naked man running towards us. He tried to manoeuvre me behind him, but I stepped aside.

"I- I'm here." I choked.

The werewolf rushed over, his eyes scanning my frame with concern. He moved closer so I could use his body as a crutch. "Are you ok? What happened?"

"I lost," I replied. "I had to be dragged out of the building."

"I`m sorry," He told me.

"It`s fine."

"Who are you?" Mr Clarke demanded. It was fair enough that he was concerned. A stranger had just run over to us, barely clothed and addressed me by the name that belonged to my dead best friend and his former student.

The werewolf eyed my teacher sceptically and then looked back at me. "Is he one of *them?*"

I shook my head. "Not a chance."

The werewolf nodded and turned back to Mr Clarke. He held out his hand for Mr Clarke to shake. "My name is Lycaon Cerulean. I was kidnapped by Veneman and she had me chained up below inclusion. Your student rescued me. Nice to meet you." Mr Clarke shook his hand, eyes wide and startled. I hadn`t realised just how massive Lycaon`s hands were until they had consumed Mr Clarke`s. Lycaon turned back to me. "Expel the smoke from your lungs. You can use your magic."

"Magic?" Mr Clarke frowned, looking more concerned by the second. The smoke must have concealed the magic when he saved me. He probably thought that Lycaon was crazy. Who could blame him? Lycaon was half-naked, claimed to be chained up below inclusion, addressed me by the name of my dead best friend and was talking about magic.

Deciding that there was no point in trying to hide my magic right now considering there`s enough crazy stuff going on and if Mr Clarke wanted to keep people safe then it would be better for him to understand what was really happening... right?

I pulled at the magic and the red dust twisted like smoke as it slipped down my throat and entered my lungs. It wasn't as uncomfortable as I thought it would have been, with a slight burn on the way down. My coughing stopped and the grey smoke pushed out from my lungs, shortly followed by the red dust.

Mr Clarke's eyes widened but he said nothing.

"How are you feeling?" Lycaon asked.

My head was clear, and I felt... fine. Tired but fine. "Ready for round two. And yourself?"

He nodded. "They got past me. I noticed Daphne wasn't in that burning building anymore, so I had to come after you." My head was spinning so much that I hadn't even noticed he'd been carrying the mirror until he held it up in front of me.

"Thanks," It was nice to know that he'd been looking out for me despite the dangers to himself. "So, what's the plan?"

"Get in contact with that vamp of yours." Lycaon suggested. "It breaks down the forcefield. Let the innocents get out and set up the forcefield again."

"Sounds like a plan." I agreed and turned back to a stunned Mr Clarke. "You need to get to the new dance studio. Protect them. Don't let in Veneman or any of the other guidance managers, Mr Small or any of Delilah Delaney's squad." It felt genuinely weird giving my teacher orders. "Those are the only members I know of but there are more. There are many more. *Be careful.* If you have a bad feeling; listen to it."

"What about you?" He inquired, concerned.

"I need to find a blue light of some kind..." Where the fuck can I find a blue light here?

"Would a Bunsen burner work?" He suggested.

"Maybe," I had no idea, but it was the best plan I've got. "But the science block has burned down. Where would I get a Bunsen burner?"

"They've ordered more in because of the recent break-ins." Mr Clarke explained. "They're probably still in reception." Then he thought about it. "But there is nowhere to plug them in..." He scratched his head. "There are some blue lampshades in the staffroom. Will they work?"

"Definitely," I turned back to Lycaon. "Take him to the new dance studio and come back up to..." I looked around for a map of the school, only to find it right behind me. There was one on the wall behind me, so I ripped it off (I've always wanted to do that) and held it out in front of Lycaon. "That's the staffroom. Meet me there. Take out as many of them as you can on the way."

"With pleasure," He cracked his knuckles with a grin. They meandered off towards the new space, taking the mirror with them.

I made my way in the opposite direction, towards the English block. I had just entered the building when I halted. I could hear something. I pressed my head against the wall.

There's someone in the library.

I got to my knees, wincing at the strain on my ankle as I lowered myself, wincing again from the pain from my banged-up knees. I crawled past the door (low enough that nobody could see me through the window) and then hobbled as best I could towards the end of the corridor. Just as I reached the end, I was greeted with a scythe. I stumbled back, almost tripping over my own feet as a short, cloaked figure stepped out from around the corner. "Did you miss me?"

Seth. "Not even a little bit." I snarled.

"You know..." He grinned, knocking his hood from his head to reveal that ugly mug of a face. "I could spare you..." He stepped forward. "If you surrender and you..." He wiggled his eyebrows. "If you come with me into that office," He pointed to the deputy head's office. "And have some *fun*."

I genuinely wanted to stab him in his face. I knew it was wrong to kill people, to want to hurt people, but I wanted him dead on the ground at my feet. "You think," I growled, clenching my fist so hard that it almost hurt. "That I would do *anything* with you after what you did to Precious."

He chuckled. "You didn`t even like her."

Precious wasn`t my favourite human being but she never did anything to hurt me and she did not deserve that. "She didn`t deserve what *you* did to her and there is no way that you could justify what *you* did to her. Go fuck yourself!"

He sighed. "Why would I do that when you`re here?"

"If you`re trying to stop me from burning you alive then you aren`t making a very convincing argument."

Seth chuckled and stepped forward. It took every ounce of my self-control not to step backwards. "You won`t do that. You don`t have the stomach to kill anything."

I rolled my eyes. "I don`t have time for this." I held up my hand. He didn`t even flinch, just arched an overplucked eyebrow. Ok, he`s asking for it. "*Hephaestus` Flame.*" I didn`t put much power behind it so the flame was small and precise. His cloak lit up (nothing else) and his eyes widened to the size of dinner plates. He squealed and dropped his scythe, rushing around blindly as if he could outrun the fire attached to his back. I limped forward, picked up the abandoned scythe and whacked him over the back of the head with the blunt end. He crashed to the floor like a sack of potatoes. I ripped off the cloak and smothered the flames. I tied his hands together with the cloak`s charred remains.

I wanted to kick him in the nuts, but my ankle still hurt. I turned to keep going but hesitate. I took up the scythe again, swinging it as if I`m playing golf and smacked him in the nuts as hard as I could (with the blunt end). That`s going to hurt when he wakes up.

I couldn`t help but smile at the thought.

That was for Precious.

Anyone around must have heard his screaming. There's no point in being stealthy. They knew where I was. Using the scythe as a crutch, I scurried towards the doors that blocked the stairs and I shoved them open. I pushed up the stairs, wishing I could move faster on this stupid ankle. Nobody's on the stairs but I tried my best to be quiet. If there's anybody upstairs, there was a chance that they may not have heard Seth screaming.

Maybe.

Once I reached the top, I returned to my knees and crawled over to the first set of doors. I peered through the window and I didn't see anyone. I pushed to my feet. *Gods, that hurt. What have I done to that bloody ankle?* I opened the door.

In contrast to the rest of the school, the staffroom's door had no window, so I crept along the corridor up to the door. I pressed my ear against the door and listened. I couldn't hear anything but I'm wasn't taking any chances.

Unleashing a battle cry, I rushed into the room, scythe raised over my head. I was greeted by a terrified scream.

"No, please!" A desperate voice whimpered.

"Mrs Kent?" I lowered the scythe, breathing a sigh of relief. "Are you ok?"

She nodded. "I've been hiding in here since those people with scythes came."

"It's the guidance managers." I replied, running my fingers through my hair nervously. Somehow this conversation with my teacher felt weirder than the fact her colleagues wanted me dead. "And Delilah Delaney's friends. The headmaster is also involved a long with several other teachers and students. They've gone nuts."

She must have been in shock because she stood there silently blinking as I hobbled around the staffroom, picking up the four blue lamps I needed for the spell. I plugged them in and arranged them in a large square.

The staffroom kitchen area was so much nicer than the canteen or the student toilets for that matter. All the taps worked perfectly, the sink wasn't blocked, their paper towel dispenser was full, and they had two *full* soap dispensers! We were lucky if there was even one. I snatched up a mug with a ginger cat on it and filled it up three quarters of the way with water. I placed the mug in the middle, trying to not spill any of it (which was harder than it sounds when you're putting something on the floor with a dodgy ankle). I used the arm of the sofa to lower myself down into a sitting position. "W-what are you doing?" Mrs Kent stammered. She scurried across the room to sit near me.

"I am calling my friend to come and help us." I told her. *Keep your voice even and calm. She's freaking out already.* She gave me a concerned look (that I tried to ignore) but she said nothing. She watched me nervously as I began.

I held Ben's face in my mind. "*Hermes, help me find what's lost.*" I opened my eyes and the water shook and rippled. I could see him and his location perfectly. He's still surrounded by those corpses and Mrs Kent gasped, staring in horror at the disturbing scene of mangled bodies piled up in unnatural angles in the mug. "Ben," I called. I tried to sound soft and calm, but nerves infiltrated my voice like an army, and I swallowed down the urge to vomit. The horror and disgust at the scene hadn't faded and my brain still couldn't comprehend the horrors I was seeing all over again. "Ben, can you hear me?"

"Ben, that's what she used to call me." He replied, his voice calm and cool. "Little One? Where are you?"

"I'm at the school." I rambled, relieved that he could hear me. "I'm trapped in this forcefield thing. The cult has trapped everyone in the school. The witch is here, and I need help. Please may you come here and break down the forcefield, so everyone can get out?"

"Yes, yes," He agreed. There's something wrong with his voice. It made my entire body tense up. "I'll see you soon, *Little One.*"

Oh no.

The image rippled and faded away.

"What was that?" Mrs Kent breathed, her eyes tearing up slightly. "What just happened?"

They'd warned me.

I switched off the lamps, effectively cutting off the spell and pushed up to my feet. "I think I just let a wolf into the hen house."

Fifteen

Don`t ever turn your back on him.
Oh, and I suggest you keep an eye out for that vampire of yours.
'Friend' mean trust, but you can never trust me.
Everyone warned me.
Even Ben, himself, warned me.

Regardless of whether or not Ben would spare me, he would kill the people here and I had no idea how many. If my hunch`s correct and Ben wasn`t himself, I had no idea how we could stop him. I couldn`t and even Lycaon said that Ben was stronger than him.

More people were going to die and it`s all my fault.
I had to find Lycaon.

Grabbing the scythe to use as a walking stick, I rushed towards the door again. "Where are you going?" Mrs Kent asked, but it sounded more like a plea. She`s frightened and she had every right to be. She stumbled to her feet, her knees shaking so hard, you could almost hear them clanging together.

"I need to find Lycaon. He needs to know what`s going on." I explained. *And if Ben`s how I think he is, Lycaon`s the only one strong enough to slow him down.* "I need to take you to the new dance studio. You'll be safer there and I need to check that none of them have gotten in."

She latched onto my arm: her wide eyes desperate and pleading. "Don't go out there! They'll get you! The dance studio is too far! They'll catch you!"

"I have two weapons," I tried to keep my voice soothing instead of harsh, impatient, or panicked but it was hard. I held up the scythe. "This is the one I'd prefer to use. It's easily made non-lethal and can knock out even the biggest of assholes." As demonstrated by Seth. I rested the scythe against the sofa and held up my hand. "This one is the more powerful." I reached for my magic with my mind. "*Thorns,*" The nearby lamp sliced in half. Mrs Kent yelped, jumping away. "We'll be fine. You can have the scythe." I could handle walking without it, but it would slow us down. If that was the price of her safety, then so be it. Please don't let her be one of them because with the scythe she could chop me in two. Being dead would make saving my classmates a challenge. "Follow me."

She hesitantly took the scythe and we made our way towards the staffroom door. I pressed my head against it and then reached for the handle. I heard her suck in a breath behind me as I opened the door to reveal the empty hallway. We each breathed a sigh of relief. I stepped into the hallway, scanning left to right. Nobody's here so we ventured further. We made our way back towards those double doors and opened them. I stuck my head over the bannister to see if there was anyone there, and once I saw that it's still empty, we made our way downstairs.

My ankle hurt far more going down the stairs than it did going up. I couldn't help but feel nervous because if I fell down the stairs with this ankle and broke something, if I couldn't move then I'd be fucked.

There were so many things that could go wrong right now, and this is wasn't an exam I could re-sit or an essay I could rewrite. My mistakes would have a body count.

I turned to where I had left Seth. He was gone along with his cloak.

Clearly, I was better at spells than I was at tying people up.

Ok... Should I go around the theatre, through the sports hall or through the front and round?

Through the sport's hall was quickest, but the cult had effectively used that space to attack me many times before so that was probably not the best way to go.

The route around the theatre was a lot of open space and there wasn't many places to run or hide. It's a very set course and it would be easy to set a trap.

Around the front would be a ridiculously long route and it would take over twice the time as the other two. However, there was a myriad of places to run or hide and I could get her out of the way pretty easily if I need to.

Though it had its own risks, around the front would be the safest route... I hoped.

Now that I was certain of our route, we crept down the corridor. I couldn't see anybody anywhere. It was the kind of empty you only saw in post-apocalypse movies. The whole school was a ghost town. They must have been hiding in wait or maybe they were circling the new dance studio like vultures.

What if Lycaon had left them to find me? What if they were undefended? What if Daphne had found him?

You can't afford to think like that. Keep going.

I gestured for Mrs Kent to crouch and we crawled along the canteen wall. My eyes darted around and in an instant, I snatched Mrs Kent's hand and tugged her behind a table.

Laughter rang out, echoing across the school. I peeked out from behind the bench as Delilah and her goons Jennifer,

Regan, and Iris strolled by, chatting loudly. "I can't believe Seth is allowed to be one of us!" Delilah complained, kicking a stone at the wall.

"Yeah," Regan agreed. "He is such a creep."

"But a rich creep, though." Iris continued. "You got with any of the men in that family and you're set for life."

Delilah frowned and shrugged. "Maybe I should marry him." The girls laughed but stopped abruptly when they realised that she's completely serious. "What? As you said, if I marry him, I'll be set for life. And, when we bring Him back, and She rewards us, I'm going to live forever. My family's money will allow me to live through this lifetime but what about the next?" I couldn't help but think of all the damage she could do if she lived forever. She had done plenty of damage by age sixteen. What chaos could she cause if she reached Ben's age or older? "I marry Seth and I could live in luxury for the next ten lifetimes without working a day in my life."

"But he killed Precious…" Jennifer blurted, her disgust openly visible for a moment but she immediately covered it and went silent when the other girls glared at her.

"And I'll kill him too," Delilah flicked her hair up with a sickeningly sweet smile. "After we're married. I just have to play the part of the grieving widow for a while. I can get away with it, I'm sure. I mean… how many women do?"

"What about Mason?" Iris' eyes glinted and she licked her lips. "Don't you think he'll run back to Kelsey when you break it off?"

"Of course," Delilah played with her nails. "But she'll be dead before that happens, besides…" Her blue eyes glinted with malevolence and her lipstick smile widened. "He'll come back to me whenever I want. I can enjoy him out of sight of Seth until Seth's dead. Then Mason can be with me forever."

I *really* wanted to punch away that smug look. Why did I feel so protective of Mason? He betrayed me. Why should I care? But I did. I cared. *Fuck.* I will *never* get back together with him. There is no way in Hell, Heaven or Purgatory. I just wished that feelings would go away already. I didn't *want* them.

"You're so clever, Delilah!" Regan cooed and the other girls nodded.

She's smarter than people give her credit for.

"I know right?" Delilah preened. "I already know how I'm going to kill him. I'll set fire to the house he's in while we're on holiday and he can *burn* for eternity."

For once, Delilah might actually have a good idea... No! Bad Kelsey.

They strutted into the PE block, reinforcing the idea that we're not be going that way. We stood up breathing sighs of relief. "Jesus," I breathed.

"Yes," Mrs Kent agreed. "I knew she was troubled but I didn't think she was this bad."

"Don't trust anyone close to Veneman." I interrupted. "She started all this." I scanned the area again. "Come on; let's get going." We crept around the side of the canteen. I stopped, shocked, when we reached the other side and we could see the carpark or more importantly, what was on the other side of it, through the front gates. I couldn't hear them, but I could see the police cars and police officers, and fire engines and firefighters all crowded outside, trying to break down the forcefield. The smashed front of the vehicles, the abandoned battering ram, and the dormant wrecking ball on the end of a crane suggested that they'd tried everything. What else could they use now? A grenade launcher? A tank?

There's a massive crowd of people behind a blockade: parents, trying to reach their children. Mrs Kent whimpered and moved to go over there, but I stopped her. "Don't. We need to get you somewhere safe."

"Adria!" I turned to see Lycaon sprinting at us, still clutching onto the magic mirror. His frightened eyes were locked on Mrs Kent. In a split second it was as if I could see through his eyes; a teacher next to me, wielding a scythe.

"She's fine!" I held up my hand in front of me in, moving it in a 'slow down' motion. "I gave it to her, so she is armed."

He sighed, relieved, and stopped running. I limped over to him with Mrs Kent trailing behind me. "I got your teacher to the new dance studio. He's fine." He looked at Mrs Kent. "I guess you found another one."

She gaped at him; eyes uncertain as they trailed up his barely clothed form. "He's ok. He's helping."

"Is he like you?" She inquired.

Lycaon gave me a strange look. Clearly, he had grown up in the Supernatural world and didn't understand how he and I could have anything in common. "Yes," I answered. Lycaon looked rather offended but he said nothing. "Yes, he's like me." The offended look was replaced with one of confusion. I turned back to him. "Let's get her to the new dance studio." Lycaon nodded. I moved to stand in front of her, and he trailed behind so that Mrs Kent was in the middle. It was reassuring to know he had my back... literally. We made our way down the path towards the new dance studio and I still couldn't see anybody. Suddenly I halted. "Um... Lycaon, don't you think it's weird that we've barely seen anybody?"

He nodded and came over to stand next to me so we could both look at the mirror. "They're outside the new dance studio." We started sprinting (or in my case limping) towards the new dance studio as fast as we could.

"What should I do?" Mrs Kent whimpered.

"Uh..." We weren't far from the carpark. "Go hide in your car. One of us will find you." She nodded and scurried back towards the carpark. Lycaon slowed to a jog to keep pace with me. "You can go ahead. I'll catch up." He nodded and he was gone in a flash.

Damn... I really need to work on my speed. It took me far longer to reach the new dance studio than Lycaon and the sight nearly made me stop.

The doors were surrounded by cult members. They were tearing off branches from the trees along the path and setting them on fire. The doors were barricaded with chairs and branches. They were flinging rocks up at the windows that were just below the roof.

Lycaon was standing between the barricade and the cult, snatching up the chairs, and flinging them at the cult members.

There were just too many of them.

"*Thorns!*" I shouted, my magic slicing through the barricade, resulting in it tumbling down like an avalanche. It was still blocking the door, but the quantity had halved. The cult jumped back and turned to glare at me.

Veneman lowered her hood so I could see her face. "You should have joined me, Adria."

"You should have gone on that quest." I countered and magic fired from my fingertips, knocking her back. "Back off!" I ordered. Lycaon puffed up. His arms didn`t look even remotely human anymore.

Veneman returned to her feet and glared at me. "*Burn it down!*"

They launched the flaming sticks through the broken windows.

I don`t know any water magic. I had no idea how to stop the fire. People were screaming and slamming against the doors. The barricade may be broken but it`s still enough to keep the door shut.

"I`ll break down the barricade!" Lycaon hollered, digging through the barricade like a dog. The chunks of chair rained down on the cult. "You hold them off!"

Nodding, I pushed between Lycaon and the cult, blocking them with my body. How can I block them off with magic? Completely unsure of what I was doing, I held up my hand and projected my magic. It`s that same dark, blood red dust, moving like smoke and then projecting into a translucent, blood-red shield in front of me. I pushed for it to stretch like a wall, keeping them contained in a little bubble.

A woman I didn`t recognise marched up to it and slammed her fist against it. She shrieked like a banshee, shaking her hand like it was on fire.

"Hit it with your scythes!" Veneman roared and her minions descend forwards, crashing against the shield, again and again. I could feel it all. It was like I was the shield. I could feel every hit on the forcefield and I wasn`t sure I could keep this up. I don`t think I can hold on.

Just when I thought I was going to break; the doors opened, and an avalanche of people poured out into the sunlight. "Get to the carpark!" I barked. "Stay together!"

They coughed, waving away smoke and scrambled towards the carpark. The shield flickered and died. Bollocks. Lycaon was quick to act, moving to act as a human (werewolf) shield to keep the cult members back. They were hesitant to directly approach him, but they pushed in different directions to move around.

I swayed on my feet. Fuck, that spell took a lot out of me.

Suddenly, the cult scattered, and I froze. Whatever this was, it can`t be good. A loud crack rang out behind me. I jumped, turning to see Lycaon`s body contorting into unnatural positions, his skin stretching as the bones beneath his skin pushed up against it. There were more and more audible cracks as his bone snapped and healed over and over again. He`s shifting. I guess he didn`t need the full moon after all. Why was he shifting, anyway?

"Did you think that I wouldn't realise he was here?" I tensed. Daphne.

"Leave him alone," I growled.

"No," She sauntered through the chaos like a model on a catwalk. "Sick her, boy!"

I span back around as Lycaon, in full werewolf form, catapulted his body at me. I knocked him back with my magic, but he just kept coming. This time, Daphne decided to join in. She spat purple magic at me, and it *burned* like acid. I screamed and dropped the magic for a second. Lycaon took full advantage and he slammed me into the ground before I could even turn to look at him. I thrusted my fist at his face. *Lycaon, forgive me.* "*Hephaestus` flame!*" The spell blasted him back and I scrambled to my feet so quickly I nearly tripped over my ankle again. The second I was on my feet, Daphne`s magic crashed into me like a bus.

"This is fun," She cackled. "It`s like tennis."

Tennis sucks.

I held up my hands, choking on the pain from the lack of support in my broken arm, and projected a forcefield over each hand but the split magic wasn't strong enough and they shattered on first impact.

They`re going to kill me.

Suddenly a loud bang tore through the school, making the ground tremble. They froze, and we turned to face the gates to see Ben, standing in front of the stunned crowd. He`s smoking in the sunlight. By that, I didn`t mean that he was attractive, I meant that smoke was rolling off his body in waves as his body blisters, bubbles and burns. He smashed his fist against the forcefield. Cracks appeared and spread.

Daphne shuddered, fear twisting her features.

Relief gripped me for a second, but it quickly faded to dread when I saw Ben`s eyes. They weren`t blue anymore. They`re red with all those veins clinging to his pupils and they were *hungry*, watching the panicked students from the other side of the forcefield.

Daphne propelled herself into the air like a rocket, spraying fire onto the earth from her fingers.

Lycaon charged for the students, ripping into them before I could even react.

Thank you. If it wasn't for you, I would have killed many people last night.

I'm sorry Lycaon. I'm wasn't fast enough this time. I stumbled to my feet, swaying slightly, and rushed at the werewolf. I couldn't use fire. It would hit the other students and Daphne's fire was doing enough damage. *"Thorns!"* My accuracy was perfect, and it sliced into him but that wasn't going to slow him down; not really. What can I do? What spell do I have could slow him down? The only thing that had ever slowed him down was the taser... Fuck, I'd forgotten I had that.

I charged forward and zap Lycaon in the chest, sending him soaring through the air... into the forcefield.

It shattered into dust and the wave of students propelled forward like a tsunami. The relief on their faces fizzled away when, Ben snatched up a student unfortunate enough to run past him, and he ripped into their throat like a savage dog. The police officers fired at, but every bullet just bounced off his body like tennis balls.

I didn't know how to make a forcefield like the cult had but I summoned my magic and focused on the feel their forcefield had given me. The word slipped into my mind. *"Seal."* The forcefield stretched from my hands, pushing as many of the innocents out as I could manage while keeping the others inside, consuming the school once more. It looked nothing like what the cult had accomplished. It was as red as my magic, translucent still but it had an ice-like pattern swirling across the dome. I wasn't sure what I had expected but there it was. Will it hold? Dozens of them had built theirs but there's just one of me and I was running low on magic before I'd even attempted making the forcefield.

It seemed that spells I wasn't used to puts more of a strain on me than familiar magic.

Now, I'm trapped in here with most of the cult members (I was sure that some of them have gotten out), Daphne, Lycaon and Ben. I reached for my magic, but a wave of exhaustion ripped through me like a dagger and the red dancing on my fingers fizzled out to nothing.

My magic had reached its limit.

Sometimes I wonder if I was subconsciously trying to get myself killed.

Lycaon's attacks turned towards the cult members. Daphne continued setting fire to everything and everyone she could see.

Ben's staring at me. "Hello,"

"Ben," I couldn't stop the tremble in my voice. *Don't show me weakness, Little One. Predators devour the weak.* Stay calm. Slow your heartrate. He can hear it. *Breathe.* "Shouldn't you get out of the sunlight? You're burning."

He licked his charred lips. I blinked and he was in front of me. Blood coated the lower half of his face. His muscles were on display as his skin had burnt away and his eyes were as wild as the fire around us. "*Run.*"

He didn't have to tell me twice. I sprinted for the closest door: the door to the sports hall. My ankle screamed and my lungs burned. My vision was blurry, and my head was spinning.

If I survive this, I have got to practise my cardio.

If I survive Ben.

When it's your best friend trying to eat you; and you can't run, and you can't hide, what do you do?

Buy yourself as much time as possible.

I rushed towards Delilah and Mason's storeroom. The smashed-up tree from my first encounter with Ben crashed into my mind. No barricade I made could keep him out. I doubted that if I shoved the entire contents of that storeroom against the door, that it would even slow Ben down. And I was certain that if Ben wanted to, he could have caught me already.

He`s enjoying hunting you.

"Why are you running, Kelsey Alexander?" Delilah materialised with her goons by her side. They wielded their scythes with their insidious smiles, standing at the doors to the hallway on the opposite side of the sports hall.

"Vampire!" I huffed.

She cackled while her goons kicked the door behind them shut. "Like I`m going to believe…"

In under a second, Ben was across the entire sports hall and slamming something against the door behind her. He`d taken one of the benches on the way, placing it as a barricade in front of the door. Ben`s face was just charred muscle, his skin completely gone. His muscles stretched horrifically into an ominous grin as he noticed at their scythes. "You brought cutlery."

They scrambled away, their eyes wide with terror, like rabbits caught in headlights. "No," Delilah whimpered.

He laughed. "Yes, dear. I`m *hungry*." He snatched Iris up before she could move an inch backwards. His mouth stretched unnaturally wide, fangs like razor blades. He ripped into her throat. Iris hung from his mouth like a rag doll. His muscles grew and healed, skin extending back across his face until he looked normal again. Or as normal as he could look when he was covered in blood.

My senses returned to me and I turned to dart for the door I`d come through, but he was in front of the door before I could take the second step. He grinned at me, blood dripping from his jaws like tomato sauce dripping from the jaw of a toddler. "Ben… Don`t do this. I`m your friend."

"And I`m hungry," He replied. He sounded like a child. He was inches away from my face before I could even blink. "And you smell *delicious.*"

Stumbling back, I cannot meet those eyes. Even though he`s fully healed again, I barely recognise him. I wanted to move but my legs were glued to the ground in fear. "Ben; please don`t do this!"

Ben slowly reached for me and gripped my skull with such force, I thought he was going to crush my head. He yanked me forward by my head, lifting me off the ground so my eyes were in line with his blood-red ones. "Perhaps you are my friend. What did they call you? Kelsey?"

"Y-yes," I wheezed. The pressure on my skull made it nearly impossible to think, let alone speak. "Kelsey. You never called me that."

"Oh?" He questioned, cocking his head to one side like a curious puppy. "And what is it that I call you, Kelsey?"

I felt dizzy. I think I`m going to pass out. I reached for my magic again, but it evaded me like a ghost. "L-Little One..." I choked. "You call me 'Little One'."

The veins on his eyes seemed to retreat for a moment but they returned just as quickly. "Then perhaps, *Little One,*" There was no recognition in his eyes or in his voice. "I won`t kill you." He didn`t put me down. "But I am *hungry* so I`m going to have a snack." Being bitten by a vampire is single-handedly the most painful experience of my life. He didn`t hold me up with his teeth like he had the others. He cradled me like a child as he gulped down my blood ravenously. My world span and it was too agonising to scream. Then he dropped me.

I lay their helplessly on the wooden floors and I watched as Ben moved across the room. I couldn`t move. It`s like I was paralysed. The combination of blood loss, vampire venom and the over-use of my magic had left me more drained than ever. I had never felt more tired.

I was completely helpless.

You cannot sleep. Not now.

He must have killed Regan on the way over to me earlier because she was on the floor too. Unlike myself, she was dead. Ben didn't speed over to Delilah. He prowled over with a swagger. She was sobbing, whimpering, and backing herself into a corner, not turning her back on him for a second.

"No!" Delilah squealed. "No! No! I'm supposed to live forever! You can't kill me! I'm supposed to live forever!"

I couldn't see his face but I could hear the smirk in his voice. "That can be arranged." His jaws snapped into her neck and she fell back. He released her neck, holding her up with one hand as he tore open his own wrist with his teeth. He shoved it into his mouth before snapping her neck. Bored, he moved on from Delilah's body to Jennifer who was sobbing in the corner, covering her face as if she still believed that if she couldn't see him, he couldn't see her, as if it wasn't real if she couldn't see it happening. He picked her up by the back of her neck, but she only sobbed louder. "Get up girl,"

Why is he…? No. He wasn't talking to Jennifer.

Delilah stood up but her body was still limp. Every limb was flopping around as if her muscles were gone. She stumbled for a second, tripping over her own limbs as if they didn't fit her anymore and then she froze. Delilah twisted around faster than I could see. She was just a blur and her eyes were on me. Blue eyes peered at my neck. They weren't Delilah's old blue eyes; no, they're Ben's. Delilah had Ben's glowing blue eyes. Blood-red veins creep from the edges of her eyes and towards her pupil. "Kelsey," She hissed like my name was a curse.

Move! My mind screamed to my body. *There is no way in Hell you're letting Delilah kill you. Move, god damn it, move! Move!*

A foreign expression crossed Ben's face and he tensed, crushing Jennifer's throat as his body convulsed. He grabbed the sides of his head and groaned, shaking.

I moved my arms and pushed against the ground.

Get up. Get up. Get up!

Delilah may not move as fast as Ben, but she was still much faster than me. She was across the sports hall in two seconds flat and she slammed me into the ground. I couldn't help but gag from the pain. "You're not going anywhere!" I yelped as my face pressed into the ground. My nose bent against the ground. "I always knew I was going to kill you, Kelsey Alexander." She snarled into my ear. "I always knew you were fucking useless but for once, I think I found a use for you." She took a handful of my hair and yanked me into the air. I whimpered but I couldn't say anything or scream. It hurt so much. "Because you smell *fucking* delicious."

There was a blur and I was on the ground again. I tried to focus on what was happening around me, but the world was spinning too fast. I made a choking sound as I rolled to my side. Ben was standing over me. Delilah was in a crater in the ground. Had that crater always been there? *"Don't touch her."* He roared.

She propelled herself up, her mouth elongating, revealing fangs as long as my thumb. "I'm *hungry*." She complained.

"I don't care." Ben countered, his voice like thunder.

"I *want* her." She demanded.

"You will not have her." She smirked and blurred forward. He caught her by the neck, and she swung in the air, dangling like a pendant on a chain. "Did you think you'd be stronger than me? Vampires in this world get stronger with age." Her eyes are widened and frightened. "New-borns can be killed by a competent hunter. New-borns can be destroyed by a strong witch." Veins spread through his eyes again. "Newborns can be eaten by elder vampires."

"I-I`m sorry." She stuttered.

He snapped her neck and dropped her again. He was crouching next to me before I could blink again, and he ripped into his wrist and shoved it into my mouth. "Swallow. I won`t turn you but this will make you feel better."

It tasted awful but I drank it. It wasn`t as if I had a choice. The more I drank, the better it tasted. He tore his wrist from my mouth, and I sat up.

Delilah was still on the floor.

"Thank you," I told him.

"Don`t die unless you want to turn." He stated bluntly.

I blinked. "O-ok." I stumbled to my feet and looked up at him. "Ben?"

"I do not know you, girl." He interrupted. "But I will not allow it to kill you."

"Why?" Stupid. Stupid. Stupid! Do not question why the homicidal vampire didn`t want you dead. You don`t want him to change his mind!

"You look like her. You look like me." He replied.

He`s said that before.

"Who?"

"You look like my wife. You look like me. I imagine she`d look like you if they hadn`t killed her." He sounded morose, tortured, but he sounded more sane than I`d ever heard him.

"Who?" I repeated. I had the feeling I knew the answer.

"My daughter." He told me. The kind of melancholy that set over us was unlike nothing I`d felt before. "She would have looked like you."

"You had a daughter?"

"You should hurry, dear Kelsey." He turned away from me, ignoring my question. How could I blame him? "She won`t be down for long and I am not the only one in this head of mine. Others may not be so merciful."

So, Delilah wasn't dead. I wasn't sure how to feel about that. "Ben, thank you."

"I will see you again." He stated. "I will always know where you are."

"Because of your blood?"

"My blood will link you to me." He explained; that sadness still clinging to his voice. "I will know how you're feeling. I will know where you are. I will be able to speak directly into your mind if I so choose."

"How?"

"Vampires like to be able to find their prey. We like to be able to taunt it... To play with our food." He mused, sitting down on a bench. "You'd be surprised how few of your kind fight back. Those are the ones most of us like best. The ones who fight back are always more fun."

"So, you're going to kill me." I breathed.

"Someday," He agreed. When he said that, I should have been afraid but I wasn't. Was that his blood or was there something really wrong with me? "But not today. Today you have your own battle and one day I will call on you to fight mine."

"Who?"

"The Vampire King of Scotland, of course." He smiled. "I should warn you, little Kelsey... You may want to hurry. There is a young man who got in before you put back the wards and he smells just like you."

"David..." I scurried towards the barricaded door.

"Who will find him first, I wonder?" Ben hummed. "The witch, the werewolf, the woman or you? Tick tock. Tick tock." I held out my hand, reaching for my magic. I grasped it and it propelled the barricade out of my way. *I can use magic again.* He laughed and clapped.

I closed the door behind me and scurried through the PE corridor.

I can't lose my brother. I won't. He's all I've got. He's been my hero my entire life. When I was little and I had a nightmare, I would go to David instead of my parents. When Peter came for me, David was the one who believed me, was the one who'd rescued me, was the one who forgave me; insisting that I didn't needed to be forgiven, was the one who moved across the country, leaving his whole life behind for me. He sacrificed everything he'd known for my sake to live in a caravan away from his family, work in a pub and to raise a teenage girl. He'd become a parent at age eighteen. I'm not even sure if he'd even dated anyone before he'd taken the role of my parent.

He's the most selfless person I've ever met and there was no way in Hell I was going to lose him especially to someone like Veneman.

I'd kill her before I let her hurt my brother.

There was no time for me to do a tracking spell and if I called out to him, Lycaon would find me immediately. With Daphne controlling him, if he somehow didn't kill me, it would still take too much time for me to save David.

Where would my brother be?

He could be anywhere in the school right now and I had no delusions that Ben would spare him for me. He might but I doubt it.

Deciding to make my way towards where the chaos had started, I left by the theatre and I marched towards the new dance studio. I wasn't sure if the fire was still burning on the other side of this block. Running back into the sports hall probably wasn't the best idea considering there was a good chance that it would be on fire soon (and that's ignoring the vampires) but I wasn't staying to find out.

I moved around to the front carpark and noticed that the police were still gathered outside the forcefield. Once they saw me, they started to shout and tried to beckon me over. I recognised one of them. It was the police officer who'd interviewed me. His eyes were desperate and worried. Was he concerned for my safety or had he seen what I'd done? Had he seen what I was capable of? Does he know what I am?

I ignored them. I couldn't open the forcefield. If I did, a homicidal werewolf would get out along with a psychotic witch and a cult that was looking to summon Hell only knows what. I knew that if Ben wanted to break down this forcefield, there was nothing I could do to stop him, and I doubted that there was much I could do to stop Delilah either. I knew she wasn't as strong as Ben, but she could in theory, be stronger than Lycaon and capable of breaking the forcefield. Hell, maybe Lycaon was strong enough to break it. There was no way I could learn how strong the forcefield I made was and how much strain it could withstand. The last one had been made by a large group of people and mine had been made by me while I was running so low on magic, I was swaying. But... I'm a witch so that could have made some kind of difference.

Making my way around the side of the building, I couldn't help but be surprised to see that there was little smoke. In fact, as I got closer, I realised that it wasn't even on fire anymore. Once I was directly in front of the doors, I could see water. There were puddles of water like rockpools everywhere. The water smelled strongly of salt. Was that sea water? It must have been Daphne who put it there but why *salt* water?

There was no time to think about that right now.

There was nobody around. Nobody. I scanned my surroundings for any sign of life but there seemed to be none.

The mirror! I looked for the mirror around me. It must have been around here. I scampered around until I found it near where Lycaon had shifted. It was a bit cracked, but it seemed to still be working. I scanned it for David and it didn't take me long to spot him.

Members of the cult had him and they were dragging him towards inclusion. He was struggling but there were four people hanging onto his limbs. He didn't stand a chance.

Mrs Veneman stood there, the only one of them without the cloak over her head, and she was looking up at the sky as if she could see me watching. She had an insidious smile on her face before she turned to follow her minions inside.

That bitch.

I began to run towards inclusion, and I had just gotten to the drama room when I saw Daphne and Lycaon. She was grinning. "You hadn't forgotten about me, had you?"

"I don't have time for this," I growled, folding my arms tightly across my chest.

She laughed in response. "You just have to keep getting in my way, don't you? If you had just let me kill them then Veneman couldn't get what she wanted. We could have killed her together."

"I don't kill people," I countered.

She laughed. "Not yet. In a world like ours you'll learn one day that sometimes it's the only way."

"Not today," I replied stubbornly.

"Not today," She repeated and sighed. "So, tell me, what do we do about this?"

"You leave," I suggested. "You release Lycaon and you disappear. I'll deal with Veneman and you don't come back here."

"Why would I give up my puppy?" She cooed. For a second, she looked like she was going to pet him, but he growled at her and her hand shot back to her side.

"Because you and I both know that if your control slips for just a second, if you start to run low on magic, he'll kill you." I was acting purely on a hunch. "You've been using a lot of magic and just keeping him like that is using more. Judging from the fact that he growled at you just now, you're running out of power. Leave."

"You're out of power now too," She smiled, her tone dripping with arrogance. "You're a newbie witch. You don't have any more power." I reached for my magic and let it dance in my hand. "Oh," Her eye sockets widened. "You... how?"

"Vampire blood,"

She cackled, fear seeping into her voice. "You have no idea what you've done by taking that stuff. It never leaves your system, not really. You'll never escape it."

"Leave here," I ordered. I'm running out of time! "Leave here, leave Lycaon, and never return."

"I'll see you soon, Adria," She breathed and retracted her magic, the purple seeping from Lycaon before she launched into the air and through the forcefield.

Lycaon blinked and fell back. His body shuddered and contorted until he was back in human form. I would have given him a covering again but all I had was a ripped shirt and burnt trousers. I made my way over to him. He looked delirious as blinked up at me. "A-Adria?"

"She's gone." I told him, gently taking his hand to pull him upwards. It was only then that I noticed that neither my ankle nor my broken arm, hurt anymore. They felt fine. Could vampire blood heal broken bones just like that?

He stumbled and rubbed his eyes, seemingly confused. "Whose gone?"

"Daphne. Daphne's gone." I stated.

The name seemed to jolt him back to reality. He immediately stood up straight, eyes alert and scanning the area around us. "She's gone?"

I confirmed it with a nod. "Are you ok?"

"I'm dizzy," He rubbed the side of his head again. "But I'm ok,"

"I need to go," I didn't want to leave him like this. "I'm sorry but they have my brother and I need to go and save him." I looked at my forcefield. Daphne seemed to have gotten through it without actually breaking it. "I think you should go," I felt sick. As much as I could really use the back-up, I knew that it was only a matter of time for Daphne to recharge her power and she'd come for him. There was no way she'd give up the power of a werewolf. Ben could attack him in this state and Lycaon would have no chance. "You should go home. I'll be ok."

He nodded. "Ok," I supported him as he limped over to through the carpark and over to the police. I focused and opened a hole in the forcefield, hurried him through it and to the police officer I recognised. I slammed it shut behind him before anyone could get in and waved a goodbye to Lycaon. Although I couldn't hear what he said from beyond the barrier, it looked like 'thank you'.

Running felt reckless. I didn't want to run out of energy. I didn't want Ben to see me moving like prey and act like a predator. I walked as quickly as I could towards the inclusion building. As I marched forward, bouncing in my step, the members of the cult stepped into my path from behind the drama room, scythes raised, and faces covered by those hoods.

I didn't slow. I kept my march, feeling the tingle in my fingers of magic. The first one swung their scythe with a battle cry. *"Thorns."* I sliced through the handle of the scythe and pushed out my magic to knock them back and into the wall. It was Mr Singh, a maths teacher.

I kicked his face and his head bounced off the wall. He fell unconscious on the ground at my feet.

I continued to march forward as the next two came at me. *"Thorns."* The scythes fell down and I launched the magic at them.

Miss Steward and a woman I didn't know toppled down. "He will rise!" Miss Steward cried.

I always knew she was crazy (she wears leopard print heels for Christ's sake) but I didn't realise she was this level of crazy. I launched the magic at her, and she slammed into the other woman, their head audibly clanging together, knocking each other out. Other cultists rushed at me. I held up my hands and projected a shield. They slammed into it and deflected with the same force. *"Thorns."* The scythes sliced up and clattered to the ground. Their faces revealed that they were Phillip and another teenager I didn't recognise. There are so many of them and they just keep coming. So many people had actually taken up Veneman's offer. It was like when you trip over an anthill and they just flood out in numbers that you couldn't imagine.

I ended up just expanding the forcefield and marching forward. What else could I do? They pinged backwards but they'd only return to their feet moments later.

David. I need to get to David.

I pushed at them, the forcefield still up and I marched forward as they pushed together against the forcefield. I shoved harder and they stumbled back. Their barely-there magical abilities couldn't stand up to me at full strength. I charged at them and they were forced to retreat.

I laughed in relief. I could do this. I could win.

I turned and knocked the doors open behind me. Just as I got inside the building, I felt something crash into the back of my head and then my world went black.

When I blinked open my eyes, I found myself back in the cult's lair. My head hurt. It felt like I'd been hit over the back of my head with a small truck by King Kong.

Against the wall were five kids chained up. One of which was the boy I saw before who'd told me to be careful. And opposite me hung David.

Veneman strutted across the room to stand in front of me, hands on her hips. "You're awake,"

"No shit," I retorted and tried to move to my brother, but I was held back by chains. Great, I'm chained to the wall.

She grinned, her eyes glinting with malevolence. "Don't bother with magic. Those chains have symbols carved into them that won't allow you to use magic." I decided to try it anyway. She wasn't lying. I couldn't even feel my magic to reach for it and at the same time as I tried, my wrists burned. I swallowed a scream of pain and tried to mask my features to look calm. "So, there is only one soul needed left to bring Him forth." There were still at least a dozen cult members in this room (some of which were the people who I'd held back with the forcefield). So much for winning. She made her way over to the table and picked up my wand.

No! Fuck, no. No. No. No. "Now, I was going to save you till last, but you *just* keep on escaping." Why did I have to send Lycaon away? I could have had back-up here. "I'm not chancing it this time."

"No!" David blurted, anger crossing his normally gentle face. "Get away from her!"

Veneman laughed and held up my wand, brandishing it like a sword at my neck. "*Mortis!*"

Sixteen

I slammed my eyes shut and waited for the pain. That agony was still fresh in my mind and the fear of it gripped me like a vice. A few seconds passed without feeling anything, before I opened my eyes and looked back to her.

Her eyes were wide and frightened, and she was frozen in place. She started to make choking noises and shake violently. Red... the same shade as my magic, appeared in the form of veins and spread across her body like spider webs and up to her face.

Beware; magic takes a toll on body, mind, and soul.
Human bodies are not built for magic.

Veneman had used a difficult spell straight away, and she was human (despite her lack of humanity). Her body didn't have the same tolerance for magic as mine.

She fell to her knees and dropped my wand as her fingers melted away into red sand. She let out a blood-curdling scream and shuddered, but nobody could help her. We were all frozen watching in horror as she started to melt away. The dark red sand melted away and eventually all traces of her had completely disappeared.

I knew it was twisted, but I couldn't help but think 'self-cleaning; nice'.

The second she had completely disappeared, the Earth started to tremble and shudder. The chains swung us around like buoys in a hurricane in the ocean, while the cult members stumbled, clattering on top of each other.

On the table, a shining golden line orbited into a massive circle. When the circle was complete, it was as if it was full of obsidian, like the centre had dropped away into space. Out of the circle twisted thick black smoke. It looked nothing like my magic. It was thick and opaque, towering above us all in moments. Just then, I noticed the salt circle around the table. I honestly had no idea how it stayed in place with all the shaking.

The salt told me one thing. They were summoning something that they didn't want to get out.

Just as the Earth stopped shaking, the thick black smoke revealed a hulking figure. It wasn't human. There was no way that thing was human. It's torso may have been human-shaped, but it was larger than the largest human I'd ever seen and was muscular enough to put the biggest body builder to shame. This creature was large enough that it could eat Dwayne Johnson's arms like I would chicken wings. Its head resembled a skull but was it it's actual face or was it a mask? I couldn't tell. You couldn't see what was behind the skull, no eyes, or facial features of any kind: just darkness. Large curling horns like that of a ram protruded from the sides of its skull. At the end of its monstrous arms were hands the size bicycle tires and it had long, thick, black claws, sharper than daggers. At first, I couldn't see the lower half of its body because of the smoke but as the smoke dissipated, you could see that its legs were like that of a massive deer or a goat? Its hooves were like that of a shire horse in both size and shape. The hair was thick and black, looking more like wire than anything natural. It also had a long, reptilian tail, that looked like it belonged on a crocodile.

This *thing* was too large to fit into the salt circle. Its shoulders stretched outside of the circle and if its hooves weren't in the circle, I was certain it would have crushed the table. It barely fit into the room. Would it still be trapped within the salt circle if its body didn't even fit completely into it?

Its magic power was so strong, it felt like I was choking on it.

What the Hell was this thing?

When it opened the abyss that was its mouth to speak, my blood turned to ice. I couldn't shudder. I was too frightened to move. "*SPEAK YOUR WISH.*" I didn't think it was trying to shout but the volume was loud enough that *everything* shook. Rock slipped from the ceiling and crashed down, narrowly missing Mr Small.

Not a single cult member could find the words. They huddled into the corner, trying to appear as small as possible. Many of their eyes were flickering between the creature and the door as if they were wondering if they could get there before it incinerated them.

How stupid were they in thinking that they could control this thing? Why the Hell did they think it was a good idea to summon it in the first place?

It turned to look directly at my brother. "*SPEAK YOUR WISH, MORTAL.*"

I wanted to shout 'don't'. I wanted to beg him to stay silent. My words evaded me and the only sound I could make was a choked whine.

"I wish..." No! Please, David, don't! "I wish that my sister will always be safe." He looked directly at me. I shook my head, my eyes pleading. "I wish that Kelsey will always be safe."

It reached out its hand to David but I couldn't see what it did through its arm.

The last thing I saw before my vision went completely black was a pair of yellow eyes.

I don't know what happened after that. When my eyes opened again, I was on the ground outside. My forearm rested in front of my face. Disorientated, I stared at my forearm as thick, ink-black veins retreated away into nothing, so quickly part of me questioned whether or not I had seen them at all.

Everything was *hot*. Far hotter than it should be in March... far hotter than it could be in the height of an English Summer. I stumbled to my feet to see that everything was on fire. The world was orange and the forcefield I put up was no longer red. It was blacker than the night's sky, the same obsidian as the circle, and you couldn't see through it at all.

I wasn't wearing my battered school uniform anymore. I was wearing a long black dress with a high collar. It had a tight-fitting torso with a flaring skirt. The dress didn't cover my shoulders and the skirt reached the ground. My feet were bare too. Despite all the rubble, scratches from before, there was not a scratch on me. My cast had completely disappeared.

What had happened?

In front of me and through the smoke marched that hulking figure from before. I couldn't see any other lifeform. There was nothing.

"*HOW ARE YOU STILL IN CONTROL, LITTLE WITCH?*" The creature boomed.

What did it mean? What control did I have of anything? I felt very out of control right now.

"Where's my brother?" I demanded. I couldn't see any sign of him. "Who are you? What do you want?"

It laughed. The sounded like a clash of thunder and lightning. "*I WILL NOT TELL YOU WHAT MY NAME IS. I WILL NOT ALLOW YOU TO CONTROL ME, LITTLE WITCH. WHAT I WANT? I WANT TO WATCH THIS EARTH BURN. AS FOR YOUR BROTHER, HIS WISH SET ME FREE AND HE IS CONDEMNED TO AN ETERNITY IN HELL. HE TOOK THE TRIP AN HOUR AGO. DO YOU WISH TO JOIN HIM, GIRL?*"

Rage bubbled up inside of me, and I felt the magic boil beneath my skin. "*DROP YOUR FORCEFIELD. SET ME FREE. PERHAPS I WILL RETURN HIM TO YOU.*"

Liar. Snarled a voice from the depths of my mind. *How dare you lie to me?*

And 'set it free'? How was my forcefield that strong? I didn't even remember making this one. Power wafted off that creature in waves. Why couldn't it get out?

"Or" I growled, my mouth running away from me before I could think better of it. "I could put you back through the portal that brought you here."

It roared with laughter.

Magic ripped from my body as if I wasn't the one wielding it. It took me a moment to realise that the violent roar I heard was tearing from my lungs. Though my magic had the same texture as before, it was no longer red. It was blacker than the abyss. It slammed into the creature like a tornado, knocking it back a few inches. It frowned and then laughed again, pressing against the magic. I pressed back harder. The magic felt limitless and hot. Almost like if I kept it in, I would burn from the inside-out.

The creature marched at me, but I pushed harder, making it slam backwards. Its face was incapable of showing emotion, but I could smell its fear as easily as I could smell pizza cooking in an oven.

Words that I had never read or heard tumbled from my lips. "*Patefio.*"

A portal ripped open directly behind the creature. It was like a vacuum, sucking in rubble and making my hair fly forwards, obscuring my vision. The force of the vacuum yanked it back for a second, but it pressed forward stubbornly. Its hoof slammed against the Earth and cracks appeared in the concrete beneath it. "*DO YOU THINK YOU CAN MAKE ME GO AWAY, ADRIA? DO YOU THINK YOU CAN BEST ME?*"

I crashed the magic into it again, shoving it as hard as I could towards the portal.

I didn't know where the portal went to or even if it was where it had originally come from but I didn't care. I just wanted it far from here.

It replied with its own magic, sending that thick black smoke back at me. I pulled up a forcefield again, fully expecting for it to barely slow the creature's magic down. It didn't. The smoke slammed against the forcefield and dissipated before it could even make a crack.

What had happened to me? Since when did I have all this power? There was no way this came from the vampire blood. I was not this powerful before… Was this David's wish? Was that where this power came from? But surely if this creature granted the wish then shouldn't it be more powerful than me?

"Yes," I replied with a growl. I did think I could beat it. As I said that one world, it was launched backwards less than a foot away from the portal, bending like a flower in the wind towards it.

"*YOU WERE SUPPOSED TO JUST BE A WITCH.*" It protested.

"I am just a witch." I forced it back and it fell through the portal. I released the magic, but the portal didn't close. The creature stood back up immediately and charged forward.

What do I do? What do I do? What do I do?

"*Occludo.*" The portal slammed shut, leaving that things monstrous hand on the ground in front of where the portal used to stand.

I strode towards it and the hand shook and started to contort and grow. "*Hephaestus` Flame,*" The hand was engulfed in flame, but it wouldn`t burn. I put more and more magic behind the spell but there was no difference to the severed limb.

"We`ll dispose of that." I flinched, spinning around to see the most striking couple I had ever seen.

The woman who had spoke`s hair tumbled like copper wires down to her shoulders with a slightly too-long fringe. Her large eyes (that kind of reminded me of Amanda Siegfried) were a swampy green and framed with thick dark lashes. She had a pale heart-shaped face with a scattering of prominent freckles sprinkled over her cheeks. Her lips were dark pink and with her mouth anime-girl small with plump, cupid-bow lips. She was perhaps an inch taller than me, but just as curvaceous, or maybe more so. She was at most in her mid-twenties.

The man was movie-star gorgeous. This man was at least six foot two, built like the main character in every action movie and had eyes the same colour as the Mediterranean Sea. Stubble scattered a long his strong jaw and his hair was a light brown, messy and with the occasional whisper of a blonde or copper hair. A light dusting of freckles coated his perfect cheekbones. His dark pink full lips were curled into a gentle smile. He looked older than her but definitely not by much. He was by far the most beautiful man I had ever seen in real life and I honestly couldn`t think of a celebrity that could compare. "Sorry to have startled you, Miss." He continued. His voice was deep and entirely comforting. "My name is Agent Carter from the Shadowsoul Agency. This is my wife Agent Adams. We came here to help you." He looked around at the scene around him. "Though it seems that you didn't need our help." He laughed humourlessly. "We'll take the hand and lock it away in a place where it cannot get out. We have people on the way to make sure that humans forget what happened here."

"Why?" I demanded. Please don't let this be another fight. I just want to find David.

"Unfortunately, humans have a tendency to kill what they don't understand." Agent Adams stated. Was that sympathy? "They won't understand and they have slaughtered witches for less." She explained. "The Shadowsoul Agency work for what's good in the supernatural world. We have more people on the way. It will be handled. You can rest."

"How do I know I can trust you?" I questioned.

She pulled up her sleeve to reveal a mark that looked like a swirling eye. "This is the mark of the Shadowsoul agency. You can touch it and it will show you what you need to know. Besides," She looked to her husband whose face was full of concern for her. Were they frightened of me? *They should be. After all, you're frightened of you.* "If you wanted to, you and I both know you could kill us in a blink of an eye." Hesitantly, I shuffled forward and rested the tips of my fingers on the mark. Images flashed through my mind. It was her life. She was showing me her life. In moments years had flashed through my mind.

I yanked my hand back, startled. "I believe you." I blurted. "Why would you show me that? I saw your life. Why would you show me things so private?"

"Because you'll know I'm not evil."

"No," I agreed. "No, you're not."

"You should go home." Agent Carter stated.

"I need to find my brother." I insisted.

The red head woman shook her head. "I'm sorry Adria, but your brother is dead. You *don't* want to see the body. I'm really sorry for your loss."

My eyes stung with tears begging to escape but I held it back as strongly as I could. "No." I shook my head. "No. I have to find him."

"Sweetheart," He didn't sound like the others who used that name. He sounded reassuring, concerned for me. "You don't…"

I ignored him, my body moving on autopilot through the ruins of my school, searching for my brother. "David!" I called to no answer.

"Adria please," Mercedes… that was her real name… Mercedes, begged but she didn't dare reach for me. Neither of them did. *They're afraid of you.*

I rushed to where my mind was guiding me. "No," I gasped, covering my mouth. I couldn't look away. "No, no, no," I was sobbing, rushing towards the charred body. He just looked like those bodies from the people in Pompeii. "No! David come back! David please!" Not him. Anybody but him. Why couldn't it have been me?

I was on my knees, bawling over my brother's body. I didn't know how I knew it was him, but I did. I choked on my tears. Why him? He was the nicest guy in the world. Why did it have to be him?

If there's anybody out there, please take me instead. The world needs him more than me. Please don't let him be dead.

"Sweetheart, we can give you a lift…" Agent Carter offered when my sobbing had slowed, and I had been sitting there staring at my brother's body. *I'm so cold.*

I shook my head. "No, thank you." I walked away.

I don't remember my walk home. I don't remember who I saw. I don't remember how I left the school or taking down the forcefield. The next thing I remembered was waking up the next morning. I caught a glimpse of myself in the mirror and stopped.

I almost didn't recognise myself.

The irises of my eyes were like pools of black ink. They were framed with long, thick black eyelashes. My hair matched it with the same jet black. My skin was so white, paper had more colour. My freckles were completely gone, and my formerly rosy cheeks had no colour. It was almost as if they'd gone pale blue grey. I could barely recognise my own face. My soft face had sharpened. I had a strong, sharp jawline and cheekbones were prominent and sharp. My lips were the same in shape but in colour they were blood red. I literally could have been drawn in black and white besides my lips. I rubbed my lips but it wasn't lipstick. My skin had been stained blood red. All the excess fat that used to be on my body had evaporated. I still had my curves but there was no excess fat. I pressed my long-nailed hand against my stomach to find that I had abs.

I didn't recognise myself.

Sergeant was whining. I was still in the same dress and barefoot. At first, I considered getting dressed before I took her for a walk but I didn't. I pretended that there wasn't an empty spot on the sofa as I stepped out of the door.

I took her through the woods. I didn't care whether or not I ran into anything. I just... I may have just woken up, but I was tired.

Once I returned home, I picked up my phone. I turned it on to see sixteen text notifications.

They were all from David. I wasn't sure which one I had read when I started crying. Each one of the texts were asking me *where* I was. They were asking me *how* I was. He was begging me to tell him if I was alive.

He was gone.

David was really gone.

I don't know how long I was bawling on the floor. I don't know when Sergeant came over to lick my tears away. It was like time was suspended in my grief. I was knocked out of the spell with a knock at the door. I stood up, wiping away my tears before I opened the door.

In front of me were two smartly dressed women and six feet behind them were a couple that gave me the chills. The couple's smiles were sickeningly sweet, reminding me of Veneman's. The women in front of me looked more morose. "Hi, we're from social services." I tensed. "Since the death of your legal guardian,"

"We're sorry for your loss." The other woman interrupted to which the other nodded her head.

"You are under the age of eighteen and therefore need a guardian. We have spoken to your family members but…"

"None are willing to take me." I finished. I would have hoped that my cousin would take me, but he drank a lot, and he had a criminal record. They probably wouldn't have even considered it, let alone allowed it.

They nodded in response. "These kind people…" They pointed to the smiling couple behind them. "Are Mr and Mrs Pink. They have offered to take you in."

I shivered at the thought.

"That will not be necessary." A voice rang out from behind everyone. Forward strode a witch. I could feel that she was a witch and she was a powerful one. She was tall, in her late forties and leaner than any supermodel. She had dark hair tied up into a knot above her head. Her jaw was sharp, and her eyes were cold. "My name is Headmistress Dhara North." She stated. "I run a school for gifted individuals. Miss Kelsey Alexander would fit in there perfectly. I have been placed as her legal guardian until her eighteenth birthday. She will be clothed, housed and be provided with the best education money can buy." She slammed a sheet into the chest of the woman on the right. "I think you'll find everything is in order."

The woman scanned the paper. "Everything seems to be in order." She looked to the other people. "Um...we'll go now."

The headmistress looked directly at me, her eyes hard and unfeeling as we waited for the others to be out of earshot. I should have been intimidated by her but I wasn't. I just didn't care. "I am the headmistress of Malachai Academy. As you can probably sense; I am a witch. You'll be safe there. You'll learn many things." She looked past me. "You may take your dog and your familiar. I was sent by Agent Carter." Her eyes returned to mine. "Malachai Academy is not run by the Shadowsoul Agency. Nor is it run by the Anderson and Light Company. It is neutral and you will be allowed to make your own decisions. You are able to choose."

"This is not an offer." I observed.

"No," She agreed. "I am your legal guardian." She pulled out another form. "Sign your name." I looked at it and she handed me a pen. "Your witch name. First name and surname."

There was only one name that fitted.
Adria Davidson.

Epilogue

"How is Mission Wild Rose coming along?" The man demanded.

"Not well," Agent Adams started, her hands on her hips. "Adria Davidson has bonded with it and Dhara North had taken her to the academy."

Agent Carter nodded. "And she has finished the name. I also feel like I should mention she is the only person known to have ever regained control after one of them had entered their body. We should get her out of that place. That woman has her believing that *we* sent her there."

"As I heard from your wife." The man dismissed, waving his hand. He ignored how Agent Carter clenched his fists. He turned to the woman in the corner of the room. "Agent Han, you will go to the academy. You will have the tattoo removed and you will go undercover. You will observe this girl and you will make sure she goes for the side of good. If she shows *any* sign of becoming what we all fear, kill her."

"No!" Agent Carter roared. "She is a child! She is an innocent!"

"She is destined to destroy the Earth." The man reminded. "But we will not do that unless absolutely necessary. Agent Carter, Agent Adams, you are to go to Brazil. There is strange happenings over there. You'll need to leave immediately." They hesitated, but they nodded and turned away. Just as they were out of earshot, they turned back to Agent Han. "If she is seen as a threat, kill her. Anderson and Light will have sent others to corrupt her and they will be particularly manipulative. Be careful."

"Why did you wait until Agent Carter had left the room?" She inquired.

"Agent Carter is a stubborn man and he may be a soldier but he isn't one for orders. If he and his wife heard this, we may have more trouble on our hands. You'll learn that you don't want to cross a man like that. As much as it would grieve me to see a sixteen-year-old girl die, it is more important that she doesn't end the world. It has found her, and she will only grow stronger. One day we will not be able to stop her."

"She can always choose not to become that."

"She chooses not to, and the fates will punish her for it." The man argued.

"We stop her, and the fates will punish us for it."

"Let's hope that she chooses light over darkness on her own."

Thank You

There are so many people I`d love to say "thank you" to but I restricted myself to only three so I can make the messages more personal.

Mr Clarkson

You are the teacher that restored my faith in teachers. I can`t thank you enough. I wish you the best of luck in the future and I hope that you continue to make the world a better place for your students. You are among the kindest people I have ever known, and you always made welfare of your students (especially your tutees) a priority. I don`t know how I would have gotten through school without you there and I know so many ex-classmates who say the same thing. Thank you so much for everything.

Grandpa

You have always encouraged my creativity. You may live on the other side of Britain (literally), but I love how we talk almost every day. You have read almost everything I have ever written. You always get involved and you always encourage me. Thank you so much. You are also way stronger than I think you give yourself credit for (which has been shown so much in the past few years, especially the Hell that was 2019). Thank you.

Mum
Words cannot begin to describe how thankful I am every day to have you a part of my life. You are so tough, and you are so encouraging. I have no idea how you balance everything and still manage to always have a smile on your face. You have read everything I ever wrote and gave me constructive criticism every time. You are so kind, so strong, so smart, and so brave… We are all so lucky to have you in our lives. Thank you.

Music I listened to while writing this.
1. Simple Man (cover by Jensen Ackles)
2. Meet Virginia by Train
3. Fire and Ice by Olivia Bray
4. That Girl by Outshyne
5. Someone You Loved by Lewis Capaldi
6. The Devil`s Backbone by The Civil Wars
7. I Caught Myself by Paramore
8. 21 Guns by Green Day
9. Make you Mine by Outshyne
10. Whipping Post (cover by Jensen Ackles)
11. Perfect by Simple Plan
12. Shine by Mr Big
13. Every Inch of You by Outshyne
14. I Wouldn`t Mind by He is We
15. Battle Cry by Beth Crowley
16. Wagon Wheel by Jason Manns
17. Empire by Beth Crowley
18. Cheshire Kitten by SJ Tucker
19. Weak by AJR
20. Numb by Linkin Park
21. Waiting For Superman by Daughtry
22. Drops of Jupiter by Train

23. Please Take Me by Beth Crowley
24. Decode by Paramore
25. Kiss it All Better by He is We
26. If I Die Young by The Band Perry

https://www.youtube.com/playlist?list=PLTO1NjBYMil7iWGYO8jlZl28BYm8PS4AV

About the Author

L.E. Hart is a seventeen-year-old college student at the time of writing this taking Criminology, Psychology and English Literature and Language. She lives in Southern England with an ogre, an angel, Sasquatch, and her dog. When she isn't working on classwork, writing novels or poetry, she spends her time in the garden shed creating her own frost giant using Dr Victor Frankenstein's notes.

Instagram: @l_e_hart

Facebook: @L. E. Hart

Book Two

Coming Soon

Printed in Great Britain
by Amazon